"Complex and haunting, *My Way Home* feelingly delineates one woman's predicament and its aftershocks many decades later—a cautionary story all too relevant to a time when a woman's right to control her body is somehow still—infuriatingly—unsettled."

—Gish Jen, author of *Bad Bad Girl*

"How do we ever reconcile a hidden past with a very different present? And who do our children really belong to? Set against the Vietnam years and pre-Roe v. Wade, Bonina's novel is a haunting look at first love, teen pregnancy, and the dangerous secrets about to erupt in a family. Magnificent."

—Caroline Leavitt, New York Times bestselling author of *Days of Wonder* and *Pictures of You*

"*My Way Home* is an often unsettling, always engaging novel full of honesty, heart, and grace. It is both seductive and disturbing, and it will remind you of why you started reading stories in the first place—to be carried away to a more vivid and compelling world. Mary Bonina knows that every story is many stories—Clare's story is Martin's story is Ray's story is Danielle's story—and she handles the complexities of the interwoven tales of loss, grief, abandonment, and love with intelligence, wit, and courage. Nothing is as it seems."

—John Dufresne, author of *My Darling Boy*

"*My Way Home*, Mary Bonina's novel with a Vietnam War era backstory, is a moving tribute to Boston, Cambridge, and those who chose the path of conscientious objectors or crossed the border into Canada. The novel reunites a pair of high school sweethearts—uncovers a painful secret hidden for 16 years—examines the role of mothers and stepmothers—gives voice to teenage daughters—and champions the challenges of a good marriage. Using multiple narrators, Bonina lets the reader into the private thoughts and motives of each of the main characters as their lives intersect and family is reimagined. A potent, provocative, and important novel."

—Anne Elezabeth Pluto, author of *How Many Miles to Babylon*

"Mary Bonina's captivating debut deftly explores themes we all must wrestle with during our short stay on planet Earth. How do we live meaningful lives while harboring deep secrets and gaping loss? What do we settle for when we cannot get what we want? What does family really mean? Written with great wisdom and acuity, *My Way Home* is a beautiful novel, full of truths about the human condition, the ways we delight and disappoint one another, the ways we save each other with our generosity and love. *My Way Home* shimmers with the honesty and beauty of being alive, each of us trying our hardest to do the next best thing."

—Mary E. Mitchell, author of *Starting Out Sideways* and *Love in Complete Sentences*

"Deeply moving, warm-hearted, and wise, *My Way Home* delves into a world of secrets, forgiveness, and "a new idea of family." Beautifully written, Bonina's novel explores the tender yet powerful ways people respond to the upheavals that love brings. I loved it."

—Rosie Sultan, author of *Helen Keller in Love*, winner of the PEN Discovery Award in Fiction

for Mark and Gianni
and for Nancy

ALSO BY MARY BONINA

NONFICTION

My Father's Eyes: A Memoir

POETRY

Living Proof
Clear Eye Tea
Lunch in Chinatown

"To regret one's experiences is to arrest one's own development. To deny one's own experiences is to put a lie into the lips of one's own life. It is no less than a denial of the soul."

Oscar Wilde

"How many words remain unsayable even between a couple in love, and how the risk is increased, that others might say them, destroying it."

Elena Ferrante

"The best way of keeping a secret is to pretend there isn't one."

Margaret Atwood

PART ONE

One

Clare, 1984

I parked the car in front of the Conservatory and Danielle opened her door, jumping out just as I braked. She rushed up the steps to the building and I hurried to follow. She didn't want to be late for her lesson—and if she had been, it wouldn't have been on my account.

By the time I caught up with her she was heading downstairs to the practice studio, not calling out as she usually did, that she'd meet me at the window seat. I headed to that favorite corner of the lobby, realizing I had no book to read and that, rushing out of my office, I hadn't even taken a notebook and pen with me. I wasn't surprised to be so scattered. I was tired from teaching all day. I was more than ready to be home, stretched out on the couch, half-watching some television program that didn't really interest me. I was hungry, too, with none of the snacks I used to carry around for Danielle. It was impossible to keep up with this eating for two business, and Dr. Aviva had recently grilled me to learn how much I'd been eating lately. *Your baby needs proper nutrition. Snacks. Small meals. Several times a day,* she advised. I ought to be traveling with a picnic basket.

Music was coming from the smaller recital rooms—the sound of strings, and a flute player in the outer corridor— and in Wolfinson 103 down the hall, a soprano was singing, reminding me of when I'd been a schoolgirl and was given a solo with the chorus. All that was behind me now.

When the hour changed and the musicians I'd heard finished with their practice, it got very quiet, and chilly, too. I thought maybe a door or window had been opened somewhere in the building. May evenings in New England were still cool, even if it had been a day as warm as this one. When the drafty silence was broken by the sound of a saxophone improvisation, I realized that the cooler air was rising from below: there was an open vent under the window seat. Whoever was playing downstairs was accomplished. I thought it might be Danielle's new teacher.

I saw a concert brochure someone had left on the bench across from me, picked it up and flipped through it, thinking that since it had been a jazz concert, perhaps my stepdaughter's new saxophone coach had played. I didn't even know his name. Her mother, Veronica, a colleague of his here, had arranged the lessons with him. Then I saw the name. *Ray Newell.* My hand shook. I stared hard at it, as if that would change it, or make it disappear. This couldn't be.

The program fell to the floor. I bent down to pick it up and stood upright too quickly, nearly losing my footing. I was shaking. My legs were leaden, and I was lightheaded, but I could move; so I went carefully and slowly down the corridor to the area the older students and parents jokingly referred to as Le Bistro, a fake café without real food or coffee, just a bank of vending machines and a microwave oven.

Across the way there was a small room enclosed by a wall that went only half way up. As open as the place was it didn't really serve as the refuge it was meant to be. Although this could hardly be considered a comfortable spot, outfitted as it was with spindly metal furniture made to look like cast iron, furniture that would have been more appropriately placed in a garden or on a patio, I could nevertheless, sit out of the way, and try to calm down while reading in a better light, the capsule biography of Ray Newell.

Mr. Newell is new to the Conservatory this year. He received his undergraduate degree from McGill University and a Master of Science in Modern American Music from the Royal Canadian Academy of Music.

All I'd heard about the teacher was that he was from Canada. Not in a million years would I have believed that Ray Newell would re-enter my life after such a long time—and never in this way—as music coach for Danielle. My heart pounded at the possibility of seeing him again. I remembered what a good sax player he was, how music had been the most important thing in his life.

The Ray in the headshot had graying hair—his would be,

just as mine might be, if I didn't color it—and he was filled out—again, as the Ray I once loved would be, a man now, and not a boyish teenager. He just might be the same person, in spite of changes that had come with age.

Had anyone ever mentioned my name to him? Danielle had her father's surname. I hadn't changed my name from Rantel to Harris, when I married Martin. But if this is the same Ray Newell and he had heard my name, would he even remember me after all these years had passed? And if so, what would that be like? What would he say? What would I say?

I heard someone coming down the hallway in the direction of Le Bistro—maybe Danielle, finished with her lesson, ready to head out and looking for me, not finding me in my usual spot. I looked at my watch. An hour had not quite passed though, and besides, these were the footfalls of a man. He was coming down the corridor, still in the shadows, maybe just passing through on his way to somewhere else. He had a confident and determined stride, as if he were on a mission, and from the sound of it, he was wearing boots. As he turned to go into the vending area, I saw them: red cowboy boots.

He stood with his back to me, fishing in a pocket of his jeans and coming up with change to feed the cold drink vending machine. There was a sudden thud of the full plastic bottle dropping down, and he reached in to retrieve it. Now that he had his drink, he went over to the stack of the new issue of *Bostonian* on the floor, and grabbed one. He stood there, leaning on the counter, flipping through the paper, his back still to the open doorway of the room where I was sitting. Maybe he was looking for something in the free paper, probably checking an event listing, the only reason anyone cared about the paper that was full of advertising.

He started to move. Now that he'd looked at everything in the issue that interested him, was he headed for the next corridor leading to the mailroom or to the library? I watched as he folded it up and put it back in the stack on the floor. He turned then—not to go on his way—but to head into the seating area to drink his Coke. He was coming right at me. I felt my heart jump and then strangely, a rush of warmth filled my empty stomach. I knew that this was Ray Newell. Danielle or Veronica must have told him I'd be waiting for the lesson to finish; he must have seen or heard my name.

"Hello," I said, looking up at him.

He towered over me. I should stand, I thought. I didn't think I could.

"And hello to you," he said. He spoke politely and formally, as if he didn't really know who I was, but was just being friendly because we were the only two people in the small room. "Ray Newell," he said, his hand stretched out to me.

"Don't you know who I am?" I asked.

When I stood, I realized that I still felt weak. He was talking but there was no possibility of hearing anything he was saying right now. I was lost in his unusual green eyes and his open face that was both familiar and strange, the way a face you once knew so well becomes after so many years. He'd left in 1968 and this was 1984. So much time had passed!

"Clare. Clare Rantel," I said, swallowing my surname. "Your student's—Danielle's—stepmom."

"Clare. Clare?"

He seemed genuinely shocked. This had to be an act. I was having none of it. And why had he left Danielle when her lesson wasn't over? Perhaps he'd given her something to practice to allow him time to come talk to me. Or maybe she was packing up her stuff and getting ready to be on her way to find me. I didn't want her to find me here like this, shaken up by this encounter with her teacher.

"You never wrote. And you didn't wait for me. I went to meet you and you had left without me. And you didn't write. I didn't know where you were."

Ray Newell stood there, looking shocked, as I rambled on.

"Oh, I did. I did. I wrote to you. You never answered. Why, Clare? Why didn't you ever answer my letters?"

"You left. I went to meet you. We were going to go together," I said.

"I couldn't. The van driver wouldn't wait."

"You could have waited for me. You said you would. I was there. You left."

I held the rolled up concert program in hand. I was trying not to slouch, consciously trying to straighten up, trying at least not to fall over, but I didn't suggest sitting down in one of the flimsy metal chairs in front of a table that wobbled. I didn't want to prolong this conversation. I wanted him to leave, to get back to Danielle's lesson, or if it was over, for him to go before she showed up.

"Did you come looking for me?"

He ignored the larger question in that, of how it had happened that he'd come home to Massachusetts, and taken on my stepdaughter as a student. It seemed an impossible coincidence.

"I thought Veronica had driven Danielle to her lesson, so I was going to say hello. She told me her stepmom had, so I thought I'd introduce myself. I didn't know. If I had known you were here, that Danielle was your stepdaughter, I would never have taken this job," he said.

"Nice to see you again, too," I said.

I changed the subject. I unraveled the concert program and held it out, thinking it might help me calm down if we talked about his work instead of our past, since he seemed to be going nowhere right now.

"I found this on a chair," I said. "I see you've done just fine for yourself."

"Yes," he said. 'It was a good concert, with some good people. Are you interested in jazz?"

I didn't answer. Why didn't he remember that I'd loved jazz? Did he think I'd changed that much as I got older?

"Can you believe I had actually forgotten you played saxophone? I thought it was clarinet."

I wanted to get back at him for forgetting how much I loved jazz. I wanted him to leave, but I wanted to keep him from leaving, until he offered some explanation of why he was here at the Conservatory, taking on my stepdaughter as a student.

"I can't believe it! Danielle's stepmom," he said.

"And you, you her teacher? Not even six degrees. How did this happen?"

"Amazing," he said.

He gave no explanation though. Then he moved closer once again, offering a brotherly kind of hug. I flinched. I pulled away, not willing to accept what felt like intimacy, since at any moment

Danielle might come sailing into Le Bistro, looking for me, and find me here with her teacher and wonder what was going on.

"Well," he said.

He paused awkwardly and gave a quick smile that made it seem that he was heading out. I took a deep breath of relief.

"Well," he repeated. "I should go back to Danielle to give her the piece she needs to practice for next lesson. She'll be wondering where I am. I've got to photocopy the music in the library and then she'll be ready to go."

He stood there looking like he didn't really want to go, that he had something more to say. I wished that he would answer the question, explain what had brought him back into my life like this. It seemed too much of a coincidence.

"I think the library closes at seven, doesn't it?"

He looked at his watch. "I'm not usually here at night. Didn't know that. I'm new here, you know."

He looked awkward, as if he knew he'd been caught in a lie, that the real reason he'd left Danielle's lesson was to come find me, and that it was all a pretense that he hadn't known who I was. I hoped he'd leave now, go before Danielle got fed up waiting for him, and headed to find him where he said he'd be, passing through this corridor to the library just down the hall from Le Bistro.

There was an uncomfortable silence then, which he finally broke asking, "You went to Stanford, right?"

"I'm flattered you thought of Stanford."

"I didn't finish," I said about phony college in California. And joking and embellishing my lie, I said, "I transferred to Bates. I was missing winter, I guess."

I had gone to Bates after returning to the east coast, but not as a transfer student from Stanford or anywhere else, and not right away.

"I see you have a baby on the way. Congrats. When?" he asked.

I was surprised he'd noticed. I hadn't thought it was so obvious yet.

"In the Fall," I said. "Do you have kids?" I asked.

"Never did decide to have kids. Never married either. It's

better that way maybe. A musician leads a crazy life."

He cut off the conversation for real this time. He said again that he had to get back to Danielle, that she'd be wondering where he was. He headed out of Le Bistro and to the down staircase to meet up with her in the practice room, and I followed. But when we got to the stairs he suggested I wait in the lobby rather than continuing on, that he wanted to explain something to Danielle before he dismissed her. I hoped he wasn't going to tell her that we'd known each other as teenagers. But maybe it was only the assigned practice music and exercises that he wanted to go over with her.

"Give me a minute and I'll send her up," he said.

He turned and looked back.

"See you soon," he said.

I lifted a hand in a weak, dismissive sort of wave and walked back to the lobby to wait for Danielle.

Two

As we left the building and walked to the car, I asked Danielle about the lesson.

"What's your new teacher like? Do you like him?" I asked.

"I don't really want to talk about it. Not now," she said.

In a way, I was grateful she didn't want to talk about him. And I thought, maybe the reason wasn't because she was tired, but because she hadn't gotten along well with Ray. A musician as accomplished as he was, would be very demanding, and maybe she was realizing that learning a new and entirely different kind of instrument was going to be too difficult. Just maybe she would drop this sudden interest in saxophone, and then I wouldn't have to worry about seeing Ray.

"I could use some ice cream. What do you think?" I asked.

"Yes! Toscanini's? Please?" she begged.

"Okay, but we can't linger. Your dad will be waiting up, wanting to talk."

I sighed and felt a twinge of worry in my stomach as I said this, and Danielle harrumphed, not knowing the half of it.

We sat in a booth, eating our ice cream. Danielle looked over at a table in the corner, and recognizing someone she knew, waved and mouthed what looked like, "Hi Chris!"

He returned a friendly but quick wave and went back to talking with his friends.

When we were finished with our ice cream, we picked up our jackets and put them on as we walked toward the door, passing Chris' table. As we did, I saw Danielle smile sweetly at him, and wave goodbye.

"Is he in your class?" I asked, once we were out on the street.

"Was. Transferred out. He's in band."

"He's cute," I said.

Danielle shrugged—of course—guarded about any feelings

she might have for the boy.

She noticed me wavering, as I thought of having to face Martin at home.

"You don't look so well right now," she said, catching my face illuminated in the streetlight.

"The ice cream, I guess. Tasted great, but it's not settling well. Too rich," I said, as if that were what was bothering me.

Martin was already in bed when we got home, and I went in to check on him, hoping he was asleep. He'd been reading though. I found him reaching toward the night table at my side of the bed, putting a magazine back on top of the stack of books about pregnancy and childbirth. He must have heard me come in. He wanted conversation, I could tell.

"Hi," he said, smiling widely, seeing me.

My stomach flipped again. Guilt had not taken long to set in. He looked so happy that I was home. Why had I hidden my past from him? I should have expected Ray to turn up someday; he had roots here.

"That was a long lesson," Martin said.

"We went to Toscanini's after. I could tell that Danielle needed a snack. I needed something, too, and thought ice cream would be good."

I took a deep breath before going on.

"This new instrument and teacher must be a challenge for her, after playing cello for so long, and becoming really accomplished at it. Don't you think?"

Martin raised his eyebrows and tilted his head, considering it.

"Wonder if she'll stick with it. By the way, I brought some ice cream for you—that weird frozen pudding flavor you like, the one that was my grandmother's favorite," I laughed. "Is it the rum base that you like so much? I thought you'd be asleep, so it's in the freezer. Want me to go get it?"

I knew I sounded like I was hiding something, talking too much, speaking too fast, so he wouldn't grill me, and then, looking for an escape, offering to get the ice cream.

Martin yawned, and said, "Not now."

"Well, it'll be there for you tomorrow," I said.

I went out of the bedroom for a glass of water.

I'd hoped, now that I was home, Martin wouldn't feel the need to stay up, but when I returned, there he was, bright eyed, propped up in bed, and back to biding his time until I returned, reading a different magazine. He wanted to hear what had happened with Danielle that her mother had called, asking me to take her to her lesson tonight.

"I don't know. Everything is always about Veronica, isn't it? About having her last minute needs met."

Martin turned away and sighed.

"So what about this new teacher? Did you meet him?"

Did I meet him? If he only knew, I thought. I hesitated, trying to respond.

"Briefly," I said. "He just introduced himself. Danielle didn't want to talk about the lesson at all, when I asked how it went. It might not have gone so well. Maybe she'll go back to cello."

I hoped with all my heart, that she'd go back to playing cello, give up lessons with Ray. I knew though, that this was wishful thinking. I remembered myself at sixteen, getting all A's in Latin, in order to impress the dark-haired, cool teacher I had a crush on. Having an especially handsome, green-eyed jazz musician for a teacher, one who wore red cowboy boots, who had lived so long in Canada he now added the question, "eh?" at the end of even declarative sentences sometimes, and pronounced *about* as *aboot*, was definitely crush worthy. I expected Danielle to be interested in keeping on with her lessons, no matter how difficult and frustrating. Besides, she'd said that Chris, the boy from school she'd greeted at Toscanini's, was in band, and I thought that maybe the reason she'd taken up sax was that she wanted to audition for it, get close to him.

I didn't want Martin to know what Danielle's new teacher had to do with me. I was tamping down panic, petrified I might slip. I loved Martin and didn't want to lose him.

It had started to rain, the gauze curtains billowed out in a gust of wind. It was one of those sudden New England spring storms that signal an extreme change of weather. At work tonight at Diamond Street, I'd heard the desk clerk talking with a student, telling her that the day's mild temperatures were expected to dip wildly overnight, that tomorrow it would seem as if winter had returned. Jean must have been right.

Grateful for the distraction, I went to the window to see if the sill was getting wet, lightly brushing my hand over it. The wind was bringing in the rain. The weightless curtains tangled me up as I tried to move quickly, to put the window down over the screen.

I hurried out of the room to check the other windows in the apartment.

A sharp flash of lightning frightened me as I rushed to close those in the living room. When a loud thunderclap followed, I stepped back and then moved quickly through the dining room and kitchen, checking the sills there, determining that they were also wet; to be fast about it, I left all the screens in place. There was the force of finality punctuating the quiet apartment, as I brought the inside windows down, one after another.

By the time Martin caught up with me to help, the windows had all been closed.

Since he was out of bed, he decided to go for the ice cream.

I went back into the bedroom to undress and got into bed. When Martin returned, I was sitting up, turning pages of the book I'd grabbed from the nightstand, hoping Martin would see I was occupied and not ask any more questions about the Conservatory tonight.

"Thanks for this," he said about the ice cream. "I'm glad you'll keep me company while I finish it."

For a few minutes there was silence again, except for the sound of Martin enjoying his ice cream, the spoon scraping the china bowl, and me flipping through a copy of *What to Expect When You're Expecting*, pretending to be reading, but really, just trying to hold onto my determination to keep Martin from knowing about Ray. It would take every ounce of will I had. A familiar and surprising feeling of affection had come over me as he'd spoken tonight, and that was both confusing and frightening. I was not a teenager as I was when

I 'd known him. I was married to Martin now, and I had never told him about the complicated past I'd had with Ray. All Martin knew was that this man was Danielle's new teacher. I wasn't even sure he'd met him yet.

What if Danielle continued with her lessons? And if she did, I would have to figure out how I was going to keep Ray out of my life, how I might avoid answering Veronica's anticipated distress calls, whenever she needed me to chauffeur Danielle to the Conservatory. But there would be recitals I'd be expected to attend, or concerts, as Danielle advanced in her lessons, as I knew she would. If I didn't find a way to avoid any interaction with Ray, wouldn't I be tempted to tell him what had gone on after he left for Canada?

The silence was uncomfortable, while Martin, oblivious to my dilemma, happily ate his ice cream. In that silence, I thought of the baby we were going to have, and that, more than anything, helped me to summon the courage I needed to keep mum, to stay calm and centered.

"I need to sleep, Martin. Tomorrow's my long day," I said.

"I know. And today was unexpectedly long," he said. "I'm sorry Veronica called on you."

"Veronica needs to be more considerate," I said. "I'm teaching in two different places, running back and forth between Boston and Cambridge. I just wish she didn't have such an influence on our lives."

I bit my tongue then, a little late. Veronica was Danielle's mother, and that meant that Martin would always feel obligated to help with her, when her mother couldn't. And when Martin couldn't, the responsibility would generally fall to me. When I'd married him, I signed up for that. I remembered what he'd said about his responsibilities for Danielle, when we discussed marriage for the first time. *You know, I'm not free*, he'd warned.

Martin let my comment about Veronica go, without responding. He had no idea of the unintentional, yet very real threat to our marriage she had now initiated, hiring Ray as Danielle's music coach. I had been so devastated, losing him. What would it mean to my marriage, to have him back in my life now?

As if on cue, another flash of lightning lit up the room. It always startled me, more than a thunderclap even. Martin saw me cringe and reached an arm around behind my back at the waist, pulling me closer to him, kissing me sweetly. I was guilty and didn't deserve his comfort. Keeping something so important from him was a kind of infidelity, I realized now, a violation of his trust, wasn't it? But I felt it would be impossible to reveal my secret, after ten years of marriage. It was too late for that.

"I love you, Martin," I said. I would have to say this to him more and more, not take that love for granted. But saying it now, felt hollow, even though I did love him.

"So, you were saying, about the new sax teacher?"

I'd hoped he'd let it go.

He had stopped eating and gave me his full attention as I tried to answer.

"He's not from Canada, " I said. "He told me he moved there in the late sixties."

"Vietnam?" he asked.

I shook my head. Martin would make that connection. After he'd lost his older brother in Vietnam he'd been a draft counselor, working out of the Quaker Meeting House, helping guys like Ray leave the country or prepare a case for conscientious objector status.

"His mother is dead and his father is old now and needs to be moved to a home. Veronica only told me he moved to Boston to help with that," Martin said.

"So he's only working here, while his dad's still alive?" I asked.

When I remembered Ray's father's anger toward him, the fact of the ultimatum he'd given him, that if he left the country for anywhere other than Vietnam, he wasn't his son anymore, it seemed impossible that caring for him was Ray's reason for returning. Maybe he'll die soon, I thought, cruelly, and if he did, I hoped that Ray would go straight back to Canada.

"You met him, didn't you?" I asked Martin.

"How would I?" he said.

"Well, I thought you must have that day you dropped Danielle off at her first lesson. Didn't you go in to meet him?"

"No way," he said. "You know how she is. She bounded out

of the car, not wanting me to go in."

His ice cream was melting and he said he didn't feel like finishing it now.

"Too late. Too much. It's rich."

Out of guilt, I suppose, I'd bought—not a pint, but a whole quart of frozen pudding ice cream for him.

He held up the bowl and said he'd take it to the kitchen.

"I have to sleep," I said.

He kissed me on the forehead.

He shut off the little lamp on the nightstand, and when he got up, he moved carefully in the dark, to head out of the room. He stopped at the doorway and turned back for a second.

"Pleasant dreams," he said.

He was in shadow now. A beam from the neighbor's crime light shone in the window and slanted across the bed.

Lying next to him in the dark, I thought not just of what might happen to us now that Ray Newell had reappeared, but I turned over in my mind, memories of that other time, when Ray had been so very much a part of my imagined life, after he'd first left the country.

Going to California with an aching in my heart—that was how the song went. In 1968, while others of my generation here and elsewhere weren't just singing about going to California with flowers in their hair, but had actually made the trek the year before, going across country driving VW buses, motorcycles, taking Greyhound or Trailways, sticking their thumbs out or boarding trains or planes. Yet, I was the opposite of free-spirited: sent to California, held prisoner in a home for unwed mothers, waiting to give birth—a mere birthing machine—a mother-to-be, but no potential earth mother. Thinking of Ray and imagining being together with him again had been my only solace. I knew that things might have been different for me, if my mother had still been alive that summer day when, after a pre-college physical examination, the family doctor had called the house, telling my father about what he called my *predicament*. My mother never would have sent me away, never kept me from letting Ray know. I wonder even now, what would have happened between us, had he known.

Martin began growling in his sleep and then sounding like he was speaking a language that wasn't translatable, but which had cadence and inflection, making me think I could decipher what he was saying, if only I listened closely enough.

"Martin, you're growling," I said, nudging him.

He turned over without waking and the growling stopped.

I reached over and rubbed his back the way I liked him rubbing mine, in a circular motion and very gently near the base of his spine. He stayed quiet then, lapsing into breathing in a barely audible, regular rhythm. If he kept to this pattern, I thought I might get back to sleep.

And I did, finally, but not for long, waking with a start, having had a terrible dream, one that was all the more frightening because it was more memory than dream. Images from the time when I had been taken away from the home to the hospital to give birth had been so vivid as to make me feel that it was happening all over again. It had been a long time since I'd been visited by this nightmare; Ray Newell had brought it all back.

In the dream there were two nuns—nurses—it was a Catholic hospital—everything seemed to be Catholic in my childhood and youth. The sisters were looming over me. To say that I'd seen them in the dream wasn't exactly true: I couldn't see their faces. It was that strange sensation you have in a dream when sometimes faces remain hidden, yet you're sure you know the identity of the characters. I had been strapped onto a gurney and the nuns were leaning over me, the nasty one ordering—*stop your hollering, will you*—that the pain couldn't possibly be as bad as I was making it out to be. *You'll remember it though, if it is, and maybe change your ways.* Then the young, pretty nun appeared—I knew she was pretty, even though I couldn't see her face in the dream. I knew who she was. When I first got to St. Ann's, she'd given me saltine crackers from time to time, when I had morning sickness. *Take small bites and chew them well.* She hovered over me, making me feel comforted, telling me not to worry, convincing me with her reassuring smile, that everything would be all right. Of course, everything would not be all right.

I considered how things had changed. Veronica had made

sure that Danielle was on the pill as soon as she began dating. And young women who weren't had had an alternative since Roe v. Wade. Keeping me awake, my mind now raced through other memories from my own time. When I was a teenager one of the neighbors who'd moved to our street from New York, so that her husband could take over as choir school director at the parish church, had been the daughter of a doctor doing research that had led to the development of the birth control pill. It had seemed so strange to learn this then. Ironically, although the husband was in church all the time, preparing his choir for Sunday Masses and concerts for holy days, this woman was something of a pariah, never climbing the church's granite steps, proudly advertising that she was an atheist. She would sit at the soda fountain at Rexall Drug every afternoon, lecturing against the Vietnam War to the regulars—some of them mailmen, just finishing their routes, and most of them World War II veterans who supported the U.S. involvement. *You'll be all right, if you stay in school*, she'd say to the University students, who came to the pharmacy to buy the *New York Times*.

When my mother was six months pregnant with my brother, our neighbor had called to talk to her about me, mentioning that since I was *now that age*, my mother ought be concerned about the Catholic Church's position on contraception, the woman telling her she thought that outlawing birth control was outrageous, that she hoped that I wouldn't *get into trouble*. In that warning she'd foretold my future. *Imagine*, my mother had said to my father, after ending the phone call that night, *imagine, talking about birth control to a pregnant woman! A child is a gift from God, and children bring so much happiness.* The irony of her comment still gave me the shivers, remembering my mother dying soon after, in childbirth.

For years after losing my baby to adoption, I'd wished that Ray had been told. I didn't think that any contentious situation would have developed back then, if he'd heard the truth. He wasn't one to run away from responsibilities, even though that was what his father had thought he'd done, going off to Canada as he did. And after all that, the fact that he was here now to take care of his father's needs was proof of his sense of responsibility, wasn't it?

Tonight Ray said he'd written several letters to me that year.

My father must have been looking out for that postmark, knowing that Ray was in Canada. I kept waiting for a letter or a postcard, an address to write to him, wanting to understand why he'd left without me. But no mail was ever forwarded to me at Saint Anne's Home. I created many scenarios in my mind during my confinement and after. And because I didn't ever hear from him again I wondered if maybe the authorities had caught up with him before he'd crossed the border, that he'd been sent off to Vietnam anyway. He might have been killed over there, MIA or gone AWOL, and then found and court martialed, or even taken as a POW. Anything might have happened, I thought. I didn't believe he'd ever written to me.

After my ordeal was over—the pregnancy and birth part anyway—I'd tried to find him by contacting his family. One day I knocked on the door of the house where they had lived, and a young woman with a couple of toddlers nipping at her ankles answered the door. She told me that she knew nothing about the people who'd lived in the house before her, that it had been vacant when the Realtor had shown it to her family, that some developer had bought the house and remodeled it for sale. Hearing this, I'd gone to a neighbor's house, hoping that the people living there were the same ones who'd lived next to the Newells. It was a good guess. They told me that after Ray's father had retired from his duties at the town hall, the family had moved to some little village in New Hampshire. *They were disgraced by a son who was a draft dodger.* "Of course they'd leave," my father had said, when I mentioned this to him. *You're lucky he left.*

I knew I was not to blame that he didn't know about the baby I gave up. But now that he was here, how would I keep from telling him that he'd fathered a child? Wouldn't I be to blame now, if I didn't? Wasn't it his right to know? And if he knew, he had every right to try to find our child. And if that was what he wanted to do, and if he found her, more than likely, our child would want to know the mother who gave birth to her as well. Then, I'd have no choice other than to tell Martin. No, Ray Newell couldn't be told about the baby. I couldn't take the chance that he'd want to find her, if he knew.

I had struggled to forget him, and thought I had. But every day, I thought about our baby girl, figured I probably always would.

I hoped that she had had a better childhood than she would have had, if I'd kept her, trying to raise her on my own, having to fend for myself, my father threatening he'd have nothing to do with me, if I decided to keep the baby. I knew nothing of what had become of her. The idea was to keep everything from the young mother, lest she suddenly have second thoughts, and not want to give up the baby, already promised to some other woman. Then, an open adoption was considered detrimental to all parties. When I heard stories these days of adopted children being reunited with their birth parents, I sometimes wondered whether my child—a teenager now—would ever come looking for me. As things stood now, the child wouldn't ever look for Ray. I hadn't listed a father's name on the birth certificate, only "unknown."

I probably would have married Ray, if he'd known about the baby, and if he'd wanted to marry me. But weren't we both better off, that that hadn't come to be? I might not have gone to college, if I'd found Ray to tell him, and perhaps, needing to support a family, Ray wouldn't have pursued his dream of a music career either. And I would never have married Martin, never be carrying his child now.

Three

Martin

It was Friday night and Clare suggested we have dinner at Elephant Parade, a new Vietnamese restaurant in the neighborhood.

I ordered a beer and she ordered ginger ale. I knew how she loved beer with spicy Asian food, but she was being careful. "No alcohol at all until the baby's born," she said. I reminded her that French women continued to drink wine all through pregnancy.

"I know. Remember when we went to dinner at Angela's?"

Angela was one of her students at the Medical Center. She and her roommate came to Boston together from Sicily. They were both research doctors. When Clare had passed on a glass of wine the night they'd invited us to dinner, Angela's roommate, whose father owned a vineyard, told Clare that if she ever came to his house he would insist she drink wine, even if she were pregnant.

"I waited so long to decide," Clare said. "I want to do this right. We did it, Martin," she said. "I'm pregnant. Can you believe it?"

I took a deep breath. It had happened fast, and even at the beginning of her second trimester, she was still amazed it had come to be.

"This time I got it right," I said.

"What does that mean?" she asked. "We never tried before."

"Oh, I don't know," I said. "This just feels right. I mean it's not the way things went with Veronica."

"Huh?" Clare said. "Can you explain that to me?"

She leaned on her elbow, no expression on her face, looking across the table at me, eyes fixed on mine. I remembered she'd had that same steady gaze that night she had said, after we'd been together for ten years, *I think we should try to make a baby*. By then, I'd thought she'd decided against it, that mothering Danielle was enough.

"I mean, this time it's different. It really is right. With

Danielle I did things backwards. I married Veronica *after* I found out she was pregnant" I said.

Clare kind of squirmed in her seat then, and said only, "Oh?"

I didn't want to talk about Veronica. It was our night, our baby that we should be talking about. But, she pressed me.

"Why didn't you ever tell me that?" she asked.

"Oh, I don't know. It's not really important, is it? We got married right away. Soon as I knew. She was hardly pregnant at all," I said.

"That's why you married her?" she asked. "Was it a good reason to get married?"

Why she cared to know the answer to that question, I didn't know, but with each answer, I gave, she needed more, listening hard— not being accusatory really—I'd heard enough of that in a courtroom to recognize it.

"Well," I hesitated, "what does it matter? I thought it was the right thing to do, at the time. She was going to have my baby— Danielle. I didn't want to do what my father had done, leaving my mother when she was pregnant. I wanted my child to grow up with a father."

I'd talked to Clare many times about how hard things had been for my mother, when I was growing up, and for me, without a father around.

"Of course, I know," Clare said. "Of course, Danielle would be your number one priority."

"Well, she is, but you are, too," I said. "You know that."

I couldn't figure out why she was pursuing this.

"I mean you've provided especially well for Veronica, so that Danielle can have a nice place to live, grow up in a comfortable situation—even though you left, right? You aren't your father, Martin. You've made sacrifices for them. We both have. I mean, look where we live, so that they can have a comfortable home."

"I want us to have a home of our own, too, Clare. I want our baby to have what Danielle has," I said. "You and our baby are my priority now. You'll see."

It had been a lot to manage with the three females in my life: Clare, Danielle, Veronica. A lot.

Clare had never liked living on Ridge Road. I got it: it wasn't luxe or anything close to that, and I knew she didn't want that, that she just wanted a comfortable place to live. She wanted what Veronica had for Danielle. That's what I wanted, too. Danielle—and her mother, too—got to live in a nice house that I helped finance, near the reservoir on an upscale, sycamore-lined street, and Clare and I lived in an old, rundown apartment building, located on a connecting road running from the route for commuters from the suburbs north and west of town, and leading to all the main thoroughfares into Boston. Rush hour happened right on our doorstep; the street even made all the traffic reports on local television and radio stations. Worst of all, was the noise: even in winter, and even with all the windows closed, the constant background of car horns, buses, motorcycles, police cars, ambulances, and fire engines, running up and down our street at all hours of the day and night, rattled ones nerves. In addition to the noise, Clare complained that all the pollution from the traffic created an oily dust, that settled in the corners of every room, adding lately, *and it's not good for the baby either, for me to be breathing that air.*

Clare and I had lived together at Ridge Road for all of the ten years we'd been married. The apartment was a choice I'd made right after Veronica and I had separated, before Clare was in the picture, and I was really struggling financially to support Danielle. I'd switched careers, leaving teaching high school history to go to law school. I'd only been practicing law for a couple of years— and working right from the start, as a Public Defender— when I separated from Veronica. I guess I got used to the apartment, but it had obviously worn Clare down, more and more. *You'd be happy living anywhere, I think. If we weren't married*, Clare would say, *you'd probably join a monastery.* And I'd agree that I could probably live in monk's cell.

"I know what you've put up with, Clare," I said now. "You're a saint."

She scoffed at that.

"As far as Veronica is concerned, I never did love her the way I love you, is what I mean. That's why I told you she was pregnant when we married. We never had what you and I have. We want this baby. We planned it. It's a mutual decision. You took your time deciding. That was fine. Even before the divorce, Veronica and I lived different, separate lives. We were just Danielle's parents really. It was never going to be right between us. People don't change all that much."

"I never thought that," Clare said. "That you hadn't loved her in the beginning or hadn't the way you say you loved me from the start."

"It just wasn't this way, the way it is for us," I said. "Please know that, Clare."

Our order had arrived. I looked down at my plate, picked up the chopsticks and pushing the food around, separated the vegetables from the noodles, banishing each to separate halves of the Chinese pagoda pictured on the blue Willow Ware porcelain. Why was Clare being like this tonight, persisting about Veronica, the way she was?

She said then that she'd always believed that having a child with someone and raising that child together meant that there was a certain kind of closeness two people have, unlike any other.

"After almost eleven years together, you'd think we'd know each other," she said, "know all the important things there are about the other person."

"I'm sorry, Clare. I just figured you knew that things were never right between Veronica and me, even if I didn't tell you that the reason I married her was that she got pregnant."

"You know," she said, "I thought I understood the shared custody thing, when we decided to get married. I thought that Danielle would be enough, that we wouldn't need to have a child together. I kept waiting for things to feel right."

"Clare, this is what we both want now. And don't you think that things between you and Danielle are right?"

"Sort of," she said. "Veronica gets in the way,"

I sighed, frustrated by this conversation. I took her hand across the table and held it.

I saw the woman at the table next to us, raise her eyebrows. She had looked up when we were being seated and had smiled at Clare, I guess, seeing that she was pregnant. Clearly, the woman had been listening to our conversation. She leaned over and whispered something across the table to the man with her. He turned and looked right at me.

"If it hadn't been for Danielle," I said, "I'd most certainly have moved on—away, I mean—from Veronica. I had, in fact moved to California and was living there."

"Right. I forgot you fell for the lure of California in the late sixties, too."

I thought she was being sarcastic now. I knew she'd lived there the year after she finished high school, but she'd never told me why she came home, what made her leave to go to college in Maine.

"I'm sorry I never told you any of this," I said. "I didn't think it was important. Veronica came looking for me, bringing the news that she was going to have a baby—my baby. It was that—only that—that brought me back east to her. Now, can we just drop this and enjoy dinner with each other?"

***

When we arrived home at Ridge Road, we discovered a line of police cars and emergency vehicles out in front of our building, yellow caution tape blocking the entrance. I stood near the cordoned off area, trying to see what was going on. A dark stained square of sidewalk at the opening to the alley between our apartment building and the house next door was illuminated by the streetlight above it. Blood, I thought.

I grabbed Clare's arm, seeing it, and steered her back toward a police officer, to find out what was going on.

"With all the traffic here, I'd been thinking I lived on the Southeast Expressway, but this—a shooting—or is it a stabbing—takes things to a whole new level," she said, pointing to the ambulance.

The light was on inside, and I could see the EMTs moving, working on the victim.

Word on the street was, that a teenaged boy was stabbed right on the sidewalk, where I thought we'd be pushing a baby stroller someday, if we couldn't find a better living situation we could afford.

The police officer in charge was keeping people out of the way of detectives and fire and ambulance personnel, and I approached him, to see if we could get into the house. The guy didn't want to hear my question, cutting me off, ordering me, as I began to talk, to "Move back behind the line."

Clare and I joined the other tenants from our building as well as several curiosity seekers, who were assembled on the sidewalk across the street, in front of Our Lady of Sorrows Catholic Church.

I looked around at the other tenants. The woman who lived downstairs from us was wearing plastic hair curlers, another one in a nightgown and robe had a pack of kids but must have left them all sleeping to come out to see what was going on. The commotion had also brought out the man who lived in the house next to ours, an insomniac, who sometimes paraded up and down the alley in the middle of the night, smoking a cigar, blowing smoke in the direction of our fire alarm sensor, setting it off.

Clare said, "What am I doing here?"

The guy with the cigar, thinking she wanted information said, "A kid got stabbed."

She just stared at him, saying nothing more.

"You've been dragging your feet about moving, Martin. Time to get out of here. We don't want to be living here with a baby. No more avoiding it."

This incident coming on the heels of our conversation at the restaurant fueled Clare's thinking about what Veronica and Danielle had for a home. This wasn't fair to her, I knew.

I moved her hair behind her ear, and leaned down to kiss her. "We'll get out of here, Clare," I whispered. "Soon as we can. I promise."

I held onto her. She looked doubtful, but shook her head *yes*.

It was nearly an hour before the last of the police cars took off in a scream of sirens, headed to some other tragedy, and we were allowed to go inside.

Once we were in the house, there was no further conversation, only activity. We fell into our usual nightly routine preparing for bed, setting out what we'd need for work the next day, keeping silent. We lowered the thermostat, set up the coffee maker, washed up, undressed, turned down the bed covers, fluffed the pillows, shut off the lights, and crawled under the covers. Clare had made herself clear; I had to get a move on, start looking seriously for other digs.

I had a hard time falling asleep. I was troubled by the thought that if we didn't find another place to live very soon, I'd have Veronica on my case as well as Clare. She would determine that my apartment was no longer an acceptable place for Danielle to live, even half of the time. She would know about the crime, of course. The stabbing would be reported in the news. A safe neighborhood was important. I knew that. Living at Ridge Road, I was putting not only Clare and the baby she was carrying in danger, but I was also now putting my daughter in harm's way. In my mind, I could hear Veronica announcing that she wanted to renegotiate the hard won joint custody arrangement she'd vehemently resisted at first.

***

Clare's first words the next morning were, "So, we should start looking for a new place right away."

"I know. I know," I said. "That's clear. We have to see what's out there."

She was willing, she said, to settle for a modest place—as long as it was clean and the appliances worked, and it wasn't on a highway or a neighborhood street masquerading as one, and if it was quiet and safe.

"And as long as we have a washing machine."

"You don't want much, do you?" I smiled.

"Just the basics," she said. "Oh, and a yard would be nice, too."

"Yes, definitely a yard," I said.

Although there was no yard for Danielle at our place, growing up she'd had one at her mother's house, a big back yard with a sandbox, a swing set, and one of those fancy wooden climbing structures that had become popular in Cambridge and elsewhere. She'd had what Clare and I wanted for our child, too.

"We can do this," I said, not really knowing how.

I kissed that sweet spot on her neck under her ear, but as if she remembered her resolve and wanted only to get to the task at hand, she squirmed away. She wasn't going to let herself be sweet-talked out of thinking about it. We had to find a new place to live. Soon.

"Where's the newspaper," she asked.

I pointed to the corner bin where already read newspapers were put. I'd placed it there, hoping to get rid of it, to keep Clare from reading the article detailing the stabbing the night before.

"It made the morning edition?" she asked, referring to the story, even before looking at the headlines. She was looking at me, the way she did to remind me that it was useless trying to hide anything from her.

Sitting back down with the unfolded front section of the *Globe* spread out on the table, she saw the story prominently featured on the front page of the Metro section, the incident described as gang related, not some stupid disagreement between two teenagers that led to an argument, and one of them pulling a knife out of his pocket.

"Pronounced dead at Mt. Auburn Hospital," she read aloud.

"I read it," I said.

The kid—he was that—just seventeen—had most likely died right there at the scene on the sidewalk next to our apartment building. The news story detailed a fight that had begun around the corner at the basketball court.

"It wasn't a random killing, Clare," I said, as if that would make her feel better.

"Hey, we made the papers," Clare said sarcastically.

I shook my head. There was nothing to say.

The phone rang. I was due at the courthouse and didn't have time for any further conversation.

"I have to go. If it's for me, let it play. I can't talk now. I'll call whoever it is back later."

The call went to the answering machine quickly. As I passed I saw Veronica Wheeler identified on the LCD display. No surprise really: she was the only one who ever called the house this early in the day. No doubt she'd been up since the crack of dawn as usual, out for a run most mornings at sunrise, even on cold winter days. *I'm warm after the first two minutes*, she'd say, whenever anyone expressed amazement, finding out on a frigid morning that she'd nevertheless done her five miles.

I stopped to hear the message, as she recorded it. It hadn't taken her long to call to get the scoop. She'd seen the early news show and the stabbing in Cambridge had been prominently featured on the newscast.

"I couldn't believe it. They were showing your house on the news," she was saying.

She signed off in that familiar way, "Give me a call, Martin."

Four

Ray

After being away from Charland for sixteen years, I should have expected that a lot would have changed. Yet, I was surprised. Several of the old Victorian mansions on the Main Street, *Painted Ladies*, as they were called, now looked rundown and uninhabited. Two had *For Sale* signs out front, one house looking like it had been completely gutted and probably modernized inside. Judging from the colorful paint job on the ornate outside trim, someone had poured a lot of money into the project.

The town diner, where I used to meet friends—and take Clare for burgers and fries—was nowhere to be seen, probably rusting out at the town dump. And the Mobil station with its Pegasus sign that was next door had been replaced by a mini shopping area with the usual: 24-hour convenience store, a Dunkin' Donuts, a pizza joint, and a drive-up bank. I was not nostalgic for that other time, though. I wondered how many people who lived here now, even knew each other. I'd hated that about the place, that everyone knew—or thought they knew—everyone else's business. Lots of gossip, and a lot of it wrong. I used to imagine what people said about me after I left.

I took the turn after the stores and continued down a road I remembered having woods on either side of it. I had taken for granted that the trees would always be there, but they'd been cleared and there were huge parking lots for new companies that had moved into town, the only trees left, those lining the road. Mercy Rehabilitation and Nursing—this place, also new—was two miles further on, according to the directions I'd been given.

Getting there, I drove into the garage, and found a spot near the entrance elevator. My father had been admitted here as a rehab patient, transferred from the hospital after his stroke. This would be the first time I'd seen him since coming home. I was experiencing a feeling that maybe I shouldn't be here. Why would I even think of this as home anymore? And so, the anxiety began. I hoped not to settle in back here, but I had no idea how long I'd be away from Montreal. This visit today, and the one I'd scheduled with the social worker, was acknowledgment of my role of caring for my father. I didn't think it would be possible to extricate myself from that role now, that only his death would make that possible.

I was here not just to try to reconcile with my old man, after being disowned sixteen years before, but I was to break the news to him that he'd be moving to *another building*, the way the social worker, in her phone call to me, kept referring to the nursing home on the hospital campus.

I walked by the physical therapy room and saw several machines and a couple of attendants putting patients through the motions. My father wasn't one of them. I scanned the community room as I passed; two tables were occupied by men playing cards—poker, it looked like. He wasn't there either. No one was walking the corridors. I'd been informed that my father wasn't very social these days, and I tried to imagine him—my gregarious father being antisocial, someone who'd had an opinion about everything, and often engaged in arguments, just for the sake of hearing his own voice, it seemed. He'd had many friends, and got along with his cronies from the town hall where he'd worked as an accountant while I was growing up. *You'll find him in his room, probably not sitting up*, the social worker had said.

She was right. He was asleep, when I arrived. I wondered if he'd been given some medication that made him sleepy. I could imagine that he'd be feisty, being here, without being given something to calm him. The social worker had also said that he repeatedly asks when he's going home, and sometimes changes that to, *I'm going home tomorrow*, or *I'll be going home this afternoon*.

I left the room and went out to ask about him at the nurse's station. There hadn't been anyone sitting there when I'd come in. Now, I found a young, perky woman sitting at the desk sipping from a soda can, while sorting through papers.

"Can I help you?" she asked.

I told her who I was, adding "health care proxy," and asked

whether he'd been given some medication, so he'd sleep.

"No. No meds for that. He sleeps after lunch sometimes."

What else does he have to do, I thought. The place was as quiet as after a Canadian snowfall.

I looked at my watch and it was nearly four o'clock. I figured that lunch had been served before noon. It was almost time for the early bird special. I'd seen the large stainless steel hot food truck being parked down the corridor when I got off the elevator, dinner steaming away inside.

"How long has he been sleeping?" I asked.

"I'm not sure. I just came on duty," was the answer. "But probably a good idea to wake him. He'll be getting his dinner soon," the nurse said.

I went back to the room. I took a deep breath, and in the voice I normally use for conversation said, "Dad. Hey, Dad. I'm back, Dad. It's me, Ray. I'm here to see you. Wake up, Dad!"

He grumbled and turned over, away from me.

I touched his shoulder and he shuddered, turning over to face me again, but not opening his eyes. I leaned over him, brought my face down next to his, and said a little louder and more enthusiastically, "Newell! Rise and Shine! Attention!"

This was the way he'd wake me for school sometimes, as if I were a Marine, as he had been.

It worked. He opened his eyes. He squinted, as if to question who he was seeing. It had been sixteen years, after all. Of course, he'd be disbelieving.

"It's me. Ray. I'm home. To see you," I said.

"This isn't home," he grouched. "This is a hospital, you goof! But it's time to go home. I'm fine now. Just a little stroke of bad luck," he chuckled.

I stood up. I could feel my shoulder muscles seizing up already. This would be difficult.

"Where's your mother? Out shopping?" he asked.

And so, the dementia the social worker had spoken about, reared its ugly head. My mother had died ten years before. My friend Eric, who never left town, except to serve in Vietnam, had broken the news to me, mentioning my mother's death, when we'd talked on the phone at the holidays, a year after she'd passed. My father had never let me know, even though, once a few years had passed and I was no longer worried about anyone knowing my whereabouts, I'd always sent him a postcard with my address—just my address— nothing else written on it, whenever I changed my living situation. It was the way I'd been located by the Mass General doctor, when he'd been brought in with a stroke. Someone had found the last postcard I'd sent, folded up in his wallet.

I didn't answer him about where my mother was.

It hurt to remember her—not to have her around, but to still have this pitiful man lay before me, totally confused about what year it was, and the two major events of his adult life, other than his service during World War II: disowning me, and losing his wife of forty years.

"I talked to the doctor," I said, thinking it was best not to bring up my meeting with the social worker.

"Now, what would be the purpose of that? None of your business. Leave it to me to be talking to the doctor. Or your mother. You're wet behind the ears still. What do you know about talking to doctors?"

He sneered and gave a little laugh.

"The doctor thinks you need more care than you can get at home."

"Your mother is perfectly capable of taking care. That is, if I need help. You can take care of yourself now, so she won't have to bother about you. Pretty soon you'll be off on your own or in the Army, whichever."

"I might want to go to the Conservatory," I said, playing along.

"And who's going to finance that? The Marine Band won't want you. But the Army will take you."

This was the way he always talked to me. After so many years, and knowing that he didn't know what he was saying anymore, it still burned a hole in my gut to hear him talk to me like this. Somehow, I'd succeeded in spite of his running criticism, and the way he'd always knocked down any dreams I'd had for the future. Maybe it hurt more, because now, given his dementia, I knew he could never really forgive me, ever reconcile with me, even if he did have any fleeting moments of lucidity. I didn't mean to cause him any upset, and I was sorry I had. I had only wanted him to listen and accept that I felt I was doing the right thing, leaving for Canada, as I had.

He grumbled and said again, "Where's your mother?"

I grabbed my jacket from the chair and put it on. I couldn't stay. I thought now that it had been a terrible idea to come home to see to his care. Why had I? Even without dementia, why did I think he'd ever forgive me. The fact that I'd come home had meant that I was willing to forgive him. He was a sad, old man now, one who couldn't remember any pain he'd caused, cursing me as he had. If it hadn't been for him, Clare would have known where I was, known how to reach me. I would have let him know where I was right away, if I'd trusted him not to turn me in. Maybe I could have explained to Clare that the driver of the van going North had refused to take her, that I hadn't had anything to do with it. If I'd been able to talk on the phone with her I wouldn't have had to write all those letters she said she'd never received. What would it matter if I told her now, explained what had happened? She was married and going to have a baby.

I blamed my father for a lot that was wrong in my life. But I did still have what mattered to me as much as Clare had. I had my music. Because I'd objected to that war, I didn't die in Vietnam, or wasn't maimed there. I didn't come home suffering from PTSD or some other deep psychological problem, as my friend Eric Belmonte had, arrested last weekend for pulling a knife on a cop after his mother had felt threatened by him and called for help. That might have been me, I thought, when I'd read the story in the morning newspaper.

Before I turned to leave, I tried again with my father.

"Dad, Mum isn't around anymore to take care of you."

He scrunched up his forehead, not understanding, and as if trying to, caused him pain.

"What? She left me now? When I was sick?"

"No, no dad. Mum's been gone a long time. For years. She died. You live alone. I've been living in Canada. Sixteen years. I'm here to figure things out about your care."

I was being cruel now. He couldn't understand anymore. I

caught myself, but too late. I stopped talking, but he went on.

"No, no. Don't tell me that. No one told me. No one. Why didn't anyone tell me she was gone?"

He seemed then, not just to think that I was a teenager still. Suddenly he seemed to forget entirely who I had ever been to him.

"Nurse. When am I going home?" he asked me. "Tomorrow?"

"I'll find out. I'll talk to the doctor when I see him," I said, and left the room.

I got into the car, and sat there, not starting the engine. Tears I hadn't shed ever, began. I wished I were in my studio, blowing my horn, able to let out some blue notes, this feeling of loss and regret washing over me now. I shouldn't have come back. Maybe what I had to do for my father could have been done in phone calls instead. I'd been naïve to think that he would be lucid and rational. He never had been with me. And now, the dementia cancelled any fantasy I'd had about reconciliation.

I started the engine. The radio was tuned to NPR, time for *All Things Considered*. The correspondent was reporting that a judge had ruled that Marvin Gay, Sr. had been declared fit for trial in his son's death. I thought about the circumstances of the Prince of Soul's death, the years of abuse by his father. I had not endured physical beatings like the singer had, but my own father's constant emotional derision had made my youth miserable. I had escaped the worst though. Marvin Gaye had succeeded bigtime, but the abuse his father had visited upon him had led to depression and addiction, and finally his death. I'd been lucky. I'd stayed clean, even working among other musicians who hadn't.

I drove back to Boston, taking the Mass Pike this time rather than the roads I'd driven on the way to the hospital, through small towns I'd wanted to see, to remember. I'd driven through Oxford and thought of Eric, who'd lived there, now in a jail cell.

With all that was going on, I felt I was really here. I should leave as soon as the semester was finished. I wondered how Veronica would take that. I'd promised to meet her this afternoon at the Conservatory and I drove there now. I'd be right on time.

She was waiting for me outside the entrance to the performance hall, talking with someone whose deferential posture pegged him as a student. She kept looking away, probably scanning the street for me, not knowing the car.

I tooted the horn and she saw me. She held up an index finger to let me know. She was nodding to the student, working on her exit.

I reached over and opened the door for her.

"Hey, there," I said.

"You got here just in time," Veronica said, leaning over and kissing my cheek. "I think that student was just about to ask me for a reference, and I'm up to my ears correcting exams right now."

"I'm glad to see you," I said, raising my eyebrows to let her know it had been a difficult afternoon.

She asked anyway.

"How was the visit with your father?"

She knew my story with him.

I groaned.

"Someone needs some hugs," she said.

She touched my thigh and I felt the heat of her hand.

"You don't have to talk about it unless you want to."

"I probably shouldn't have come back," I said. "What was I thinking? It was crazy to expect anything different from him. And now, he doesn't even know what year it is. He doesn't even know me. He thinks I'm still in high school and that my mother is still alive."

I sighed then, remembering, "He even called me nurse."

"I'm so sorry, Ray," she said. "I'll make you feel better. We can go to my house today. Danielle will be at school until her lesson with you. And please, don't think of leaving. Things will work out."

At her house, we went inside to the kitchen. She poured a glass of wine for herself, and started to pour one for me. I put my hand over the glass to stop her.

"I have the lesson, remember? And don't you have to go back for a rehearsal tonight?"

"I do. I just thought one glass, to take the edge off."

I reached out and put my arm around her and pulled her close to me.

"I can help with that," I said, burying my head in her hair that smelled like grapefruit.

"Mmmm," I hummed.

She put her glass down. We started toward the entrance to the dining room, to go upstairs. We stopped, hearing the front door creak open, and suddenly there was Danielle's voice calling out, "Hello? Mum? You here?" We rushed back into the kitchen, unsure of what to do, realizing we had no escape.

Five

Danielle

I'd told my Mom that I'd be doing some work at the school library, and that there was a class meeting with the college counselor before my lesson with Mr. Newell. I had actually been hanging around at Mona Lisa, the pizza shop near the high school, hoping that Chris Seagate would stop in for a slice after jazz band rehearsal. He actually had transferred out of my Chemistry class, dropping it to take Biology, I'd found out. That meant I didn't have any classes with him now. I'd passed him in the cafeteria, but he'd been involved in some group conversation and hadn't even noticed me. Figuring he'd gone straight home after, or that the rehearsal was still going on, I gave up and took the bus home to Mum's house.

I didn't think she was at home since the Toyota wasn't in the driveway. I was glad. I'd been hoping to be alone, that she wouldn't have a student at the house for a lesson, or wouldn't be here rehearsing for a performance or planning a lecture. It was rare to have any time home alone, and I wanted to practice the embouchure exercises Mr. Newell had assigned. I was still having trouble with them and wanted to do better at my lesson tonight. I didn't want Mum to hear me practicing, didn't want to hear her suggestions or comments.

But when I opened the front door, I heard a man's voice and then my Mum's, answering him. They were in the back of the house, in the kitchen, it sounded like. The man's voice was familiar, but I couldn't immediately place it or hear what he said. Perhaps it was one of her students I'd met in the past. I didn't hear any music being played though, so maybe they weren't having a lesson, but a meeting about a recital or something.

I did hear a counter stool scrape against the stone floor, and figured Mum was coming out to see me.

"Danielle?" she called. Her voice got closer, and then she appeared.

"Your car wasn't in the driveway, so I didn't think you were home. Do you have a student?"

And then, my mouth dropped open. Behind Mum, standing in the kitchen doorway, frozen there, the way I felt, was Mr. Newell.

"He was just leaving," she said. "He gave me a ride home. My car is in the garage."

"Oh, what's wrong with the car?" I asked. "Wouldn't it start?"

"Nothing's wrong. It's in the Conservatory parking garage. I'm going back to meet with a student, so I left it there."

I didn't understand. This made no sense. She'd said Mr. Newell was just leaving.

"How are you getting back to school, if he's just leaving? Aren't you going, too?"

"Hi, Danielle. How's the embouchure practice going?" Mr. Newell said.

My heart jumped a little, when he acknowledged me.

"I came home to practice. I didn't think anyone was here. I didn't see the car."

"He was just leaving," Mum said again. "Hang on, Danielle. Ray has to pick something up at his apartment, before we go back to campus. I want to talk to you, so he'll come back shortly to get me."

She walked toward Ray and then walked him back into the kitchen. What were they up to?

A few seconds later, he left by the kitchen door, calling out, "See you later, Danielle."

When he was gone, I threw my backpack down on the floor with such force that the vase on a side table nearby rocked a bit, but luckily, didn't fall. I had brought home all of my heaviest textbooks this afternoon, and I had put all of my anger at finding Mum here with my sax teacher into pitching the bag.

"So, why didn't you drive yourself home? Why did he take you home? I don't get this."

She reached for my arm to guide me to the couch, and I resisted. But she was strong and I felt weak in this situation. It seemed all wrong to have found him here with her in the middle of the afternoon, when she would ordinarily have been working—if not teaching, then seeing students or preparing a lecture. This was my teacher. My new teacher. She couldn't have a thing going with him, not yet anyway, could she?

"I'm so sorry, Danielle. I should have said something."

I moved to get up off the couch but she pulled me back down next to her. She was crying. This always happened when I got angry.

"You should have said something about what?" I asked. "He's my teacher. What are you doing with him?"

"Sometimes things happen. You don't expect anything. And sometimes you can't explain it. How was I to know that anything would come of getting to know him?"

I wanted her to stop talking, to let me go, if she wasn't going to answer my question.

"I don't know. I don't know," she said through tears. "I don't know if this is anything serious, anything that will go on. So, I didn't tell you, didn't want you upset if it was something that wouldn't go on."

What was wrong with her, not to think this was serious that she was involved in a thing with my new music coach? She kept shaking her head in dismay, and then she said something I just couldn't believe. How could I believe her when she'd been keeping something like this from me?

"Okay, if you can't handle this, I'll end it. He's your teacher. I know."

Suddenly it made sense to me that she'd tried so hard to keep me playing cello, not switching to saxophone. It wasn't about me. It was all about her. About her and Ray Newell, not about what I needed, what I wanted to learn. She wasn't looking out for me. She was looking out for herself.

"This is the reason, isn't it," I asked, "that you didn't want me to give up cello? You had something going with him."

She shook her head *No*, and said, "Danielle, please listen."

I didn't want to listen. I wanted to block my ears, but I knew that would be childish.

"I didn't even know Ray Newell, until I went looking for a teacher for you. He might not even stay around. He has a temporary position at the Conservatory, covering for someone on sabbatical."

I knew I couldn't stay here and listen to her any longer. And I certainly didn't want to be here when Ray Newell returned to pick her up to go back to the Conservatory.

"Call Dad," I said. "Tell him I want to stay with him and Clare tonight. And I don't want you driving me to my lesson. You aren't coming there with me!"

I knew tears were about to gush and I went into the bathroom, slamming the door behind me. I splashed cold water on my eyes, while she made the phone call. I hoped my dad would answer.

"Well?" I asked her, when I came back to the kitchen where she was sitting at the counter, drinking a cup of coffee.

I saw a full wine glass next to it.

"Well what?" she asked.

"Did you call him?"

"Not yet. I will."

"Well, tell him to pick me up outside the auditorium. I'm going back to school for a class meeting."

I hoped he wouldn't try to talk to me on the way to the lesson, about what had happened, about Mum probably being lonely. I would tell him I didn't want to talk about it, that there was nothing really to talk about. I'd keep saying it, until he gave up trying.

I didn't want to stop learning saxophone. I wanted to get into jazz band, to get close to Chris Seagate, to get to know him, get him interested in knowing me. I didn't know how that was going to happen now.

I'd been planning to skip the meeting this afternoon with the college counselor, but decided to go, thinking Seagate would probably be there, even if jazz band rehearsal was over. Just seeing him would probably make me feel better.

I picked up my backpack, and rushed out the door, before Mr. Newell got back.

Six

Martin

That morning, when Clare asked about my schedule for the day, wondering if I'd be working late again, not wanting to give her false hope, I'd mentioned nothing about my plan to check out the neighborhood where a friend of mine had a house for sale. I had no idea what to expect.

"I'm seeing a client at the prison," I said. "Then back to the office after lunch. So, hopefully I'll be home tonight at a reasonable time. Maybe even for dinner, for a change."

"Seeing a client at the prison," Clare repeated, as she rinsed her coffee cup and put it in the dishrack.

She said she wondered how those words, after so many years, still surprised her, how they always made her stop to mull over what, on the surface, seemed so contradictory to my nature: that I'd become a criminal defense attorney.

"I thought maybe you'd become one of those attorneys who take on big corporations that pollute ground water supplies, endanger drivers, the food supply, or babies."

She said that she thought that would still be in line with my desire to "do good."

"Wouldn't it?"

She smiled, something Veronica wouldn't have done, prodding me to think about a higher profile kind of legal work. I knew Clare was just teasing, that we had in common, a desire to have work that gave us the opportunity to help individuals who were often left behind, that that was the reason she was teaching immigrants the English language, rather than joining the faculty of any one of the several universities in the area. She knew that Veronica had wanted me to join a firm or go into private practice, and she understood why I hadn't. My decision meant we were struggling financially, the reason that I wasn't sure if buying a house was even within the realm of possibility, and didn't want to tell her what I planned to do today at lunchtime.

I said the same thing I always said, about practicing criminal law.

"If, every once in a while, I keep a person from doing time he or she doesn't deserve, then I consider I'm doing a worthwhile job."

I said the same thing to certain relatives who nagged me that I ought to join a firm or get a partner and go into practice for myself, just as Veronica had been nagging me to do, those years leading up to the divorce. Rarely these days, Clare and I would have dinner with old friends of mine from the early seventies, who walked with me on picket lines to support the United Farmworkers, prisoner's rights, or some other group that was getting a raw deal, and I'd find myself being interrogated by my old buddies, too, about the work I was still doing. Like Veronica, they'd expected that I was cut out for something different, *There are so many people—some of those same friends even—who've done a one hundred and eighty degree turn, haven't they? They must seem as if they'd been wearing masquerade costumes, when you knew them back then, they're so different now.* Clare wanted to know why I felt I needed to explain myself to one or two of those old friends. *Frankly, I don't know why you want to have anything to do with those people anymore. You're so loyal.* But they were friends of my youth, and for that reason alone, I kept in touch. I knew that many of my old friends had been trying on different beliefs, different life styles. And that many of those who may have actually been motivated by idealism, couldn't keep the faith. I accepted that idealism fades for many people, that life can break you down.

"I'm off to jail, Clare," I said, hurrying, kissing her goodbye. Being late for an interview was frowned upon.

***

I walked up to the glass double doors and the guard inside pushed a button that opened them. I saw from the large wall clock, that I was only five minutes late for the appointment with my client. I was lucky. I knew the guard on duty to be a bully. I'd been here once when he'd denied another lawyer a private consultation room, when he was fifteen minutes late after being held up by a traffic accident on Route 2. I didn't want to have to meet in the visiting room set aside for the general population, as that lawyer had to do. It was my first meeting with this client and I wasn't sure what to expect.

The guard reached out to take my folder and identification for inspection, and waved me toward the metal detector, all without a word. The guard there, looked down at his clipboard and said, "Name?"

"Martin Harris," I said. "Attorney to see Eric Belmonte."

He made a mark with his pencil on the sheet and he waved me on.

The guard, whose job it was to view the camera, slid a small plastic container from a stack of them, down the conveyor belt toward me. When it reached me, I took off my hat, sunglasses, and put them in the bowl, and then removed everything from my pockets—lose coins, my keys, a couple of pens. I even took my watch off, knowing how often the alarm sounded here.

I walked through and nevertheless set off the alarm. As always, I was told it was probably my shoes, and I took them off and walked back and forth.

The beeping began again.

This time, the guard at the detector said, "Move aside, sir."

I did and knew it meant a pat down.

"Raise your arms," he said.

His beefy hands slapped my shoulders, under my arms, my chest and back, my sides, my buttocks, my thighs, my knees, my calves, and then he felt around my ankles.

"Spread your legs," he said.

He slapped my inner thighs, and reached his hand up to find my balls.

I wondered if he got a thrill out of doing this, or if he was just trying to keep his job.

The guard who'd met me as I walked in approached, said something inaudible under his breath to the one who'd patted me down. They both laughed. The guard then handed me back my folder. He waved me on toward the first steel door.

I was let inside by another guard, into a concrete, elevator-sized room, facing another steel door, hand-operated by the guard. I held my breath in that little room, waiting for him to move the lever. He hesitated, as the door operator in this room always did, sadistically, I thought, to emphasize the power of confinement. I always looked up in this place: the ceiling was painted with constellations of stars, someone's idea of a joke, or someone's attempt to remind everyone who passed through, that another world existed outside these walls.

Let out, I breathed again. I was always a little nervous, meeting a new client under these circumstances, and today was no exception. Another guard led me down a tunnel-like corridor, to a private room where my client would be waiting. My escort opened the door, delivering me. The man, who was my client, didn't look up, but kept his head buried in his arms on the table. Another guard was standing behind him. I nodded to him, and he said, "Thirty minutes. I'll be back." Then I was alone with Eric Belmonte.

I put a hand lightly on his back.

"Hey, buddy," I said. "We're alone here now, Eric. Let's talk."

Eric lifted his head, drowsy.

I reached out for a handshake. We hadn't met, so I introduced myself.

"Martin Harris. Your counsel."

I wondered if he'd been given some medication, and asked.

"My meds. My regular meds, I guess," he said.

I wondered if his doctor had been called and he'd upped the dosage, or added a new medication.

"Had you been taking your medication before the incident?" I asked.

I figured that losing it with his mother, and attempting to assault a police officer meant that he hadn't been. His mother had felt threatened by him, she'd reported. He'd picked up a knife from the kitchen counter when the officers had entered the house. He was lucky he didn't stab him, lucky the situation didn't escalate, or he might not be here now to talk with me about his defense.

Eric shrugged.

"Do you live with your mother?" I asked.

"Since my wife left me," he said.

"And how long ago was that?"

"New Mexico. She went to live in fucking New Mexico with her sister. Five, maybe six months ago," he said.

He laughed.

"She said she couldn't deal with my issues."

He put a lot of emphasis on *my issues*.

"And I need you tell me what happened with your mother. She's not well, is she?"

At this question, Eric took a deep breath and sighed.

"I can't keep taking care of her. She can't even walk. She needs help with everything."

Ah, here was yet another example of a client needing a social worker—and some decent mental health care, which might have prevented things from getting to the point that an attorney was needed. But now, I tried to steer the conversation to questions and answers that might help Eric Belmonte's case.

"What did your mother do for help before you moved in? Did she have outside help?"

"She told them she didn't need them anymore. She has me, she told them. I can't do everything. I'm a guy. I told her I'm not going to help her with the toilet or taking a bath anymore."

I wondered how this woman who needed so much help, according to her son, was able to manage even her basic needs now. But she was resourceful and knew how to use a telephone. She'd called the Police, hadn't she? Wouldn't she be able to call the home care people she sent away when Eric had moved in?

"What happened? Why did she call the Police, Eric?" I asked.

"I was yelling. I told the officer that. That's all. I was just yelling. I can't do everything. She needs this. Then that. Then this. All day. Every day. All day long. I had enough. I'm not in the Army anymore."

I asked him where he had been deployed, but since I'd seen in the record that he was just a year older than I was, I knew the answer. He was a Vietnam Vet. A Vietnam Vet with lingering *issues*. He told me he hadn't worked since he'd returned to the States, more than a decade before. I told him my brother was in Vietnam.

"Was he from Boston? Around here?"

"I didn't grow up in the area. I came here for school. Where did you grow up?" I asked.

"Same place. Oxford. My mother still lives in the same house."

I hadn't noticed, but now I glanced at the notes in my folder and saw that he'd grown up West of Boston, in a town neighboring Charland, where Clare had grown up. In reviewing the notes before coming to see him, I had also noted that Eric Belmonte had no record. He had stayed out of trouble. He hadn't been physically wounded in Vietnam, and had served his full time and then some. I thought that since he had only threatened the officer, who had actually been able to get him to drop the knife, that perhaps his service, his clean record, along with a psychiatrist's report and testimony from a character witness—if he had one—maybe even additional testimony from his mother, who had benefited in the past year from her son's help and companionship—such as it was—that a deal that avoided a trial could be negotiated, one that might keep Eric out of prison, on probation, and under court-ordered out-patient psychiatric care. Maybe a VA social worker could help him find alternative housing and make sure his mother got the home care she needed. There were a lot of ifs, but I wanted to help keep Eric out of any kind of institution, not just prison. He seemed like a good person, who'd been damaged by that war.

"Can you think of someone, Eric, who you could call on to be a character witness for you? You understand what that is—you know, someone who could attest to your character. I see you've been clean, not so much as a speeding ticket shows up for a record. Do you have some friend who might be willing to testify that you're a good person, and you don't mean harm to anyone?"

Eric was silent for a while. I looked at the clock on the wall behind me. Time was almost up.

"We've only got a few minutes left to talk, Eric. Can you think of someone I could call on your behalf? I already have the name of the prescribing psychiatrist, but someone who knows you personally, as a friend, might help. If you have a name and how to reach them, I'll get in touch, and let you know if the person is willing."

I pushed a paper with my notes on it, toward him, and

dropped a pen on the table next to it.

"Just write it here," I said, pointing to a blank spot on the page. "The phone number, too, if you have it."

He wrote something on the note paper, then said, "I don't have his number here. It's at my mother's house. I wrote it on a message pad on the night table in my bedroom."

"Can you write your mother's phone number there for me? I can give her a call."

"If she'll talk to you," he said, writing it down.

***

Before going back to the office, I decided to use my lunch break to check out the house an old friend from law school had for sale. He'd been having lunch at the coffee shop when I'd seen him last week, and hearing this, I'd mentioned that Clare and I were looking for a new place to live. He'd given me the address, so that I could check out the neighborhood, see if I wanted to make an appointment, take a look inside. Since Troy had inherited this house from a client he'd worked for, he'd told me he wanted to sell, not be bothered renting the house, that he'd never expected this. He hadn't known that the woman had revised the will he'd prepared for her *pro bono*, that she'd enlisted another lawyer to amend it after the relative she'd willed the house to, had died. Armed with this information, I was hoping a reasonable deal might be made, if the house was in good condition. Clare and Veronica were both on me about moving to a better, safer place, and I wanted that, too, with a baby on the way and Veronica threatening to revise the joint custody arrangement for Danielle—*so she won't be in danger living at Ridge Road*—as she put it. But with Clare's freelance teaching not bringing in much, it was a long shot that we'd be able to afford a mortgage in the Boston area.

I hadn't mentioned the house to Clare yet. I didn't want her to get her hopes up, before I knew the situation. I did want to please her. I did want us to have a home of our own.

The neighborhood where Troy's house was located seemed a lot like the one I'd grown up in. Providence had many neighborhoods like it, originally working class and still retaining some of the same character. I'd never expected to find a neighborhood like this one in a section of Cambridge called Fern Hill. I'd imagined that, like in other Cambridge neighborhoods where young professionals now were outnumbering the old timers, that the place would have taken on a new character. I could easily pick out the houses of each group here: the young families—it did seem like a family neighborhood— were those who'd built dormers so they'd have attic rooms for their offices, because they had different kinds of work than the long-time residents, who'd made this a real neighborhood. Or the attic rooms might provide for their out of town guests because the occupants hadn't grown up in the city, but had come to Cambridge for college and stayed, or they'd come here from away to take jobs with the new biotech company in town, or other high-tech startups, that would surely follow, according to news reports. Improvements had been made to the front entrances of the dormer houses and they were all freshly painted, while the others still had aluminum siding, probably installed in the early sixties to save money and the effort of having to paint every so many years to keep up with New England winters.

I guessed that the old-timers were Italians, considering obvious clues. In many yards there were brick patios and carports, pergolas for grape vines, trellises for roses and tomatoes, making me nostalgic for those later years of my childhood, after my mother had moved us from the Midwest to our Providence neighborhood.

Rounding a corner near a small tot lot I felt confirmed in my analysis of the neighborhood's ethnic makeup. There was a house that had a tall flagpole out front and the Italian colors were flying. And there were the colors again, in stripes painted on the asphalt, right down the center of the street in front of the house that advertised this year's date for the annual St. Anthony Festival. Oddly, there was a little chapel attached to the house there, a throwback maybe to a time before the large Catholic Church had been built on the main avenue. Or perhaps, the chapel had been established for the faithful who wanted to worship with their own kind, divisions separating new immigrants from the rest of the flock; as unchristian a thought as that was, that had been the inspiration for so many churches being built. There was the French Church, the Polish Church, the Irish Church, and yes, the Italian Church. Cities like Providence had churches on every corner, it seemed. Who knew though? The house chapel might even have been built by the family that lived in the house, as an expression of their devotion and gratitude for favors granted by the saint; I had relatives who had favorite saints they swore interceded for them, when they were in need.

There was a recreation hall, too, on the other side of the house and the same sign about the entrance that advertised the festival months away, also gave the phone number for information about rentals. At the end of the walkway leading toward the entrance, a sign was tacked onto a post, listing the schedule for Sunday Masses; the chapel was still used for services, not just prayer. I imagined the St. Anthony congregation now, a few old women who had trouble walking, dressed for Sunday and every other day of the week in black dresses nearly down to their ankles, just as my own grandmother had dressed. I'd passed a woman like that sweeping the sidewalk on Lawn St. and had said hello as I went by. She just stared, knowing I was an outsider. She might not have spoken English either.

I walked for a while, circling around, going up one street and then down another, returning more than once to the same spot, noticing this was a much greener neighborhood than Ridge Road, which had so few trees and in alleys between houses where grass might have been, asphalt had been put down to create parking spaces for tenants.

I liked what I saw. Returning for a third time to the spot where I'd started out, I went then in the other direction. I counted no house over two stories high, except the ones that had had dormers built up out of the attic, raising the pitch of the roof. Everything seemed to be of manageable size, reminding me of the diorama in the lobby of the courthouse. Here there was a small grocery store, where I watched kids let out for recess from the school across the street, crowding in for ice cream bars, Coke, and packaged cupcakes. There, I was overcome by a feeling of longing, thinking about having raised Danielle as I had on Ridge Road, wondering what it would have been like if our family situation had been different. The house I rented for her and her mother was nice though, and it was a single-family home on a far more residential and certainly quieter street than Ridge

Road. I was happy to have been able to provide that for her. But there was something else here—a community—and that had been missing in both of Danielle's houses. Hers was a real Cambridge childhood—there was such a thing these days—one with a full social life and many scheduled activities—a fortunate childhood, yes. But it was one with little time for chatting up neighbors who were gardening or trimming hedges or sitting on porch rockers. I was a little regretful that Danielle had had an upbringing so much less innocent. When I first talked to Troy about the house he had for sale, I thought that buying it was a longshot. Today though, I really wanted to make it happen, and I believed it might be possible.

I turned the corner onto Stevens Road. The street was lined with some kind of ornamental fruit trees just beginning to bloom. They blossomed on streets all over the city every spring. Why hadn't I learned the name of this tree? It wasn't crab apple or Chinese cherry trees, or dogwood; I knew those. These were filled with tiny white flowers, lush with them, and the fruits that appeared in the Fall were small, making me think that they were a dwarf fruit variety. I would find out what they were.

Speaking with my new client, Eric, reminded me today, how fortunate I was to have avoided Vietnam. I thought of my brother dying there, when his helicopter was shot down, thought if he'd come home physically intact, he might have ended up traumatized like this new client of mine. Eric came out of it alive, but hadn't life as he'd known it before that war, ended for him?

Close to the house, I slowed, wanting to take my time, dillydallying a bit to take a closer look around. Everything seemed so benign. I peeked through gates and over fences and hedges, the small yards where jonquils were growing, yards where there were poles woven with string waiting for climbing beans, where rows of lettuce were already poking up through the soil in small gardens, and where I saw fig trees no longer swathed in winter burlap dresses. Spring had advanced enough that forsythia, too, was in bloom out front of many of the houses. I was happy that winter was leaving. It had been a hard one: cold and snowy. I noticed lilac buds were opening on some bushes. It wouldn't be long before even those in shady spots would burst open, releasing their intoxicating scent. I spent much of my days indoors, often working late, until dusk or after, even at this time of year. I hardly noticed the seasons changing. I was glad to have the afternoon free to pay attention.

Clare absolutely loved springtime. *I know*, she would say, *it's a cliché, but spring restores my sense of purpose, gives me hope for possibilities in my life*. I loved her for entertaining romantic notions, as much as for her realistic attitude about life.

There were plenty of neighborhoods in the city where you'd be inviting trouble if you put out flowers in fancy planters. Apparently not this one, since several houses displayed them in expensive looking pots— begonia and geranium placed on front doorsteps. At one house a child's plastic wheelie toy was left out in the driveway and a sandbox in the yard of another was full of toys, heavy metal dump trucks and tractors left out, without worry that they'd be taken. This would be a great neighborhood for us to raise our son or daughter.

As I approached the house, I thought that the man I saw coming off the path at the side of the house for sale was Troy. I didn't want him to see me snooping, even though he'd encouraged me to check out the neighborhood. He was about the same height as Troy, I thought, seeing him duck to walk under the overhang of lilac bushes bordering the neighboring yard. Thinking he'd seen me, I raised my hand to wave and quickly let it fall down again by my side, hoping the guy hadn't seen the gesture, realizing once he'd stepped down onto the sidewalk, that he appeared to be a good head taller and much thinner than Troy, who had put on some weight since law school days.

Good. I didn't think the man had noticed me waving. He was heading up the street in the other direction. I saw him get into the red Honda I'd noticed as I passed. It had been parked near the corner and it got my attention, as I went by, because it displayed a Conservatory decal across the back window, making me think of Veronica. I was curious, wondering if he were someone Veronica knew. Perhaps he was a workman though, a carpenter or electrician come to see Troy about something he thought needed to be done to make the place more attractive to a potential buyer. The guy might not have anything at all to do with the Conservatory himself; he might have bought the car used from someone who did—a student or faculty member—and perhaps just hadn't removed the decal.

Then I did see Troy coming out the front door of the house, and I watched him from my distance, as he went over to the lilacs and pulled a branch toward him. He bent his head into the barely blooming flowers and looked like he inhaled. Lilacs made people you'd never expect to see inhaling the scent of a flower do that. I was envious, since lilacs made my allergies go crazy. The lilacs were in along the path at the side of the house. I could always pull them up.

Otherwise, from the outside anyway, the house looked as Troy said it would: a well-maintained Philadelphia style, built in the early part of the twentieth century. It did not stand out from the others, but fit in well. From what I could see as I got a little closer without being noticed, there was a small yard in back, and a narrow walkway between the house and the yard next door. There was a driveway; some of the yard on the other side had been paved for off-street parking. I couldn't see from the street, whether like in other yards, this one had a patio.

Satisfied that it was worth taking Clare to see the house inside, I headed back up the street to where I'd parked. School was back in session by the time I walked past the building and I could hear singing, because the day was warm enough for the windows in the classrooms to be open. The streets were almost empty now. I saw no one except the mail carrier and a woman hurrying up the steps and into the school. Reaching the car, I still had a half hour before I'd be expected back at the office; so, I delayed a bit longer. I took the path into the park. An older couple was taking a walk around the pond, and some kids flew past them on trikes. I really liked this neighborhood. Having another chance—this time with Clare—it would be a perfect place to live and raise our child together.

At this time of day, there were mostly mothers with toddlers in tow, or day care workers leading strings of preschoolers along the path around the pond. A couple of adults were doing exactly what I was, enjoying a beautiful early spring day, taking a break from eating lunch at their desks or in coffee shops. I watched the toddlers sipping juice from small boxes with mini-straws, collecting pine cones and sticks that littered the path, and I imagined being here with Clare and our boy or girl at this very park a couple of years from now. I could see myself teaching my son—we might have a boy, since I'd had a brother and there'd been only brothers in my father's family, too—to ride a bike or zoom around on a scooter, or how to skip a stone across the water. There was a big hill on the other side of the pond, and I'd driven by when there was snow and it would be filled with kids wearing bright red and blue jackets and scarves, dragging sleds up the hill or flying down on aluminum saucers.

***

Back at the office, I plowed through the pile of briefs on my desk, expecting it to be a normal day for me, no working late tonight. I had thought that I was making progress, until mid-afternoon, when the call came from Veronica, telling me that Danielle needed me to drive her to her lesson.

"Danielle needs me, or you do?" I said.

"Well, both of us actually," she said.

Then she told me what had happened, that she was involved with Danielle's new saxophone teacher, and that she hadn't thought she ought to talk to our daughter about it. I listened while Veronica described Danielle coming home from school unexpectedly, deciding not to stay doing homework at the school library until a class meeting, after which Veronica was supposed to pick her up. Discovering her teacher at the house with her mother in the middle of the afternoon, she had blown up at Veronica, and rightly so, I thought. I was worried about Danielle, so, of course I agreed to pick her up. Poor Danielle, always second fiddle to her mother's needs. I knew she wouldn't get to the Conservatory on time, if she tried to get there on her own. I wished she wouldn't go tonight.

So much for getting home in time to have dinner with Clare. Covering once again for Veronica, I would be working late, going back to the office after I dropped Danielle off. And worse, I'd have to ask Clare again to pitch hit for Veronica, and pick Danielle up when her lesson finished. Once again, we'd be breaking her house schedule, having her stay with us to bail out her mother.

***

She must have been sitting in the back of the auditorium, because when the college counseling meeting finished, she was the first one out the door. No sooner had Danielle jumped into the passenger's seat, that the sea of students who'd exited right behind her, hemmed us in. Not only that, but the car was also blocked in by a charter bus that entered the roundabout and pulled up right next to the car to load up the basketball team, to take them off for their away game. I recognized Remy Atwood from the neighborhood, wearing a sport coat and tie, and climbing the stairs into the bus. I wondered why Danielle never mentioned him. He was a handsome kid, even more so, dressed up as he and the other members of the team were required to be on game days.

"Great," Danielle said, seeing the bus parked there.

She leaned over and hit the horn.

"Don't," I said. "We just have to wait."

I saw a boy who must have been frightened by the horn give us the finger.

"I'm already late. Great. Stupid class meeting. We waited forever for it to start."

I knew her temperament wasn't just about the school bus being in the way. She was angry at her mother. Probably angry at her teacher, too, though I knew she would put most, if not all of the blame on her mother, for getting involved with him.

I remembered that the sandwich I bought for lunch came with a cookie, and I hadn't eaten it. Danielle was more likely to act out when hungry— low blood sugar probably. The cookie might change her attitude, calm her down and soften her up, especially if the bus got moving any time soon.

The driver must have been as anxious to get going as we were, because in just a matter of a few minutes, he was pulling the lever to take in his STOP sign, and heading out of the school driveway.

"I got you something," I said.

"What?" she said, as if I were disturbing her.

Before I started to drive away I reached into the backseat for the little white bag that held the giant chocolate chip cookie.

"Here," I said.

She took the bag from me and looked inside tentatively, her

expression immediately changing when she saw it.

"I'm starving. Thank you, Dad," she said.

I avoided lecturing her, knowing that what had happened earlier in the afternoon wasn't anything she wanted to discuss with me. I was worried about her, worried that it might be a mistake for her to see her teacher this evening. She was staking her claim, it seemed, hoping that she could keep him as a teacher, that her mother would not interfere with that. But Veronica had already done that. I wondered if he'd talk to her about what had happened this afternoon. I knew teenagers just wanted to be left alone to figure things out for themselves. They learned from their mistakes. Danielle didn't want my perspective to influence what she did or how she was supposed to feel about anything really. That was typical, but as her dad, I was more than a little concerned. Why hadn't Veronica considered her feelings and told her about being involved with this guy, before she had to find out as she did? I didn't understand.

As we approached the Conservatory campus, she said, "It's the brick building on the right."

I could see that she couldn't wait to get out of the car.

"Wait until I stop completely," I said, when I saw her touch the door handle, like she was going to open it, jump out before I'd braked.

"There he is," she said, about the man who had just climbed out of the car parked at the curb across from the steps into the building. "That's my teacher."

I moved to open my door, thinking to introduce myself.

"It's late, Dad. You don't have to meet him now. And you don't have to come inside," she said. "You can do whatever --- get coffee or something and come back to get me when it's over."

"Well, I would like to meet this new teacher, you know. You don't want me to introduce myself? And I'm not picking you up. Clare will. I have to go back to the office."

"No, Dad, I'm late already. You can meet him another day then."

Then she did jump out the door and ran toward the steps of the building, turning around before she caught up with him, waving me away. I read her lips ordering me, "Go," her hand sweeping my car down the street.

I waved and smiled and pulled out. I'd seen the teacher get out of the car that was parked just a few spaces ahead. Checking it out as I drove by, it looked like the same red Honda I'd seen this morning, parked up the street from Troy's house. It wasn't just the same color, but there was the Conservatory decal on the back window and the same dent in the driver's side door; this was the car I'd seen earlier today. I didn't get a look at the teacher. He was already heading up the steps to the building, his back to me, by the time Danielle had identified him as her teacher. Although I'd only seen him from a distance, he looked to have the same longish dark hair, and he was tall, like the guy I'd seen coming out of Troy's house, who got into this car—I was sure it was the same car. If this was Danielle's teacher, then what was he doing at Troy's house?

Seven

Clare

The phone in my office at Diamond Street rang, just as I'd settled all the evening tutorials, opened my salad container, and had started to eat. It was Martin.

"Clare, I'm still at work," he said, "and Danielle is at the Conservatory for her lesson."

"And?" I said, chewing on my lettuce loudly, figuring that Veronica must have messed up the schedule again.

She had, and royally this time.

"Danielle will be spending the night with us," Martin said.

I said, "But it's not her night with us."

I said this as I had many times before, even though I knew that it was a useless comment.

Martin sighed deeply.

"I took her to her lesson, and that's why I'm working late. She went home after school and found Veronica in the kitchen with her new saxophone coach. Apparently, there's more between them than the fact that they're on the same faculty, and that he's Danielle's saxophone teacher."

The lettuce caught in my throat.

"Wait a minute, Martin," I said through my coughing.

I put the phone down to catch my breath.

"Are you okay?" he asked, when I picked it up again.

"Something caught in my throat, " I said. "Danielle went to her lesson tonight? After that? That's pretty bold," I said.

I was more than a little surprised to think of Veronica and Ray together. I was panicking, hoping this was just a fling, nothing serious.

"Bold, or something," Martin said.

"Yes, it's something," I said.

"She wouldn't let her mother drive her, so she called me.

That's why I had to come back to the office, finish up."

"So, I guess her mother won't be picking her up either? And you aren't quite finished yet? Right?"

"I'm sorry, Clare. I'm sorry this keeps happening, and you have to fill in for Veronica."

I didn't blame Danielle for being so upset about what was going on with her mother and Ray—*Mr. Newell,* as she referred to him. I could just imagine how awful Danielle had felt, when she came home to find him with her, even if they were only just talking in the kitchen. Danielle was a pretty typical sixteen-year-old, and sixteen-year-old girls were a lot less naïve now than when I'd been that age. I'm pretty sure that it had crossed her mind that, although they were only talking in the kitchen when she'd walked in the door, there was a good possibility that that wasn't all they'd been doing—or had planned to do— before she'd arrived.

I couldn't imagine the two of them together really. She was so demanding, and I thought Ray would resist someone like her. I thought of how I'd felt talking with him after so many years, how, in spite of feeling that he'd abandoned me back then, I had also felt affection for the person he used to be to me, and I was curious about what he'd be like to be with now. Veronica and Ray as a couple—yes, that seemed as unlikely to me, as it had been to Danielle, who'd said, according to Martin, *My new music coach! And besides, he's just way too cool for her. I mean, she plays cello in a chamber music group. Really?* When Martin told me that it made me smile; just about a month ago, Danielle had also still been playing cello in a chamber music group.

But it probably meant something, that Veronica and Ray had music in common—even if what they played was vastly different. And what did I really know about Ray Newell anymore, other than what he'd said about coming back to the States to take care of his father, plus what I'd read in the concert program the night of Danielle's first lesson. Our encounter had been brief. He had revealed very little about his life in the past sixteen years, other than that he *never married and never did decide to have kids.* But he did have a child—our child—somewhere, and I felt that twang of guilt which had become all too familiar since he'd showed up. Powering that guilt now, was my worry that if Veronica didn't decide to end things with

Ray—for Danielle's sake—if she got through to Danielle and had her blessing to keep on with him, that Ray would stay in Boston, even if his father were settled in a new living situation, even if he died. I was certain that if this thing between Veronica and Ray wasn't just a fling, I couldn't possibly continue to keep my secret from him, from everyone. It would haunt me even more than it had been.

    I finished some paperwork for my program while waiting to drive to the Conservatory, leaving my office just before the lesson was scheduled to finish. After running into Ray that other time, I'd told Danielle that thereafter, whenever I was picking her up, instead of waiting inside at my usual spot at the lobby window seat, I'd be waiting in the car, and she should come out to find me in the parking lot. I hoped she hadn't forgotten that. I didn't want to see Ray, and I couldn't trust that he wouldn't come looking for me again. I was a bundle of nerves as I sat in the car, waiting for her, afraid that seeing him would begin to eat away at my resolve to keep my secret.

    The scariest thought associated with telling him kept surfacing: *What if Ray wanted to find our daughter, to make things right*; Martin would have to know then. I dialed back that worry, since Ray seemed to like his freedom too much, drifting wherever his music career took him, without the responsibility of family—other than his father at the moment— something he knew was temporary, not the way that being a father to his own child would be. The reason he'd come home to see to his care was probably more a way of hoping to make amends, not wanting him to die before he did.

    I could just imagine what Martin would think of me giving up my child if he knew. Hadn't he told me that night at *Elephant Parade*, that he'd gone to the extreme of marrying Veronica because he felt he should be a father to their child, that that sense of responsibility, one that his own father had not lived up to, was the real reason he'd married her. What would he think of me? Would he even listen to my explanation that the decision to give my daughter away had really not been mine to make, that I was powerless up against my father's will. I couldn't imagine Martin understanding why I'd been hiding something so important from him. And then—to learn that Ray Newell, who'd been hired to teach his daughter to play saxophone, was actually the father of that child I gave up—of course, that would be just too much for him to handle. Surely it would fuel a belief that Ray had calculatedly insinuated himself into our family life in order to get close to me. Would he consider that I may have planned that with Ray? Any of these possibilities could be devastating. Martin would never trust me again. My marriage and the family life we believed we were going to have together, would be doomed, even before our baby was born.

I thought, too, about Veronica, and how she'd feel if she knew. Certainly she'd be jealous of what she thought Ray and I had had in the past, most likely also believing that Ray had come back to find me. I couldn't help but wonder, if maybe he had.

I saw Danielle coming out the side door of the building into the parking lot, alone thankfully. I was relieved.

"It's been cleared for you to come home with me tonight, and not to your Mom's house," I said, when she got in the car.

"I know," she said, as if that had been a given. "I don't want to see her."

Danielle had no idea what I was hiding from her. Good God, what would *she* do if she learned that, not one, but *two* of her mothers had been intimately involved with her teacher? Would it matter at all to her, that what went on between Ray Newell and me had happened before she was even born? But even if it did, wouldn't I seem like such a hypocrite, trying to offer solace about her mother hiding her involvement with him, when I was doing the same, and what she'd probably consider much worse since there had been a child involved.

"How was the embouchure?" I asked. "Any better at it tonight?"

My concern was false: I was hoping the technique would frustrate her and she'd go back to cello, and be done with her *Mr. Newell*.

She ignored my question and said only, "You could have cut the tension in the room with a knife."

This was a cliché Martin used sometimes when he talked about his day in court, particularly about when he was successfully cross-examining a witness.

"I never knew what Dad meant, saying that, not until

tonight, when I was shut up in that tiny practice room with Mr. Newell after this afternoon."

Tell me about it, I thought, remembering my own chance meeting with Ray in Le Bistro.

"The room where I had my lesson," she continued, "is barely big enough for one person with a sax, never mind two, with that baby grand in there, taking up so much space."

She said she'd felt so rattled and awkward, when she first walked in, that she knocked down not one, but both collapsible music stands.

"You didn't," I said.

"Can we stop at Toscanini's for ice cream again?" she asked.

I supposed that ice cream might make her feel better. I supposed, too, that she was hoping to get a glimpse of that boy, Chris.

"Okay. Ice cream, it is. But, you know you're going to have to sit down and talk to your dad about setting a time to meet with your mother to straighten things out."

"I know," she said. "I know, but I just don't want to talk about it right now. Not tonight."

Once I'd agreed to take her to Toscanini's, she relaxed. She mentioned she'd seen some girl tonight in the performance hall, sitting in a back row, intently listening to the orchestra rehearsing. Danielle said she'd poked her head in when she passed by, to hear what they were playing. Maybe she was missing the classical pieces she was familiar with, playing cello.

"She's pretty. I think she was there another night, too. It's weird. I've seen the same girl recently hanging out in The Pit. She's not the kind of person I usually see there," she said. "She just suddenly appeared."

The Pit in Harvard Square was the place where Goths, punks, freaks, and kids Danielle called posers hung out. A lot of them were runaways or had drug issues. There was always a social service van from Bridge Over Trouble Waters parked near the corner at Holyoke Street.

"Maybe she works for the Bridge?" I said.

"Maybe," Danielle said. "But I don't think so. She might just have nowhere else to go and so she's hanging out at the Conservatory when people are there. I guess it would be better than the street. She has nice clothes, not like the rest of those that hang in the Pit."

The ice cream shop was crowded as usual. MIT students flocked there every evening, and Central Square was a busy place; lots of foot traffic meant lots of customers. The place was listed in all the guidebooks, too. Already there were tourists in town in spite of what could be fickle weather at this time of year, and they were jamming up the line, buzzing about never before knowing of such unusual flavors of ice cream and sorbet, as those offered here.

When we were waited on, Danielle asked for samples of ginger chili pepper and arugula peach. The scooper consented, handing her a tiny wooden spoon of each and waiting for her verdict, while Danielle applied and then swirled the ice cream on her tongue, first one kind, then the other, just as if she were tasting fine wine. Then she ordered ordinary chocolate. It was admirable that the girl wasn't afraid to try new things, yet she knew what she liked. I went for the vanilla bean, which was comforting, because it was so creamy. Chocolate would keep me up, especially with all that was on my mind.

As she'd probably hoped, there was that boy Chris in a corner booth with two of his friends.

We'd been seated, eating our ice cream, savoring it, when Danielle saw him and waved to him when he looked in her direction. Not noticing her, he didn't wave back.

She had said that the boy was also a sax player.

"Maybe you should get together with him to talk about his teacher, see what he thinks of him. I know you don't want to talk about this now, but if your mother stays involved with Mr. Newell, you might not want to keep having lessons with him," I said, praying that she wouldn't. I was overstepping, giving this advice, but I was feeling desperate.

Danielle just shrugged and said, "Yah, maybe, but really, Mr. Newell is totally great."

I realized that if she ditched the lessons with him it might not solve the problem of Ray being around. Her mother might think she then had permission to continue to be involved with him. I could only think the worst about that. What if he moved in with

Veronica, and would sometimes drop Danielle off at our house or come to pick her up, or bring her something she needed that she'd left at her mother's house? Veronica, if she knew I'd been involved with Ray, might let on to Martin or Danielle. I didn't think though, that he'd tell Veronica, if he wanted to keep on with her; she'd be jealous of him having anything to do with me. I was more worried, though about the weakening of my own resolve, to never tell Ray, or anyone, about the child I'd given up.

"I'm really tired," I said, finishing up, wanting to leave the ice cream shop. "I just want to get home and lie down."

"I can drive," Danielle offered. "As long as you're in the car, it's okay. Remember, I'm going for my license soon, so I'll be fine."

She had barely taken the wheel, when there was a sudden jolt and the car stopped. It was a gentle crash, but a crash nevertheless.

"No! I can't believe this! This didn't happen!" Danielle yelled.

For a moment I couldn't respond either to Danielle or to the situation. But then, as if struck by an impulse that I needed to prove that I could still speak, that I was intact, all right, this wasn't too bad, I answered my stepdaughter with the motherly reality check she needed.

"Well, it did happen. Are you okay?"

"Great. Just great. I don't know how this happened. I wasn't doing anything wrong!"

I generally ignored her when she acted like this, having learned that that was the best tactic in the face of teenaged defensiveness. Right now though, I asked, "Weren't you paying attention to your driving?"

What had I been thinking, letting her drive? Before this evening, Danielle had driven only in empty office parking lots or Sunday afternoons on mostly deserted country roads out in Lincoln and Concord where, other than the occasional car exploring new territory, the only moving vehicles she encountered were tractors going at a snail's pace, heading from farm fields to barns. And she'd never driven at night, as far as I knew. I tried to reassure myself. It wasn't so crazy to have allowed her to get behind the wheel. Danielle was right: in less than a week, she'd be taking her road test. She ought to have been capable of driving home.

Uncharacteristically, she grew silent, and looked worried, watching in the rearview mirror, as the well-dressed, middle-aged man got out of the car she'd backed into. He was moving slowly, but deliberately. He was moving at least. That was encouraging. The damage couldn't be too bad. It wasn't much of a jolt. But he was massaging his neck, I noticed, and I hoped that was just a nervous tick and not the result of any injury he'd just sustained. He looked like the kind of person who was all business. In fact, he probably was a businessman, dressed in his charcoal gray suit, driving a Mercedes (a Mercedes!), probably on his way home from some important dinner meeting that had topped off a hectic day, now delayed by a teenager driving a beat-up Toyota.

"I was pulling out. Didn't you see my brake lights and my turn signal?" he said, as he was bending over to put his face right at the open window.

"I'm sorry, really sorry," Danielle said.

"Where's your license?" he asked gruffly.

He stood up to wait for her to produce it, moving back from the car.

We both watched him as he efficiently took a mini memo pad from the inside pocket of his jacket, and then started searching furtively in his two outside pockets. He looked back toward his own car, as if he were thinking of going there for whatever he needed. A pen, so that he could take down information, I guessed.

"I have a pen," I offered, though he hadn't asked for one.

I rummaged around in the glove compartment until I came up with one, and I reached over Danielle to hand it out the window to him.

The man didn't say thank you or even glance over at me. He was tall and awkward, leaning down to the window to engage Danielle.

"I have a learner's permit," Danielle said, handing it to him.

He looked at her picture.

"You're wearing glasses in the photo. Where are your glasses?" he asked. Then, looking over Danielle, and directly at me for the first time, he said. "Didn't you see that she wasn't wearing her glasses?"

His head was a moon in the window. He must be a lawyer, I thought, or maybe a risk manager for a large corporation.

"They're reading glasses. I put them on to read the bottom line of the eye chart. I don't need them to drive," Danielle testified.

"You'd see the code for 'corrective lenses' under 'restrictions,' if she did," I pointed out.

I'd learned something about countering with facts, living with Martin for ten years. Once when I'd been in the car with him, he'd been stopped for something minor. I couldn't remember what now, but pulled over, he had gotten out of the car just as the police officer was. He'd advised Clare later that she should do the same, if ever stopped for a traffic violation or if she had an accident. It was better, he said, not to remain in a seated subordinate position, to level the field. Martin's life was about equalizing power if he could, and he was pretty good at it. That hadn't worked for me though, when I'd tried it after being stopped for going through a light that had turned red halfway through an intersection. The officer, seeing me getting out of the car, had ordered, "Remain in the car, Mam."

I knew that I ought to at least get out to check for damage now, but I didn't feel like moving. Not that I was in pain or emotionally paralyzed or anything like that. I simply didn't want to get out and have to stand next to this man, whose manner was downright insulting, not just gruff; and I knew that his height, the fact that he was well over six feet, meant that he would tower over me when I stood near him, and that would simply emphasize his superior attitude. Instead, I asked Danielle to have the man show her the damage to his car, and to check out our car as well. It was the right thing to do anyway, to have Danielle take account of the results of her actions.

"I think you should come look at this, too," the man said, addressing me now. "You are the responsible adult, aren't you?"

Danielle and I got out simultaneously, and walked over to inspect the man's car, which had sustained no damage whatsoever, since there was a rubber strip on the rear bumper, and that had reduced impact. We walked past the man, going to look at our car.

He caught a glimpse of me sideways.

"And you're pregnant!"

He turned to address Danielle again, to lecture her.

"Don't you know, you have precious cargo? You don't want to be responsible for anything happening to precious cargo, do you?"

Danielle looked worried then, and I took her arm and whispered, "I'm fine," when the man turned around to walk back to look at our car. There was only a very small dent, that according to Danielle, "wasn't there before."

"Great," I said, happy that the car could be driven and we wouldn't have to call Martin to come take us home.

Against my better judgment, but because I remembered the importance of "getting back on the horse" after falling, once Danielle and the man had finished exchanging the necessary information and he'd gone on his way, I allowed Danielle to continue down the road home, and the rest of our journey took place in silence, and without incident.

Martin was still up when we got to the house.

"Where have you been?" he asked. "I thought you'd be right home after the lesson."

He must have been worried about Danielle, after what had happened with her mother and Ray, I thought.

I took a deep breath and let out a sigh. Danielle and I had conspired to keep the little accident a secret from him, since there'd been no damage to the other car and only a tiny scratch on the Toyota, unnoticeable, unless you were looking for it. We didn't think he'd notice. He was always so busy, running from courthouse, to office, to jail—and sometimes, like this afternoon, to drive Danielle to some appointment—that he barely noticed anything about his car, and had recently ignored my warning, that I'd noticed that the front tire treads were almost bare; letting it go had led to a flat in Harvard Square during morning rush hour. Hey, if he didn't notice when I was wearing a new dress or had changed the color or length of my hair, probably a small scratch on the bumper of my car that had resulted from Danielle's inattention tonight, wouldn't be on his radar.

"We went to Toscanini's," I answered.

"Again?" he said.

"Well, it was a tough day for her," I said.

Of course, his reaction to what Veronica had subjected Danielle to, was one of fatherly concern. He was angry at Veronica's lack of sense when it came to her role as a parent, upset that she'd been "sneaking around with the guy."

I told him I thought Danielle had handled seeing Ray for the lesson well, but that, of course, she said it felt awkward.

"She stuck it out. And she might keep on with the lessons, even if her mother continues to see him," he said.

"Did she say that?"

"Well, no, not exactly. It's just her attitude, the fact that she went tonight."

"But do you think it's a good idea for her to keep on with him?" I asked. "I mean, there must be other sax coaches out there. It was a little crazy, don't you think, for her to have gone to the lesson tonight? Maybe the jazz band teacher knows a sax coach he could put us in touch with?"

"Was Veronica seeing this guy before Danielle had said she wanted to learn saxophone? Do you think that's why she found a teacher for her so fast?" he asked.

"Hmmm," I said. "I did think it was a bit odd, since she's a classical musician, not into jazz. But I don't know. They could have met when she was looking for a teacher for Danielle. Maybe, it happened just the way she told Danielle it did, that they hit it off right away. That happens, doesn't it?"

I remembered that it had been that way when I first met Martin. He'd forgotten we'd been head over heels when we met.

"Veronica had put up quite an argument with Danielle when she'd told her that she wanted to play cello, though. Protesting too much perhaps?" he said.

But I thought that the objection she'd voiced had sounded simply like the snobbery of a classical cellist.

"Prejudice against the saxophone, maybe," I said.

It was a mystery to me that anyone wasn't in love with the sound of the instrument, a sound I thought was closest to an honest human voice.

Now that Martin had mentioned Ray, I wished that I could talk to him about what I was feeling, wished that I'd told him what had happened to me, told him early on, when we first met, when things were not as complicated as they certainly were now. It's not that I didn't trust him. I did think that he would have understood back then. But I kept the knowledge of my child secret, believing I was protecting myself. I didn't tell him because I wanted to get past what had happened to me. I didn't want Martin thinking about it or mentioning it ever. I knew that could happen. I'd thought, what if he wants a child and I decide I don't; he might try to convince me that I needed to have a child to get over the first one. Back then, I hadn't been sure if I'd want a child, after what had happened to me. I knew now that I would always think of the daughter I gave away, always feel the hurt of having lost her. But back then I'd considered the secret was my own private sadness, one that I would always carry with me, and that no one who hadn't experienced what I went through, could ever really understand. Keeping my secret was the best thing to do, I thought. How could I have been so wrong?

Lying next to Martin in the dark, I wondered what was going to become of us.

Eight

Ray

That night, after Danielle discovered me at the house with her mother, I told Veronica I wasn't up for going out, even though we'd planned to take in a concert at Berklee. I needed some time to think about what all this meant, whether I actually wanted to get in any deeper with Veronica. I hadn't realized the complications of seeing someone with a teenaged daughter from a failed marriage, had thought it would be easier being involved with Veronica, since Danielle was older. But I was wrong. I had begun to worry that Veronica might expect too much of me, wanting me to fill a void that had existed for too long, when I'd only been hoping to feel less lonely.

I hadn't really expected to get so involved with anyone, so soon after coming back, but Veronica seemed always to be there. I had been learning a lot from her about the Conservatory. She generously imparted a wealth of information, helping me navigate in a new position, showing me the ropes at the place she'd been teaching for two decades now.

She'd been on the hiring committee, so she'd seen evaluations from colleagues and students of mine, when I'd taught in Toronto, before moving to Montreal to focus on performing. She knew, too, that I'd been making inroads as a performer and recording artist, doing back up for some well-known musicians, and that I was now heading the Newell Group, which had been getting good press for our regular gig at a popular Cambridge Club in Inman Square. She'd come to hear me play one night, I learned, that day she showed up at the door of my studio, looking for a coach for a daughter who wanted to learn to play saxophone.

***

My studio was in a basement practice room in one of

the Conservatory buildings. Since I was new, I'd been given that claustrophobic interior room, one without even a small window in the door—which I didn't mind, since it meant I might have fewer visitors.

When Veronica knocked on the door, I was alone, but blowing my horn. Since she knew I was there, hearing me play, she kept knocking, even though I didn't answer right away, getting louder, ignoring the implied message that I didn't want to be disturbed. Maybe she thought I couldn't hear her over the notes I belted out.

I swung open the door finally, perturbed but wanting to put an end to the knocking. She was looking down, as if she'd been about to slip under the door, the piece of paper she held in her hand. She stared at my feet a second longer, before looking up at me, to tell me what she wanted.

"Nice boots," she said, smiling. "Red. I don't see cowboy boots on classical musicians too often."

And then she looked up, directly at me.

"You know, you're unique around here. Not too many jazz musicians in this place. I'm surprised you didn't end up down the street at Berklee."

She was all compliments, even though she didn't apologize for the interruption. She was no longer shy or nervous, asking me to explain myself.

I tried to let her know from my lack of response to the compliment—if that was what it was—and by not showing any enthusiasm, that I didn't like being interrupted. She looked awkward though, as if she were embarrassed to have shown up unannounced, and I felt I was being mean, not to be friendlier to her.

"Hi, I'm Ray Newell," I said. "Here from Montreal and just getting settled," I said.

"Since Montreal has such a good reputation for being a hotbed for jazz, why would a saxophone player—especially one of your reputation—move to Boston?"

I hadn't met many others at the Conservatory then, and I was grateful to be asked anything bordering on the personal, as long as she didn't get too personal. I'd explained to her that I'd grown up in a small town west of Boston, and that my dad was old and ill and needed some help, and that I was the only one he had on earth, who he could call on. Maybe I'd already said too much, and should have left it at that, but I went on.

"Boston is a good music town, so I landed here, got some gigs while getting him settled into some kind of assisted living place or whatever. I plan to go back to Montreal after that."

I had added also, that I was taking on private students.

"Boston is one expensive town, and I didn't give up my apartment in Montreal, so there's that, too," I said.

Veronica found that to be the perfect segue that day, to ask about lessons for her daughter.

"Why Canada, if you grew up here?" she'd asked.

I let her know about leaving right after high school, so I wouldn't end up in Vietnam, like so many of my friends had. She looked to be almost my age, and she'd immediately understood, and began pouring out her own story, of how she'd met her ex-husband—emphasizing the ex in ex-husband—who'd become a draft counselor, she said, "after his brother was killed in Vietnam." She'd been staffing a booth in Harvard Square, when they'd met, signing up students and others to take buses to D.C. for demonstrations.

"I never knew anyone who'd taken his advice, and I've often wondered what happened to guys like you," she said. "You didn't get counseling at the Quaker Meeting House in Cambridge, did you?"

I'd suddenly felt that I'd been sharing too much in the way of personal details, with a woman I didn't know at all, someone entrenched at the Conservatory, and I thought that maybe I should be more careful, as someone new to the place.

Then, she handed me the paper she'd been holding in her hand.

"My phone number. So we can talk about lessons for Danielle," she said.

We'd spent a lot of time together since that day. I enjoyed being with her. She'd insisted I go with her to The South End Jazz Fest, and it had been a memorable sunny day that had led to connections with several other sax players. She'd introduced me to the best restaurants in Cambridge and Boston for whatever food I craved.

We went to the cinema to see movies, when it had been a long time since I'd watched any on the big screen, being alone and choosing instead to view videos at home. I'd even been considering that, if offered a longer-term position at the Conservatory, I might stay, even after settling my dad's living situation, at least for a while longer, until I figured out what it might mean to return more permanently to the Boston area. Veronica had, in recent days, told me about a position she knew was going to be opening up, and had encouraged me to apply as soon as it was posted. She didn't think that anyone eligible with seniority was interested. But now, I wasn't sure about staying, whether I could handle the fallout from a relationship with Veronica. Things were already becoming more complicated, not to mention that her ex was married to Clare. Coming back now felt like I'd unleashed too many obstacles to having the kind of life I'd made for myself in Canada. I'd gotten used to an easy-going lifestyle there, one in which I didn't have to worry much about how my personal preferences affected others, a life that had seemed much freer than what was possible here, being involved with Veronica Wheeler.

***

Waking the next morning, I remembered immediately, that I had made an appointment with my father's social worker. We were to meet in Charland at the nursing home on the hospital campus, so I could decide about the move. With the events of the previous afternoon, I hadn't remembered the meeting before going to sleep. I hadn't planned well for this morning, and had to hurry to get there. No time for breakfast, I showered quickly and dressed, getting out the door with coffee mug in hand, and on the road in just enough time so as not to be late.

The social worker had instructed me to ask for her at the lobby desk. The secretary made a quick call to let her know I'd arrived. She hung up the phone and said, "Follow me, and led me down the hall to Leslie Williams' office.

After introductions she discussed insurance and additional payments and the possibility of when there might be an available room for my father. *An available room* meant, I knew, that a resident had permanently left, as in died. She suggested we "take a walk through," so that I could "view the facility."

As we walked the corridors after taking the elevator to different floors, I was struck by the contrast between the entrance floor and the actual living space. This was called Mercy Home, and it was less like a home, and more like a hospital, no matter the attempt to convey a different atmosphere, with its well-appointed lobby, dining room for mobile residents, and sitting rooms located on the first floor. I knew that that floor was designed to immediately engage family members considering placing relatives here, hoping that those images would stand-out in their memory, as they made their decision.

Each floor, I noticed, had its own community room as well. When I came through with Ms. Williams, residents were sitting around tables, waiting for their lunch to be served. Both the television and a tape player were on in the room, that cacophony—some music from the 1950s popular hits in competition with the Eyewitness News noon report on the television. There was no talking among patients, but one of them was reciting what seemed like a litany, but repeating only one word, over and over, like a plea for help. "My, my, my, my, my," she sang, over and over, pinching her forehead, as if trying to understand her situation.

"Is there much, if any, interaction between patients?" I asked Ms. Williams, not having noticed any.

"Well," she said, "that depends on so much. Our residents may not feel well, or be too tired to talk after a bad night. Some—many, I suppose—just aren't capable of carrying on a conversation anymore."

"And none of these people can walk? I see they're all in wheelchairs," I said.

I noticed this not just on one floor, but on several, and I wondered if the place was primarily one for immobile patients.

"No, no," she said. "It's just a precaution. They aren't too steady on their feet anymore. We don't want them taking a tumble."

I supposed, having seen so few aides and nurses on any of the floors, that staff couldn't possibly watch out for all the patients, if they were allowed to roam the corridors with only a cane or walker for support. I supposed too, that the nursing home didn't want any lawsuits for negligence. Yet, I thought that those who were able to walk when given a wheelchair, probably wouldn't be for long, losing muscle strength.

"We have chair exercise sessions," the social worker added.

Seeing the place, I now considered that there was another option. Perhaps what made the most sense, was to find a Veteran's Home, where more care might be provided. It was, after all, a benefit my father was entitled to after his service. An earned benefit, and he might be more content in a place like that. Perhaps he'd see it more like a posting, that he was called up to be there, his duty, if he were with other Vets. He could recount his experiences during the War, something he never spoke of, when I was growing up. Many Vets never did, though the nightmares and changes in personality persisted. In a Veteran's Home, I knew that there would be Vietnam Vets as well as those like my father, who'd fought in the Second World War. I wondered if that would make him resent me, his unpatriotic son, or if, in his dementia that allowed him to misidentify others, according to whatever delusion was playing in his mind, maybe he would think that I was one of those Vietnam Vets living there, and would that give him comfort?

I thanked Leslie Williams for the information and the tour, making no commitment to have my father put on a waiting list at Mercy. Instead, I gave myself another assignment, to check out the Veteran's Homes in the area.

"I'll give you a call after I've seen a few other places," I said.

We shook hands and I left. I headed home, hoping and praying that I would never end up in a place like that. As bad as things had been for me with my father, I wouldn't want him to spend his last days there. "Whoa, Mercy, Mercy," I sang out loud. "Oh, things ain't what they used to be..."

So many things were weighing heavily on my mind. I hadn't had so much worry since right before and after I'd left the country for Canada. Yesterday, after seeing my father, being with Veronica had helped me to feel calm. I thought maybe just talking with her would help.

I was about to call her when the phone rang. I didn't

recognize the number, but answered anyway.

"Hello, this is Martin Harris, attorney for Eric Belmonte," the voice on the other end announced. "I believe you're a friend of Mr. Belmonte." he said, more a statement than a question.

"Yes, I know him," I said. "We grew up together. What's this about?"

"Mr. Belmonte has suggested you as a character witness. You have heard about his arrest?" he asked.

I wondered if Eric had burned bridges with his friends or if there just weren't any of them living around Charland anymore. If any of them did still live in the area, there was a good chance he'd worn them all out. And since I'd been away, not there to be called upon to help him out whenever he got in a jam, I guessed that he figured he could call on me for help, now that I was back.

I sighed, thinking this was yet another expectation someone had for me. But what would become of Eric if I didn't help—and if I did, would it even matter for him?

"Yes. Yes. I read the news story in *The Globe*. What exactly does it involve, being a character witness?" I asked, adding, "and do you think that it even matters what I would say? I mean, I've been away for sixteen years living in Canada, and Eric threatened a police officer with a knife, which I think is a pretty serious offense, am I right?"

The attorney explained that he'd like to set up a time for an interview with me.

"In person, to go over everything involved," he said.

"We can't do this over the phone?" I asked.

"I'd prefer if we met in person," he said.

I figured he wanted to get a look at me, see how I'd go over in front of a jury, if the case went to trial. Hey, one never knows about jazz musicians.

We settled on meeting the following day, when I had no classes at the Conservatory. I didn't know if Danielle would continue with her lessons, but even if she did, an early meeting wouldn't conflict. We were to meet at a café near the courthouse.

***

I was glad we were avoiding the lunch rush. At 3:15 p.m. no one was seated at the café. There were only a few customers picking up take away orders at the counter. I took a seat at a corner table, away from the hustle there. A few minutes later, the man I pegged for a lawyer entered. It was a hot day and he carried his sport jacket over his arm, and his tie was loosened. He was wearing a fedora though, tilted on his head in a roguish way. I thought that maybe this wouldn't be so bad, dealing with him, rather than a stiff suit from a private firm, not a court appointed attorney. I took a chance that I was right about who he was, and raised my hand to identify myself as the potential character witness-in-waiting. I stood up to shake his hand, as he approached. He pointed to my coffee.

"I see I can't even get you a cup. Hope you haven't been waiting too long. Always a magic trick to slip out of the office without being stopped by someone with a question."

So, he was considerate, too. Perhaps Eric hadn't fared too badly in landing this guy to defend him. But weren't most attorneys who chose the kind of work he did, instead of practicing law that would bring in the bucks, drawn to the work, because they were decent people?

Once he had his coffee, we got down to the details of Eric's case.

"I have my work cut out for me, but I think I've persuaded his mother to testify to the help he's given her, while living with her since his wife left him."

I raised my eyebrows. "She had called the Police to come deal with Eric."

"I know. But she seems regretful that she'd called them in the first place, but she said she couldn't get him to calm down that day, that he was off his meds and she was scared. You can't really blame her. Eric's a big guy, and she's pretty frail, uses a walker to get around, she said. And, she's been relying on Eric for everything, and he'd reached his limit, I guess."

Martin Harris had been stirring his coffee the whole time he was talking, but then, as if he just realized he hadn't added any cream to make the stirring necessary, he said, "Excuse me."

He got up then with his cup, to go to the counter for cream.

I thought about what he'd said, about Eric being a pretty big guy. I hadn't seen him yet, since I'd returned, only talked to him once on the phone. Back when I knew him, he'd been a tall, skinny guy, who was a star shooter on the basketball team, regularly earning the most points in a game.

"Does it make things any easier for him, that he didn't actually attack the cop, only threatened to?" I asked.

He took a sip of coffee.

"Perhaps," he answered. "It really depends on the psychiatric report, and the people who can testify on his behalf—or give a sworn statement, if we can keep it from going to trial. A lot of ifs, but the help he gave his mother counts for a lot, provided she gives a good statement. And that's where you come in, too."

He wanted to know how much contact I'd had with Eric since I'd been out of the country.

"Phone calls once in a while. He didn't use email—probably doesn't own a computer—and who writes letters anymore?" I said.

"Hmm," he said, disappointed I thought, that Eric hadn't ever visited me, or sent any letters or emails I might still have that could help his case, help establish his good character in his own words.

He was a silent for a moment, drinking his coffee, which had been getting cold.

"And what is it that you do for work?" he said, putting the cup down.

I'd thought that Eric might have mentioned this to him.

"I'm a jazz musician," I said. "While I'm here arranging care and a new living situation for my father, who had a stroke and has dementia, etcetera, I've taken on teaching a course at the Conservatory, and I've got a couple of private students, too, as well as a regular gig at the club in Inman Square.

Attorney Harris was now staring off into space, and I wondered if he'd even been listening to what I'd said. But his eyes were wide open and his mouth hung open, too. Was he surprised by what I'd said?

He looked down at one of the papers he'd spread out on the

table in front of him when we'd first started to talk, checking some information. Perhaps something I'd said jogged his memory. Maybe Eric had told him I was a musician, and he was checking what else he'd said about me.

He pushed the paper aside and looked me in the eye.

"Ray Newell. I thought the name sounded familiar. I've been busy. A lot going on. Your name didn't even register with me. Wow," he said.

"Oh?" I said. "Have we met somewhere before? Or did you come by the Club, hear us play?"

He smiled, a little uncomfortably, I thought, and he moved his hat that he'd placed on the wide window ledge next to our booth, back and forth, back and forth. I thought for a moment that he was going to pick it up, put it on, and leave. But that wasn't it.

"Ray Newell. Veronica Wheeler. Danielle," he said.

He didn't need to say anything else for me to understand the connection he was making, that we were all involved in some way with the same woman. Veronica either hadn't ever given up her maiden name when she married, or else she'd gone back to using it, after the divorce.

"Veronica," I said. "Yes. And you're Danielle's father, Martin."

He shook his head and I thought maybe he was thinking, *Of course. You're the guy who's upset my daughter.* But he didn't say it. Maybe he put the blame more on Veronica.

He said only, "It remains to be seen whether Danielle will keep on with her lessons. I'm sure you understand that things have become complicated."

"Sure. Sure," I said. "I get it."

Like a real pro, he stayed then with the matter we'd come to discuss. This, too, made me think that Martin Harris was a pretty decent guy.

"So, what do you think about writing up something about how you know Eric, how you know him to be as a person? You could mention his service in Vietnam. I don't think you want to mention that you didn't serve, though. That could make you seem a less reliable witness to some people. I don't mean to me, but to some people — you know how people looked down on *draft dodgers*," he said.

He put *draft dodgers* in air quotes, so I'd know he meant no criticism. I knew from Veronica, that he'd helped scores of kids like me from being sent off to South East Asia.

"That, taken with the fact that you're a musician performing in clubs—we all know stories about some of them, right?" he explained, "might go against your character, and we don't want that to be in question. So, maybe don't mention why you went to Canada in the first place, but just that you went to school there and then taught in Toronto. Emphasize the teaching over the club dates," he advised.

I got the picture. I told him I'd call his office and let him know what I'd decided.

"Eric seems like a good person, just a victim of circumstances," he said. "I wouldn't want to see him put away."

"He is. He is," I said, standing up, shaking his hand, and moving to leave. "I'll call you," I said.

He thanked me and we each went our separate ways.

Nine

Clare

  It seemed that Boston had skipped spring entirely, as it will sometimes, giving up winter for summer-like weather, rushing the season. Temperatures in the high seventies caught people off guard. Like me, many of them were inappropriately dressed. Knowing the fickle New England weather, I'd left the house this morning wearing a light wool dress and a cardigan sweater under a jacket. That was the way to go in spring, to dress in layers, I thought. I was now going to be carrying the jacket over one arm everywhere I went all day. And this would be a long day. Once I finished up at the medical center I had the tutoring sessions at Diamond Street to supervise. Given this weather, when I got home, I'd have to search the closets for skirts and sundresses to wear with lighter linen jackets for the cool mornings and evenings of the new season, just in case this heat held. But then I remembered: if anything still fit me, it probably wouldn't for long, given my new body, all the baby weight I'd been putting on. It was almost the end of the school year for academic classes, but my teaching would go on all summer, both at the medical center and the community center. I had some clothes shopping to do.

  The summer-like weather made it seem as if it had been months since I'd found out that Ray Newell had returned, yet Danielle had only been having lessons with him for a little more than three weeks. So much had happened since. I wondered if, when it really would be summer according to the calendar, and the semester at the Conservatory ended, if Ray would return to Canada and free me from nagging worry. There was a strong possibility that Veronica might continue seeing him, somehow contrive to get him to stay in Boston, if his dad died, and whether or not his position at the Conservatory was renewed. I didn't think I could avoid telling him if he stayed, I couldn't live with the secret any longer if I were regularly seeing him at the Conservatory or otherwise; it would continue to eat away at me.

One thing I knew for certain was that if he didn't leave I had to stay away from him. Maybe Danielle would give up her lessons, too frustrated with the embouchure thing, and then, with our paths not crossing, the opportunity for a conversation would be eliminated. Even if he left and I hadn't told him about our child, would the worry be gone with him? I didn't know. I already thought of my child every day, wondered where she was, how she'd fared. I didn't want to add to that, and I feared that my marriage and the family I wanted now, with the child Martin and I were expecting, all my plans could be topsy-turvy at any moment. It would be disastrous for everyone—not just Ray— to know my secret.

Whenever the weather suddenly changed for the better, warmer temps really taking hold, there were always several days like today, when the heating system would continue to blast for riders on commuter trains. And in office buildings, the maintenance crew stuck to a schedule that management had created on some snowy, frigid winter day, when it had been hard to imagine the weather ever being like it was now. Everyone will be sweltering, cursing the fact that none of the windows in the building open, to let in a breeze.

I got off the train at South Station and took the escalator to the ground floor, climbing the moving steps as I always did, rather than standing stationary to let them take me up to the sidewalk level. Out the door to the street the salty breeze brought a slight sting, a fine mist hitting my cheeks. I inhaled deeply. Last night's thunderstorm hadn't signaled a change in the weather, nor had it cleared the air; it was still humid. No matter: the briny air always felt clean and refreshing. It was wonderful to be working near the waterfront.

I stopped for a moment and stood looking toward the horizon to catch a glimpse of the harbor. It was not a working waterfront, unless you counted the ferries that took tourists out to the Harbor Islands or to Provincetown at the tip of Massachusetts. There were mostly pleasure boats docked along the wharfs, large yachts and small sailboats alike. The clouds in the sky seemed far off, much farther west, and I hoped that any other storm that might be brewing would fizzle out or change direction before it reached the coast. I looked across the water, watched a plane land at Logan. I thought of the first time I'd ever flown alone, when I was returning from the West Coast, after giving up my baby. I remember thinking how my life had changed then, that I would never be the same after what I'd done.

***

I started college in Maine that year, and not wanting to go home for summer break, wanting to see my father as little as possible after the decision he'd made for me, I took a job as a cook at one of the hotels on the southern coast, one right on the beachfront. I lived there, too, since "the working girls," as we were called, were allowed to rent rooms at a reduced rate.

At night in my room, I'd leave the window open. It didn't face the ocean, but I could still hear the waves breaking and get the scent of the salty air coming in with the breeze. The working girls had rooms in the back of the house. Premium rooms were for tourists who stayed at the hotel for the ocean view, and paid a pretty penny for the privilege of waking up to it.

At the restaurant I hadn't been prepared for how busy the kitchen would be, serving the dining room, and the beachgoers as well. At night I was as tired as I had been after working at the *Home* with the other girls. The sleeping quarters were also reminiscent of that other place. At the hotel, besides being relegated to the back of the house, we were also settled in attic rooms. Mine was to the right of the narrow stairway, a large, but not exactly spacious room, since it had four double beds set up infirmary style, as the rooms were at St. Ann's Home. Three other girls—two sisters and their cousin—occupied the other beds, arriving a week or so after I moved in. Most nights I fell asleep as soon as my head hit the pillow. The ocean, combined with hard work, did that for me.

Being at the ocean the summer after I gave up my child, had brought me the comfort I desperately needed. I love the salty air, the sound, and I don't know what pleased me more: the reliability of the waves breaking, or the fact that the sea is always changing. On nights when the sea was calm, and stayed that way, I fell asleep and never woke until morning. Other nights I was awakened by a wild roaring, because there was a storm at sea, a high wind whipping up the waves.

The storms inspired me to get out of bed and dress, quietly leaving the hotel to walk down to the beach, my bare feet squeaking as I scuffed the smooth sand to reach the water's edge, to watch the show. I climbed the ladder to the lifeguard's stand and sat there, my curly hair frizzing from the moisture in the air, and I thought deeply about how I might get on with my life. I stared past the breaking waves to the horizon, trying to count lights burning in towns all up and down the coast, sparkling like jewels studding the black sky.

After going out in the middle of the night, I dreamt of living at the ocean under better circumstances. Living on an island would be nice, I thought. What would it be like, I wondered, for a child to take a water taxi instead of a bus to school? Or, to live on a larger island, one with its own school, or enough children to warrant a real ferry to bring my child to the mainland?

***

I headed to Chinatown Gate, moving slowly today, not trying to dilly-dally, not at all unhappy to be heading to my job. I loved teaching these students. There wasn't any other work I'd rather be doing, except being a parent to a child of my own. It was the weight of the worry of having Ray Newell back in my life that was slowing me down, that combined with the need to search for a new place to call home, a house or a better apartment in a safer neighborhood, where Martin and I would raise our child. My students would lighten my spirits, keep my mind focused on other things. They always did. The Wednesday class was held in one of the older brick buildings on the hospital campus, down an alley lined with others just like it, a piece of nineteenth century history preserved in the middle of Chinatown, which itself was steeped in tradition, yet, all along its perimeter there were new glass and concrete towers going up. It seemed that the decision about where my classes were scheduled was totally arbitrary, as if—ironically—no one in the Department of Human Services cared to spend much time considering which available space would be most conducive to a decent learning environment for the employees. A room would open up anywhere, and a staff person would book it.

I went up the stairs to the fifth floor seminar room. The only downside to this new spot was that there wasn't an elevator, since the building was ancient. That wouldn't have mattered except that I was always transporting books and materials for a long day, having a freelance position with no office space assigned to me.

Opening the door, I found Ying already waiting, seated at the seminar table, no matter that it was a half hour before the start of class. I just couldn't seem to get in ahead of her.

"Hi, my teacher!" she called out energetically, smiling broadly.

I'd encouraged the students to call me by my first name when they greeted me. The Haitians and some others from Central America and Eastern Europe generally complied, but the students from China—especially the older ones—continued to address me as "Teacher," which was culturally more respectful, I knew.

I smiled and returned the enthusiastic greeting Ying had offered, and set to work preparing the materials for class.

Spread out at her feet, Ying had the same transparent red plastic shopping bags carried by the older men and women outside on the street. Many of the hospital employees shopped in the markets during lunch break or on their way to or from work. I looked at Ying and took note of her clothing. She always dressed in the kind of layers that certainly weren't necessary for warmth on a day like today. Her layers of clothing seemed a protective padding, as if Ying hoped that two undershirts and two sweaters and a jacket would keep her safe— from what, I wondered. Not only was the weather warm, but also, as could be expected, the room was stifling hot. But Ying didn't take off any of the layers, except the outer jacket, which she hung up in the closet.

She was the oldest student in any of my classes, how old, I didn't know. Ying herself was no help in determining her age. At one class, she'd answered *hundred* to the question, *how old are you?* The other, much younger women in the class had scoffed at her, shaking their heads in disbelief, and they'd rolled their eyes at me, something they often did when Ying spoke. They were trying to warn me not to pay Ying any mind. But I liked Ying and felt badly that I hadn't been able to help her make better progress with the language. I guessed that she came early to every class for the extra conversation practice.

I handed her a booklet from the stack as I went around placing one on the table in front of each chair. Ying put hers down without even looking at it.

She was here for conversation, not for browsing in the booklet. She grilled me about family life. If she only knew the half of it, I thought.

"How is your Dawtah?"

I cringed, hearing Ying's pronunciation of the word daughter, recognizing my Boston accent in it, only more exaggerated. Dawtah. Ah, there it was: the Boston *h* that found its way into so many words where it didn't belong. Whenever Ying asked about Danielle, I wasn't sure if she understood the difference between "birth child" and "step-child," even though I'd tried to explain it to her many times. I didn't dare complicate things further by introducing "adopted child." Not yet anyway. It was always a mistake to offer too much at once. Whether she understood or not, Ying always smiled and said, "Thank you, my Teacher."

If she asked about Danielle, I never just said, *she's fine*, but instead mentioned something current in her life, to try to give Ying the conversation practice she wanted. I had to be careful not to start a complicated conversation, though. Today, I said, "Danielle is learning to play saxophone," and there was the sought after teaching moment. This class hadn't yet learned to use the verb "to play" when speaking of musical performances. I wasn't sure that Ying knew what a saxophone was, if she'd ever heard the word before. Surely, she must have heard saxophone playing in canned music in an elevator, at a store while shopping, or on a sound system in a restaurant where she went to eat, or even, from a street musician in Chinatown or at Downtown Crossing.

Because I'd recently taught the students in this class the meaning of "to play baseball," as a way of introducing them to the verb phrase—interchanging baseball with football, volleyball, basketball, and even Mah Jong—Ying was confused.

"What game sassaphone?" she asked.

"Sax-a-phone," I modeled.

Aside from her faulty grammatical construction and incorrect pronunciation, Ying's question pleased me. It meant that she remembered the lesson on "to play games." All was not lost.

"Sax-a-phone. Repeat, Ying!"

Ying tried hard to mimic my pronunciation, getting it right once and then losing it again.

"What game?" she repeated.

"Not a game. Play sax-a-phone. Make music."

Ying scrunched up her brow and the furrows went deep. She struggled with English.

"Music. Play music. La, la, la," I sang.

Then I mimed playing a piano, and then a horn. I tore off a sheet of newsprint from the easel, rolled it up into a poor substitute for a horn. Without keys, it became a megaphone, and of course, the shape wasn't correct for a saxophone. It would have to do. This pitifully constructed phony cousin of the woodwind family would make my point. Ying grinned widely, this time indicating that she was very happy to have learned something new, even if she could not pronounce the word for the instrument. From my facsimile, she couldn't really know either, what the instrument looked like. To correct the problem I tried to at least get the shape right, drawing one on the easel pad; then I made a note in my calendar to look for the book that featured the lesson on the names of musical instruments, illustrations included. I also made a note to remember to bring the box of pocket mirrors to class next time, to help Ying with her pronunciation—the others, too—so, they'd be able to look in the mirror to see how well, or not, they were imitating the way I moved my lips and what I did with my teeth and mouth, and whatever facial expression I made when pronouncing sounds that were new to them.

I'd left the door to the room open, and I could hear the footsteps of a crowd coming down the hallway, getting closer. The others were here; I'd be able to move on to today's lesson.

The students entered the room, still deeply engaged in conversation with one another. I loved hearing them talk, never mind that today, the energy level of this group gave rise to a bit of anxiety for me. I'd have to work hard to keep up with them, feeling—if not exactly weak—very tired, not having had more than four hours sleep the night before, worrying.

The conversation of those most vocal was in Chinese. It

heartened me that they liked to talk; that always helped in learning a language. The shy students had the hardest time.

"This is English class. We speak English in English class," I announced, when they didn't settle down right away. I tried not to sound like an impatient American who would holler out, *Speak English! Speak English!* from the back of the line at the teller's window of the bank or at a fruit and vegetable vendor's stall at Haymarket, whenever there was a customer struggling with the language, slowing service down. Speaking English only was my rule, though admittedly, it was a rule sometimes broken in order to avoid total frustration, when some students understood my meaning and others did not.

I wasn't always sure if my corrections were helpful, my explanations understood, and I worried that the distractions of my personal life, eclipsed my enthusiasm for teaching. These students deserved better. They were smart. They didn't miss a trick. They would know when something was bothering me. I was trying hard to hide my troubles from them today.

I hadn't stood to greet the students, as I normally would, but rather had stayed seated at the round table where they were to join me for their lesson. My laziness immediately registered with Mei Lin, who was very perceptive; she was the student who fancied herself as arbiter of proper behavior in this group. Mei Lin clearly looked perplexed, recognizing that it was out of the ordinary for me to be so reserved.

"Clayah, you sad today?" she asked.

I ignored her perceptiveness and focused again on the Boston accent that made me cringe. I opened the desk calendar once again, and on the page where I'd written the note to remember to bring pocket mirrors to class, I added, "pronunciation exercises for the letter r." Then I answered Mei Lin.

"Am I sad today? No, I'm not. I'm tired."

I wondered, would I be able to keep up with my students, be effective, even before the baby came? It wasn't just the worry about the secret I was keeping from Ray Newell and everyone else that zapped my energy and gave me insomnia. There was not just the search for a new place to live, but then moving. If I could not find the enthusiasm for my students, how could I continue teaching them?

Without the income from this job Martin and I would never have the money to move. Thinking of the dilemma further exhausted me. We couldn't possibly stay at Ridge Road once the baby was born. But I needed this job for another reason besides the money I earned. It made me feel as if I were contributing. My work meant something, helping these people. Yet plodding through classes was something I couldn't imagine I'd be able to keep doing.

I would not talk about the real reasons for my demeanor. It was evident though that I couldn't put anything over on this group. They had found me out. These women treated me like a daughter, a treasure to be looked after, someone who not only gave advice, but who needed it herself.

"I am tired," I tried again, remembering that this was a beginner class and I ought to be modeling the verb "to be" at every opportunity.

"Say that. I am tired."

They looked blankly at me, and then they repeated, "I am tired."

"Clare is tired," I said.

"Clare is tired," they said.

I pointed at Ying and asked if she was tired.

"No, Ying not tired," she said.

Ordinarily, at this point I would get up and go to the flip chart and write the correct sentences for them, underlining the different forms of the verb "to be," to reinforce meaning and to help Ying understand what the others would get more readily. But I let the opportunity pass.

"Is Mei Lin tired?" I asked.

"No, Clayah tired," Mei Lin said, adding, "Why no sleep, Clayah?"

"Clare is tired," I repeated, to correct her. "Are you tired?" I asked her again.

This time she surprised me, taking the lesson one step further.

"No, Clare is tired."

***

On the trip back to Cambridge from Chinatown the train stopped and started, then stopped again on the Longfellow Bridge over the Charles River. It was rush hour. The MIT sailing club was out on the water, taking advantage of a good wind that had blown in from the ocean. I looked at my watch, realizing that I'd be late getting to Diamond Street. I didn't know how long I'd be able to keep up this intense freelance schedule running around between Chinatown classes and my work at the Center in Cambridge. Hadn't Dr. Aviva been correct, reassuring me that I'd have more energy once I was out of the first trimester? I was halfway through my second now and still feeling drained.

A woman plugged into an oxygen tank sat on the bench across from me. The advertising poster above her was for St. Aloysius Catholic School. I looked at the girl pictured in the classroom and thought of being her age, in a similar situation—an adolescent, except I'd have been wearing a green gabardine jumper and underneath it, a white blouse with Peter Pan collar, matching forest green bowtie clipped on. The uniform requirement had even specified green knee socks with loafers. Looking at the advertisement for today's Catholic education, it didn't seem that the student in the desk chair was even wearing a uniform.

Things had changed a whole lot in Catholic schools, if this photo was any indication. The camera's perspective was from the viewpoint of the teacher, the student seated in the front row. She didn't seem to be wearing socks at all, and looking at her from what was, for me, a familiar position at the front of the room—I wondered why the classroom was empty, except for this girl. Probably meant to convey the message that the school was big on individualized attention, although all I could imagine was that the girl had been required to stay after school for misbehaving. That was about the only time I'd ever been alone in a classroom with a teacher. Today's student was seated in an all-in-one chair and desk, and she was leaning on the desk part that folded down when not in use. She didn't look like she'd been reprimanded and there was no exam booklet for a make-up test on her desk. Her legs were crossed and even her inner thighs were showing in the picture, since she was wearing a very short skirt. *You could almost see everything God gave her*, I thought—something my grandmother would have said about me, reporting to my father, when he came home from work, that I'd been chastised, letting him know that the principal had seen me using a belt to hike up my knee length uniform, making it into a mini-skirt. Could Catholic schools have changed this much, that now a girl wearing a miniskirt and seated as she was, would be the image chosen to represent a typical student?

***

At the convent home in California, recommended by the high school principal at St. Agnes School, where my father had inquired about homes for unwed mothers, one of the Sisters was always watching—as if a girl might try something. Who could seriously consider escaping from the place—though we all longed to—because where was there to go, being pregnant, and without money, and knowing no one in the area, all of us from other places—the Midwest, the Deep South, the East Coast? We were helpless, totally dependent on our captors, sent away from family and friends.

Did every girl love the father of her baby the way I loved Ray? He was on my mind then, whenever I wasn't occupied. I had brought a wallet-sized copy of his high school yearbook photo with me, had hidden it in a sock in a bureau drawer. I took it out whenever I thought it was safe to do so, whenever there was no chance I'd be seen. Looking at it kept me dreaming. There was also a delivery guy, someone who looked so much like Ray, he could have been his older brother. Once a week he brought produce to the kitchen. I volunteered to work there cleaning, when I realized he came on the same day every week. He smiled like Ray, and he was polite like he was, too, when I checked the crates of fruits and vegetables against the invoice he handed me, my hand brushing against his.

Luckily, we were assigned chores, when we weren't expected to be praying or studying. Tired as we were from the hard cleaning work we were expected to do, sleep came easily and was welcomed, generally obliterating worries. I tried to keep dreaming of Ray, but sometimes nightmares took over.

Like most of the young girls, I didn't think that I was capable of taking care of a baby on my own then, but there was the question that haunted me. *How will I feel after the baby is taken away from me?* We were told we wouldn't even be allowed to rest our eyes on the baby's face, probably not hear its cry, the child scooped away so quickly into a room with a door. I would have to imagine what my baby looked like. I was sure it was a girl I was carrying; I even spent time thinking of a name for her, settling on Julia Rae, or maybe just Rae, her father's name in sound anyway. I wished over and over again that Ray had taken me with him as he'd promised. I just didn't understand why he hadn't waited for me, why he hadn't written to explain, once he got settled in Canada. I got no mail at the home.

There was never any privacy at Anna's House. One of the nuns was always standing sentry, even outside the bathroom door, which we were required to leave open—again probably because they wanted to be sure we didn't try anything. There was gossip that the year before, a girl had saved a sewing needle after she'd been assigned some mending of a Sister's coat, hidden it inside the cuff of her blouse, and used it to dig out a vein in her wrist.

After being sick in the morning, I went to the sink and splashed cold water on my face. Seeing myself in the mirror after, my face was ghostly white and I didn't recognize it as my own.

"Are you sick to your stomach?" the kindliest nun asked. She looked to be nearly as young as we girls were. She'd heard me heaving, and through the doorway was watching me at the sink. She saw me look in the mirror, horrified. Sister came to me. She reached up and wiped my sweaty brow, scratching my cheek—though not meaning to, I could tell—with the stiff, starched handkerchief she took from a pocket beneath her white half-moon bib. Was it made of cardboard, that bib that hid her breasts?

It wasn't always the good Sister finding me in distress; less kindly nuns sometimes stood in the doorway as I was going out, forehead damp with beads of sweat. There was the tall one I hated. Some of the girls called her "Slats." Slats would order me into the kitchen and stand over me, making me chew and waiting, watching me swallow down saltine crackers with milky tea that had too much sugar in it. I'd prefer to take it without milk, I would say, but the nun would whiten it anyway, removing the tea bag when it had barely left a stain. I can't be heard. My preferences don't matter anymore. Have I disappeared, and is that the reason?

I had no proof of it, but I believed that the baby I was carrying now was a boy, and had begun to wonder what to name him. This time I didn't have morning sickness and was grateful for that.

At Central Station I disembarked and slowly climbed the stairs up and out of the subway, feeling the weight of the tote bag of books slung over my shoulder, and so much more. The air smelled of curries, Szechuan spices, hamburgers, and fried foods. I needed to eat and settled for a take-away salad from the Middle East Restaurant, watching hungrily as the waitress added feta cheese to the vegetables, and then wrapped half loaves of sliced pita bread. I was eating for two and trying to be diligent about meals, even having several small ones during the day; but sometimes, like today, I'd be so involved in classes and commuting from one place to another, that there wasn't much time to eat and I'd forget the snack I had in my bag. I would eat my salad tonight, as soon as the tutorials were settled.

I rushed down Diamond Street, still hoping to get to the Center before the first of the students arrived. At the reception desk I stopped to pick up mail and phone messages, several from the same person: someone identified only as "young woman." Who was that? I'd been waiting to hear from Fernande and Marie Desir, the two sisters from Haiti, who'd stopped in to see me one night, just minutes before closing time. They were going to call to make an appointment to register for the program. And there were a few more students who had problems with schedules because of changes in their work hours. I wouldn't consider that any of these women, who came to mind, were "young" though. All were middle-aged and only one of them I'd describe as youthful. The rest showed their age in many ways, having lived difficult lives. Maybe the message-taker had been fooled. Voices could be deceiving.

Guy Paul was on desk duty tonight and he emerged from the Men's in the far right corner of the lobby. His initials were the ones on the message slips. In addition to not identifying the "young woman," he also hadn't recorded a phone number at which the caller could be reached. Although my work here, like at the medical center, was with recent immigrants, the Diamond St. students were different. To be part of the program here, they had to know enough English to be able to understand the explanations of the tutor, who wasn't an English teacher by profession, but rather a volunteer who worked in an entirely different profession. So, it surprised me that the caller hadn't left a message. Some of the staff—the office support staff especially—resented my freelance position and didn't like having to do anything to help with the program. They followed their job descriptions to the letter. Guy though, wasn't one of those who'd ever seemed resentful, and instead he tried to support the program, helping me to carry out some of the responsibilities, even if it wasn't part of his job description.

"What was her accent like, Guy?"

"Nope," he answered. "She didn't have any accent at all. This was an American woman. She said she'd call again."

Well, she had. Two other times. And Guy still had not been able to extract a hair of information from her. I let it go. There was no message in the pile of them from Lucille, a student who had disappeared. I'd been trying to track her down since she'd missed two consecutive tutorials. I'd even left a message for her at work. I saw a reply Guy had recorded, from the owner of the salon where Lucille cut and styled hair. He hadn't seen her either and he wanted his message relayed, when I caught up with her. Guy had written that Lucille's boss had said, *When you find Lucille, tell that woman I got an angry mob waitin' for straightenin' and dye jobs*. Guy had been able to get that one down.

Here was Amelia, one of my most dedicated students, coming in the front door. Even from a distance, and without wearing glasses for nearsightedness, I could identify her. I wasn't the only one who came to Diamond Street straight from work. Amelia was a dark-skinned woman from Antigua. She wore a snow-white food service worker's uniform—and soft-soled shoes, just as white as her dress. I didn't know how those white shoes could possibly stay so immaculately polished, since she wore them on the street. Those shoes made her approach perfectly silent. She often startled me, if I had my back turned, or if I were looking down reading or doing something at my desk. Sometimes, while searching the lower shelves of the program's library, looking for a book to recommend to a tutor or student, suddenly Amelia snuck up on me, calling *Clare! Clare!* She spoke in a tone not unlike what I imagined the Biblical voice heard in the wilderness would sound like—both assertive and beseeching.

But approaching straight on now, Amelia was chatting away in her other voice, a soothing Caribbean lilt, intending to keep me company at the unreliable copy machine, where I'd been trying to locate a paper jam in order to get on with the task of photocopying a vowel exercise one of the tutors had requested. I loved listening to Amelia, when she spoke in this voice. Island people had the rhythm of the ocean in their voices. It made sense: they'd been rocked to sleep as babies while the sea was churning in the background. The sound of the ocean wasn't just their lullaby, but the soundtrack of their lives as they were growing up. The same rhythmic rise and fall could be heard in the Irish lilt of Moira Harrington, one of the tutors.

"Keep talking. I'm listening," I told Amelia, who'd stopped relating her story to watch me pull out of the copier machine, sheets of inked-up white paper, responsible for the jam.

Black goo was all over my hands, but I had to wait to head to the staff room to clean up, so I wiped off as much as I could with tissue from the box on the desk. Amelia had a story to tell and she pressed on with it, something about radio broadcasts in Antigua.

"The radio gives the word to us. Everybody know who was dying, who have babies coming into the world," she said.

I hadn't given much thought to how important community news was relayed before there were readers and newspapers, other than through the grapevine. Of course, the radio would be the way. I knew the literacy rate in Antigua was very low when Amelia was a child, having researched it when she first came to register at the Center. I'd learned that before the 1970s, when she was born, no child was even required to attend primary school.

"Your baby, when she be born, announced on the radio, if you live in Antigua," Amelia said, obviously proud of this practice in her homeland.

She pronounced it Antika.

The students had learned the news of my pregnancy only

recently. I figured it was time. They must have begun to notice anyway. They were happy for me, offering well-meaning advice illustrated with anecdotes from their own experience. Some of them brought containers of food they'd made for me to eat for dinner. My favorite had been the Moroccan chicken with olives. Amelia, who had no children, didn't want to feel left out and had commented about the radio broadcasts, as a way of participating in the enthusiastic response of the students who were parents, I thought.

Amelia had said, "When *she* be born." My heart skipped a beat, remembering the daughter I'd given up. I didn't tell her I'd begun to think of *this* baby as a boy. I did so, I guess, because to have another girl, would probably always make me wonder what my first had been like growing up, at each age, the way I wondered now about what she might be like now at sixteen, the same age as my stepdaughter Danielle. Was she like Danielle, I wondered? Did she play a musical instrument or have a crush on a boy in the jazz band or one in her chemistry class?

"So then, you were announced on the radio when you entered the world, Amelia?"

"True. True," she said, proudly again.

Amelia remembered that, as a young girl, from time to time, her mother brought her to the home of the radio broadcaster. She didn't go for afternoon tea and conch fritters, but to ask for a letter or some other important paper to be read for her. There was a letter that her mother didn't know held the news that her brother had died in a London hospital. Curtis had been the first to leave the family behind on the island.

The man who was the broadcaster didn't have the heart to tell Amelia's mother right away, that the letter she wanted him to read for her held the information that her brother would not be returning to the island ever, that he was gone from this world. He gave her only the name of Middlesex Hospital, where Curtis had been taken, and then died. The broadcast man had been feeling ill himself that day, he told Amelia's mother, and stalling for a better moment to break the sad news, he told her that he would call the hospital from the radio station, for word of Curtis' condition.

"Just go home and pray for him is what he said."

Her mother had again taken Amelia along with her, going back the next day to see the radio broadcaster. Then he did tell her, but by that time, her mother already knew, having shown the letter to the village minister, reminded by a neighbor that *he got educated in America and then had come home to preach.*

Why? Why? Why? Amelia remembered her mother wailing at the radio broadcaster. *You should have told me yesterday. Prepare, you say. Prepare? Ha! Who prepare for death? We go 'round closing our eyes to that.*

As Amelia was relating all of this, I thought of how I played the same role for my students that the minister and the radio announcer had for Amelia's family. I was the person they came to, to read and interpret the doctor's lab report they received in the mail, informing them of sometimes good/sometimes bad results of a blood test, a pap smear, mammogram, prostate or other screening, asking me to explain what it all meant. They showed me silly letters that came and frightened them, informing them that under penalty of law they had to appear for jury duty, no matter that many of them were only just learning to read in English. So how could they possibly examine the documents shown in Exhibits A, B, or C? And sometimes when they came, they had a letter from home, written on old-fashioned blue airmail sheets that folded up into envelopes bearing foreign postage stamps. When the students brought them to me, it wasn't likely that I'd be delivering good news from home. These letters were probably not written by family members themselves; many of them could neither read nor write in English or in their own language either. They would have paid someone to do it for them. A man came in and took one out of his back pocket or from his billfold. A woman rummaged in her messy pocketbook, first pulling out receipts from the pharmacy, her subway and work passes, the papers she had to bring to immigration. Finding the letter from home they'd press it into my hand, saying, *read it for me please, Clare.* Mine is an old-fashioned job. To them, I'm the educated one, the scholar in the community, the wise woman. I am scribe to them. I give the word in this village.

What could I say to Amelia about her brother's death all those years ago, and about her mother's reaction to it? It brought to mind my own experience of not expecting my mother's death, thinking only that I'd be hearing about a new baby brother's birth. I stood on the porch, waving goodbye when my mother had climbed into the taxi that afternoon, headed to the hospital in labor. There had been excitement in the house then—joy, I would call it now. A sense of anticipation, while waiting for news of the new baby, was palpable. How quickly it had all turned: my father's promised phone call never received, and then the unexpected arrival of my grandmother. She sent away our beloved neighbor, Ingrid, who'd been watching me after my mother had left the house. Then, bewilderment had set in. How it had washed over me and erupted in questions like the one Amelia's mother had cried: *Why? Why? Why?*

I'd had no day of faith, praying, hoping for my mother's recovery, as the radio broadcaster had tried to offer Amelia's mother. My own grandmother had been cruel in her matter-of-factness. I wanted to say to Amelia now, that I thought the man had been kind to wait, to give her mother a little time, a little hope. *Your mother won't ever be coming home,* is what my grandmother said to me that awful day, and her words sounded as if the cover of the piano had been slammed shut over the keys; they conveyed that kind of finality.

Heaven was a place I'd tried to imagine again and again in childhood. The Sisters at school seemed so capable of it themselves. But for some reason I couldn't dream it up at all, and so had settled for believing it was just the way they'd described it. In my mind I saw only angels living there, having decided one night when having trouble falling asleep, that angels were what happened to the dead. My mother has become an angel I would think. Being quite fond of angels, the idea had given me comfort.

Ten

Martin

I had been so busy lately, that I'd let two weeks pass, since finding out about the house my friend Troy had for sale. I still wanted to try to make an appointment to see it from the inside—that is, if it was still on the market. This house was especially worth pursuing if it really was the gem Troy had described that morning having coffee with him at Valhalla. I kept thinking that because he hadn't bought the house and therefore had no investment to recoup, other than the lost client fees that he'd never expected to receive anyway, since his work for her had been pro bono, then perhaps the place might actually be more affordable than anything else on the market. Besides, Troy considered the house to be a burden, and since he was an old friend, perhaps a deal could be struck.

I knew that Clare wanted to take some time off after the baby came, and that meant we'd have less income. Before hearing of Troy's house, neither of us had been thinking of buying, but only renting a decent, safer place to accommodate the new addition to the family. But now I was thinking that a mortgage payment, if the price was right, might be equal to or less than the rent for a larger, nicer apartment. Rents in Cambridge had gone sky high.

Ever since the afternoon I'd played hooky to walk around the neighborhood where the house was, it had been impossible to avoid thinking about living there. I was envisioning those streets I'd walked in early spring. Seeing Clare so overwhelmed by what she kept referring to as The Search, crying this morning at breakfast, I had promised her that today I would get in touch with Troy, see if he would take us through the house, to get a look inside.

I was back at the office, making a few notes about another meeting I'd had with Ray Newell, and still trying to wrap my mind around the fact that this character witness that Eric Belmonte had come up with, was Veronica's lover and Danielle's teacher, not to mention that he'd said he'd grown up in Charland. Given his age, I realized that he grew up there during the same years Clare had been living there. Newell knew Belmonte, he said, from high school; he'd attended the regional high school, which drew students from several area towns, including Oxford, where my client had been raised. I didn't think Newell had mentioned to Clare that he was from Charland, since all she'd said was that he told her he'd grown up in a town west of Boston. However, knowing that in small towns everyone knows everyone else, I was a little surprised, that his name at least didn't ring a bell for her, even if she didn't know him personally when she was growing up. Then again, she hadn't lived there in years, and I suppose that unless you lived in the same neighborhood or played on a sports team, there wasn't a lot of connection between kids in public and private schools. If she remembered his name, I thought she'd have said so, that night she'd first met him.

Finished with the file, I put it away, I looked at my watch and realized that it was time to head over to Valhalla, see if Troy was there. I'd been there to grab a coffee to go most afternoons, and had made a note that Troy generally occupied the same booth at the back of the diner at about this time of day. Before raising Clare's hopes higher—and my own—I wanted to know if there were any potential buyers since the last time we'd talked. If not, I'd make an appointment to take Clare and Danielle to see the house.

Carli, the new secretary, stopped me as I was heading out. She'd just finished writing out a message slip.

"I didn't realize you were back from your interview. For you," she said, holding out a message slip.

"I'm back but I'm going for coffee. Do you want one?" I said.

"Sure, I'll have a cup. Cream only," she answered, and waving the message slip at me added, "I know that she's on the list of those who are allowed to interrupt you. She called just a few minutes ago."

She was on the list, but Veronica was under instructions never to call me at work unless there was an emergency involving Danielle. My heart beat faster. I tried to remember that there had been a few times when she'd broken the rule, although it had been a while. Turning back to my office, as much as it irked me that she called me here, I hoped this was one of those times.

When she answered the call, Veronica's voice sounded surprisingly upbeat for an emergency.

"What's up? Something wrong with Danielle?" I asked.

"Oh, no, nothing like that."

"I did tell you not to call me here, except in an emergency," I said.

She was silent. She must have been counting to ten, something the counselor we'd seen had advised, when Veronica still hoped there was something we could do to save our marriage. I could hear her now, *I know you're angry, but take a breath. Count to ten. You don't want to say something you'll forever regret.*

"I'm sorry," Veronica admitted. "I just thought you might run into Troy. He said he'd seen you at Valhalla, had coffee with you not long ago."

I wondered if she had planted some surveillance device in my brain before I left her, one night when I was dead tired and out cold. How did she know I was headed to see Troy? She was always one step ahead of me, always scheming about something. If it wasn't the schedule or some financial need, it was something else.

"He called me," she went on.

"Huh?" I said. I was confused.

"Troy. Troy called. I didn't even recognize his name at first, it'd been so long. He had to remind me that we used to have dinner with him and his wife—ex-wife now— sometimes on Friday nights at that Chinese place near the Law School. It's funny how you can be so close to people at a certain time in your life, and then just not see them anymore. You forget about them just like that."

I could picture her snapping her fingers at that last comment. I wondered if Troy was still single. Had he called to ask her out?

"Yes," I said. "I did see him. What is this about anyway? Can't this wait, Veronica? How about if I call you tonight after dinner? We can talk then. But since you called—how about getting together with Danielle—for a family meeting. At Patel's tomorrow evening. We'll have an Indian meal and talk over some of the things Danielle is going through."

We hadn't talked since she'd called to let me know that

Danielle had found her with Newell.

Danielle's house schedule had gone out the window since she refused to stay in the same house with Veronica.

Veronica said nothing about meeting.

"This is important, Veronica," I said.

"I've already made plans, Martin."

"With Ray Newell?" I asked. "Is he more important than your daughter? And didn't you tell her you weren't going to keep seeing him, if it upset her? Well, guess what? Danielle's upset!"

I was losing it, but she kept calm.

"You're late in asking about getting together for dinner tomorrow, "she said. " I generally have things to do on the nights Danielle is with you. And she's supposed to be with you on Thursdays."

"And where was Danielle supposed to be since Tuesday night?"

"I didn't change the schedule. That is Danielle's doing," she said. "Her idea, not mine."

"Your daughter's problem is your problem. Who brought this on?"

"I have to have a life, you know."

"I'm all for live and let live. Okay, if you have dinner plans tonight, we can meet after Danielle gets out of school tomorrow. I'll change my schedule and leave the office early afternoon."

"Oh, don't put on the martyr act," she said.

"I am being put upon, and so is Danielle, so that you can have your life. What about us, huh?"

"Who gave up work to be home with Danielle when she was a baby, when you didn't think my work was important enough to take on a better position that would have allowed us to hire a nanny after the first few months? Turning down offers from firms so that you could be a Public Defender, as if you were some Super Hero. So, yes, I have a lot to make up for right now."

"Enough. We've been over this already," I said.

"And did you consider Danielle, when you got involved with Clare, when your daughter was too young to even understand what had happened between her mother and father, that they were no longer living together, and she was being shuffled back and forth between homes?"

"I'm not going to get into this. And do not call me here, Veronica," I said firmly.

I was hoping Carli, and no one else would absent-mindedly pick up this line, not realizing the button was lit and a call was in progress. I wanted to end this call, get to the diner and see Troy before he headed out.

I wasn't going to let on that I was hoping to see Troy now, to arrange to have Clare and Danielle see the house as soon as possible. It was always better anyway, to have a fixed time, so that these family meetings didn't drag on.

"I'll let you know if I can rearrange an appointment I have tomorrow, and we can meet with Danielle after school, instead of at dinner."

She kept talking, and I was about to hang up, when she said, "Just listen a minute. I'll be quick. Troy says he's got a house for sale."

Great, now she wants me to buy Troy's house for *her*? I thought. It's not enough that I've been paying the rent on one. It would probably be cheaper in the long run, but no: she wasn't getting this house. If it was going to be anyone's house, it was going to be Clare's. And what was it with Troy approaching her? *What* did he think? That Veronica was paying rent to live where she did with Danielle? He was a lawyer; he ought to know about child support.

Having now counted to ten myself, I said as calmly as I possibly could, given the implications, "You know, Clare and I are going to have a baby, and we need to move to a new place ourselves. Remember? You didn't think it was safe for us to stay there, if Danielle spends time with us? It's going to cost a lot more for us to live in a better neighborhood—even if we rent and don't buy."

"Ha. No, no, I'm not interested for me and Danielle. We're fine where we are."

So, maybe she won the lottery, and she was going to buy *me* a house?

"I know why you're interested. It's for me, isn't it? You must have been saving all that money I've given you to rent that sweet little house that you and Danielle have been living in, and now you want to give it back to me for a down payment on the one Troy wants to unload. Right? In fact, I *was* thinking of taking a look at it, thank you."

"I can't believe you still harbor such anger and resentment after all these years, Martin. You've been providing a home for Danielle by paying rent on that house."

I was about to hang up, even though it had been weeks since a phone call between us had ended that way.

"Okay. Okay. You've already made me late. So what's this about?" I demanded instead.

"Well, if you're interested in the place yourself, you'll be none too happy to hear what I was going to tell you. Yes, in fact Troy had called to see if I might be interested in the house. He said he was *putting out feelers to everyone he knew*. I told him I wasn't in the market for one, but I did put him in touch with Ray Newell, Danielle's new sax teacher—or rather, former sax teacher—she's giving him up. I'm sorry. I didn't know you were interested in buying. I was calling you because Troy said he'd seen you recently, and I figured he might have mentioned where the house was. I didn't ask. Just wondering if you knew anything about the neighborhood."

So, now it made sense that I'd recognized Danielle's teacher as the guy I'd seen coming out of Troy's house for sale, when I was checking out the neighborhood. Veronica was going on and on, and I was now more anxious than ever to get to the diner to find Troy.

"Ray doesn't know the city very well, and I thought I could give him the scoop," she said. "He hasn't lived in the area since the late sixties, and you know how things have changed. He was one of those "draft dodgers."

Here, she gave a little extra emphasis to draft dodgers, her way I knew, of referring to our past—my draft counseling work out of the office in Harvard Square, and her own work, recruiting volunteers to head to Washington for protest marches during the Vietnam War. I didn't say anything, only sighed, waiting for her to continue, once she realized that I wasn't going to remark upon the reference. She didn't seem to care that I wasn't interested in being chatty, or hearing about this guy.

Ray Newell had now become involved in my work, with my daughter, my ex-wife, and Troy. And he'd seemed like such a nice guy.

Who'd imagine he could be so disruptive? Ultimately, it was Veronica who'd let him have such reach, by hiring him as a teacher for Danielle.

"There's the possibility that Ray might be offered a tenure track job at the Conservatory next year," she said. "He said he'd consider it if he could find a house. If so, he wants to buy something, now that he's seen how high rents are here."

Tell me about it, I thought, though Veronica made no connection between what she was saying and my situation.

It was also uncharacteristic of her to be so altruistic, intervening to assist the guy who was—or had been, as she had just informed me—Danielle's new teacher in his search for real estate—unless she was also interested in continuing to be involved with him, and not just a fling with him. Now in his mid-thirties, he was still unattached and maybe wanted to remain that way. I thought of Danielle, and how this situation was for her. I wondered how she'd ever accept her mother having long-term involvement with the guy. Now, according to Veronica, Danielle had probably given up the sax, after having fought so hard for the lessons. What on earth did Veronica think? Ending the call, I wondered when, if ever, she would stop having such a disruptive influence on my life.

If I'd been hesitant about the house, thinking maybe we couldn't afford it, this conversation sent me flying out the door to Valhalla now, sweeping past Carli before she could remind me of another responsibility, announcing as I went, "I'm taking a half hour away from my desk." I hoped Troy would be seated in his usual booth when I arrived, and that he'd be alone, so we could talk.

He was there, but holding court with another lawyer, someone I didn't really know, but recognized from the office down the hall. I approached and Troy introduced us. His friend took the opportunity to scoot. I wasted no time in asking Troy not to decide on a buyer for the house until Clare and I had seen it, that I knew that he'd called Veronica and that she'd put him on to Newell. He apologized for calling Veronica, saying he didn't mean to offend, but that he just wanted to settle things with the house as soon as possible. He repeated what Veronica had said he told her, "I'm putting out feelers everywhere."

I learned that Newell hadn't made an offer on the house. Perhaps he'd been distracted by the situation with Veronica and Danielle. Something good had come of the upheaval maybe.

I made an appointment for early afternoon the next day.

***

When I went home that evening, I told Clare that I'd finally met the saxophone teacher.

"Or maybe he's now the ex-saxophone teacher," I said to her.

"How? Don't tell me Veronica involved him in your family meeting?"

"No, no. That didn't happen yet. It'll be tomorrow. But," I said, "it turns out that my new client—the guy who threatened the police officer with a knife, the one in the Globe article—happens to be an old friend of his from a town near Charland. Ray Newell grew up in the same town you did. You didn't know him?"

Clare had been doing the dishes and she didn't turn around when I started talking. She didn't answer right away either, but when she did, she said, "No, no. I didn't know him. I think he must be older than I am. He looked older," she said. "What town is your client from?"

I told her. She said she didn't know anyone who lived in Oxford, when she was growing up.

"I didn't know him. No, I guess Ray Newell must have run in different circles than I did. And he must be older, too."

"I'm surprised," I said. "Charland is a small town, even if he isn't your age."

"Well, if he knows this guy you're representing, then maybe he didn't spend a lot of time in Charland, having friends in other places.," she said.

"Right. He and my new client went to the regional high school together. That's how they knew each other.

I didn't tell her about the phone call from Veronica, how she'd put Ray Newell on to Troy, and that he'd looked at the house Troy had for sale.

"We have an appointment to see the house, before I meet

with Veronica and Danielle. I figured we ought to look at it before he shows it to too many people. We don't want to miss our chance."

Clare, finished with the dishes, said she was looking forward to seeing it.

"I hope things will work out," she said. "So much going on," she sighed.

She looked tired, and I knew that what was happening with Danielle weighed heavily on her mind. She was tired of Veronica's interference. If she only knew that as part of her engineering Ray Newell's stay, Veronica was not only trying to help him get a more permanent position at the Conservatory, but she'd also been helping him find a house, including introducing him to Troy, and that he'd toured what I had begun to think of as *our house*.

Eleven

Clare

I went down the list of truant students, making calls to learn why they'd missed meeting with their tutors. Christian James' excuse for not getting to his tutoring session the night before was that he'd had an accident on the way to the Center. That he drove a car was a surprise, since he wasn't able to read much of anything in English yet—and there were street and traffic signs. Marlena Mercurio didn't get to Diamond Street because she had been stuck taking care of the twins that belonged to her unmarried teenage daughter, Delfina, who hadn't come right home after her GED class. Octave, also a beginning reader, wasn't at the Center the night before, because she'd been scheduled to work at the hospital, where she transported patients to surgery, and that called to mind newspaper stories of surgeons operating on the wrong body part, when there was a patient mix-up. And Grevil Marshall didn't meet with his tutor because he was upset that he had lost his job that afternoon, learning that the Jamaican restaurant where he was a cook, was going out of business; and if that wasn't enough, his roommate was threatening to move out, because Grevil, who'd been making some money on the side, doing baking for other restaurants, had been keeping him awake, whipping up spice cakes in their kitchen in the middle of the night, banging pots and pans around, and filling the air with the scent of ginger and clove, and a host of other enticing aromas, that made his roommate want to get up to eat.

Who could find fault with any of them for missing their lessons? Tracking them down though, made it less likely that they'd give up trying to learn to read and write and drop out of the program. They were adults. They had jobs. They had families. And many of them had troubles. Day to day life made it a challenge to get to their sessions at Diamond Street. I'd come to realize that, for many of them, being at the Center for tutoring was a luxury.

Once calls were made for all the names on the list of truant students, I went into the kitchen to make lunch to take to the Medical Center for the brown bag class with my ESL students this afternoon. Martin and Danielle were sitting at the kitchen table—it was going on a half hour that they'd been there, a record for a morning talk. Seeing me, Danielle saw the opportunity for escape and stood, lifting her backpack of books up off the floor, and hoisting it onto her shoulders.

I reached out to help adjust the straps and tested the weight of the bag.

"That's heavy," I said.

Danielle shrugged off the comment and headed for the door.

"Remember not to make afterschool plans for tomorrow. We're getting together with your mother," Martin said, as she went out.

***

She was only six years old when I'd moved in with Martin, and she couldn't relate to me then as a person, never mind as an auxiliary mother. Danielle's resistance toward me hadn't been entirely eliminated. I thought she still held some residual longing for a different situation, one that didn't involve her parents divorcing. But there was no denying that things had definitely improved from the early days.

In the very beginning there were mornings at the breakfast table when she'd ask Martin, *Why don't you still live with Mom and me?* Or pointing an accusatory index finger at me, she'd scrunch up her mouth, nose, and eyes, and say, *Why is she here?* And as time went on, I'd sit in silence when she'd say, *Why is she **still** here?* I tried to steel myself against Danielle's hurtful words. It really was a wonder that our marriage had survived all that. I had had my doubts, and at one point, had actually left for a week to stay with a friend, when I didn't think I could tolerate the situation any longer. But I was the adult, and all through the turmoil with Danielle, I thought I'd acted like one. I loved Martin and told him when I returned, that I wanted to love Danielle, too, as impossible as it might have been in the beginning.

"Do you think I tried too hard with Danielle?" I asked Martin, now that Danielle had left and was on her way to school.

I'd thought I'd been doing everything right, as she was growing up. I indulged her, taking her to see every new Disney film that hit the theaters, baking cookies so often I thought I was running a bakery. I drove her and her friends to the best parks and indoor gyms for play dates. I invited her friends for sleepovers. I tried hard to win her affection; maybe I tried too hard.

"You've been a great mom," he said.

"Stepmom," I corrected him.

He recalled the little game his daughter had loved, one that I had dreamed up to underline family unity. Sometimes, when Martin showed any spontaneous affection for me—a hug or a kiss while we were making dinner together, both of us standing at the stove, one of us sautéing vegetables, the other whisking a special sauce—we'd catch a glimpse of Danielle in the background looking on, though we hadn't heard her approach, didn't know she'd been watching.

"And when we noticed her, we'd call out, 'Sandwich! Sandwich!' And then Danielle would come running, worm herself in between the two of us for a double hug, the filling in our sandwich," Martin remembered.

I remembered that after a while, Danielle had taken up the game on her own.

"She'd announce, whenever she wanted to, *Sandwich! Sandwich!* She enjoyed the power she wielded in our little family, didn't she?"

Martin looked surprised at that comment.

"She was just a kid, Clare."

"I know. I know. But I've been thinking there might be more bothering her these days than her mother's antics. Do you think she's also worried about being displaced by our baby? I've been worried some of her feelings about us being together might resurface, when you're preoccupied with someone else—the baby, this time."

Secretly, I worried, too, that now that Ray had become so involved in our lives—now even with Martin, with this court case with Ray's friend, Eric—if he were to learn of my history with him, Martin might worry that *he'd* been pushed aside. But he didn't know, and I intended to do everything in my power to keep him from knowing.

Martin said that today he was going to confirm the appointment to see Troy's house, now that I'd agreed to look at it with him.

"I'll pick you up tomorrow around noon, since Troy said he'd be available to show us the house." he said. "Okay?"

I nodded.

Back when I had realized that Martin couldn't move into my old apartment, because it was too small, I'd suggested that rather than living at Ridge Road, we look for new place, one big enough to accommodate Danielle; then, we'd have a clean slate, beginning our life together. There was no argument about it; Martin hadn't really been happy with this apartment either, having rented it well before I had come into the picture, when he'd finally admitted to the reality that things with Veronica were irreconcilable, that she'd never let up about wanting him to join a law firm or get into private practice, so they could live more comfortably. So, leaving her, he'd chosen the apartment, in spite of all its flaws, just to be near Danielle, to be in the same neighborhood to promote the consistency he knew his daughter needed during the transition.

We were both still idealistic. I knew Martin wanted to please me now, just as he had then, when we had toured available apartments together, looking for something better. Any that were affordable turned out to be in worse condition or in a less desirable neighborhood, or both, and some of the landlords were asking even higher rent than what Martin had been paying here at Ridge Road. So, he stayed, and I moved in. Reluctantly.

At least this one has potential compared to what we've seen, I remembered Martin saying about this apartment at the time, trying to put a positive spin on the idea of staying put. *I'll fix it up. You'll see. It's big—Danielle has a good-sized room of her own here. And it's sunny.* And *yes, sun is a plus*, I'd said, thinking though, *it does expose all flaws*. I had to give Martin credit for trying to make the apartment comfortable. In the weeks before I'd officially moved in, he'd worked hard every night after returning from the office or the courthouse, dead tired—a whole month—trying to make me feel better, scraping away at the layers of old varnish, filling in holes in the plaster, then sanding the walls smooth. *Clean white paint throughout will make a huge difference. You'll see.* And I had thought of Doctors Without Borders, their task of creating sterile clinics in less than ideal outposts.

I had expected when I moved in with Martin, that it would be temporary. We'd been living in the apartment together for almost ten years now. I remember how I'd hated to give up my place that had views of the Boston skyline through its top floor windows that faced east toward the Longfellow Bridge. All the while I'd lived there, I'd considered it a privilege. I could watch the sun rise over the city on days when gray winter shoved off and the sky was blue. Here on Ridge Road, when we looked out the side windows, all we saw were the apartment houses next to us. At least we saw the church from the front windows, but there were no trees to speak of on Ridge Road. Martin tried humoring me about moving in, predicting that I'd receive many blessings, living across from a Catholic church, making a bad joke that in summer, when the doors of the church were flung open, and we could hear the amplified voice of the priest reciting the Mass on Saturday evenings and Sunday mornings, that we were fulfilling our religious obligation (both of us being raised as Catholics, although we no longer subscribed.). *Multiple blessings if you're home for more than one Mass,* he would tease.

As I was thinking about getting out of this disappointing living situation, Martin leaned down and kissed my cheek. I had begun to feel like a two-timer, even though I told myself that there was no longer anything between me and Ray. Yet I found myself thinking of him often during the day, every day since I knew he'd returned. I was living with the worry that he might stay in the area, and what might happen if he did.

Lunch made, I was ready to leave the kitchen. These thoughts went too deep for so early in the day. Time was slipping away, so that suddenly I felt I had to hurry to get to class on time.

"Here's hoping we like what we see tomorrow," Martin said, "and can negotiate something before someone else scoops that house up. It looks like a great little place."

Because Martin had been talking about this house with such enthusiasm, I worried not just that we wouldn't be able to finance it, but also, that I might not like it. If it fell through, for one reason or another, he'd be crushed, and if I got my hopes up, I would be, too. Martin's enthusiasm for the house had even made me stop reading listings for rental apartments. I did know that life was too tough not to have some place that was yours, to take comfort in knowing that you could create a haven for your family within that space, and that not everyone had that: a place to celebrate, a place to soothe your troubles, to rest from cares and everything that would beat you down, just living each day. I hoped we could have that. And I hoped that the daughter I'd given away, had that, too.

"If we're going to find a place, it will have to be soon. I can't imagine traipsing around, looking with a babe-in-arms," I said. "And if we have to stay, we'll be pressed for space with Danielle living with us half of every week. She needs to feel it's her place, too. She can't give up her room or share it with the baby."

"Of course not. And so you know, she's already made it clear that she won't be babysitting," Martin said.

Our "office" would have to become the nursery, if we had to stay in this apartment. But that room faced the loud and busy street, and the baby might wake or be startled by the sounds of motorcycles and sirens, having a crib on that side of the house. I remembered that when our friend Sara's children were babies, she used to have parties on weekends. Being such a young mother, only in her mid-twenties, they'd play rock and roll the whole time, stereo cranked up and the place crowded with friends dancing, the floor actually moving up and down, so many people were packed into the place. *Noise never bothers my babies*, she would say, when I marveled that they slept through it all. *You have to get them used to it.*

Martin drew me back to him, touching my hair, wanting to kiss me, but not the way I'd kissed him goodbye, the peck on the cheek. He held me for a moment, but I felt the need to pull away.

"I really have to get going," I said.

***

That evening, after teaching all afternoon at the medical center, I went straight to Diamond Street. When I got there, my first appointment had already arrived. She was right on time; the desk clerk said. I was a few minutes late. I saw a woman—she was young and well-dressed, like a professional. She was seated next to Mrs. Lila Jenkins who was dressed in a light pink nursing aide's uniform, Bible open on her lap, mouthing silently whatever scripture she was reading—hellfire and brimstone, no doubt. I'd seen her coming into the building ahead of me, heard her quoting something harsh to a homeless man on the steps, something brought on when she'd noticed him drinking whiskey from a pint bottle wrapped in brown paper. He'd been too far gone to answer her, never mind to manage to get out of her way. She'd stepped over him, as I had to, following her inside, hearing her continue to mumble the same Biblical passage under her breath as she walked to the chair in what was clearly her favorite corner of the reading room.

I finally had a name for the caller who hadn't previously left messages.

After I'd put my bag and papers in the office, I went over to the girl and introduced myself, asking, "Are you Judy Kneeland?"

I led her downstairs to my office, what I called *Headquarters*. As we reached the basement level, I said, "Come into my cave," imitating a Boris Karloff kind of voice. The place was something like a cave, smelly and dank, but definitely not dark. I felt I had to explain, if not apologize for it.

"The place floods when it rains," I said. "It's cozier upstairs though, where the tutoring sessions take place."

I didn't want to scare this potential volunteer tutor away, didn't want her to think this is where she'd spend her evenings.

"This is just a conference room and we keep our program library here, too."

I pointed out my office in the back, an office with a window instead of a wall separating it from the rest of the large room, so I could pretend that I could look outside, though all I saw was the conference room and the door to the stairs beyond. Everything was painted white, set off by loud, orange, uncomfortable, plastic chairs that were placed around the table where I held meetings, interviews, and occasionally taught classes. The overhead fluorescent tube lighting emphasized the whiteout effect and made everyone's skin glow unhealthily. It *was* the atmosphere of an interrogation room, and calling it *Headquarters* seemed appropriate.

"And I always feel like I ought to put sunglasses on, being here; it's so bright," I said.

.Judy Kneeland was beautiful though. She had a healthy glow, even in such terrible light. She looked, if not pampered, as if she paid good attention to what she ate and that she kept physically active. She might even be an athlete, I thought. Her eyes, dark brown, and her hair like my own, curly, and frizzy in the humidity. But her hair was darker than mine—black—and it set off her milky complexion and rosy cheeks.

"I'll try," I said, when Judy asked me to describe some of my students. "But no one's typical really. They're all different with similar themes and challenges running through their stories."

I sighed, overwhelmed for a few seconds, thinking of several of them at once, how hard their lives had been—and still were—how much courage they needed in order to stay afloat, and how resourceful and positive they were, to have searched and found me, to have discovered this place at all. I admired them greatly, I told Judy.

I visualized the room full of students at the last film night I'd held here, and began describing for her what it was like. I saw them seated in rows of chairs I'd set up to face the screen, waiting to watch the film on the history of the Civil Rights Movement. They'd been excited that there were going to hear Dr. King give the "Dream" speech. Most students who attended that night had not been born and raised in the U.S., and I'd selected the film, I told Judy, "disguising a history lesson as entertainment."

I made popcorn for them and they pretended to be at the cinema, eating it out of large paper cups."

"What a great lesson!" Judy said.

"There are new problems every day in a program like this. It's all trial and error to find what works best."

"You sound like an expert," she said.

"An expert would have it all figured out," I said. "It's hard to know how to reach them sometimes."

"Nothing in life is simple, is it?" Judy said.

I raised my eyebrows at that, thinking that it was a very mature comment, for someone who looked so shiny bright and youthful. It also piqued my curiosity. I wondered what it was that was so difficult in *her* young life. Dressed as she was, in a jacket color coordinated with her skirt, she looked professional. It was difficult to tell her age, but she appeared to be in her early twenties.

Judy looked uncomfortable after her comment, as if maybe she thought she'd said the wrong thing. She straightened her short skirt, trying to pull it taut underneath her, trying to resettle herself in the visitor's chair I'd pulled up to my desk.

I took an application form from my desk drawer. I saw a couple of bite-sized snickers in there.

"I could use a little treat, couldn't you?" I said, hoping to help her relax.

I held one of the chocolate bars out, and she took it from me.

"I needed something sweet," she said.

She asked if she could take the application form home to fill it out.

I handed it to her.

"Should I drop it off or mail it back to you?" she asked.

"Either way, if you don't have time to fill it out now," I said.

Perhaps I'd scared her away, meeting with her here in my office rather than taking her up to the tutoring room. But she smiled broadly as she left and promised to fill it out soon.

"I'm happy to meet you," she said, as she headed to the stairs.

Martin had called earlier, to let me know that he'd be staying late at the office, since he had the meeting with Danielle and her mother in the afternoon the next day, and he'd have work to catch up, if he didn't.

Even leaving Diamond Street at nine o'clock, I got home before Martin did. Being tired after a long day, and not having any reason to stay up, I went to bed, thinking I'd read for a bit, hoping to stay awake until Martin got home. My eyes were heavy though, closing as I tried to read. I couldn't force them to stay open, and gave in to sleep, shutting off the light.

I woke in the middle of the night and felt Martin beside me. What comfort it was, to have him there. I moved in the bed, reaching out to touch him, and realized that my lower back ached. I resettled myself, thinking that it had something to do with the way my body had been positioned and tensed during sleep—a physical response to the stress of all that was on my mind. Or was it from being jarred in the little crash Danielle had involved us in the night before, coming home from her lesson? I'd felt nothing though, when that had happened; it had seemed so minor an accident, the other driver making something out of nothing. But maybe, although I hadn't noticed it at the time, I had pulled a muscle and carrying my tote bag of books for class at the medical center, or crouching down to find a book on a bottom shelf of the Diamond St. program library, I had aggravated something minor, made it worse.

Hoping I wouldn't feel the ache, I tried to breathe more shallowly, remembering that was the way I'd dealt with pain after a sledding accident that had left me with a broken rib as a kid.

Unsuccessfully, I tried to push away the thought that the pain had something to do with the baby, my mind going to another fear I'd been living with ever since I learned I was pregnant: what if I lose this second baby, too? I tried to change focus, to be positive. At the last visit to Dr. Aviva, only days short of beginning the third trimester, she'd said at that checkup, that this was a *viable pregnancy, a keeper*, and we'd listened together to the roaring heartbeat of my baby.

I got out of bed carefully, so as not to wake Martin, or the pain I'd felt.

In the kitchen I poured a glass of milk and sat down at the table to drink it. Although it was very dark I didn't want to put on the table lamp or the overhead light. Instead, for light I thought to move my chair nearer to the door with a window onto the back porch. I got up and slid my chair out from the table and as carefully and quietly as possible, gently pushed it over the tile floor, with my foot, not carrying it. I didn't want to wake Martin or Danielle. I moved slowly, not wanting to feel even a little twinge of that worrisome pain, lest it bring back the anxiety I felt, that maybe something was wrong with the baby. I needed to mother a child of my own. It seemed the only way to make up for my loss.

I was bathed in moonlight streaming in through the porch window. I sat down in the chair, saw that the light illuminated the back of my hands, made them look old, exposing large veins. I turned them over and looked at the palms, but without enough light I couldn't see the lifeline and the lines that told how many children I'd have. I didn't think I remembered anyway, which lines were which.

I stood up to look at the moon, which was still waxing, but now almost full. Outside there was only stillness—nothing moving out there—no cats, raccoons, or skunks that I could see, and too early in the morning for birds to be hopping and flitting about, and singing. The porch chimes weren't even tinkling; the wind had completely died down.

I heard footsteps behind me. Martin. He was rubbing his eyes as if I were some kind of apparition he was hoping to smudge out, rather than his wife, the woman he thought he knew almost as well as I knew myself.

"Oh, did I wake you?"

"In that long, white nightgown you look ethereal in the moonlight," he said.

But he looked worried.

"Deliberating about something?"

He understood I'd be troubled, he said.

"Why wouldn't you be? It's perfectly understandable you'd be worried. This thing with Danielle and Veronica does complicate things for everyone involved. It's a lot to consider."

He pulled another chair away from the table and dragged it over nearer to me and sat down. He reached out, put his arms around me, carefully drawing me to him, guiding my head to rest on his shoulder, like Ray used to when I went dancing with him at that club, all those years ago, when, at the end of the evening, the band played slow songs. Martin thought he knew how complicated matters were. I wished I could tell him my secret, wished I could let him know how very complicated this situation between Ray Newell and Veronica was for me.

I left my head on his shoulder. I liked resting there. I had danced with Martin after drinking a little too much champagne at his colleague Carl's wedding, not long ago. Martin must have thought of it, too, because now he had the idea to waltz me around the kitchen, as he had the evening at the wedding. He stood, took my hands, and gently pulled me up to him.

I hadn't said anything to him about the pain. While slowly dancing he sang quietly, *Everything's gonna be all right...*

"I'm a little dizzy," I said, afraid the dancing—even a slow waltz—might wake the pain.

He steadied us to a stop and said, "Sorry, I didn't mean to make you dizzy. Come back to bed now, will you?"

"I'm feeling a bit sick to my stomach," I said. "It's why I'm dizzy. It's not the dancing. It was the reason I got out of bed," I lied.

I still didn't mention the pain. I didn't want him to worry. It was probably nothing.

"Should I make peppermint tea?"

I wondered how he could be so sweet at this moment, at this hour of the morning, when we were both exhausted. I knew, too, that our world had shifted, and people were in new places, as if moved by a powerful force, one that I wasn't able to stop.

"No, no mint tea. It's chamomile anyway that helps with sleep, not mint. My Chinese students said so. Ying told me she used to put it in her baby's bottle when she would wake at night."

I wondered if that was safe for a baby, if it actually was what Ying had meant to say, her English being so poor. I didn't think a baby should have anything but milk for a long time, preferably mother's milk.

At the mention of the word *baby*, Martin, still holding me to his chest, moved away a bit and looked down at the little rise of my belly, as if he'd just remembered the baby. He put the warm palm of his hand there.

I immediately warmed inside, when he did that. "Mmmm."

I moved close to him again.

"Let's remember that business about putting chamomile in the baby's bottle, and ask the pediatrician," Martin said.

He sat me down again and went to the sink to fill the kettle and set it to boil on the stove.

"Mint should settle your stomach, I think," Martin said.

When the tea was ready he handed me the cup, watching as I sat there in the moonlight, slowly drinking it.

I finished and we went down the hall, Martin with his arm around me, heading back to bed.

***

Oddly, when I woke later that morning, I felt fine and was relieved, chalking up the nighttime pain to tension and worry. I told Martin the truth about the reason I got up out of bed in the middle of the night.

"But we're supposed to see your friend Troy's house this afternoon before your meeting with Veronica and Danielle?" I said, when he told me to call him if the pain started up again.

"We can see Troy's house another day, if you aren't feeling well. I can call him. Please, let me know, Clare," Martin said.

I vowed that I'd excuse myself from class to call him, and agreed that, if it happened, a call to Dr. Aviva was a good idea. Then, I set off for my classes at the Medical Center.

***

I pulled open the door, leading onto the floor where my first class would meet, and the pain—very low in my back—returned. Sharply. So sharp, it took my breath away. What was the reason for this pain? I had worried in the middle of the night, when it wouldn't subside for so long, that it wasn't caused by the stress of new decisions I had to make. What if it wasn't a pulled muscle from carting an itinerant teacher's tote bag of workbooks back and forth from home to the Medical Center, then after to Diamond Street. I considered that it was possible I'd eaten something bad the day before; perhaps the egg salad at the deli had been left out of the fridge too long? But I discounted that possibility: the pain was situated in the wrong place for that.

And then, I thought again, of the worst possibility. What if the accident with Danielle had caused this pain; what if there was something wrong with the baby?

The classroom door was unlocked. The repurposed room looked like it had once been a doctor's large examining room, or an outpatient surgery. Nothing had been done to bring it into the last decades of the twentieth century, except that the walls had been freshly painted white. Even the furnishings were from another era: in the center of the room there was a round Mission-style heavy oak table and matching chairs, and over in the corner, a free-standing oak and glass cabinet, its shelves empty now, but I could easily conjure up images of apothecary jars filled with swabs, potions, and cotton. I'd found the door of the cabinet unlocked, trying it the first day, and when it was opened I got a whiff of the same medicinal smell I would get, opening the little drawers of the cabinet built into the pantry wall of the house where I'd grown up, which had once belonged to a doctor, who'd had his office in his home.

Not all the rooms I was assigned were so welcoming; some were in rented office space with nothing else in the room but a brown-imitation wood covered metal table, plastic stacking chairs with aluminum legs—and, if I were lucky—on a window sill above the heating and air-conditioning vent, someone would have been thoughtful enough to have placed a telephone, in case of emergency.

The young Chinese women who were students in this medical terminology class were employed typing information onto insurance forms, listing patient names and contact information, medical diagnoses and treatment, and policy numbers. This meant that they would have to consult records and be able to spell and type the names of diseases and the procedures for which the hospital was billing. Because the handwriting on hospital forms was often difficult for anyone to decipher, never mind one of my language students, I was charged with familiarizing them with the most common diseases and remedies, hopefully making it easier for them to recognize what they were looking at. I was doubtful the class would help much, but many of the women were very bright, so they enjoyed the spelling drills I gave them, and the game I made of learning Latin and Greek prefixes and endings.

The course was new this year. I preferred teaching conversation, but the company I worked for was always coming up with new ideas for classes—*keeping current* was what they called it—increasing revenue was what it really was. I was never sure how much these classes actually helped the hospital workers advance in their jobs, although that was the way the company marketed them. *It's about empowerment*, they told me. I felt some pressure to *sell* the classes; that, taken with the unbridled optimism of the students, made me uncomfortable. I didn't want to be someone who was taking advantage of my students' genuine faith. I did want them to succeed, in whatever class I taught.

In a few minutes these students would come into the room, that faith shining through in their clear eyes and on their smooth faces, and in the smiles and enthusiasm with which they greeted me. They seemed always very happy to see me, not like some of the American students I'd taught in high school or college classes, those who wanted to stay on friendly terms because of what they might need—a reference, a good grade, or an intro to a professor or some other person who might help them in their education or career advancement. Like all of the students at the hospital, those in this group came to this country after escaping trouble and the lack of basic necessities and opportunity in the countries of their birth. As difficult as their lives in those places had been before coming to the U.S., I knew that many of them still had lives here fraught with difficulty; yet they never seemed to harbor bitterness, showing gratitude for even the smallest gesture of kindness. The hope they held onto was for the future—not their own, they would tell me—*for daughter*, one said. *For son*, said another. *Family. Children. Not me. Too old now. Too old to learn too much.* I thought of my own daughter. I gave her away, so that she would have a future. Not having the means to care for her on my own, I knew that I could not raise her myself without help, and there was no one to help me.

I believed that most parents hoped for a better future for their children. Martin cautioned me against generalizing, having seen too much at the courthouse to persuade him otherwise. There were times, that as a criminal lawyer, a public defender, whose cases sometimes had involved parents who had perpetrated serious crimes against their children. I didn't want to think about the fact that I didn't know what kind of future my lost daughter had, that I knew nothing about the family raising her. I hoped that she'd been loved and nurtured. I realized since seeing Ray again, that I'd been pretending that I was over the loss, over the fact that I had signed away any influence on her future. But I knew that a bright future was what Martin and I wanted for our child. I knew that we would both do everything in our power to make that possible, and I hoped that would lessen my loss.

Before seeing Ray, when I thought about the past, I'd focused on myself, on what I was missing out on, as my child grew without my help, grew to be the sixteen-year-old she would be now, same as Danielle. Knowing that Ray had not married and had not had another child—didn't even know he had one—I was thinking of him, thinking that possibly, he would not ever know what it was like to raise his own child. At least I was being given a second chance.

Margaret Kwan was the first to arrive. Like the others in this class, Margaret was bright, but her English was better than the rest. Nevertheless, she had complained of always being passed over for promotions. She believed though, that if she took every new class that came along, management might eventually notice her. She'd been taking classes for three years now. She looked to be about my age, was matter-of-fact in conversation, and serious bordering on bitter—an exception to the generally open and enthusiastic students in these classes. She'd been here longer than the others and seemed better educated—perhaps something in her experience had shaped a more critical approach to life. She did not hide from anyone, the fact that her work didn't provide the kind of challenge she would have liked, that she knew she was capable of much more. But she gave the impression that something else, something bigger than all of that, had hurt her in life.

Margaret was married, as all the women in this class were, though she was the only one who said she had no children. When I'd announced that I was going to have a baby, Margaret alone had remained silent, foregoing the congratulations and enthusiastic response the others had shown.

"I'm not feeling well and may have to leave early today,

Margaret," I said, after we exchanged hellos.

Margaret looked as if she wondered if I might be contagious.

"Must have eaten something I shouldn't have."

Margaret seemed to relax, hearing this.

"Maybe you should stay home. Why come to work?"

It was useless to try to explain that I didn't have sick days because I worked freelance, and therefore showed up unless I was very ill. It would have been unfathomable to Margaret, that as an educated professional, someone she considered to be important for having achieved the status of teacher, would not have the benefit of paid sick days. My students had taken jobs at the medical center for that reason, and because they had paid vacation and personal time, and health insurance; the benefits were good, even if their hourly wages were on the low end of the scale.

"I know. I probably should have stayed home. But since I'm here now I'll start the lesson when everyone arrives. I was thinking that if I do have to leave, you might dictate the list of words to the others, so they won't waste class time. They can practice spelling them until the class is finished."

Margaret looked pleased that I thought her capable of taking over.

"Make sure you tell my Supervisor," she said.

"Of course. I'll write it in my report."

I hated doing those reports and was never paid extra to write them at the end of each course. But although the reports took hours to do, I diligently compiled them, wanting the effort and progress of the students to be documented for their managers, honestly hoping that they would advance as a result.

One after another the students arrived, and then the last four came in a group, speaking loudly, sounding as if they were arguing, just the way my mother's Italian relatives sounded during an ordinary conversation.

As was generally the case, we spent some of the class time informally talking before settling into the boredom of Medical Terminology.

"Catching up with each other," I announced, segueing into it, explaining the idiom as best I could when they crinkled up their foreheads and formed their mouths into the letter o.

"A few minutes of conversation about what's new—what's happening—before we begin the lesson."

"What's new, Qui Qui?" Margaret asked.

Qui Qui always had something going on. Calling on her to speak first had become routine; it was a light-hearted way to start class listening to her entertaining descriptions of her latest escapade at work or with family.

A couple of students laughed and one or two raised their eyebrows, anticipating her tale.

She was a good sport, enjoying her ability to make others laugh.

But today Qui Qui shook her head *No*, when Margaret called on her.

"Is something wrong?" I asked, concerned.

During news sharing, students sometimes brought problems to class and they were allowed to present them for a kind of group brainstorming session. They were usually about a son or a daughter, a husband's job, or their own work situation, the difficulty almost all of the time related to not understanding something about American culture. Sometimes it was the school system, sometimes someone needed to have an explanation for some business paper that had to be filled out.

Qui Qui covered her mouth with her hand. She looked at her friend Mei Lin, as if to say, "Okay, go ahead and speak for me."

"New teeth," Mei Lin said in her always sweet, semi-hoarse voice.

The rest of the group looked as perplexed as I felt, until Mei Lin began to explain that Qui Qui had had new dentures made and they didn't fit her mouth."

"Not good. I tell her, complain," Mei Lin said.

"You told her to complain," I said.

"She pay a lot of money."

"She paid a lot of money?" I said.

Mei Lin then began, what sounded from her tone, like a chastisement, growling and coughing up Chinese words at Qui Qui.

"No, don't, Mei Lin. She feels bad," I said.

"I tell her, show you. Very bad. Very bad doctor," she scoffed.

Her hard pronunciation of the letter c in doctor seemed to stab Qui Qui in the heart. She winced and looked lost, obviously wanting help, but not believing there was anything to be done about her terrible new dentures.

She let her hand fall from her mouth. She smiled and we were all able to see they looked to be ill-fitting horse teeth; quickly she covered her mouth again, putting her head down in defeat.

There was something far more important than medical terminology to teach today. Using the most basic English possible, I asked how she'd found the dentist, the one who had taken the impression to make her new teeth. I asked her also, whether she had any pain from them. She must have. Finally, I asked if she'd already paid the bill.

How could she chew without hurting her delicate rosebud lips? She was a pretty woman, not much older than thirty; suddenly she'd aged—criminally so—the teeth robbing her of her naturally good looks. Looking up the phone number of my dentist in my little black book, I found it and wrote it down on a piece of paper, and handed it to her. Taking it from me, she looked only a bit more hopeful about seeing another dentist. But maybe he'd take a look and at least report or call the charlatan on her behalf, maybe refer her to someone who might help her without charge or for a minimal fee, if he couldn't.

"I'll call him and let him know you will call for an appointment."

I nodded to Margaret, who recognized the sign as a request for a Chinese translation. Margaret then repeated in Mandarin, what I'd said about calling my dentist, to make sure that Qui Qui understood.

Gratefully, Carlene announced that she had "some good news."

"Baby going to China to stay with grandmother."

"Your baby is going to China to see your mother—her grandmother? That's wonderful," I said. "How long will your baby be gone?"

A couple of students gasped and said something in

Mandarin, which might have been interpreted, judging from their expressions, as disapproval, or possibly jealousy.

I repeated what it seemed like the student meant, but using better English, modeling the correct form again for Carlene, hoping she'd hear those helping verbs.

"You are taking your baby to China to stay with her grandmother. How long is your family going to be in China?"

"Only baby stay in China."

Perhaps Carlene had misunderstood the question. A simple declarative rather than a question might be better.

"It will be a nice vacation for your family in China."

"Not vacation. My sister coming, take baby to China. Grandmother taking care of baby."

"Your sister lives in China? She is coming to take the baby to your mother—her grandmother—in China?" I asked, trying to understand.

I was perplexed. Carlene, who must have already talked to Margaret Kwan about the news, looked at Margaret, who again fell into her role of interpreting what stymied me.

"The baby will stay in China with Carlene's mother for a while," she said.

I felt the sharp pain in my lower back once again. Was hearing that—the idea of Carlene giving up her baby, even for a little while and not the way I did—forever—the reason the pain had returned? I tried to ignore it, to go on trying to make a lesson from this conversation.

"I work hard. My husband work. We save money. Buy house. Then bring baby back."

"Your husband works hard," I corrected her.

"I work hard, too," Carlene said defensively, not hearing the emphasis on the letter *s*, the correction of her verb.

I went to the easel then and began to parse the present tense of the verb *work*, and as I lifted my arm to write with the marker, the pain in my back was so bad that it took my breath away.

Margaret saw me wince and said, "Let me." Then she got up from her seat by the window and walked to the front of the room to take over.

The other students, not knowing the agreement I'd made earlier with Margaret, gasped and looked as if they thought their classmate had shown disrespect for their teacher.

Mei Lin clicked her tongue.

Qui Qui, surprised, showed her big teeth.

I went to the back corner of the room, where there was a telephone on a small table. I dialed Martin's number at the office and was relieved to learn that he was there. He would call Dr. Aviva and leave immediately after to pick me up. "Leave in about twenty minutes," he said. "It will take me at least that long to get there." Since it was raining now, he said to wait in the foyer until I saw his car in the alley.

The students were whispering among themselves, and when I finished with the call and turned back to face them, they immediately fell silent. There had been no privacy for the conversation, and they couldn't help but hear, and even if they couldn't translate the content exactly, they most likely had recognized the fear and worry in my voice, as I spoke to Martin. And surely, they'd recognized the word *Doctor*.

They looked deeply concerned, but I couldn't bring myself to say, *Don't worry. Everything's going to be okay.* I did say, "I have to leave in twenty minutes. Margaret will help you with the lesson."

Margaret who had understood every word of what I'd said to Martin, motioned that I should sit down and wait; then, keeping her eye on the clock, she began the lesson as she'd been instructed earlier to do. She had them open their books to the page with today's vocabulary.

"Abdominal. Repeat and spell."

Why couldn't today's words be about the brain or heart?

They all tried saying *abdominal*, struggling with it, but Margaret went on to the next word, after they'd spelled it twice.

"Amniocenteses," she called out.

The students growled.

Margaret broke the word into its root, prefix, and suffix to make it easier for her classmates—a good instinct. It was fortunate that they needed only to familiarize themselves with the words, that their jobs did not require them to know how to pronounce them.

Margaret kept looking at the clock every so often, and when she saw that twenty minutes had passed, she nodded to me, and looked back at the clock, so that I would know it was time to leave.

When I stood, Carlene offered to carry the tote bag of books downstairs, and Margaret, now firmly in charge of the class, nodded again to indicate that Carlene was excused.

We went down to the foyer, taking each step carefully, Carlene in the lead. I kept thinking of what it must be like to send a baby a continent away—of her own volition—as Carlene was planning to do. For all I knew, the baby I'd given up might have been raised or might now live as a teenager, on some other continent. But at least Carlene expected to have her baby back, when she and her husband had saved enough money to buy a house. I hoped it wouldn't take them long.

To whatever beneficent power watched over the universe, I prayed that Carlene's baby would return to her safely, and thinking this, I could not help but feel saddened that the now grown person—grown to be a teenager now, from the baby I never knew—might never return to me.

Now, also truly worried for the new life inside me, over and over in my head I prayed, begging the Divine to let this new life stay with me. *Allow me to be the mother I want to be.* My faith came back in moments when I felt powerless, knowing the worst could happen, going over in my mind how something horrible might come to be, imagining it, right down to the smallest detail. And now, I was running with this new fear that the life inside me might not be viable, try as I might to believe what Dr. Aviva had proclaimed last visit, that the baby was *a keeper*.

I would have to be more detailed in my prayer maybe, the way I would have been as a child, once conscious of just how elaborate creation really was, the fact that keeping track of it all meant that God—then I did believe in God and not some Divine Intelligence without face or name—had so much to do; there were so many streets in the universe, where so many people with needs were living. Specificity was required, I thought. So, I hoped now, that this discomfort was only from the egg salad sandwich bought at the new deli that had recently opened on Mass Ave. in Central Square, the place where I'd eaten a late lunch with Sarah from Diamond Street, the day before.

In spite of the fact that everywhere one looked on a city street, black Toyota Corollas like Martin's could be seen, I knew that the one turning off Washington Street and heading into the alley, moving toward the doorway, where Carlene and I stood waiting, most certainly belonged to him. The fact that Martin was here in the middle of the day during a busy work week—not to pick me up to take me to see his friend Troy's house—but to take me to see Dr. Aviva— made me focus on what I now believed to be inevitable; our baby was in real trouble.

I bent down to take the tote bag from Carlene, who pulled it away.

"No, no. Let me," she said.

Carlene went out of the foyer first, opening the heavy door and stepping aside to hold it for me, as if I were some kind of celebrity, not someone who felt ill. She then opened the car door as well, handing the book bag in to Martin first; then, she remained standing on the sidewalk, waiting until I was settled. When I was, Carlene gestured protectively, tapping my shoulder twice, making me think of a magician tapping a wand on a top hat, to make magic happen. She then carefully shut the car door, but didn't go back into the building right away. She stayed standing by the curb, waiting for the car to leave. She reached for the proper gesture then, giving a little salute, making the okay sign after, followed by a thumbs up.

I surprised myself, smiling, seeing this. Martin was pulling away quickly. The window beside me wasn't open, so I waved and mouthed *Thank You* to Carlene. Then the car was out of the driveway and into the alley that led to Washington Street.

Twelve

Martin

Clare leaned over for a kiss, nicking my hat with her forehead as she did, unsettling it. I lifted my hand to adjust it, then looked away from the road for a second to glance in her direction. She looked at me through the blur of tears that had now begun. I shook my head and my eyes met Clare's. I saw that her eye makeup had been smudged when she'd tried to wipe the tears away. I kept one hand on the wheel, while fumbling with the other, reaching into the pocket of my jacket. I remembered I'd taken a napkin from Valhalla Diner, where I'd bought coffee this morning to take back to the office, and I hadn't used it. Searching, I found it and passed it over to her.

"It's all I've got," I said.

"I hope there are no complications," Clare said.

She shut her eyes. She was thinking, she told me, of that day her mother went into labor with her brother, the baby delivered without complications for the boy, except that the birth ended her mother's life. I couldn't imagine how her father had stayed at work to finish up with clients, as she'd told me he had. He should have rescheduled those appointments, not let his wife get to the hospital on her own in a taxi.

"By the time, he did get to the hospital," Clare said, though she'd told me this before, "my mother was gone."

I took her hand.

She said that she believed, that if her father had been there at the hospital, he might have talked to the doctor who was covering for her mother's obstetrician, who wasn't available—away on vacation or administering to another patient in equally dire straits at the time—she couldn't remember which. Clare insisted that her father might at least have asked some questions or requested some intervention that might have saved her mother.

"That was then—your mother's situation. I'm here for you,

Clare," I said, trying to offer the comfort she needed. "Don't think about complications," I said. "This is a different situation than what you remember of your mother's. Thinking of that serves no purpose in the present."

"I thought I'd been doing pretty well," Clare said.

I looked away from the road, and over at her, saw fear, defeat, and disappointment in her eyes. Any feigned courage was gone. I didn't say it, but despite keeping a positive attitude, I was feeling what she was, that something terrible was happening.

"Didn't you think I was doing pretty well?" she pressed on, wanting, I suppose, to feel that this trouble was not her fault.

"You have. You've been taking excellent care of yourself, eating well, going for long walks to stay fit, and keeping all your appointments."

I truly believed that she'd been inordinately conscientious. There were all those books about prenatal and infant care that she'd been reading like crazy. She'd been trying so hard to make everything go well for her, for our baby.

I drove, negotiating the city's busy afternoon traffic, coming into Government Center, up New Chardon Street, and then I took a right turn onto Cambridge Street, making my way to Longfellow Bridge, heading back over the Charles to Cambridge.

"She took my call right away," I said about the doctor. "I didn't even have to leave a call back number."

"What did she say?"

I didn't answer, just shrugged, and then switched on the car radio. The news had ended and the announcer was giving the weather report. Heavy rain coming this afternoon.

At the health center we checked in and walked down the hall to the lab, where Dr. A. had said to stop first. We went to the desk together and Clare gave her name. She was handed a plastic cup, and pointed in the direction of the restroom.

"You can have a seat," the woman said to me, pointing to a corner of the waiting room where there was an empty seat. To Clare, she said, "Come back and sit here when you finish, and we'll call your name when the clinician is ready to take your blood."

Clare went off as directed, and I sat waiting for her to return. The front section of the *Boston Globe* was on the table next to my chair, and I glanced at a headline, about some states considering laws to re-criminalize abortion if the Supreme Court were to overturn Roe v. Wade. It was amazing how much had changed so quickly in the years after 1968, and it was disturbing to see a movement to set back the clock.

When I heard the click of the interior door closing, I looked up and saw Clare coming back to the waiting room. Her face was pale, paler than it had been, and she looked like she'd seen a phantom. I thought she might faint, so I stood and went quickly to her.

"It's started," she said, trying to bury her head deep in my shoulder.

She didn't need to explain. I understood. When I'd called her doctor, she'd asked if there was spotting. *I don't think so. She didn't mention it*, I said, and the doctor's response had been simply, *Not yet?* She'd been expecting this to happen.

A door opened and the phlebotomist appeared.

"Clare Rantel?" the woman said.

"Yes?" Clare replied.

"You can come in."

She got up and I followed. The young technician didn't object.

"How are you?" she asked Clare cheerily, without really looking at her.

The woman's demeanor quickly changed, when she looked at the form the doctor had sent to the lab with her request. She did look at Clare now, and seeing her tears, pointed me to the ledge in front of the window behind the vacant next booth. I helped myself to a few tissues from the Kleenex box, handing one to Clare, putting the rest in my jacket pocket for later.

When Clare's blood had filled the two tubes the technician then slapped a STAT label on them and fixed a band aid onto Clare's arm, where it had been punctured, and said, "The results will go right to your doctor."

We checked in upstairs and took a seat in the OB/GYN

area. It was still lunchtime, and the flow of patients in and out of the examining rooms had slowed, so there was now a crowd waiting.

"I hope it won't be long to see her," I said to Clare.
Just then Dr. Aviva herself was coming toward us to bring us into the examining room, rather than the usual medical assistant, who was going to weigh Clare and take her vitals.

"Great," Clare whispered as the doctor approached. "Maybe my blood pressure won't be so high this time, since she's taking me right away."

My mind was not really at ease, though; the fact that we didn't have to wait, and that the doctor was the one to come out to the waiting room for us, only assured me of the seriousness of the situation.

"We'll sit in my office first, where we can talk more comfortably," the doctor said.

On the way, we were led through a small staff kitchen, where half-eaten bagels and cream cheese containers littered the counter. In the office, Dr. Aviva's brown leather bomber jacket hung on the unvarnished birch coat tree that looked like she might have gathered the large branch herself on a walk in the woods, hauled it in here. The jacket must go nicely with her red sports car with the OVUM license plate, I imagined. I'd seen the doctor driving away in it one afternoon when I'd come by to pick up a prescription at the pharmacy.

There was a nice lamp on the desk, too, like the one Clare had wanted to order from a favorite catalog, although she'd never purchased anything from that store, only drooled over some of the offerings. The lamp, like everything else in the catalog, was too expensive.

"Sit. Be comfortable," the doctor said.

We obeyed, about the sitting part anyway.

Clare stared past the doctor, not looking into her eyes, even as she explained the purpose of the blood test. She said that when we were finished talking, she would listen for the fetal heartbeat, and then do an ultrasound.

"By then I should have the results of the blood test."

Directly behind and above the doctor's desk was a bulletin board covered in a collage of photos of babies and young children.

Clare trained her eyes on it. I knew—and Clare did, too, from our previous meetings in this office—that these were photographs of babies Dr. A. had helped to bring into the world. Across the lower half of the pictures, there were labels identifying the names and birthdates of the children she'd assisted in delivering.

I remembered that at our first visit after learning that Clare was pregnant, she had asked Dr. Aviva if age was important to a healthy pregnancy. She'd been told she was *still young, only thirty-five. If you're in good health—and I would say you are, since you had no trouble conceiving—and if you take care of yourself—it makes a difference.* And when Clare had neared the end of the first trimester and the doctor had been so very positive, telling Clare about the fetal heartbeat being *so strong*, she'd declared what I could not get out of my mind now, *Looks like a keeper!*

There was a knock on the office door, and Dr. Aviva said, *Excuse me*, and went to answer it.

She came back with a piece of paper, some form, presumably the lab report. She did not look at it, but put it down on her desk. Perhaps it pertained to another patient.

"Come with me," she said, and led us both through another door and into the examining room. She took a dressing gown from a drawer under the sink, and said, "Put this on. I'll be right back."

Then she left the room.

Clare reached back to unbutton her dress, and I helped, pulling the zipper down, so she could worm out of it. She put the gown on and then got up on the table. I sat in the chair across from her. She sighed, and looked tired. I knew she hadn't slept much the night before, even after drinking the peppermint tea I'd made for her. I reached out to her and she gave me her hand. I was still holding it a few minutes later when Dr. Aviva returned, pushing a portable ultrasound machine into the room. She had the paper in her hand, and I figured it was the lab report that she was going to go over with us.

"Lie back, please," she said to Clare.

I let go of her hand and pushed my chair back closer to the wall, to be out of the way.

The doctor took her probe and passed it over Clare's stomach. I heard no swish and energetic heartbeat, as I had the time before. The room was still.

"You know, this may need a battery," she said about the doppler. "Let me see," and she rushed out of the room.

Clare started to cry uncontrollably. I went to her and held her to my chest, kissing the top of her head. Her hair was so soft. The night before I was struck by how fragile she had seemed to me when I went to her, finding her sitting in the kitchen, looking out the window at the moon. She seemed so much more fragile now. Her vulnerability was palpable. I felt fragile, too. I had resigned myself to having just one child, and had been surprised when Clare had come to me and said that she wanted to *try for a baby*. It was disarming, hearing her say it, but I had quickly become invested in *our* baby, aware that it was something we both had finally admitted we wanted, that it would be a different experience than the one with Danielle. Like Dr. Aviva, knowing how healthy Clare was, and since she had no trouble conceiving, I had vividly imagined that the pregnancy would proceed without a glitch.

The doctor returned, a new probe in hand.

"We'll try this one," she said.

When there was still no heartbeat and the screen showed no activity, Clare, who had wiped her tears just before Dr. Aviva had returned, expressed a loud, "Oh," and reached out for me. I reached out and took her hand again.

"I'm sorry," the doctor said. "I've seen the lab report, and you've experienced a complete miscarriage."

I got up and went to Clare. The doctor moved away from the table.

"I'm sorry," she repeated. She put a hand on Clare's shoulder.

Clare pushed deeper into my chest, as if she were trying to climb inside. My heart beat hard and I felt like I couldn't breathe properly.

"I'll leave you. Take as long as you need. I'll meet you back in the office when you're ready," Dr. Aviva said.

It was raining when we came out of the health center. I told Clare to wait inside the doorway, that I'd go get the car in the lot and drive over to pick her up.

"No, don't. I'll go with you," she insisted.

She didn't want me to leave her there alone for even a minute, I could see. But I also saw how shaky she was, and I didn't want her walking the distance to the car.

"I'll hurry. You stay here." There was a bench in the foyer. "Sit," I said.

When I drove up, I got out with the large black umbrella I kept in the trunk, and met her at the door, putting my arm around her shoulders, as we walked to the car. It was a hard, heavy rain, of the kind that precedes a thunderstorm on a day as hot and humid as this one was.

"This umbrella is like those the undertakers held above the mourners' heads at my mother's funeral. It was a rainy day then, too. Where did you get this umbrella?" Clare asked.

It was dark.

"Big storm coming," I said. "Maybe it will cool things down. It's too early in the season for this kind of heat."

After that we were silent all the way home, as I drove down Memorial Drive. Illuminated in the headlights from the oncoming cars, Clare's eyes were teary, glistening, her cheeks wet. I felt tears coming, too. I tuned the radio to the oldies station. Dylan was singing—the DJ playing a string of rain songs. *It's a hard, it's a hard, it's a hard rain's gonna fall.*

Clare said nothing almost all the way home.

I didn't think that I wanted her to go through anything like this again. Even if another pregnancy was healthy, would she always be worried and anxious that it might not be? And I thought that I would be worrying about her all the time.

And then she spoke words that made me feel that she had some regret now.

"If I were young again," she said.

"Younger?" I said. "I'm not sure that would have made a difference."

"Oh, it might have," she said.

When we got to our street I turned and parked outside the house. The headlights exposed a wet skunk running in front of the car. Because the day had turned dark as dusk, the skunk had been fooled. Or was it rabid maybe?

We didn't go into the house right away, waiting to see if the rain would let up. We just sat there in silence, leaning into each other, holding on.

Once inside, Clare went to the bedroom and I followed. I got into bed with her and then the phone on the nightstand was ringing. It was Veronica. When I didn't pick up, she was leaving a message that she'd called my office just to make sure our meeting was still on, but she thought she'd call here, see if I was home yet. *Are we meeting at your house?* She wanted to know.

"I'm sorry, Clare," I said. "I have to let her know."

"NO, no, don't. Don't tell her," she begged.

"I have to tell her we can't meet and ask her to leave a message at the high school for Danielle, that she doesn't have to hurry home."

"Danielle, oh, no."

"Yes, she'll be here tonight," I said.

This meeting was supposed to straighten things out, get us back to the house schedule.

"I'm sorry, Clare. I have to answer."

I picked up the phone reluctantly.

"Hi. I can't really talk. I have to cancel. No way around it, Veronica."

I didn't get into an excuse. I simply asked her to please let Danielle know, to get a message to her that she won't be meeting with us this afternoon. "We'll talk later," I said.

I hung up before she could ask a question or offer an angry insult.

I lay back down beside Clare.

"I'm so sorry," I said.

I held her close. We were both crying now.

"It's all such a mess," she said. "My life."

Thirteen

Danielle

When I came out of gym class, Mr. Burns, the assistant principal, was standing outside the door, like he was waiting for some troublemaker.

"Danielle?" he said, as I was about to pass him.

He seemed unsure, when he called my name. I didn't think he knew me. My heart jumped, even though I wasn't one of those students who would regularly appear in his office for breaking rules or causing disruptions in the classroom or halls. I hadn't done anything out of the ordinary for him to be looking for me. I thought that he might just be practicing getting to know all the students, some new effort to "improve the sense of community" in the school, greeting students by name. *Community* was a topic of discussion at class meetings all the time.

But no, Mr. Burns was delivering a message for me.

"Your mother called," he said.

My heart jumped again. A message being delivered by Mr. Burns sounded serious. I'd always thought students only got messages from the office in an emergency.

"I wrote down what she wanted you to know. You don't have to call her though," he said. "I told her I'd call her, if I didn't find you to pass this on."

"Thanks," I said, wondering what was up. *Good*, that I didn't need to call her.

When he'd gone, I read what was written on the pink message slip—only four words—*Meeting this afternoon cancelled*.

"Yes!" I yelled.

All the students walking in front of me down the hall, turned to see who'd yelled and why.

I crouched down, looking innocent, pretending I was trying to find something in my backpack, so no one would recognize me as the one who'd hollered out.

Not having the family meeting today meant that when school let out, I didn't have to take the bus to my dad's house right away. I'd stop in at Mona Lisa, where several of my friends were sure to be. I knew that Chris Seagate didn't have jazz band rehearsal this afternoon, so he'd probably be there, too. Now, I had something to talk about with him.

Coming out of the school building, I crossed Cambridge Street and walked down to Mona Lisa. Inside, I saw my friend Stephanie and a few other friends sitting in a corner booth. There wasn't room for me. I walked past them, waving as I did, looking for anyone else I might sit with. Chris was in a back booth with his friend, Robert. I conjured up every ounce of boldness in me and headed to his booth.

"Hi Chris," I said, smiling to hide my nervousness.

He looked up from his conversation.

"I need some advice. Can I talk to you?"

He looked at me as if he were surprised that I would want to talk. *Hi* and *Goodbye*, were the only words I'd ever said to him.

"Sure. Sure," he said.

"Hi, Robert," I said.

His friend looked at Chris, not me, and raised his eyebrows and said, "Later?"

"Later," Chris said to him.

He got up and I took his place, across from Chris.

"So, what's this about?" he asked.

Just then, the man at the counter yelled, "Small pepperoni!"

"That's mine," Chris said, and got up to get the pizza he'd ordered.

He brought back two napkins and two paper plates. I figured he'd planned to share the pizza with Robert, who'd now moved over a couple of booths away, to sit with other friends. But no, I guess he hadn't planned to share it with him. He slid one of the paper plates over to me and handed me a napkin.

"Have some," he said.

"Thanks, I'm starving."

"So what's up?" he asked again, swallowing half a slice.

"Oh, nothing, I just wanted to find out about your sax teacher. I think I'm looking for a new one."

"Sax?" he said. "I thought you played cello."

"Well, I did, but I stopped."

I hadn't even considered he might not know. I realized I hadn't been on his radar for a while, not since the last school concert, when I was still playing cello—that was probably the Christmas concert. Since we'd never talked about anything, he wouldn't know unless one of my friends had mentioned it to him, and obviously no one had.

"I started taking lessons with Ray Newell," I told him.

"Ray Newell? *The* Ray Newell? Wow! How'd you get him for a teacher?" he asked.

He was clearly impressed, which made me realize that what I was going to ask him, would make me sound stupid, to even consider giving up lessons with someone he admired so much.

"Well, I was taking lessons with him, but I think I'm not now."

He looked confused. I was confused, too, I realized.

"Why would you even think of doing that? I mean lessons with Newell? How great that must be. Pretty lucky," he said.

I didn't answer right away, thinking of what to say. I was surprised that he'd heard of him, since he just came to Boston from Canada.

"You didn't like playing sax?" he said. "It's not cello—not at all—and it's hard, but you get it, if you want to, if you keep going."

"My Mom teaches with him at the Conservatory. That's how she got him for my coach, when I told her I wanted to give up cello, and play sax," I said.

"I wish I had that kind of luck," he said. "And connections. You could learn a lot from him. Our jazz band teacher got us tickets to hear him play with his new group. They're great."

I sighed. I took a bite of the pizza and the cheese dribbled down my chin. I was glad he'd given me a napkin.

"Maybe I made a mistake," I said.

"Giving up cello?" he asked.

"No, I was going to ask you about your teacher, if he was any good," I said.

"Well, he's not Ray Newell."

Even before hearing what Chris had to say about him, I had been thinking maybe I was making a mistake, telling my mom that I didn't want lessons with him anymore. I just didn't know if I could handle seeing him all the time at my house, where he might be hanging around with her. I knew she wouldn't end things with him, unless it was his idea. He might even move in with us. My sax teacher moving in with us. How weird would that be? She might even have him pick me up at my dad's house sometimes, if she got too busy. I knew she said she was going to give up seeing him, if that was what I wanted, but she'd broken promises before—a lot.

"Maybe I should stick with him as a teacher," I said to Chris.

"Well, yah. If do you want to play sax," he said, shaking his head in disbelief. "You can learn more from him than I will ever learn from Jeff Marinello. A lot more. I mean, starting out with someone that good for a teacher? Wow. I had a shitty teacher before Jeff. Jeff isn't that bad, but Newell has a lot of passion to pass on."

Passion. Right. He did have passion, and not just for saxophone.

"He does. He does," I said.

"I'll give you Jeff's phone number if you want to call him. But damn, I wouldn't switch, if I were you. You're pretty lucky."

He kept saying how lucky I was. I hadn't felt lucky after what had happened, but I had before I found out about Ray Newell and my mom.

"Would you switch to Newell, if you could?" I asked.

I suddenly thought that if I did go back to lessons with him, maybe I could mention Chris' name, maybe he was still looking for new students. And maybe Chris would be ever grateful to me for an introduction.

"You could introduce me, if I did want him for a coach?" he asked, getting the possibility, just as I did.

I shook my head *Yes*.

"No kidding?" he said. "Hey, I'd give up my guy, just like that!"

He snapped his fingers.

I shook my head *Yes*, again. "I'll let you know if I stay with him," I said.

It felt like it was all I could talk about with him right now, so I said, "I should let you get back to being with Robert."

"I can talk to him when we walk home," he said. "Help me finish the pizza."

I smiled and he smiled back. Something new had happened. It felt good to be sitting with him. He didn't even laugh when I dribbled cheese down my chin.

***

Getting home later that afternoon, I walked into the house and my dad was sitting on the couch, staring off into space. It was not like him to sit there, when he wasn't reading some work papers or a book or newspaper. He looked like he was intently watching television, except the TV was off.

"The meeting with your mother is cancelled," he said.

"I know," I said. "That's why I didn't come home right after school, like you said I should. I got the message."

He hadn't offered his usual greeting of *Hello*, didn't ask about how the school day went. He gave no explanation for why the meeting was cancelled. Since he was home, it meant he'd taken the afternoon off from work, so I figured that cancelling the meeting must have been my mom's fault.

I stormed off to my room, noisily, mad that I'd had nothing else planned for the afternoon. I thought of leaving again, but didn't feel like socializing, now that I was home. I flipped the radio switch. Bruce was singing about wanting to change his clothes and his face, *You can't start a fire....without a spark.* I lay on my bed, dreamy about Chris.

My dad suddenly burst into the room.

"Lower the volume, please!" he bellowed, his own volume on high.

It was an order, not a request. This, too, was not like him. I turned the volume off.

"What's going on?" I asked.

I thought he was mad at my mom for cancelling the meeting, and he was taking it out on me.

"Clare is sleeping," was all he said, and then he went out of the room.

I hadn't even realized that she was at home. She must be sick, I figured. She never went to sleep in the afternoon. I thought, too, that maybe her days for teaching classes downtown might have changed, and because she was sick she wasn't going to Diamond St., as she usually did today.

I followed my dad out of the room.

"Is Clare sick?" I asked.

We were standing outside their bedroom door.

He shook his head, *No.* "Whisper, please," he said.

"Well, if she isn't sick, then why is she sleeping?" I asked.

"She's tired and needs to sleep," he said.

I shrugged, knowing how out of the ordinary this was, and went back into my room and turned the volume up a little, but not as high as before.

There was a strange atmosphere in the house this afternoon. Now, I thought maybe it wasn't my mom who'd cancelled the meeting. Maybe my dad had, because of Clare. What was wrong with Clare? I didn't like the quiet in the house. I didn't like the idea of her sleeping during the day, or of my dad being here in the afternoon for no apparent reason, now that the meeting was cancelled. Generally, he would go back to the office. He was always at the office.

Clare didn't have dinner with us. We got takeout food from the Chinese place around the corner, something we generally did only on Friday nights, so that, too, was unusual. If Clare didn't cook, my dad usually did.

He tried making conversation, but his spirit wasn't in it. He did finally ask how school was, and I said, "Fine." He didn't mention my saxophone lessons, even though talking about whether I was continuing with them or giving them up, was supposed to have been discussed at the family meeting.

"Did you go with Clare to see that house?" I asked, trying to get him to talk to me.

"Oh, God," he said, and jumped up from his seat at the table. "I have to make a call."

He got up and went down the hall to his study.

When he returned, he said, "the house viewing was cancelled."

"Did your friend sell it already?" I asked.

"No, no. It was just cancelled. That's all."

"Are you going to see it another day?" I asked.

"I don't know, Danielle. I don't know."

"Okay, okay. I'm only asking, so that I can know if I have to go with you, so I won't plan anything else. I thought we were all going to see it, after you and Clare did."

He didn't answer that. I didn't understand why he was acting like I was bothering him every time I asked a question. It wasn't like him at all, but something was on his mind, distracting him.

"I said, I don't know, Danielle."

"Never mind. You can see it whenever you want," I said. "I don't have to go."

Then I took my plate, scraped off what was left of the rice into the garbage, washed my dish, and set it in the tray to dry.

"I have homework," I said, and I left him sitting there, leaning on his elbows, with his head in his hands, and I went into my room and shut the door.

***

At breakfast the next morning, Clare was up—or sort of. She was lying on the couch. My dad had brought her breakfast into the living room, but she was waving the tray away.

"You should eat something," he said.

"I told you, I'm not hungry," Clare answered.

It seemed as if they had had some argument, and my dad was trying to be nice to make up for it, and Clare wasn't ready to accept his apology. He'd made pancakes, unusual for a weekday breakfast. He didn't say *Good Morning*, as I passed through the room, nor did Clare. I didn't think either one of them had noticed me. They were off in their own world.

I went into the kitchen. When my dad came in, he seemed surprised to see me, so I knew he hadn't noticed me as I walked through the living room.

"We need to talk," he said.

"I thought we were going to talk yesterday."

"I know you might not want to, but you're going to have to go to your mother's house, even though it's supposed to be your weekend to be here, and even though we didn't hash things out with her about your music coach."

I was even more confused now. Were my dad and Clare going to get a divorce, because Clare was sick of him always being at the office? Maybe that was why he stayed home all afternoon yesterday, even though the house viewing and the family meeting had been cancelled. Or was something else going on?

"What is going on?" I demanded. I put my juice glass down hard on the table and some of it spilled. "You need to tell me. First you cancel the BIG meeting and don't tell me why, and then you tell me this—that I have to go to my mom's."

I got up to leave, but my dad sat down now, and quietly asked me to do the same. He looked like he was about to cry.

"Lower your voice," he said.

"What *is* the matter? Tell me, dad. *Please.*"

Then I saw tears streaming down his face. I had never seen my dad cry before and I didn't know what to do. I got up from the table and took a Kleenex from the box on the counter, and handed it to him. I sat back down at the table.

"Clare lost the baby," he said.

"Oh, Dad, no."

I moved my chair closer to his and hugged him.

"Oh, Clare. No. She must be so sad. Can I go talk to her?"

"I don't think she wants to talk right now, Danielle. She's very sad. And I am, too."

"Can I at least hug her?"

"When you're leaving for school," he said. "But call your mother now, and tell her she needs to pick you up after school. She doesn't have to be at the Conservatory today."

"Can you call her for me?" I said.

"No, she doesn't know, yet. She needs to know, but I don't want to talk to her right now." he said. "You make the arrangements. And don't argue with her when you see her. Maybe talk about what happened with your teacher. You're a young adult. Take responsibility," he said, recovering and going into lecture mode.

I went to the phone on the counter and called.

"I have to come home to stay there tonight. Can you pick me up after school?"

She agreed without any hesitation. I figured, not that she'd missed me, but that the day before, my dad must have talked to her about me coming home, after he'd been with Clare to the doctor and called her to cancel our meeting.

I went off to finish getting ready for school. In my room, I collected my books and papers from my desk and put them in my backpack. Then I went into the living room to give Clare a hug goodbye. But she had fallen asleep. My dad was sitting in the armchair right next to the couch, and he warned me away.

"Let her sleep," he whispered.

***

My mom had sounded like she was happy to hear from me, when I'd called to tell her I was coming home. It had been a whole week, since I'd left to stay with my dad and Clare at their apartment. I walked down Broadway, to where she said she'd pick me up after school.

Traffic was crazy. All along Broadway kids just randomly walked out into the street, expecting cars to stop and allow them to cross, ignoring crosswalks and walk lights, stalling a long line of cars. I looked for my mom's Honda Accord, and didn't see it. She'd said she'd meet me in front of the War Memorial. I scanned the line of cars parked at the curb. It was raining, and I wished I'd waited a few minutes inside, to make sure she'd be there. She was always late.

I saw that there wasn't anywhere she could park, so I thought maybe if she had been on time, that she'd driven around the block, hoping I'd be out front by the time she returned.

I was standing alone, away from others, at the curb, right

where I said I'd be, so she could easily see me.

When I saw her car, I put my arm up and waved her down the street, where it would be easier for her to pull over and park. She'd showed up pretty quickly, and I was glad not to be too wet or too stressed out, wondering where she was.

"I'm surprised you didn't have plans with friends this afternoon. It would have been much easier to pick you up later," she said about the traffic. "Your dad didn't say why he was cancelling our meeting when he called yesterday. Something come up at work for him, and he couldn't get away?"

She looked happy, but what she said cancelled out her expression. I got the message that it was a hassle for her to pick me up. I didn't answer. She was also fishing for information. When I didn't say anything, she asked again.

"He said that Clare and he had some things to take care of this weekend. I can't stay with them then either—not just tonight," I said.

I figured that she was thinking that there was some trouble between them. She always seemed to be looking for any problems they had. There *was* something wrong between them, but not that they didn't get along. Clare understood about my dad's work, even though I knew she wished he were home more to share giving me rides. Clare worked a lot herself, back and forth between the medical center and Diamond Street, and she took other work, sometimes tutoring or editing. I didn't mind. It meant that if they were at work, or they were home busy, they didn't bug me about stuff, the way she did.

"Even though he cancelled the meeting, I'd still like to talk with you about what happened with Mr. Newell," she said.

I laughed to myself about her calling him Mr. Newell, like he was only my teacher to her. I sighed loudly, but I was prepared, had figured she'd want to talk. I'd decided not to resist, so she went on.

"I know I owe you a huge apology. I should have told you right away, not let you find out as you did, especially since he's your teacher. I was wrong."

"Was my teacher," I corrected her.

"I hope you'll reconsider that," she said. "If you do want to learn saxophone, he's tops."

I didn't want her to know yet, that after talking with Chris the day before, I *was* reconsidering. She was trying to get me talk about my feelings, but all I could think about now, was how things were with Clare and my dad. I needed to tell her, needed to talk about it with someone. I took a deep breath.

"Dad and Clare lost the baby," I said. "Dad told me this morning. Clare's just lying around. She's sad. Really sad. Dad is, too. And I am, too. It's too much, not to talk about it."

The light ahead had turned red from yellow. She hadn't been paying attention to her driving, listening to what I was saying. Registering suddenly that the light was red, she slammed on the brakes.

"Oh my God! That's awful. Of course you needed to talk about it. It must have been tough, getting through the school day, Danielle. God! And being there last night! You should have called me then."

"I didn't know then," I said. "And I had to be there. I had two tests today, or actually one in English, but I had an oral report due today for History. "

"How could you focus, if you'd just found out this morning?"

"I did okay, I think," I said. "Better than I would have if I'd been distracted from studying last night, if I found out then. I wouldn't have been able to concentrate, thinking about what had happened to Clare. I didn't get called on for the oral report. We didn't get to mine, ran out of time."

We each stared straight ahead. The world blurred. Winged seeds from the leafing maples along the street slid down the windshield on rivulets of rainwater, piling up on the wipers. We didn't talk about the hard rain, or about the crowd of students darting across the street, preventing us from going anywhere. I wished I were with them, as they headed to Harvard Square, where they'd be with friends at Newbury Comics or the pizza shop in The Garage.

"I really want to do something for Clare, to cheer her up," I said.

My dad said he would let her know that he told me what had happened, so I felt it would be the right thing to do, to show her I was thinking about her, that I cared.

"Maybe send some food for dinner?" she suggested.

"No," I said. "She won't eat anything. She's not hungry right now, she says."

"Maybe flowers would brighten her spirits, make her feel better?"

"Maybe," I said, although I didn't think anything could right now.

She drove into Harvard Square, and because it was raining and not that many people were out shopping, she easily found a metered parking spot. We walked together down Mass. Ave., sharing her big umbrella. It was different, walking side by side with her, where I might see friends, or even Chris Seagate. I usually walked behind her when we were together in the Square, trying to act like I didn't know her. Today felt different, though. I needed to be with her, with someone. I guess, I needed to be with someone in my family. What had happened was something I didn't think I could talk about with any of my friends, not now anyway. At least I had her.

At Brattle Florist we entered the store, and seeing the pots of bright flowers on the floor and ledges, the cut roses and gerbera daisies and other flowers in buckets of water, cheered me. It was nice on a dark, rainy day. The store smelled sweet and fresh.

"What should we get?"

"Not roses," I said. "Something not so serious."

"A plant or cut flowers?" she asked.

"Flowers die. Maybe a plant instead," I thought.

That seemed right to her. Since it was spring, but felt like summer, we looked around to see what was in season. Cyclamen seemed too ordinary, although the purple and pink colors of those we looked at were pretty. Clare's loss was big, so we needed to get something special.

"We could buy a hydrangea plant, and then if they buy that house, they can plant it in their yard," she suggested.

She worried that a plant growing in their yard might remind them each year of their loss, especially if the plant flourished, and they didn't ever have a child.

"Who knows, if they will?" she said.

"Are they buying the house?" I asked. I thought maybe my dad had said something about it to her.

"Well, I know they're considering it. Or they were. Because of the baby, your dad said. They had plans."

I was silent then, realizing that the loss might be lasting for them. I let my mom put an arm around my shoulders. She led me to the back of the shop, to look at hibiscus.

"These are pretty," she said. "And if they do still move to a house of their own, they can plant it outside, if they want to. And if not, it can live inside, too."

I agreed, and we picked one with orangey peach-colored blossoms, and brought it to the counter."

"Should I wrap it for you? Or do you want it delivered?" the clerk asked.

"Delivery," I said, before she had a chance to answer. Then, under my breath, I whispered, "They want to be alone. That's why I called you to come get me."

She paid for the plant and gave the clerk the address.

At home, I went to my room to do homework. She went into her music room. I heard her talking on the telephone—someone at work, I figured.

"You just might have a shot at the position. They don't necessarily want a classical musician," I heard her say.

She was silent and I thought she'd ended the call, but then she said, "And you do have classical training. I do think that's a plus. It's a tenure track position."

When she mentioned the classical training I wondered if it was Ray Newell.

And when I heard what she said next, asking the caller—"Move on or move back?"—I was pretty sure that he was on the phone with her. It sounded like he'd told her he wanted to move back to Canada.

Fourteen

Ray

Veronica called again the next day. She was working hard to try to convince me to apply for the permanent position opening up at the Conservatory.

"I'm sure they must be committed to hiring a classical musician," I said again.

"Not necessarily," she repeated.

I knew that she was hoping I'd stay around and we might find a way to work things out, that Danielle might come around to forgiving her and accept me in her mother's life.

"You do have classical training," she said. "I do think that's a plus."

She was quiet, waiting for my response.

"It's just that I don't know about taking a tenure track position anywhere. I might decide to move on, so I'm not sure I'd want to make that commitment, but maybe...."

"Move on? To Berklee? Or move back?" she asked.

I hesitated, then I said, "I really don't know, Veronica."

I didn't tell her about the call that my dad had been brought to the hospital, that he'd had another stroke.

She changed the subject then, asking me if I'd gone back to see the house her friend had for sale, as I'd said I was going to. I was feeling a little guilty now, even thinking about it, knowing from Veronica that Martin had told her that he and Clare were considering it.

"No, no, I didn't," I said.

She pressed me on it, and I knew that this house viewing was a part of her strategy to get me to remain in Boston.

"Didn't Troy ever call you to set up another appointment?" she asked.

"He did. But I haven't had time," I said.

She told me that Martin had been going to take Clare to see the place the day before, but had cancelled the viewing.

"Not interested anymore?" I asked.

"No, not that. They've had some trouble. Have. Have some trouble," she said.

"What kind of trouble?" I asked.

Had they been having trouble in their marriage, I wondered? He seemed to be a good guy. But he was buried in his work. That was obvious.

Veronica seemed to consider if she should tell me more. But she couldn't help herself.

"Well," she said, "you knew that Clare was pregnant?"

"I did notice," I said, not knowing what that would have to do with anything. It seemed to me it was more a reason to buy a house of your own, if you were going to have a baby.

"She lost the baby," Veronica said, flatly.

She might have been talking about someone losing car keys, something that insignificant, her voice showing absolutely no emotion.

I gasped though, hearing this, the last thing I expected her to say.

"It was a surprise to everyone," she said, again matter-of-factly.

"Terrible. Just awful. She must be devastated," I said.

"They are," Veronica said. "Danielle told me both of them are."

"I'll talk to you soon," I said, having nothing more to say.

"Think about applying for that position, now that it's been posted. It would be great to have you around," she admitted.

"I have a lot to consider," I said, and ended the call before she mentioned getting together.

I hung up the phone and stayed leaden in the armchair, where I'd dropped down, after getting this news from Veronica. That, combined with the pressure I felt from Veronica to stay in the area was plenty to immobilize me. I didn't think I wanted a long-term position at the Conservatory. Also, now knowing that Clare and her husband were interested in the house that Veronica had suggested I look at, I certainly didn't want to get in the way of Clare's dream of a house of her own, by pre-empting any offer that she and her husband had made—or intended to make, especially now. Veronica wanted me to stay in Boston for her own reasons, I knew. I wasn't sure yet about keeping on with her or remaining in Boston.

After I'd decided to leave teaching at the Royal Academy in Toronto, and head to Montreal to focus more on making— rather than teaching— music, I was enjoying not being so tied down. That accounted for my reluctance when the call came from Massachusetts General. I wasn't sure of coming back to Boston for my dad—not because he'd given me the ultimatum that he'd disown me, if I refused military service and headed North— I didn't think he'd have carried that slip of paper with my address in his wallet, if he didn't want some sort of reconciliation with me. What made me hesitate was that I knew that once I came back and got involved with his care, there was no telling how long I'd need to stay to settle things.

It was worse than I'd expected, I'd immediately realized that there would be no reconciliation, given his dementia, and it was complicated trying to move him to long-term care. And now, after receiving the call this morning that he had had another stroke and had to be hospitalized, what the doctor had called "a seriously debilitating stroke," it seemed not to matter that I had not yet secured a place for him at a Veteran's home. It seemed he was not long for this world. But he'd rallied before, I knew. I'd seen how feisty he was, dementia and all, and talking with him, I thought he might go on living for another ten years. Yet, at his age and with his general condition, this new stroke was most likely, an insurmountable crisis. Right now, I didn't want to think beyond the temporary position I'd taken at the Conservatory; anything involving a longer commitment than that made me nervous.

I thought now about Clare losing her baby. Ten years was a long time to be childless in a marriage, if you wanted children. Veronica had offered nothing more, and I didn't want to keep on asking questions about Clare and making Veronica wonder why I was so interested.

I thought it would be even more devastating for Clare, if

this were not her first baby lost. But maybe she hadn't been pregnant in the past. For all I knew, the baby may have been an accident. Or maybe in all that time, Martin hadn't wanted another child, that having Danielle was enough for him. Perhaps Clare had been the one to want a child, and had only this year been able to convince Martin to start over. Who knew what went on in people's lives? I knew zero about Clare and Martin's relationship in the past, but I had to admit, that I wondered now, what would happen between them after such a loss.

I'd been surprised at how quickly I'd begun to have fantasies of what might have been between Clare and me, even after learning that she was married and going to have a baby. One would think that learning that would have put an end to it. I was sad for her now, but that only made my feelings for her stronger. I wanted to see her, to offer some comfort, crazy as that was. But I knew the impossibility of that.

I had a class to teach and needed to get on with the day. I forced myself up and out of the chair. I retrieved my horn from the study, and gathered up my music and some student papers and put them in my instrument case. I grabbed a light jacket to take with me, in case the temperature dropped this evening, and I went out the door. I drove, stopping at the corner grocery, a misnomer really, since the place wasn't what you'd think of as a grocery store, selling lion meat, quail eggs, alligator sirloin, iguana, and ostrich. This wasn't your local bodega. I was stopping in to pick up a lunch of Asian noodles to take with me, just about the only thing sold in this gourmet food store— Cambridge had many—that wouldn't break my budget.

I was trying to hurry, negotiating my way around older men and women taking their time, a shopping trip presumably the day's major event, blocking the aisles as they stopped to read labels on products or stretched to reach a higher shelf for something they wanted, or called a clerk to do it for them. I was stopped in the aisle displaying gift baskets. I got the idea to send one to Clare and Martin. A fruit basket was a good idea, I thought. I asked the clerk behind the counter if she could make up a basket of Anjou pears and Fuji apples, and to add some *Chocolate Therapy* bars. She handed me a small card and asked me to write a greeting on it, and also to fill out a form giving the address for delivery and the specific order. I addressed the card to both Clare and Martin. The loss belonged to both of them. I pulled out my lesson book from my sax case and turned to the list of private students, finding Danielle's address at her dad's house.

I got into my car and headed to Storrow Drive, making my way to the Conservatory. Thoughts of Veronica telling me about Clare pestered me, and I began to worry about the fact that I'd just admitted that I knew of their loss, by sending the fruit basket. It hadn't been Veronica's place really, to let me know about Clare, or mine, to acknowledge that. It was for Clare and Martin to reveal, if they wanted to, and I didn't think that either of them would. I wondered why Veronica had told me. Was she trying to elicit sympathy for herself, that she was having to find her way dealing with Martin and Clare, and her daughter? She would have to comfort Danielle, who surely must have feelings for Clare's situation. And I was sure that Veronica must have realized, too, that she would be needed to carry more of the family load for a time, until things got back to a normal routine. I shouldn't have sent the fruit basket.

I was passing the chemical storage tanks at the edge of the Mass Pike, one of the most heavily trafficked highways out of or into Boston and Cambridge. The tanks were painted in pastel colors: pink, mint green, lavender, and lemon yellow. It was obvious that Veronica resented the fact of Martin's marriage to Clare, longed for what she thought they had. I thought about how there are often risks just underneath the surface of a situation that seems perfectly ordinary—picture perfect, even—the way Veronica seemed to view Clare and Martin's marriage, the way the chemical holding tanks would seem to anyone, who didn't consider what might be inside. But one little chink in one of those tanks could lead to irreversible harm for unsuspecting drivers on their way to work, or heading out for a day of sightseeing, or to celebrate a milestone, ending life as they'd known it. I didn't really know if the loss of the baby or anything else threatened serious change in Clare and Martin's marriage, but very few relationships were perfect, even if they seemed so, viewed by others.

I took the next exit to get to the Conservatory, and

trying to put all of this out of my mind, I attempted to focus on the improvisation class I had to teach in exactly twenty minutes. Improvisation was better than giving a music history lecture this morning. It seemed right, with all that was going on in my life right now.

Fifteen

Martin

It seemed so quiet in the house without Danielle. I had become accustomed to the background music coming from her room, her regular trips to the fridge for something to eat or drink, and having to answer the phone when her friends called. With Clare sleeping, it was certainly quiet enough for me to complete a substantial amount of the work I'd taken home from the office. But I was distracted, hoping that Veronica and Danielle had been able to talk. Veronica would be expecting me to call this evening, to see how things were going. I didn't want to have to worry about Danielle and her mother arguing, so I decided that making a call was better than imagining the worst between the two of them.

I dialed Veronica's number and just as I said "Hello," the doorbell rang.

"Hold on a minute, will you?" I said when Veronica answered. "I have to see who's at the door. Clare can't get to it."

But Clare surprised me, coming out of the bedroom and heading for the door, just as I was.

"Who could that be?" she asked.

She looked dazed as if she were not yet quite awake after napping.

"I'll get it. It's okay. Go back and lie down," I said, kissing her hair.

She moved away, but didn't go back into the bedroom. She stood waiting to see who it was that rang the doorbell.

A delivery man was standing there when I opened the door, holding a large hibiscus in full bloom, the plant decorated with a shiny red ribbon.

"This is for Clare Rantel," he said.

I said, "Yes, she lives here," and he handed me the plant.

When I turned around, I saw that Clare was open-mouthed.

She came to me and kissed me, thinking, I guess, that I was the one who'd sent the flowering plant.

She took the card that was tucked under the bottom leaves and read out Veronica's name and Danielle's. "So sorry, Clare," was the only inscription.

"What? You told her? Why did you tell her, Martin?"

The deep emotional pain she felt was clear. Clare stood before me, folded her arms over her belly, and rocked her body, her eyes closed.

"I didn't. I didn't tell her," I said.

I went to her and held her. She pulled away and looked at me.

"Well, how would she know then, if you didn't tell her?" she asked.

"Danielle," I said. "Remember? I told Danielle. I felt I had to, to explain why she had to go to her mother's. And she was worried about you. She could see you were hurting, that something was terribly wrong. I wanted her to understand that we needed time alone. I was afraid she wouldn't go unless I did. We hadn't had that meeting we were supposed to have, and she was still angry at her mother. Oh, Clare, I'm sure Danielle is very sad for you, and she needed to talk to her mother. Veronica was going to know eventually anyway."

I wanted to change the subject. Clare looked stunned, but I didn't think it was only because of the delivery of the flowers; it seemed this was her general state of mind right now. It was the first time she'd been out of bed all day.

"Why don't you sit down, Clare?" I said. She did and she put her head down between her knees, and I realized that maybe she was feeling faint.

"Let me get some water," I said, going to her and getting her to lie on the couch. "And maybe you should eat something."

I went for a glass of water.

She took a sip as I held it for her. I went on talking.

"Are you mad at me? I'm sorry, Clare. I'm hurting, too, you know. I love you," I said.

She didn't respond. She pushed away the glass of water,

having had only a couple of sips.

I suddenly remembered that I'd called Veronica and she was probably waiting for me to go back to the call. I went to the phone and hung up the receiver, so she'd know I wasn't going to talk to her. Now was not the time. I thought she'd probably call back, so I disconnected the phone, wanting a busy signal to play, if she did. I would call her when Clare wasn't around. I brought the plant out to the kitchen and left it on the counter and then went back to Clare. She had left the living room and gone back to bed.

She turned away from me, when she saw me coming into the room, feeling betrayed, I guess, about letting Veronica know we'd lost the baby.

"It was thoughtful, Clare. Veronica meant well," I said, about the plant.

Now she sat up and looked at me.

"What goes on between us is none of her business," she said. "This is a private. This is our grief. Between us. Does she have to involve herself in *everything* that goes on between us?"

"Yes, she does get into too much of our life together, I know, Clare. But this time, I do think she was only trying to...."

She cut me off.

"I don't want to hear you defending her. Not anymore. I'm tired of it! And what will we do with that thing?" she said, gesturing dismissively, as if the plant were right there in the bedroom and not out on the kitchen counter. "That's an outdoor plant! We have no yard. Remember? We rent here, and now that there will be no baby, now that we'll have no family, there'll be no need for a house of our own. You heard Dr. Aviva mentioning *other possibilities*. You know she meant IVF or any of those interventions other couples resort to, and I'm not interested."

There was such finality in her pronouncement. I sat down on the bed beside her, hoping to calm her down. I tried to take her into my arms, to comfort her. I needed comfort, too. But she pulled away, covering her head with the blankets. Her shutting down like this felt awful. I needed her. I felt this loss just as deeply as she did.

"Clare, we can still look at the house, whether or not we have a child of our own."

I waited in silence for a while, hoping we could talk this out, but when I figured she'd fallen asleep, I left the room, shutting off the light as I went out.

I wasn't ready to go to bed. I knew I wouldn't be able to sleep right now anyway. I went into the kitchen, found the bottle of scotch, and poured myself a drink. Then I settled in, on the living room couch, thinking of the mess I'd made while trying to balance two households, wondering how I'd deal with Veronica's continuing interference.

***

At dawn the alarm clock went off and I scrambled to silence it, before it woke Clare. I climbed out of bed, drew open the window drapes: a gloomy day. I'd hoped for sun, but got fog. The yellow day lilies along the walkway leading to the church across the street looked a little too enthusiastic about heralding the new day—shockingly bright—gauche, really.

I pulled the drapes closed again to let Clare sleep. I wished that I could stay home with her, not leave our bed, but the backlog of cases was already overwhelming, and I had a deposition scheduled, too. And besides, yesterday Clare had said not to worry about leaving for the day, that she'd like to be alone.

I'd gone to sleep early the evening before, so I was up for the day now, wide awake at five a.m., more than an hour before the time I usually got out of bed.

I took a long, hot shower, then stupidly and frantically searched the closet for the suit I'd planned to wear today but couldn't find. The appointment to see the house hadn't been the only thing I'd forgotten. With the events of the previous day, I hadn't remembered to pick it up at the dry cleaners.

Normally I'd have just coffee and eat only an apple and a muffin, or a bowl of cereal with milk and berries for breakfast, but this morning I raided the refrigerator, gathering ingredients for an omelet, wanting to stave off hunger. Getting home from the doctor's office yesterday, I'd crawled into bed with Clare. I'd held her while she'd sobbed, until we both fell asleep. When I got up an hour or two later to make something for dinner, Clare said she just wanted to sleep when I'd tried to rouse her. I hadn't felt much like eating either, and ate only a little. And after the plant episode, I had no appetite at all. I couldn't sleep for a while after going to bed either. Veronica's plant delivery had left me wound up, confused, not knowing how to comfort Clare, how to make her understand that I felt this as my loss, too.

I enjoyed cooking as much as the eating. Ironically, I'd hated the job that had first required me to cook. It was the Summer of Love and I wasn't feeling it. I'd just finished high school in Rhode Island. It was a few months after my brother Larry's flag-draped coffin had been lowered into the ground. It was my first summer living away from home. There was a busy diner near Horseneck Beach, over the Massachusetts border, and I took a job there as a short order cook. The owners of the diner also had a hotel on the property, and they rented rooms to anyone on staff who wanted a place to stay, giving us a discount on the rooms in an annex. I was glad actually, not to have to be in an apartment with friends who partied and stayed up late, talking, and playing music. I didn't feel much like partying that summer after we lost Larry.

The diner's menu was a play on the name of the beach, all the omelets named for famous racehorses. Sometimes the kitchen staff used to bet on which of the omelets would be most popular on any given day. I had luck at predicting the winner and often took home the small amount of cash the kitchen help and waitresses contributed to the pool.

To distract myself now from worry, I counted off what I could remember of the names of the special omelets: Seabiscuit, Man O' War, Sir Barton, Citation, Dr. Fager.

The onions were browning much too quickly. I turned down the heat to low, so they'd barely simmer, while I got the other ingredients ready. I sliced up a handful of baby belle mushrooms. I felt like I was in slow motion today, but strangely, not in a fog; my senses were heightened to sharp awareness, the way they'd be after making love. Ah, that odd dichotomy, the recognition of the fleeting quality of pleasure—of life—a somewhat anxious feeling surfacing at the loss of intimacy, mixed with an alertness that seemed to sharpen the vision.

I slid the sliced mushrooms off the cutting board with a knife, and into the melted butter. I chopped parsley and garlic finely, also scraping that mix into the sauté pan. I grated some sharp cheddar and Parmigiano-Reggiano, poured beaten eggs over everything, and waited for the eggs to puff up. When they did, I spread the cheese on top. I even considered making hash browns. Instead, I toasted hunks of yesterday's baguette under the broiler, just long enough to let the butter melt.

When I was ready to leave the house, I looked in on Clare. She was still sound asleep. She needed rest but I also wished she'd open her eyes long enough for a goodbye, so I could tell her I loved her, and that I'd call her this afternoon. She looked to be so soundly asleep that it seemed she wouldn't wake for hours. Looking at her I deeply felt the pull of our shared loss and had a strong urge to curl up beside her. I would carry my loss with me—it *was* mine, too—would hold it inside, as I went about the workday. I leaned over the bed and kissed Clare's forehead. She did not stir.

***

Today I had to depose Eric's psychiatrist. The judge had asked for an independent evaluation, ordering him to the State Hospital for observation. Knowing that he was being evaluated, I wanted to have a strong sense from Eric's doctor of his history, and I hoped that I was up to the task. This was an especially difficult case, and I hoped I'd have the emotional wherewithal to do right by Eric.

I wished now that there was someone else to take a few other cases off my list. I'd actually volunteered to help out Crandall, another lawyer in the office; only two days before, when he'd asked if anyone could take on any extra cases, to lighten his load, since he had some family issues. He was going to have to use some of his personal time. That day, I'd thought my family life was perfect, so I'd stepped up to help a colleague.

I drove down Memorial Drive along the Charles, going over in my head the list of calls I had to make to gather information that would help in preparing Eric's defense. I'd ask the secretary to hold any messages or requests, telling her only that I had some family responsibilities and that I'd be leaving the office early again today. I didn't want Clare to be alone for too many hours. I'd take home another stack of files with me, to work.

Arriving downtown, I searched the lower levels of the parking garage for an empty space, ending up on the eighth tier—the open level. What was going on that the garage was so full so early? I collected my brief case and fished for the umbrella that had rolled off and under the seat. Since I'd parked at the top, I walked to the edge of the floor to look out at the city. The financial district with its skyscrapers on the horizon had gone missing in the fog, giving the sense that the harbor was closer than it actually was.

Too impatient to wait, I didn't take the elevator. In the stairwell there was the sharp stench of urine, so I descended all eight flights as if being chased by a ghost. I did feel like a ghost was tailing me this morning. Outside I longed for the soothing warmth of early summer sun, but minus that, I was grateful that it was only misting and not a hard rain like the day before.

Today, as on most days, I walked by the Vets shelter on my way to the office, passing homeless men congregating on the sidewalk or in the alley next door, sent out for the day in the early morning, because the shelter was primarily a place to sleep. These men on the street were my age—the Vietnam generation—although many of them looked much older. The guys I saw braved the elements, no matter the weather, just as they had in battle. Still practicing esprit de corps, they never asked for spare change, a cigarette, or even a cup of coffee. They kept to themselves, talking quietly with one another. The War still took its toll, never mind that it seemed now so long ago. When I saw them, I couldn't help but think of my brother Larry, wondering if he'd have been like them—so damaged—had he lived through the War. Who was to say either, that Larry wouldn't have been as messed up as my client Eric? Who could really say what would become of anyone so young, sent off to war like that?

But I knew the aftermath of Vietnam—or any war—was so much larger than these hurt men, or my brother. There were so many other casualties on both sides. There were families like mine, who struggled to deal with their loss, and I also counted among the wounded, the families of those soldiers who came back maimed in one way or another, as these men had. There were the mothers, fathers, siblings, friends and lovers, who so desperately wanted to help these men and others like them, to be whole and healthy again, and how they suffered frustration and sadness, when that was not possible. I remembered now, that Danielle had said that Ray Newell volunteered at this Vets' shelter, presenting evening jazz programs with his quartet. That earned him points in my regard, never mind the disruption the guy had caused in my family life, getting it on with Veronica. I figured he must be a good guy if he'd do that, especially since the reason he'd been living in Canada was to avoid being drafted for Vietnam. Obviously, he had empathy for the guys who'd answered the call or enlisted. I wondered if I might even have counseled this Ray Newell fellow, at the Friends Meeting House or the Unitarian Church. Kids came from all over Massachusetts to Cambridge and Boston for help. After Larry was killed, I'd volunteered to help guys like him, who were resistors and conscientious objectors. Even if I hadn't met him face to face back then, I might have answered a phone call, given him advice.

It was a sad day all around, made sadder, thinking these thoughts. But I was helpless to push them away, while realizing the casualty of the hour, the loss of our baby. I'd been reluctant at first, when Clare approached me with her decision after ten years of marriage, that she wanted a baby, *to try for one*, she said. My initial reluctance was no match for her will, and when she got pregnant, I was all in. But we had lost our child.

Walking toward the office, I gazed over at the Valhalla. I wanted a cup of coffee. I thought, too, that I ought to stop to get a sandwich to take with me, but I knew I didn't have time for an involved conversation with Troy, and I couldn't take the chance that he'd be holding down the back booth at the diner. Instead, I settled on deciding that when I got in, I'd ask Dorothy to pick up a sandwich for me, when she went out for her lunch. Once in the office with the door closed, I wouldn't venture out today, if possible.

I hadn't called Troy until last night, to apologize for not keeping the noon appointment with him to view the house with Clare. Not going into detail, the message I'd left for him only mentioned that I'd been sitting in Doctor Aviva's office with Clare at the time I'd promised to go to the appointment. I hoped he wouldn't think that we weren't interested anymore, but it would be impossible to consider rescheduling at this point. I hoped Ray Newell wasn't serious about buying, but I was beginning to wonder if it would be good if he did stay in Boston. It might change things, reduce how much Veronica relied on me, or interfered in my own family life with Clare and Danielle—that is, if he continued to see Veronica, and if Danielle could accept that. I didn't know how, when—or even if—Clare would consider moving. But the prospect of leaving Ridge Road, of finally becoming homeowners, might eventually lift her spirits—and mine---even though, when we had first begun to consider it, it was with the intention of providing a better environment for the child we'd thought we were going to have. Still, if we didn't see the house, the chance to own a home might now slip away; we'd been told that the real estate market in Cambridge was heating up and Troy could have other potential buyers looking at the place. Although I didn't want to take the time to talk to him now, when he was in his usual booth at Valhalla, I'd try to remember to call him tonight, let him know what had happened. It would be easier to cut short a phone call than to get away quickly, if I engaged him over coffee at the diner.

Having decided to skip Valhalla, I went looking for a cup of good, strong coffee. Crossing Cambridge St. at Court, I walked toward the café with the steaming kettle, an oversized fairy tale-like brass teapot, protruding from the building near the roof and actually letting out a continuous puff of steam. It had gone dead for a while when the owners put the place up for sale, and I'd missed it, had counted on seeing it, finding it somehow reassuring, just as the Citgo sign had been to me, when I was a student living at Kenmore Square.

My apartment used to face the Citgo sign, a flashing and ever-changing tri-color neon light show. Veronica and I were new lovers, when I lived there. We argued about the sign's artistic merits. She hated it, calling it a blight on the landscape, complaining that it kept her awake, whenever she spent the night. Even the closed venetian blinds didn't keep the room from lighting up. I enjoyed the sign for its sense of movement, the way it seemed to embody the city, calling up new energy over and over.

I had a head full of confusing thoughts this morning. I was Clare's husband, Danielle's dad, and Veronica's ex—like the Trinity, the nuns and priests would have explained God was, magically being three persons in one: Father, Son, and Holy Spirit. It was an odd connection to make, but sometimes I felt like I was expected to be super-human, dealing with all that this triple role implied, pleasing the three main women in my life, no matter that their purposes and needs were often at odds with one another.

As I got closer to the waterfront the breeze off the harbor this morning held a chill.

***

After the deposition, I worked steadily for several hours, going down the list, making one after another of the phone calls I had to make while heartsick. At four o'clock I got up and went to the bank of oak cabinets against the wall, and drew out some files for other cases on the docket this month. I packed them in my briefcase, took my trench coat and hat off the rack and headed out, putting them on as I was passing through the outer office, calling to Dorothy as I did, "See you in the morning." I was grateful that she didn't stop me to ask any questions and did not hand me a bunch of message slips either.

Arriving home, I was surprised to find Clare at work in the study. When I poked my head into the room I saw that she had the roster of her students at the Medical Center open on her desk. She looked like she'd been about to make a phone call and I'd interrupted.

"Good to see you up. How are you?"

She gave me a look as if to say, *how do you think I am, buddy?*

"Trying unsuccessfully to take my mind off things," was what she said.

"Have you eaten anything?"

I lifted my right arm, robot-like, so that Clare would see that I was holding a foil bag, the kind designed to keep food warm. She recognized the bag; I'd bought a chicken from the Armenian place around the corner, a take-out restaurant, which we affectionately referred to as "The Chicken Lady," because the owner, an older woman, had for decades sold only one entrée—rotisserie-cooked whole chickens, that came with sides of rice pilaf, salad, pita bread, and her special garlic sauce. It was her life, she said, when Clare once remarked that she kept very long days at the restaurant.

"If she ever closes up shop for retirement we might waste away to nothing," I said, trying too hard to cheer Clare up.

It was true though, that at least once a week, sometimes twice, if it were a particularly busy or stressful week, one or the other of us stopped there to buy a cooked chicken for dinner and to have lunch leftovers, too tired or just not interested enough to prepare something in our own kitchen.

"I'll leave it on the stove—or should I put it in the oven at a low temp, so it'll stay warm?" I asked.

She got up and followed me, as I headed to the kitchen, and I thought maybe that meant that I could get her to eat something.

"Don't do either on my account. I haven't been hungry," Clare said.

"Well, you might be later."

She didn't answer. I figured that she wouldn't be eating anything anytime soon. I knew that being upset caused people to relate to food differently. I sought comfort in it, eating more than I generally did. Clare was just the opposite; being upset—especially if depressed—led her to fast. Nevertheless, I turned on the oven, setting the temperature at 200 degrees, just to keep the chicken warm.

She stood looking as I did this, resting her arms over her little belly, encircling it, as if the baby were still growing within. Then, as if suddenly realizing that now-hollow space, she jerked her hands away, pulling her arms back to her sides. This was supposed to be a good time in life, and in our marriage. The baby was supposed to give Clare the family she'd finally decided she wanted.

"We'll get through this," I said.

Truth was, that I was worried that maybe we wouldn't. I knew that, for all the positive energy Clare expended working with students and others, trying to help them succeed, always trying to figure out new ways of reaching her still idealistic goals—goals we shared—when it came right down to it, in a crisis of her own, she could be completely thrown off course emotionally. I'd seen that early on, when she'd had to deal with Danielle's unwillingness to recognize her as her stepmom. I didn't know why Clare hadn't expected that, had been so invested in Danielle accepting her right away, when I thought she'd have realized it was a process, and it would take time for them to bond. I wondered then, if something more had happened to her in the past that had made it so difficult for her. If so, she'd never let on.

"Things will work out, Clare. You'll see," I said.

"It's confusing, so damned confusing," she said. "Here we are just living our lives, kind of going along with some good things finally happening, when they hadn't been for a long time. And then, all of a sudden, out of the blue, look what happens."

She gestured then, throwing out her arms, as if to indicate that everything important to us was in a heap on the kitchen floor.

Her words—that good things had just been starting to happen finally—stopped me.

"Really? Is that the way you've felt—that good things hadn't been happening?" I said. "I didn't think that."

I told her that I'd considered our life together was good—yes, especially good recently, when we'd thought the baby was coming—but I wondered why she'd said that, why didn't she think our life together had been good, while I did. Then, I began to list all the things I thought were good in our marriage.

"My job is all right and I don't think I complain too much about the frustration I sometimes feel with a client, or a judge, or the system. The two of us get along, don't argue much. We certainly aren't a bickering couple. You have work you love, even if it is freelance and doesn't bring in much money—and I don't bug you about that. Danielle does well in school and doesn't generally act out any more than what would be considered typical for a kid her age."

I took a breath, realizing this sounded like a summation, something I had a good deal of practice with, being accustomed to the courtroom.

"And," I added, "we've both gradually been getting better at dealing with Veronica, who hadn't been insinuating herself into our lives as much as she used to—not until now, anyway. What exactly did you think had been wrong in our life together before all that's happened now? I want to know, Clare. I want to fix it, to make things better for us."

How was it that I didn't realize how much influence Veronica had had on our marriage, how demanding—not just financially, but how much Clare sacrificed so that Veronica's life with Danielle would be, on the surface anyway, better? This was not the way I wanted to end my day. It had been hard enough already. There was a weakness in our marriage, I thought now. I hoped we could fix things.

"I know you've put up with so much for me and Danielle. I promise things will be better going forward. It may seem an impossibility now, but we have to try," I said. "I want to make things better for us."

As Clare moved to leave the kitchen, I took her in my arms. "I want to help," I said. "I need you."

She didn't pull away, but I knew she didn't want to talk further. This was all too much on the heels of losing the baby. I wished this conversation had never happened, never accelerated, as it did. I let her go and went to hang up my coat.

Going out of the bedroom, I glanced again into the study as I went by, hoping Clare had gone back to try to work, but she had left the room. I could see through the doorway, down the hall, that she'd settled herself on the couch in the living room, and I heard the television. She was watching *The News at Six* on one of the Boston stations.

From the other end of the corridor I heard her gasp.

"That was you, Martin. Wasn't that you on the news report?" she called out.

When I went to look, I found her stretched out, taking up a good two-thirds of the couch. I squeezed in next to her feet.

I'd been in court briefly for an arraignment the morning before, and the news was catching up or repeating the news I hadn't watched.

"It's better when they don't allow cameras in the courtroom," I said. "When they do, I always feel like I want to be like one of those defendants who pulls his jacket or hoodie up over his head to hide."

Because Clare was so distracted by her thoughts, she paid only fleeting attention to the news. She sat up and took this week's

New Yorker from the coffee table. She was paging through the magazine, stopping to read the cartoons as she encountered them, maybe trying to feel something—anything. Her face showed no expression though, just as she hadn't seemed to register what had really been happening on the news. Her gasp had only been an indication of surprise at recognizing me. She had put up a wall not to feel anything, it seemed.

I missed Clare's usual responsiveness, never mind that it was often a bone of contention between us, that whenever she read something in a book or magazine, something she found interesting, enlightening, humorous, or beautifully written, she could not keep herself from sharing her pleasure—or in the case of reading or watching something on television that disturbed her—her outrage. She was like this even when I was in the same room, obviously engaged in case work brought home, or if I had my head buried in my own book. Generally, she didn't think twice about interrupting to share what engaged her. Tonight, nothing held her interest for long.

I wanted to change the channel, put on some national and international program on PBS, MacNeil/Lehrer maybe, something without the sensationalism and cataloguing of local tragedies on regular network news. Television for Clare was a way of tuning out though, usually when she was just too tired to think anymore that day. She also seemed to have the television on sometimes, just to feel like she had company, when I was in the study working on case files in the evening, or still at the office.

After a while, Clare put the magazine down and stretched out again on the couch. She lifted her legs and rested them over my lap, allowing me to claim more space. I switched the television channel, looking for a station that had moved on to sports. Not finding one, I decided to get up to get a drink. I turned back to ask, "Can I get you one? Or how about that chicken dinner now?"

When Clare didn't answer, I realized that she had fallen asleep. Getting up carefully, I gently moved her feet, resting them on a pillow.

In the kitchen, before making a martini, I shut the oven off, took the chicken out to cool. I wasn't hungry either.

Sixteen

Clare

I didn't know if it was dawn or dusk when I opened my eyes. I felt for Martin in the bed beside me, and realized the empty space. Had he left for work already and kissed me goodbye, and had I not known it? He never left the house without a goodbye kiss, a promise he'd made when I told him of the day my grandfather had died, how he'd run out of the house, when he felt a heart attack coming on, and then collapsed in the street out front without even a goodbye, never mind a kiss for my grandmother, his wife of fifty-one years.

"Martin!" I called, hoping he was still at home.

I reached for my watch on the night table. Of course, he wouldn't be here; it was nearly noon. I'd slept around the clock.

And then there was the remembered knowledge, as I focused—that I was truly alone—I'd lost the baby. How many days had it been. Yesterday? No, I had missed all of yesterday. Up but not out, for only a short while, I had tried to make work calls, but my heart wasn't in it, and I'd slept most of the day away. I didn't ever want to go through this kind of loss again, and I knew that Martin wasn't interested in adoption. My body stiffened, as if to brace for a fall. There would be a succession of mornings like this, when I would meet the day with a sense of dread rushing back, as I remembered my loss all over again, sleep only temporarily erasing the memory. Perhaps this feeling would last for six months, like the grief brought on by the loss of a lover. Or it would last for years, as the grief I'd felt ever since my first child was taken from me? Would that old grief that I'd thought was finally passing, return with a vengeance now, merging with this new one, overtaking me because the two combined would be so great?

Beside me on the bed, fitted in the impression Martin's body had left there, I saw the heavy maple breakfast tray, and on it a thermos of coffee and my favorite large pottery mug. He hadn't wanted to wake me up. He loved me. Leaving the coffee for me, I knew he'd wanted me to *Seize the day!*—what he always said, waking me. He was up before me every morning, rarely able to sleep much past dawn, even on weekends.

I wondered how long it had been since he'd left and whether he'd been able to wake at his regular hour, get to the office early, as was his routine most days. How on earth could he have propelled himself to get to work at all yesterday and today? Was this what all men did, keeping on, not taking time for grief? I sat up and collected the several pillows on the bed and made a cushion to rest against, resettled myself, and filled the cup with coffee. Generally, I complained when Martin made such strong coffee, but I knew it was what I needed today.

The phone rang, and I figured he was checking up on me. I wasn't yet awake enough to talk. I would call him back after downing the rest of the coffee. The answering machine went on, and I heard my voice repeating the standard announcement about leaving a message, but it recorded only a dial tone from the caller. Someone had hung up—a telemarketer or a charity, someone looking for something, just making sure the right number had been called. I had nothing to give anyone today.

After finishing the thermos of coffee I showered, dressed, and drank a glass of milk, wanting not solid food-not breakfast or lunch—yes, it was already lunch time. Then, I didn't know what to do. I had tried to read the newspaper, but I hadn't been able to concentrate and didn't think that I could settle into a book either. The house felt too small. Was this what my grandfather had felt when he ran out, his heart breaking? I thought, too, of my neighbor, of when he'd been dying of cancer and still trying to fight it. His wife had to be at work, and he'd be alone all day, but couldn't tolerate staying in the house, even though he had nowhere to go, except to his medical appointments, and his strength was waning too much to take a leisurely walk. Those days, he'd go out and sit in his car—sometimes for hours at a stretch—sit staring out the window of the car that he was really no longer able to safely drive. He needed to be out in the world. I wondered: had that made him feel less frightened, not as lonely, or more alive? I thought that maybe he felt a combination of all three. When I used to see him sitting there in the car, behind the steering wheel, I would tap on his window, trying to get him to talk to me, though he was reluctant.

I knew I needed to get out today, too, but when I went about the house, drawing open the curtains and pulling up the window shades to see what kind of day it was, the outside world was no more inviting than the apartment was, when it was dark and dreary; both gloomy places looked like a reflection of my inner weather. Even though I thought I'd have a hard time talking to anyone, I wished now that someone would call, that a voice would address me, offer an affirmation that I meant something to someone.

The phone did ring again eventually. This time I didn't wait for the message, but went right to it.

"Hello?"

No answer. The second caller had listened to my voice, but left a dial tone as a message. Perhaps it was not from a telemarketer or a charity. The unspeaking caller may have been someone wanting to know if I—if anyone—were at home. Was it a potential intruder calling, someone who might be planning to rob the place? If so, it was good that I'd answered this time. But it could have been someone too shy to speak—one of my students perhaps, lacking confidence in language skills, afraid to talk to me personally, calling back, having conjured up the nerve to leave a message—one practiced diligently—but then scared off, surprised that I'd answered. Or had it been Martin, wanting to know if I were awake and not sleeping the day away, looking for some sign in my voice, of how I was doing? But no, Martin would have spoken. I was sure of that.

But then I thought to check the caller ID from the first call with the dial tone for a message, the one that I had not interrupted. The call, I saw, had come from the Conservatory. Most likely, it had been Veronica calling. But why hadn't she left a message for Martin? Perhaps she hadn't expected him to go to the office today, but when no one answered, she'd decided to hang up to call there. Now what did she want?

A little while later there were footsteps on the porch outside the front door and my heart beat faster, remembering the caller hanging up. But then, there was the familiar sound of the swinging brass mail slot opening and closing. The outside door slammed shut and I went out into the hall to collect the mail. I opened the heavy wood door, knowing that tucked between it and the storm door, there would be a hefty bundle of catalogues and magazines. There was, but there was also a large food basket, wrapped in yellow cellophane paper and tied with a bright yellow ribbon. Was Veronica still up to her antics? Wasn't the plant enough? What did she want, sending me these gifts? I bent down and picked it up by its handle, saw chocolate bars mixed in with fruits, and little bags of nuts. The card from the sender was attached to the bow, and I took it out of its tiny envelope. I gasped reading that it was from Ray, not Veronica. All it said was, *I'm so sorry, Clare and Martin.* I shivered, thinking of what Martin didn't know. *I hope these treats bring you a little solace, knowing I'm thinking of you.* How did he know? Had Danielle resumed her lessons with him? No, probably not. Probably Veronica. Yes, Veronica again.

  I sorted through the catalogues delivered with the mail, determining which ones to leave in the recycling box and which to take in. I flipped through the ones I'd decided to discard, making sure that there were no stray envelopes stuck in their pages. I'd missed a friend's wedding once, finding the invitation too late, only seeing it when packing up the catalogues I'd put in recycling, getting ready for pickup.

  There was one piece of mail jammed in between the pages of the *Beginnings* catalogue, full of baby items that I wouldn't need now. In the bunch of them there were three other catalogues marketing goods to expectant or new parents. I discarded them all, putting them in the wooden box on the porch, slamming the lid hard as I did.

  Engraved in the left hand corner of the envelope, the card or letter that had been hidden in the catalogue had a California return address. I didn't think I knew anyone who lived in California who corresponded with me anymore. Martin's Aunt Lara did, and his west coast cousins but this wasn't any of those addresses and they would be writing to Martin, not to me. This envelope from San Diego was for me. I hadn't ever known anyone in San Diego, only an old high school friend I hadn't seen in decades, and she might not even live there anymore. I tore open the envelope to see who'd sent it. I was so foggy that when I took the letter out and found a signature, it took me a few moments to remember who Judy Kneeland was, never mind that the writer mentioned in her note that she had visited me at Diamond Street to discuss volunteering to tutor. She was apologizing for not getting right back to me, but said she'd had some personal things to take care of first, that she had to move and was looking for a new place to live.

Judy Kneeland was after a meeting now. She was writing to see if she might set up an appointment for training and orientation, and there was also something she said she'd discovered and wanted to share with me. I assumed that she'd been living here with her father, since she told me that her mother had lived in California, hence the envelope with that return address. I imagined that she'd been there visiting and had just borrowed one of her envelopes, that her parents were divorced.

I actually welcomed having something to think about rather than my sadness. Maybe I'd match Judy up with Grevil, one of my Jamaican students who'd told me in his initial interview, that when he was growing up he'd only attended school sometimes, that he and his brothers and sisters shared books and shoes and therefore had to take turns showing up in the classroom. If not Grevil, then someone else; any of the students at Diamond Street would have a good deal to teach a young woman like Judy. I liked the learning to be mutual. I knew nothing about Judy yet really, only that she wanted to volunteer to be a tutor. I'd done most of the talking at our meeting, explaining how the program worked, what would be expected of her, and the help I provided. It was, after all, an interview. Straight Q & A, but Judy didn't need to ask many questions to get me started because, as usual, I was off and running with the first one. Neither of us actually had revealed anything personal, except that which couldn't be ignored at the time. Judy Kneeland had commented on my pregnancy as she was going out the door, slipping in the question, *When is your baby due?*

I brought the fruit basket in with the mail and put everything on the kitchen counter. What did Ray want, sending this? Was he simply hoping that he'd be in Martin's good graces, and that he'd then try to convince Danielle to return to her lessons? Or was it meant only for me, and he'd added Martin's name, not wanting him to suspect that he had any interest in me? Was he looking for friendship, or something more?

There was a telephone number included in Judy's note, and she was hoping to set up a meeting some time the following week, when she would be moving, she said. I would probably call her once I felt stronger. Right now I needed time away from work, away from everything. I had to get used to this. Reminders of loss would be everywhere, appearing as they had in the catalogues I'd just thrown away, or in the memory of the evening Judy Kneeland had come for an interview and asked when my baby was due. My emotions would take free reign and whenever objects and memories brought the loss to mind, I would feel untethered and unable to concentrate. Thrown for a loop was the way Dr. Aviva had described how I'd feel for a while, just as if I'd been sucker punched. That had been the good doctor's attempt at counsel. Yet, when my first child had been taken from me, no one had given me even a shred of advice or empathy, and I'd been left trying to sort things out on my own. It took too long for me to realize that it had been wrong that I'd been made to think that any feelings I had—of sadness, depression, loss—were the price I had to pay for giving in to desire.

PART TWO

Seventeen

Clare

Two weeks passed. I'd decided to wait a little longer to return to work at Diamond Street, but to go back to teaching at the Medical Center, where a substitute had been hired to cover my classes. I'd begun to worry that I might be permanently replaced if I extended my leave any longer than the two weeks I already had. I knew, too, that my students would be concerned about my health. Someone in the Human Resources Department had let them know that I was on medical leave, and I felt they might be thinking I wouldn't return because of some serious illness. Letting them know that, calling my leave a medical leave was wrong on another front; since I was a freelancer, I didn't have the benefit of medical leave, not even a sick day.

I knew that I would have to tell my students that I'd lost the baby. It was an odd expression, to lose a baby, as if my offspring were floating around somewhere in the sky, like a kite, when the string I'd been holding had broken—or that my baby had been misplaced, like car keys, sunglasses, or one of my winter gloves. Misplaced: now that was what had happened to my first child. Misplaced. The child Ray and I had made, had been given to some other woman.

Whether to tell Ray Newell about the child had been eating away at me, more and more, my mind not occupied with work. My thoughts kept going to him, and to the baby he never knew I had. I felt trapped in the kind of lethargy that can set in during a time of personal turmoil. I knew it was going to take all the energy I could muster to return to my students again, and if I decided to see Ray, to tell him what I'd been keeping from him, finding the energy I'd need for that, was unimaginable. Where would that kind of strength come from? How could I conjure it up? But I had to tell him, for my own sanity. I had to take the risk that he'd understand, and that Martin would, too. I wasn't convinced that either of them would. And what words would help them to listen, so they would understand that it wasn't my choice to have or to give up our baby, and that I'd felt powerless, at the mercy of my father's will? If only I'd known how to reach Ray? If only I'd been free to make my own decision, to have had some choice in the matter. At the Conservatory, Ray hadn't believed that the letters he said he'd sent, had never reached me. He didn't know how that could be. So many had been sent, he said. He didn't know that they had come most likely after I'd been sent away to the home and that my father must have destroyed them. The home—now that was the biggest misnomer of all, calling that place a home.

While imagining various scenarios that might result from telling Ray about his child, I suppose I was trying to prepare myself for any possibility. And finally, I thought I had. I'd decided that I couldn't live with myself if I didn't tell him, difficult and risky as it might be. I needed to be free finally, of this secret. Maybe he wouldn't care that I'd given up the child, that he'd realize how much of his freedom he would have lost, had he taken on the role of father. For a long time, after going back and forth about calling him, once I knew I'd be returning to teaching, I decided to make the call.

***

Ultimately though, the decision was not mine to make. It was a quiet Saturday afternoon, when the phone rang. Martin was out grocery shopping, and I was free to talk. I wished that I'd been the one with the nerve to initiate the call. The conversation would have been on my terms then, directed by me, and I thought that I would have felt more in control of my feelings. As it was, hearing his voice, so kind and careful, I was taken in by it.

"I hope your husband wasn't offended," he said, when I thanked him for sending the food basket.

"Why? Why would he be? It was thoughtful. Martin thought so, too. And he doesn't know that I knew you in the past. I've never discussed that with him," I said. "I know you're involved in one of his cases—Eric's—very sad. I hope you haven't mentioned knowing me in the past."

I said nothing about having been upset that he'd learned

that I'd lost the baby, though I felt betrayed that Danielle had told her mother, and I was angry at Veronica, who'd then made our private loss the topic of conversation with him. I figured it wasn't Danielle who'd told him, since as far as I knew, she hadn't resumed her lessons with him. I didn't bring up either, the fact that I knew Veronica had promised Danielle she'd end things with him, and that since she'd been talking to him about my personal business and not just as a colleague, it meant that she hadn't honored that promise to her daughter, that nothing had changed even though Danielle was so upset about her mother not telling her of their relationship.

Ray was quiet, as if he were hesitating about his reason for calling. It seemed obvious that this was not a call about Danielle's lessons, and when he spoke again, he made that absolutely clear.

"Can we get together sometime, to talk?" he asked.

"I'd like that," I said, surprising myself at how quickly I'd consented after being so hesitant for weeks. But this was my opportunity to tell him.

I thought he sounded as if he'd rehearsed what he was going to say, just as I would have. What did he want to talk about? I knew what I had to tell him, but I wasn't sure what he wanted. Did he think that perhaps we could pick up our relationship where we'd left off? Had the loss of the baby given him reason to connect with me now, a time when I would be vulnerable? Was he afraid that if Danielle didn't return to her lessons with him, that he'd no longer have a connection to me? I did need to see him to let him know what I'd kept secret for too long, but where that might lead frightened me. I'd had a lot of time to think about the possibilities.

There were many responses he might have. I didn't want to hear anger from him, if he expressed that emotion. But what if he were not angry, only curious about what had become of his child. And if he wanted to find her, what on earth would Martin do, having to know about that, especially now that he wouldn't have a child with me? Would he be jealous to know that Ray did, the way I'd been sometimes, about Danielle being the child of his relationship with Veronica? But Martin was an empathetic soul, and given that we'd lost our child, if Ray wanted to find our daughter, wouldn't he want me to know about the one child I did have? Yet, I was confused; I didn't know if I even wanted that now. What worried me most about telling Martin was that Ray Newell was the father of the child. Surely, he'd think that Ray had found his way into our lives, intending to get close to me.

Again, as before at the Conservatory, talking to Ray—even on the phone and not in person— I realized, that I felt a warmth in my belly, and now, where only emptiness had been these last couple of weeks. He was so attentive, as we spoke. Could he tell that I enjoyed that, but that it also rattled me? This was the kind of warmth I usually felt with Martin, but had not in some time.

"I can't believe you're back here," I said. "When I looked in that jazz program booklet, just to kill time, waiting for Danielle's lesson to be over, there you were, big as life, your photo and bio staring me down!"

I paced the floor as I talked. Though I could not land and had to keep moving about the room, feeling only a little shaken, I was aware of speaking to him with greater ease than I'd been able to manage, when talking to him in person, having to look him in the eye, while knowing what I was keeping from him.

"You mean you actually recognized me from that photo?" he said.

The headshot was a recent formal studio portrait, he said. Yes, his features had become stronger—more chiseled—as he'd aged, but I had immediately recognized him.

"I might not have known it was you, just from the photo. But with the bio, it all added up." My voice cracked and trailed off. "It was a good thing though, that I didn't see your boots in the picture, only later, when you came into the Bistro. Otherwise, I wouldn't have thought that was you, wearing boots like those. But by then, I'd already convinced myself."

I paused and laughed, teasing him good naturedly, the way anyone would give a friend the business for wearing something that seemed out of character. But it had been years, and what did I know about him now? As a teenager, he went in for the semi-preppy look. As a jazz musician he would get over that, of course. Though certainly there were Canadians who wore cowboy boots, I wondered if he'd chosen to wear them as a way to identify himself as an American, while living in Canada.

He didn't take offense from my comment about the boots, but instead laughed, too. He'd intended to call sooner, he told me, but his father hadn't been doing well.

"He's back in the hospital. Another stroke. This one debilitating. Not a good prognosis. There's no telling though, how long he'll be with us."

"I'm sorry," was all I could manage to say. I wondered how it must feel, to be back here to take care of the father who had poisoned his relationship with him, declaring, when he told him he was leaving the country to avoid service in a war he didn't support, *I can't think of you as my son anymore.* That night at the Conservatory, Ray had said that more than fifteen years had gone by without them having any contact with each other, except the postcards Ray had sent home, the only message on them, his new address, whenever he moved to a new place. Although he'd written to his mother a few times, he'd never received a letter back—or even a birthday card. The news of her loss, learned a year after, and not from his father, but from a friend, he said, had further devastated him, because he'd never harbored any anger toward her, knew she was powerless to change his father's mind. When she'd begged him not to leave the country and he couldn't be deterred, she asked him to promise to write to her. He never did know if she'd ever received and read his letters, or if instead, his dad—like my own, who most likely had destroyed the letters Ray had sent—had intercepted them. That was what Ray said he suspected. After leaving the country, he'd missed his mother terribly, he said.

I blamed his father, too, as well as my father, for losing Ray. If he had not disowned him, had given him his blessing when he left for Canada, I might have talked to him, found out where Ray was, to let him know I was pregnant.

Ray was offering so much of his personal feelings in this conversation. I could tell he wanted a closeness with me, and that was tempting, but I didn't think that I was capable of offering him solace now. I only wanted to offer him the truth of our past, which I was convinced I could no longer avoid.

He was obviously lonely. Who did he have in his life now? I didn't know what was happening with Veronica. She was so needy. I thought he might like his freedom too much, to make any long term commitment to her, especially with the demands she regularly put upon those close to her. But maybe she wasn't so demanding with him, and it was only her history with Martin that made her act that way.

Ray's father was dying. His mother was already gone. He was an only child. He wasn't married, and as far as he knew, he didn't have any children. And any friends he'd made in the sixteen years since the time when we'd been together, were in Canada.

"Who are you in touch with from home now? Anyone? Have you seen anybody?"

"Only Eric. I went to see him in the lockup, and I wrote something for him, a statement of his character. But I have a friend from back in the day, who's at the Conservatory. He's the one who recommended me for the faculty opening, and for the regular gig at the Cambridge Club."

He was not distracted from returning to the conversation about his personal difficulties with his father, unresolved now, unresolved forever, since the strokes, and the dementia that had set in, taking his long-term memory.

"My father seems to remember nothing at all of what went on," he said. "I'd weighed whether I should or shouldn't come back to help with his care. Truthfully, I was shocked that he'd given my name as next of kin. But who else? He had no one. When the hospital called, I didn't know that he'd forgotten what I never could, so it was even worse. I'd foolishly thought there might be the possibility of reconciliation."

I had too much to consider related to my own losses. I knew that I couldn't be there for Ray now. I had my own problems, and I was only concerned with my own truth-telling now.

"So, let's figure out when we can meet," I said, trying to steer the conversation back to what I needed. "I'm going to return to teaching at the Medical Center next week. Could we meet downtown before my class?"

"If you want to wait to arrange something, that's fine," he said.

I wondered why he was so nervous, why he would so easily

offer the opportunity to postpone our meeting, when he'd called to see me. But now that the contact had finally been made, I didn't want to wait to tell him. I was grateful he'd called, since I'd been having so much trouble calling him. I might have gone back and forth ad infinitum, to the pros and cons list I'd drafted in my mind, maybe never connecting with him at all.

"I'm teaching next week. I'm ready to go back," I said, forcing courage. "Maybe we can meet before my Chinatown class. If that doesn't conflict with your own. Mid-day? My class is early afternoon."

My voice cracked and he was silent for several seconds before responding, as if he were trying to interpret what that meant. I thought, what if he stood me up again, as he had years before, when I went to meet the van taking him—and me, I thought—to Canada. It angered me all over again to remember it, but I didn't want that anger to interfere with what I had to do.

"Let's meet on the waterfront, at Long Wharf. We can pick up a sandwich on the way. I know a place nearby that's good, if you need a recommendation."

I pictured where I wanted to be with him. Not in a booth or at a table in one of those tourist trap restaurants, but sitting out in the open air at the edge of the water on one of the large slabs of granite that made a low wall wide enough to sit on, or—if a person felt like it—even to stretch out like a cat and bask in the sun. Sometimes, when I was early getting into town and needed to waste some time, I went there and saw people doing that. I'd switch trains and ride one stop on the Blue Line and get off at Aquarium, which brought me right to the wharf. Then, I'd relax there for a while before heading over for my class.

The waterfront was heaven on a nice day. The cobalt blue of the harbor and the lighter azure of the sky was streaked with wispy clouds, and every so often, the blue yonder was pierced at the horizon by planes landing and taking off at Logan; below small sailboats floated by. The place was the perfect combination of invigorating and calming, exactly what I'd need, given what I had to say to Ray. I'd need the deep breathing that salt air encouraged, slowing my heart rate. Grown up now, the ocean air didn't make me sleepy the way it had when I was a child, falling asleep on the porch hammock at the family cottage in Maine, coming home from a day at the beach. Now though, salt air put me on high alert, when I sat at the waterfront, all senses fully functioning.

I wondered, would he try to comfort me and be understanding? Or would he walk away, when he heard what I had to say. And what was his reason for wanting to meet me? I was partly relieved, to have finally set our meeting, but still, I couldn't believe I'd agreed to it.

"We do need to talk," I said. "I'll meet you then, and we'll talk."

We said goodbye.

Suddenly life seemed more unreal. I thought of all those clichés people toss around at times like Ray was going through, like I was going through. He'd uprooted himself to take care of his dad, coming back into my circle as he had, unaware of what I had not told him. *You're only given what you can handle. Someone leaves your life and another one enters.* Clichés were spouted so conveniently because they were true, an old coworker had once said. I'd complained that she was too fond of using them. *Life takes detours and sometimes you get lost and have to back track to find your way again.* I hoped to be able to summon the kind of fortitude Ray must have had to conjure up in order to leave his life in Canada. Or maybe he hadn't really left? Would he go back when his dad died or what would he do? I had the sense that my life right now was teetering on the edge of something new, that I was in risky territory, that my life was changing in a big way. Was Ray looking for a new life here, I wondered.

***

When the day came, I wished that I hadn't decided to meet him on my first day back teaching at the Medical Center. I'd had trouble sleeping the night before, obsessing about how to tell my students I'd lost the baby, in addition to being worried as well, about Ray and how he was going to respond to what I had to tell him. My students had been so invested in my pregnancy, thrilled by the auntie role they'd taken on, a way of welcoming me to their clan: The Great Clan of Motherhood. Losing a baby was an idiom

I couldn't be sure they knew. They might think of money lost, the Red Sox losing a game, or of their relatives back home in China. But wouldn't they see the real meaning in my demeanor, and in my eyes, especially? They would surely notice my belly, gone now. I'd resort to mime sometimes, when words failed me, especially with the beginner students. If I had to, I'd simply cross my hands over my stomach and shake my head No, and then I would bow my head. Surely, they'd get the meaning of that.

Language For Working hadn't even sent a card or a get well email. The Human Resources staff at the hospital though, had told the students that I was ill, so they had contributed toward a flower delivery, and with the bouquet there was a fancy card that had been signed by students in all of my classes.

I went through the clothes closet, frantically trying to decide what to wear, wishing I'd chosen an outfit the night before. As I slid the hangers along the wooden pole, I saw a dress from the past and took it down to look at it. It was a fancy dress—certainly too fancy for work—a black silk number with subdued splashes of colorful abstract lines and shapes. Why did I keep it, a relic of the past, something I'd never even worn? I'd bought it years ago at a local Greek church bazaar, where other kinds of things were being sold: a carefully curated collection of flea market items, crates of vegetables and fruit, as well as bags of nuts and figs shipped from the old country. Next to the café, which sold spinach pies, moussaka, and good strong coffee to have with honey and walnut pastries, I'd wandered into the "Boutique" area, a rummage sale featuring clothing of surprisingly good quality, looking like it had never been worn. This was a wealthy congregation located in the elite Brattle Street neighborhood. I'd admired the dress, talking to the well-coifed white-haired women, who were acting as sales people. *Try it on; go on*, they had encouraged me about the dress, and I did, to their *oohs* and *ahs*, as I emerged from the makeshift changing room—what had been a closet, before the organizers had removed the door and hung a curtain so that customers would think they were at Saks or Bloomingdales. *It fits you perfectly*, they'd gushed, exchanging glances with each other, as if they were suddenly missing their thinner, more youthful figures. *But where would I wear it? I have nowhere to wear something like this*, I said to them. *For a fete,* one offered. *Wear it around the house,* another suggested, making me laugh as I thought of vacuuming or making dinner in such a dress. But the woman had meant her suggestion to be taken seriously—apparently, they had help for those kind of ordinary household tasks. I'd bought the dress, imagining I could wear it to a concert, with high black boots, to make it less formal and more bohemian, thinking also to add a thick black patent leather belt to replace the silk ribbon tie. I now noticed the dress label, securely sewn, that of a New York atelier, some small designer's work, no doubt. My dream of wearing it hippie style had never been realized; my life had changed—Martin's work seemed all consuming, and mine, too, leaving little time for concert going— and the dress stayed in the back of the closet.

Today, I settled on wearing a simple tunic and a skirt with an elasticized waist, one which I thought ought to fit me again. I dressed, finished my coffee and headed to the subway station.

***

There it was, approaching. I didn't run or walk fast, my usual inclination if I hadn't yet reached the platform, when I heard the train rumbling through the tunnel, getting closer to Harvard Station. I took my time this morning. Although I didn't hurry, I got to the platform, just as the train arrived. It screeched to a halt, a door opening right in front of where I was standing. But on the spur of the moment, I froze and couldn't board. I backed up into the pack of mostly men in business suits, who'd crowded in behind me, waiting to get on. I went against the tide, weaving through.

"Excuse me. Excuse me. Excuse me, please."

Reaching the wooden benches that lined the back wall along the platform, I sat down, choosing one near the middle-aged Haitian man, a musician, a regular performer here of ballads he sung in French. He had a repertoire of heartfelt songs, not all of them dealing with gloomy romance, some in fact quite spirited. I needed this music to release me from my anxious mood. On the floor to my right, the man had set up his microphone and suitcase amplifier. He'd opened out his guitar case in which he collected contributions of change—and even dollar bills sometimes—from appreciative commuters. Next to the case, and resting on a little fold-up stand, he displayed CDs for sale, and a sign stating, *Available for Parties and Events*.

His music was soothing, too. I was thankful that the man had chosen to work this station today. Some of the students in my *English as a Working Language* class at the hospital—Octave, Fernande, Andre, and Champe—had said, when I told them about this musician, that he was from their community. He played for festivals and celebrations and at their church sometimes. He was famous, Champe said, on the day I taught them that English word, asking them to name people as examples. Delores, star student, remembering the sonogram picture I'd showed to the class that morning, the image with surprisingly perfect features of the unborn son I'd then believed I would have, said, *Your son will be a famous movie star. Very handsome.* This had led to a flurry of other predictions for his future—that he'd be *a famous scientist or singer*—on that day, when my life and my son's life had seemed all about possibilities, they had continued on and on, using the vocabulary I'd taught them, offering good wishes and many blessings for him. My heart ached now, remembering the moment.

The Public Address announcement—*We are experiencing delays on the Red Line. We apologize for any inconvenience*—drowned out the music once in a while. It was well past rush hour now, and the makeup of the crowd had changed. It was larger and louder, with crying babies strapped in carriers at their mothers' breasts, and toddlers squealing and chasing each other, perhaps a little too close to the yellow line at the platform edge. I wondered if I'd changed my mind, not boarded that last train, so that I could be here now, among women who'd been successful at becoming mothers. Would I ever be one of their tribe?

I sat through four or five tunes before another inbound train arrived. Then it was a scramble to get on, never mind, that for a few minutes after making the decision not to board the last train, I'd actually been the only person waiting in the station. Students now pushed their way in, bumping up against me with their backpacks and large shoulder bags to clear a path. The mothers nudged strollers at my ankles. Tourists with shopping bags, jockeyed for a seat.

I fell into the first empty seat, happy not to have to stand, hanging onto a pole. I was still feeling a little weak, not having been out and about for so long, except a couple of times, taking trips in the car with Martin, to go to the doctor and the pharmacy. The train jerked its way toward Central Square and on to Kendall/MIT, where most of the students exited. As it came up from underground and out into the light onto Longfellow Bridge, I was surprised by the view of the Charles River and the Boston skyline. I'd hoped that seeing it once again, I'd feel relieved to be resuming almost daily trips across the river to see my students; instead, the view saddened me. It was hard to believe that I'd lived in an apartment where I'd wake each morning to this view, that I had given it up to live with Martin on Ridge Road, where we seemed to be stuck.

Loss still held me firmly in its grip, and I felt a twinge that might be pain, indigestion, or simply the anxiety I was trying to keep at bay, anxiety that accompanied thoughts of meeting Ray. What would his response be, hearing me tell my secret? Would he believe that I had wanted him to know, but that the choice had not been mine to make?

The Charles River looked calm, no sailboats, but some of those land and water duck boats, packed with tourists today. It was a new season—or it felt like one anyway—an early New England summer having taken hold. By evening a thunderstorm would arrive and shake things up, hopefully reducing the uncomfortable humidity. I'd heard the weather report before leaving home, and now saw the needle atop the John Hancock tower. Just as there was a little ditty to remember how to set the clocks—*Spring ahead! Fall behind!*— there was one to interpret the lights on the tower needle—red or blue, steady or flashing—as a way of forecasting the weather. Today it was *Steady Red— Steady Red! Rain Ahead!* At least it was spring; in winter, when it was flashing red, it meant, *Snow Instead*. Besides having a view of the skyline, to the left of the window across from me, the advertisement that used to appear frequently on Red Line trains, had been posted again. I hadn't seen it in some time. A man who'd been standing, blocking it from my line of vision, made it visible to me, when he took an empty seat as the train jerked to a stop on the bridge just before the Charles/MGH station stop.

The sperm donor recruitment posted used to amuse me, but that was before I'd lost this other child. The poster was newly designed. Worse. The tag line—*Help Prospective Parents Realize Their Dream of Starting a Family*—didn't have the effect that it used to, when the purpose was more straightforward, and when I still dreamed of being a parent, not just a step-parent. Sure, the plea was right where it should be if it were going to be the hook to draw in men, who might be able to help couples have a chance at conceiving. But viewed along with some new graphics and their message, the supposedly altruistic appeal didn't have the importance that its placement was supposed to give it. In fact, the message nearly vanished, once you looked at the illustration.

There was a huge dollar sign to the left. Some squiggles—the universal symbol for sperm—had attached themselves to it. Other squiggles were swimming their way west across the slick paper, to join the others where the money was. Central to this was the job being advertised: *Sperm donors needed in Cambridge. Earn up to $1100.* I thought it sounded like any other job, hardly different from delivering packages for UPS. A post office box number to which one could confidentially apply, was given, and the restriction printed below: *Applicants must be 18-38 years of age.* Seeing the poster, I thought of Ray and me, when we made love, just before he left for Canada. How easy it had been to get pregnant. I thought of the child we conceived and realized what our child had in common with the children of sperm donors, that like our daughter, chances were, they wouldn't know who their father was either. California still had closed adoption records, and I didn't know if the maternity home had had some connection to adoption agencies in other states, where records had been opened, since those days of *The Baby Scoop*, when so many young women, like me, were directed to have and then give up their children. There was the very real possibility that the agency taking babies from the home was in California; then, even if Ray wanted to find our child, it might not be possible.

Seeing the poster made me think, too, of a story reported on *Sixty Minutes, Dateline*, or some other one of those news magazine television shows. The program presented the story of a doctor who'd set himself up in business in a fertility clinic and was inseminating women all over town with his own sperm. Had he done this to save having to pay donors, or was there something narcissistic in his motivations? The town was small enough that some of the mothers had begun noticing similarities in the appearance of their children, as they compared them to other families in the community—their build, hair color, and features—all seemed similar. They realized that the children had all been born to women who'd enlisted the same doctor's help in conceiving. The recollection gave me the shivers.

Wasn't it fitting that this poster was done in black and white? No gray areas in this business. No one else on the train seemed to be looking at the poster, no matter that I thought it screamed for my attention.

But then, a child distracted me from it.

The boy—about two—was strapped into a stroller. He was pleading for his bottle. "Eh, eh," he kept saying, stretching out his arm to reach it, twisting around and pointing to it, tucked into the rear mesh pocket behind him. After a minute of this, the woman—presumably his mother—took him out of the stroller and pulled him up to sit next to her on the window bench. She had the bottle in hand now, filled with something yellow—apple juice probably. All the mothers I knew gave their children apple juice in their bottles, or in little rectangular carboard boxes that came with tiny plastic drinking straws.

"No, you don't behave. You're a bad boy. Sit straight," the mother kept repeating, withholding the juice bottle.

As if to prove her right, the boy squirmed to turn around on the bench, to look out the window she didn't want him looking out of, his neck stretched sideways and back, though she held his hips down, trying to keep him from seeing into the dark tunnel, to notice what he might, whenever the train passed intermittent lights.

"No, you sit straight," the woman insisted.

"Look! Look!" the boy begged, pointing toward the window, each time saying the word louder.

"I want you to sit straight in your seat."

"No! Look! Look!" he now demanded, furious.

"Do you want the juice?" the woman teased.

When the boy became excited about having it, and did turn

around as she'd been telling him to, she smiled and said, "No, you can't have it. You don't behave. Sit straight."

I had all I could do to restrain myself, watching this disturbance. What force denied me and Martin the possibility of a child, yet gave this woman who seemed so obviously incapable of the patience parenting required, a little boy to torment? All around me were people reading their books and newspapers, oblivious—or pretending to be—or dozing off with their eyes closed to the scene unfolding. My longing for motherhood made me want to get up out of my seat and take the boy in my arms, hug him tightly, and hand him that bottle of juice.

He let out a long, loud screech, and I wanted to cheer him on. I winced, knowing what was coming next.

The man, who was sitting on the other side of the woman, the boy's father perhaps, had said nothing up until this point. But now, he reached over and slapped the boy's face.

"Are you going to behave now?" the man asked as the child wailed and then shook his head, "yes," and sat back in his seat.

"Give him the juice then," he said to the woman.

She did, and then the boy stuck his tongue out at me. I'd resorted to trying to distract him from further trouble by making silly faces and playing peek-a-boo behind my paperback book.

"Don't look at her," the mother ordered. She took his chin in her hands to turn him away from me.

The boy ducked at that, and looked again. Seeing my changing, foolish face, he let out a raspberry in my direction. Then he sucked in hard on the bottle nipple for a minute. When he'd had enough, he feigned choking, so he could spit juice on the floor. He grinned after he did.

At this point, the father got up and sat on the other side of the boy, each parent pressing in on him.

I couldn't keep quiet any longer, watching this scene.

"Why are you mistreating that child? Let him be, or I'll call Social Services about your cruelty." I stood, deciding at Charles Street Station to move to another car of the train. I couldn't bear to watch any longer.

"Mind your business, lady," the man said, as I did.

***

When I got to the waterfront, the afternoon was bright, sunny, and warm, with a southwesterly breeze. At Long Wharf people were lined up for boat trips out to George's and Spectacle Islands. I saw the New England Aquarium exploratory boat docked. I was glad not to see what I called *the rock 'n' roll boat*, an excursion boat that made several one-hour trips each day, out into the harbor and around the islands, playing loud music, which the advertising brochure touted as state of the art with more than two dozen marine grade speakers. Their motto was *Don't even think of asking us to turn the sound down*. It was fast, too, not for the faint of heart or lunchtime boaters on a brief trip around the harbor, looking for a quiet escape from the office, serenity in the midst of a hectic work day. *Codzilla*, as it was called, was a huge version of a speedboat, the name alluding not only to the Boston cod, but also, to its size, as the brochure described, *seventy feet of marine aluminum and bad attitude*. The company that owned this monster wasn't kidding. It was painted with wild colors reminiscent of my psychedelic youth, when that style of design was reflected in everything from clothing to album and concert posters, like the one of Bob Dylan in silhouette with curly multi-colored hair that I hung on the wall in my college dorm room in 1970. The speedboat attracted young tourists and an older clientele, too, that appeared to have come of age in the sixties, as Ray and I had. Relieved not to see the vessel, thinking that it must be out on the water, I hoped it wouldn't return to port to drown out our conversation. If it did, I'd ask Ray to move around behind the old Customs Buildings, to the next wharf over where the wealthy docked their yachts—or to the much quieter India Wharf in the other direction—though I thought that might add too much solemnity to our conversation; India was a wharf where the scale of everything was very large, and I already felt quite small in the scheme of things. My words might reverberate in a place like that.

I looked around to see if Ray was waiting. I spotted him, able to recognize him, even from a distance. My heart jumped and my legs felt weak, the way they had that night when I'd found him—his photo, his story—in the jazz program booklet at the Conservatory, and he'd come looking for me. It was the way I felt, too, being left in the lurch the day I went to meet the van that I thought was taking me with him to Canada. I tried to breathe in the salt air that I thought would relax me.

Looking at Ray's posture, I thought he seemed anxious, too. He was sitting facing the harbor, his head moving back and forth as if he were scanning the small boats moored alongside the wharf, waiting impatiently for someone who'd just returned from sea to disembark. But I knew he was looking for me. I looked at my watch. I had an hour before class was to begin, and it was a fifteen minute walk to the medical center. I didn't know if that would give us enough time for this meeting, and who knew if there would be others? Would I want others? What if he wanted to find our child? There might be many times we'd meet, if so. I didn't think I wanted that, but what if he did? How terrible it was, that what I had to tell him would be news to him, although it had happened sixteen years before. It was so long ago. I had a husband and life now, and he had his life. Whatever he wanted, though, I would have to be strong enough, capable of dealing with any possible outcome.

When I approached he was still looking out at the harbor, away from those who'd crowded onto the wharf, since it was such a good day to be on the water or just to drink in the scene. Standing behind his right ear, I said, "Hey," unintentionally startling him. He turned quickly, nevertheless greeting me with a wide grin.

"This is great," he said, pulling at strands of his still long hair, fighting the wind that had blown it across his face as he'd turned to me. "Great to see you. And such a great location! I'll miss Boston. What a day, huh?"

I would not hide in small talk. I would scream out what I had to say, if that was the only way to tell him.

"You'll miss Boston? Why? Are you expecting to be finished teaching soon? To go back?" I asked.

I'd been unable to hide a sense of panic in my voice. If he were leaving to return to Canada in the near future, I absolutely had to tell him today—no postponing it—just take one very deep breath, then spill it. I couldn't bear to harbor this secret alone anymore. I needed to be free of it, to put that child behind me, to accept that I might never know her, to accept that first loss.

Ray tilted his head, as if he were affected by the fact that I cared that he might be getting ready to leave Boston soon.

"Not right away. I'm in Boston through first semester of the next academic year anyway," he said. "Maybe longer. It depends if the musician on sabbatical decides to return or not. Though I don't know yet, if I'd stay if asked."

"I've always thought of Boston as a good music town. All kinds really," I said.

"Oh, it is. It is."

He hesitated and then I thought he was about to begin to say what he wanted to say, why he wanted to meet me to talk.

He didn't, so I did.

"Martin and I have been through a lot these past couple of weeks."

"I'm so sorry, Clare," he said.

Although obviously moved, knowing I'd lost this baby, he kept talking, as if that set him off.

"I left my car in the Conservatory garage. I rarely take public transportation."

He jumped up suddenly, as if on a spring, and he looked away for a moment, in the direction of the train station, as if he might be considering bolting. What was wrong?

"You aren't thinking you have to go so soon, are you? Sorry, I was little late getting here. The train was crowded."

But I misread him, not knowing why he was all of a sudden acting so strangely.

"Don't worry," he said. "I'm not going anywhere. We came here to talk after all these years, didn't we? You know, taking the subway train today, looking around at the commuters on the platform, seeing how they boarded on cue, when the train pulled up and the doors opened," he said, "I noticed a homeless woman, managing her cane like a staff, rather than a tool to help her with mobility, since she had so much else with her—all her earthly belongings probably—in a large, plastic garbage bag she dragged along. She just kept on. We do, don't we? Or some of us do anyway," he said.

His words, acknowledging that not everyone could keep on,

given profound challenges, felt now, that they were meant for me. I didn't know how I could. Not yet. Would I? I didn't know.

"I have something important to tell you," I said.

Ray turned to look at me; he was no longer anxious and in need of an exit. What did he think I was going to say? His green eyes seemed to be pleading for me to say it. But suddenly I felt shy—that teenager thing again, pulled back to the time when we had known each other intimately. I had never said what I was about to tell him, not to another soul.

I looked at Ray's red boots and couldn't help smiling. He had cleaned them up and they looked almost new, though still a bit worn—but fashionably so. Had he spiffed himself up for me?

I reached out my hand. Ray took it and I drew him back to sit down next to me on the chunk of granite. This is it, I thought. But before I could speak I began to cry.

"Hey, hey," he said. "It's all right. It'll be alright."

"What I have to tell you is going to make you want to run, to turn on those boot heels, walk fast along the granite walkway and right into the subway station, all the way down the flight of stairs to the boarding platform," I rambled on through my tears. "These tears aren't just about this baby I lost," I said. "They're about another one."

"I'm sorry it happened before, too," he said.

He softly brushed the back of his hand across my cheek to wipe the tears away, and he put his arm around me, gently pulling me to him in a *that-a-girl* sort of way. And he tilted my head to rest it against his for a second, my soft hair touching his face. I thought he was going to kiss me. What was he thinking?

I pulled away, not sure of what he meant by this gesture. It was brotherly, yet it stirred up confusing feelings. I felt as if it were 1968 in his father's Galaxy, parked outside Spider Gate Cemetery, or dancing at The Cove, when the floor cleared for the last dance of the evening and only serious couples swayed so slowly they hardly moved, holding each other as close as they could, feeling the heat of each other's bodies. We weren't teenagers anymore, though. We were adults with complicated feelings and responsibilities. I was married, but I hadn't felt like this with Martin in a long time.

"That baby wasn't the only one," I repeated.

My words hovered in the air a moment before taking off just as the pair of gulls I was watching did, when shoed from the pier by a child running toward them.

"What do you mean, not the only baby you lost?" he asked.

I didn't turn or avert my eyes, but looked at him straight on when he said this. The intensity of his returned stare frightened me. I saw in his eyes, the same longing that I felt must be reflected in my own eyes. Was it the longing for what we once had, what had been lost between us, what we had been denied?

I shook my head and Ray shrugged his shoulders.

"What? Tell me," he said.

"I know nothing," I said. "Nothing about what happened to the child."

I paused and then continued.

"But really, I am not to be blamed."

"Who's blaming you? And for what?"

His voice had become softer until it was merely a whisper.

I told him then, how I'd been sent away and made to give up our child, how I'd never seen his letters, so I didn't know how to find him. And he told me that he hadn't wanted to leave for Canada without me, and that he'd explained that in his very first letter.

Ray stood again. This time I thought he really was taking off. But seeing more tears, he turned more confrontational than impatient, and he said, "What could you do? You could have let me know. Yes, you could have kept the baby. I would have done something. I would have tried, you know, had I known. I did write, after I was settled. I didn't know why you didn't answer. I never heard from you."

"My father must have destroyed your letters. He wouldn't let me try to find you."

I was crying hard now. A little boy walking by stopped, seeing me, and stared for moment and then skipped on.

"So where is the child?" he asked.

"Not a child," I said. "Not anymore. But she is our child though."

A gull atop one of the wooden pillars swooped down to snag a french fry from the cardboard lunch tray of an unsuspecting tourist standing on the low wall nearby. Suddenly there was a flock of the cranky birds wanting to be fed.

I couldn't think straight.

I wanted the man to go away, to take the birds elsewhere. Let them follow him, the way they'd follow a trawler coming into port.

"I have no idea at all about her," I said, collecting my thoughts after the tourists at the railing shooed the birds away. "I couldn't even give her a name. She was whisked away right after birth. I barely got a glimpse of her."

"A baby girl?"

"Not anymore," I said. "Not a baby, I mean. She'd be sixteen. Danielle's age."

"Don't you want to know her? I want to know her. And I think you need to know her, too," he said.

"I don't think I can handle knowing," I said. "Think of the possibilities. She could be anywhere, in any circumstances. Think of the emotional energy we'd have to invest, searching for her. And what if we searched and didn't find her? I gave birth in California, and I'm not sure what adoption agency she went to, whether it was in a different state, one with open records. Or what if we did find her, and she didn't want to know us. For all we know, she might not even know she was adopted."

"Well, I want to know," he said.

He was firm in that, and I was shocked.

"Why? Why would you?" I said.

"If you didn't think I'd want to know, then why did you bother to tell me? For what purpose?" he said.

"Think of my marriage to Martin. If he knows...."

I shrugged, sighed, and searched my pockets, and then my tote bag for a tissue or even the napkin I thought I'd taken earlier from the coffee shop, where I'd bought the sandwich for which I now had no appetite. Ray realized what I needed and couldn't find and reached into his own pocket and pulled out a napkin he had in there. "It's all I've got," he said.

He handed it to me and I took it and looked at it. It was marked with the name of a French restaurant, Le Biarritz, something no doubt from the last time he'd worn this jacket, when he was still back in Canada and this scene was one he might not ever have imagined.

"What time do you have to teach?" he wanted to know.

I hoped he realized that there was too much to think about, and we hadn't even got started.

"I have to ask if things are serious between you and Veronica?" I said.

"I'm not sure. I just don't know if I can manage it, seeing what it's doing to her relationship with Danielle. Isn't it strange that I'd become involved with her through Danielle, and that would lead me to you?"

I pressed him.

"Aside from Danielle, is it serious between you and Veronica?"

"I don't know how I feel, and I'm confused about how she feels. I'd been asking her about you, after seeing your name on Danielle's registration form as a contact, even before that night at the Conservatory, trying to determine if you were who I'd hoped you were."

I bristled at that, hearing of his hope. Hope for what?

"Veronica questioned my motives, asking about you. That led to an argument. She'll think she was right to question me, when she finds out about us. That could put an end to things, I'd think, since I'd kept our history from her. She'll know how right she was."

We sat there then, saying nothing until the relative silence along the pier was broken by the horn of a sightseeing boat about to leave the dock. What a mess things were, I thought.

"I could come back and meet you later this afternoon maybe? When your classes are over? We could talk more then. I can get my car, if you're free to have dinner?"

Then, as if he'd suddenly remembered how things had changed for me since he'd been gone, that I was now married, and not free on a whim to follow a suggestion like this, he said, "I'm sorry. You have Martin to go home to. I don't know where my head is."

"He's working late tonight. I can call him."

"Of course you must have told him. He must know you gave up our baby. Even if he doesn't know I'm the father. Or does he?"

"He doesn't know anything. Not about you, and not about the baby either."

He looked shocked to hear this. I supposed he was thinking my marriage was built on a lie.

I sighed and stopped talking. Ray didn't say anything.

After a few minutes, I said, "I have thought of little else these past months since knowing you were back, except how to talk to you about this and what might happen after I did."

"I'll walk with you to your class, so we can keep talking. We have to talk this out. I didn't buy a sandwich, so maybe I can get dim sum, wait for you to finish teaching, and we can meet up after?"

"It's a little late for dim sum now," I said.

I was frozen in indecision, just as I'd been about whether or not to call him to arrange this meeting.

"I don't know," I managed to say.

"You don't know which is a better plan, or you don't know if you want to continue talking?"

"I don't know," I repeated.

This would not do. I wasn't prepared for this, had never expected that he'd want to know what had happened to our child, thinking that he valued his freedom too much. He could probably see that I hadn't even expected him to care. I had considered that perhaps he might deny the baby was his, when I told him. But this—his interest—his genuine concern and caring—had thrown me, and was sure to turn my life upside down. If I'd thought that losing Martin's baby already had done that, I could now imagine how much more complicated things might get.

"Well, you don't want to be late for your first class back," he said.

"Teaching my class feels so unimportant right now in the scheme of things," I said. "And I need time to think, Ray."

"Your class is important. Everything is important," he said.

I looked at him and thought, yes; my students are counting on me to be back today. They'd missed me, and said so in their card and notes, and I had missed being with them, too. I could call Martin and even if the meeting he planned to have after school with Danielle and Veronica didn't involve having dinner with them, he could go back to the office after, on the way there, pick up something to go from the diner, and eat at his desk. I could tell him that I wouldn't be home until a bit later than usual, that I wouldn't be eating with him tonight. There was trust between us. I didn't question him, when he was working late at the office, or when he had to meet with Veronica alone, to discuss something about parenting Danielle. He trusted me as well. I didn't really want to make up a story about why I wasn't coming home until later, tired of secrets, tired of pretending things were hunky dory, even if they were not, but I'd have to explain why I wouldn't be home for dinner, would have tell him something. This was my life and I had to deal with it, just as Martin had his life with Veronica and Danielle. I knew what it might mean for him to know everything, but now he'd have to know, even if it did mean the end of our marriage. I expect that the trust we'd built between us would crumble when he learned that my secret past was suddenly very alive in the present.

Still, I questioned whether I could go on talking with Ray without first doing some thinking on my own, about what to do next. Maybe we ought to wait to talk more another day, after all of this has been processed.

But no, what I really wanted to do was jump at the chance to actually figure things out, to start on a plan to resolve what I'd never had the courage or support to deal with alone. Yes, a search could send us in circles, but I needed to believe that I was strong enough to manage that.

When we saw *Codzilla* coming into port, we found a spot where we could sit on a step of the open pavilion. The office workers having lunch there, had dispersed, and there we were, just the two of us, sitting together, no longer talking. The pavilion had the feeling of a temple, a house of worship.

I was the one to break the silence after a few minutes.

"Okay," I said. "What do you say, you get your car and meet me near the Chinatown gate at 5:15 after my classes? We can eat dinner and talk. There are a few relatively inexpensive garages, just outside the gate."

I hurried to the building where my class would be held. There was a phone in the room, and I would call Martin, tell him my students had planned to take me out for a welcome back dinner, and it was impossible to refuse them. He would still be at the office, since Danielle wasn't out of school yet, and his meeting with her and Veronica was scheduled for later in the afternoon.

Eighteen

Danielle

I knew that Chris wasn't going to be at the pizza shop on Broadway this afternoon. He'd told me at lunchtime that a last-minute band rehearsal had been scheduled. We'd been going to go the Square and get pizza at a different place, the one in The Garage on JFK, so we could talk without so many kids we knew being around. Things between us had been going okay, ever since our conversation when I'd promised to introduce him to Ray Newell, convinced I should continue with the lessons. I'd been planning to tell him when I was going to start up again.

I was meeting Stephanie, instead. I came out of the career services office and first took a detour to the auditorium. I didn't go in, but stood outside, listening to the jazz band. I could pick out Chris' sax. I was still dreaming of a day when I might join the band as another sax player. *We need another one*, he'd said to me, when I'd told him I was taking lessons. *Get good and we'll see.* I didn't know how it would be, if I did decide to go back to lessons with Mr. Ray Newell. What if my mom did keep seeing him and I was having lessons with him? Awkward, I thought.

Outside the building I met up with Steph. The pizza shop was crowded, so we decided to skip our usual afterschool haunt; that was fine with me, since the star attraction, as far as I was concerned, would be missing. Instead, we continued down Broadway, turning to take a short cut through Harvard Yard, where we passed a tour group of older Japanese tourists stopping to take photos on the steps of Widener Library. It was weird living in a city that was a tourist destination, and I often wondered what it would be like to live in some ordinary town. I sometimes thought that if any alien creatures from another galaxy were to land in Cambridge, they might mistakenly think, so this is what earth is like. And did Clare's students from other countries, who'd come directly to Boston and settled in Cambridge, have the idea that the City was typical of others in this country?

Expert at traversing the maze-like paths of the campus, the two of us quickly found the one that led to Dexter Gate, and walked out onto Mass Ave. across from Toscanini's.

"I don't want ice cream," I said, seeing Steph raise her eyebrows at the sight of the place. The memory of the last time I'd been there with Clare— that awful night after finding my mother with Ray, and Clare picking me up at my lesson, letting me drive, hitting that old guy's car—was still fresh in my mind.

We crossed the street and there was the usual clog of Goths and faux hippies hanging around in The Pit, the sunken brick area behind the subway station. I noticed the girl who didn't seem to belong there, the one I'd told Clare about, and she'd thought maybe she was someone who worked for Bridge Over Troubled Waters, but I didn't see the van anywhere. She really stood out, wearing a nice sundress, and she had expensive-looking sunglasses on, and really nice leather sandals. I wondered why she was there with all those strays.

We walked not aimlessly, but in the direction of Brattle. Getting there, we stopped in front of the florist shop to admire the potted blue hydrangea and the bright pink azalea standing in puddles after a good watering. Last time I'd been here was that day with my mom, after Clare lost the baby.

"I want pizza," Steph said. "I just didn't want to wait for a table at the place on Broadway."

So, we passed up the Algiers and walked back in the direction of JFK, heading to the place in The Garage. I was wishing I was going there with Chris instead.

It was quieter in the Square, now that most of the Harvard students were gone on summer break, though there were already a fair number of tourists taking photos, like the group we'd passed in the Yard, taking photos of places that were so familiar to us, that we took them for granted.

Once in a while, Clare talked about when she'd first moved to Boston, about walking to Faneuil Hall Marketplace at lunchtime, for sandwiches or chowder, and even on some days for a whole meal that was more like dinner, at Durgin Park. She'd sit among the tourists who flocked to the place, considering it a special attraction for its history, which was the way Clare said she'd thought of the place before she moved to Boston, when she made occasional trips from her hometown. But when she started working nearby, she said Faneuil Hall Marketplace became just ordinary, just a place to eat and shop. I wished that I could feel the same excitement about Cambridge, as these tourists did. I was spoiled. I knew though, that somewhere in the mountains or farmland of New Hampshire or Vermont, or Down East in the blueberry barrens, or in the flatland of Ohio, a young girl thought of escaping her own situation, too, assigning to another place—maybe even Cambridge, the city I took for granted and was even bored with some days—the highest value in her dream for another kind of life. Harvard Square. Cambridge, just one stop on the subway train from Boston, the Hub of the Universe. Cambridge: the People's Republic. I knew girls like me, who were stuck in less interesting places might think of me as a spoiled brat, to be bored with a place like Cambridge.

I watched the tourists taking photographs of passersby, and thought, how silly they are if they think they're capturing images of the local citizenry. You could see them aiming their cameras at the crowds of other tourists sitting along the stone wall to watch the acrobat outside the florist shop, or those sipping coffee at patio tables at Au Bon Pain, where other than the chess players, there weren't many locals at this time of year.

"So what about your plans for summer?" Steph asked, once we'd placed our order for the Primavera Veggie Special, and had settled into a corner table that looked down on the little park outside Grendel's Den.

"Well," I said, as I unwrapped a straw and fought to sink it into a can of ginger ale. It kept bobbing up and down from the carbonation, almost jumping out. I took a deep sip, which allowed me to think before answering Steph's question. I didn't know yet really what I was going to do, and I didn't like it that she'd been pressing me to decide before I was ready.

"I've been talking to my mom's friend, Molly." I said. "She's the one I babysit for on weekends sometimes. She needs a nanny at their Cape house this summer. I'm still getting the details—like when they're leaving town, when they plan to come back. If I decide to take the job, I want to have a few days after school ends and before it starts again, to get ready. The kids know me, so I don't think it would be so bad being with them all day. The older two boys will be in day camp most of the time. So, I'd have the little guy to watch."

"And how about a few days to have some fun? It's summer, you know. Did you ask about days off? And what about Chris? Don't you want to see what happens with him? And what about your sax lessons?"

I didn't want to get into my real reasons for wanting to leave town—my mother's embarrassing involvement with my sax teacher. I hadn't told any of my friends about my mom and Mr. Newell. I didn't want Chris to hear and think that was the reason I wasn't sure if I was going to keep taking lessons with him.

"I didn't ask about time off," I admitted. "Not yet. But I'm going to," I said.

I ignored her question, pumping me for info about Chris. She didn't seem to notice that, or that I hadn't answered about the sax lessons.

"I think you should apply for some jobs around here anyway, just in case. Now is the time. If you change your mind about going to the Cape, or if it falls through because she found someone else for the job, and then you go looking, you know you won't get one here. They'll all be taken.

Steph was sounding the way my mother would when she tried to push me to do what she thought was best. I didn't need another mother. I had two already.

"Enough, Steph. I need to think this out myself."

She stopped then with her aggravating questions that she liked to answer herself, and in a matter of seconds, got up from her chair and went to the counter.

I hadn't heard the cashier call our number to let us know that the pizza we'd ordered was ready, and it turned out it wasn't. Stephanie returned to the table with two applications for employment. When we'd entered the shop she hadn't missed the Help Wanted sign in the corner at the door.

"Here," she said. "We should each fill one out. It would be fun to work together."

"What? You think I want to work in a pizza shop all summer? The ovens! What are you thinking?"

"But you do want to work with kids all summer? Forget it. I'm filling one out. It's better to have *a* job than *no* job," she said. "And besides, this place is hangout for guys who are jocks. They need their carbs, you know, after tennis at the courts around the corner. And what about the runners along the Charles, coming back into the Square, feeling hungry? And maybe even a hunky Italian tourist craving a taste of home?"

"You're ridiculous, Stephanie. Jocks and teeny-boppers. Who needs them? Mostly thirteen- year-olds who think it's cool to eat real pizza in Harvard Square instead of at their neighborhood Greek spot."

Stephanie was a dreamer, always imagining the best possible outcome, although I noticed that in doing so, she rarely fared any better than most of our friends who had a more realistic attitude.

"I think your hunky Italian tourists would choose cappuccino at one of the cafes, like Pamplona or even Au Bo Pain, before they'd come here," I said, pronouncing the French word for bread ironically, as my friends and I sometimes did, pronouncing it as if it were the English word, pain, which is what I thought Stephanie was intent on being about my summer job situation.

There were a lot of reasons it might be better to leave town, spend the summer at the Cape. There was my mother and her embarrassing affair with my teacher, and how she was constantly bickering with my father over my schedule, and pressuring me about thinking about college applications already. I was getting tired of having two mothers. Clare was always trying to be the peacemaker, to help me figure things out by giving me *guidance* that I didn't ask for, and then my mom seemed to mess things up for everyone. Yet, if I leave for the summer, what if Chris finds some other girl. I heard him telling someone that he wasn't going to music camp this summer and would be in Cambridge the whole time. I wondered whether he would have a summer job and where.

When we finished the pizza and Steph had gotten nowhere,

trying to convince me to stay in Cambridge and look for a summer job in Harvard Square, instead of traipsing off to Cape Cod to work as a nanny, I decided that since I was scheduled to be at my dad's house this weekend, I'd go straight there, rather than pick up a backpack full of clothes at my mom's. I had a whole wardrobe at each house anyway now, no longer wanting to feel like a traveler with a suitcase, having always to bring things back and forth. When I'd done that, I'd always leave some favorite or necessary item of clothing behind, and not realize it until I needed it. Retrieving something, even if I did notice right away that I'd forgotten it, would become a major operation, especially when I was younger, not old enough to be expected to get it myself; this would often lead to arguments between Mom and Dad, about whose responsibility it was to bring the jacket or shorts or whatever to me. It was just simpler to have two separate wardrobes. At this time of year I didn't need much in either place anyway, since I rarely dressed up—a couple of pairs of jeans, tee shirts, tank tops, and a light sweater in case the weather turned chilly, and a slicker in case of rain.

  Steph decided to take the train one stop to Central Square, rather than walk home to Cambridgeport. I headed the other way, down the platform and through the doors to the tunnel, where I'd get the bus to my dad's house.

  I rarely had the opportunity to be alone in the afternoons, often having afterschool meetings, a lesson, and sometimes track meets, so I was looking forward to some time to think about what I was going to do with my summer, how I'd navigate the craziness of my family if I did decide to stay in Cambridge. On free afternoons, if I went to my mom's house right after school, I'd usually find her at home, giving a private lesson. And now, after what had happened, if she had no lesson scheduled, I was afraid I might find her again with Ray Newell, or even with someone else, if she'd moved on from him, as she'd promised me she would, when she saw I was so upset. Perhaps she'd finally decided though, that she didn't want to be alone anymore, as my dad had suggested, when we'd had our little talk. I wondered if he'd spoken to her and she'd told him that.

  I knew though, that on certain days of the week, I could usually count on being the only one at dad's house in the afternoon.

Clare had gone back to teaching at the medical center and had a class scheduled on Friday afternoons. It wouldn't get over until four-thirty, and then she'd take the train home. Given the time of day, and the fact that she had to transfer to the Red Line downtown, the trip could easily take an hour or more. Plus, she might have to take the bus from the Square, like I was, since my dad was staying a little late, until he came to pick me up to take me to dinner with my mom. I thought I should have a little time alone, before either of them arrived.

    I got off the bus at the corner, walked past the Quik Mart, and then crossed Mass Ave. to walk down Norland, which would bring me closest to my dad's house. As I was approaching home—my sometimes home—from a distance I saw a woman who looked like Clare going up the front steps to the enclosed porch. Why would Clare be home now? Had no one showed up for her class this afternoon? It wasn't a holiday week or any special day, as far as I knew, so her students wouldn't have been missing. I hoped she hadn't dismissed them early because she felt sick. I'd been worried about her ever since she'd lost the baby. She'd been in a daze most of the time, not her chatty, helpful self. I knew that another teacher—a substitute—had replaced her while she'd been on leave. But had she maybe been permanently replaced now, because she'd missed too many classes? Clare wasn't on a medical leave payroll, I knew, because she worked freelance for some private company that had a contract with the hospital. She loved working with those students from China, Haiti, Central America, and other places around the world, and she'd be crushed if she couldn't go back, if that teacher who'd substituted for her had actually replaced her.

    As I got closer to the house, I saw that this was not Clare, who still had kept a little of the extra weight she'd put on in the months when she'd been pregnant. This was a much thinner, and younger woman, someone who looked like a teenager, about my age. And when she turned around, because she'd heard me approaching the steps to the porch, I saw that this was definitely true. I recognized her. She was the girl I'd been seeing hanging around The Pit, the same one, who sometimes sat in the back of the auditorium at the Conservatory during a rehearsal. What was she doing here!?

I saw now that she really did resemble Clare a little, being the same height, and having exactly the same peachy complexion. I'd been fooled, too, seeing this girl from the back; the humidity had curled and frizzed her hair in exactly the same way Clare's hair would rebel in this weather, too.

As if she knew that I wasn't the person she was looking for, she turned away without even a casual *Hello*. I climbed the steps to the porch and saw she was not ringing the doorbell for Mrs. Cook, who lived on the first floor, but rather, that she was bending down to the mail slot in the front door that led up to my dad's apartment. She was trying to push through a large envelope.

"Hello?" I said, and she did not let go of her envelope but stood up, still holding it firmly in her grasp.

"Hello," she said, looking back at me. "Do you live here?"

I wondered if she'd been stalking me.

"Who are you looking for?" I asked, not wanting to reveal any information until I knew just what business the girl had, being here. In situations like this, Dad always advised me to get the facts first.

"Clare. Clare Rantel," she said. "I sent her a note letting her know I'd be around and was hoping to talk with her. I'm not sure if she got it, since I didn't hear back from her. You aren't her daughter, are you?"

"And she knows you how?" I asked, still not feeling right about identifying myself for this stranger.

"I met her at Diamond Street Center. I went there about volunteering. That was a while ago. I had to leave town, so I didn't follow up right away." She hesitated, and then matter-of-factly said, "My mother died. I'm moving here from California."

"I'm sorry about your mother," I said, feeling bad now that I'd been giving her a hard time, being so evasive. I'd always been the kind of person to whom strangers told personal things—people sitting next to me on buses or trains, and last summer, when I'd been on vacation in Maine with Mom, I'd gone for a walk alone, and just as I turned down the avenue toward the cottage, a woman ran out of the front door of her cabin and bounded down the steps, stopping me in my tracks, crying and telling me that her father had just died. I was upset, not knowing how to respond to the grieving woman I didn't know.

"Sorry," I said again to the girl—a teenager actually, I thought. "So are you staying with your dad?" I asked.

"No," is all she said.

"Clare's not home," I said. "I think she's still at work."

"Will she be home soon?"

I shrugged. "Depends. She's taking public transportation. You never know."

The girl smiled. "Right," she said, holding out the manila envelope she'd decided not to drop through the mail slot, when I'd startled her.

"Could you give this to her, if you're going to see her?"

"Sure," I said. "What's your name?"

"I'm Judy Kneeland," she answered.

"Okay, then. I'm Danielle, by the way."

I was feeling that I'd been rude to her and didn't want her to leave with a bad impression. I didn't want her to mention to Clare, that I hadn't been very polite.

"Is Clare Rantel your mother?" she asked.

"Sort of. She's my stepmom. She's married to my dad. When I first saw you, as I got near the house, I thought you were Clare," I said.

"Do you live with your dad and not your mom?"

"Well, both," I said. "They share me."

I was unable to avoid sighing, when I said this.

Judy Kneeland didn't look like she was leaving soon. Too many questions, I thought, and she kept on with them.

"Oh. Have they been together for a long time?"

I thought that was a weird question. Why would this stranger care about that?

"Why do you ask?" I said.

"Oh, I was just thinking about my dad leaving my mom to live with some woman in the U.K. when I was little. I haven't seen him since then."

"I was little, too."

"You're lucky though that you live with both of them still," she said.

"I guess," I said.

It wasn't always easy, the back and forth, I knew, but this girl seemed sad, and I didn't think it was only because her mother had died. What must it be like? She was an orphan now.

I was about to ask her who she was living with, when she turned to leave. She didn't seem any older than I was and wasn't it illegal to live on you own if you weren't eighteen? Wouldn't she need a guardian? Maybe she had an aunt or somebody living around here.

"Okay, then," Judy said. "Thanks for delivering the envelope."

I nodded, smiled, and then watched her walk away. She stopped when she got to the sidewalk and turned back, not to look at me again, I didn't think, but it seemed like she was getting a long view of the house itself. I waved and she went on her way.

Who was this girl? And why would she care that I'm Clare's stepdaughter anyway? Probably it made her feel sad, not to have one parent, when I had three. She must be feeling abandoned now, with no one. I hoped she at least had a nice aunt or uncle who'd taken her in.

Nineteen

Clare

"Teacher! Teacher!"

Without looking to see who was calling out, I knew the unmistakable, always sweetly raspy voice of Mei Lin, the youngest of my students in this class.

While keeping on with setting up, removing workbooks from my canvas tote bag and distributing them around the room, I said, "You can call me Clare."

How many times had I said this to my Chinese students? It wasn't just Mei who resisted.

Of all the students this semester, only Margaret Kwan in one of my other classes, who'd lived in the U.S. the longest, seemed to enjoy complying, even emphasizing the hard C in Clare, when she spoke my name; when she called it out, she sounded the way someone wanting to share a tidbit of gossip might, in order to get my attention.

I stopped what I was doing and looked at Mei Lin, a characteristic scowl spread across her wide face. Her expression might have let me know that something was amiss, except that Mei Lin's scowl was as permanent as her sweet, raspy voice—not that she had a sour personality; in fact, she was the liveliest person in this class. I thought that perhaps she had some nerve or muscle damage to the face, like the network television news anchor who had—not a permanent scowl, which would have been more appropriate, given the nightly news reports— instead though, he always wore a fixed smile, even when reporting the world's latest horrific events and atrocities: famine, gun violence, murder, killer earthquake, or bombing. Yet even though Mei Lin's scowl held no foreboding meaning, her way of pleading for my attention right now did. I realized that I'd indeed been too optimistic to think that I could make up for any lost class time with today's lesson. Something was the matter, and that meant it had to be addressed and I'd accomplish little of my goal of catching up after missing nearly two weeks of classes.

The sharing session that I'd instituted before we would begin each day's lesson and activity had really taken off. At the start of every class, I'd been encouraging the students to ask questions having to do with ordinary difficulties they encountered—at their children's schools, at a supermarket outside of Chinatown, at the DMV, anything anywhere that was related to adjusting to life in the United States. I wanted them to receive the help, information, or goods they sought, as well as the respect everyone deserves. Admittedly, the sharing routine had gotten somewhat out of hand. Discussions seemed to take up nearly one third of class time—and sometimes longer, if a topic interested the whole group. But I kept on with the practice, because what was the point of learning a language if it didn't help you to survive in the world in which it was spoken? I didn't want to teach them English the way I'd learned French—memorizing vocabulary, verb declensions, and La Fontaine's *Fables*, never having real conversations, only pre-written dialogues, so I was always translating in my head, unable to think in the language, and therefore helpless to spontaneously apply it to everyday life. I wanted my students to have what I wished I'd achieved—fluency.

In truth, this was a survival skills class as much as one given for mountaineers or scouts hiking the Appalachian Trail. These students needed to communicate in their new life and to understand a culture that too often seemed mysterious to them. If they couldn't, it was as bad as being lost in the woods or going off a mountain trail and not being able to find the way back.

Their questions generally did come out of real life situations, more often than from the material covered in a lesson. One of them would walk into class and simply blurt out, "What meaning?"

They would plead actually, the way Mei Lin had just now pleaded for my attention. They brought letters from the schools their children attended, housing leases, medical reports, and court and immigration documents.

Today, there were two problems, Mei Lin said. With the first, sadness came rushing back to me, the way it would—in waves—when something set me off, triggering my grief.

The first had to do with Carlene, who had announced a few weeks back that she and her husband were sending their six month old baby boy to live in China with Carlene's mother, as a way of avoiding childcare costs; that way, she and her husband could keep working and save for the down payment on a house. I supposed that Carlene's mother was thrilled that she was going to have her grandson with her, happy to introduce him to the family and their cultural practices and preferences. Seeing Carlene now for the first time since I'd lost my baby, I wanted to tell her not to be so foolish, that she'd miss her boy. And what if something awful were to happen to him while he was away?

Mei Lin pointed, to tell me to sit down in the empty chair next to Carlene at the big round table, where we all sat for class. Carlene had an envelope in front of her. I saw from the cellophane window, and the return address for Metro Labs, that it was either a bill or a medical report. *Please don't let this be bad news I have to convey.*

"What is this?" Mei said, like an angry parent defending a child.

It surely was a lab report. Carlene was squinting, scrunching up her forehead, and when she did, she created lines like an old woman would have, although her skin was smooth, shiny, and youthful-looking.

Opening the envelope, I saw that it was not a report of the results of a mammogram, a precancerous lesion, or worse. It was confirmation of pregnancy.

I froze, seeing it, then quickly put the letter back into the envelope. My student saw the baby she already had, as interfering with her American Dream, and now she was pregnant with another child, a child not planned, the way she'd carefully planned how she was going to amass the down payment for a house in the crazy Boston Real Estate market.

It was shaping up to be a very difficult first day back.

"Excuse me," I said, getting up and rushing to leave the room before tears began to flow.

Somehow, I propelled myself past the other students seated around the table, all of them puzzled, pushing their chairs back, too, as if they were all going to get up and try to follow me, find out what was wrong. Out the door, I broke into a jog going down the corridor—not to the nearest rest room—but to the larger women's lounge that was farther away, some place where they might not think to come looking for me.

I burst through the swinging door and ran smack into Margaret Kwan from the medical terminology class. She was standing, drying her hands with a paper towel, in my way, as I tried to get to the sink to splash cold water on my face.

Margaret's expression showed that she was not just surprised to see me, but she saw that I was crying.

I looked away from her to the mirror, saw my red face, and tried to calm myself to regain some composure.

"Hello, Margaret," I said, looking at her in the mirror.

I moved back a bit from the sink and turned to her.

"You're back, Clare. What's the matter? Are you feeling sick?" Margaret asked in perfect English. "I can help," she said.

"No, no, no one can help. Nothing can be done. Nothing at all," I said.

I was now openly crying again, and I moved closer to the sink and began splashing cold water on my face.

"This is just life, that's all," I said through my tears. "I lost my baby."

"But you are strong," Margaret said, sounding like her usual Spartan self. "Sometimes, I don't think," she stumbled and then tried again. "Sometimes, I don't think I can survive something terrible, but then..."

She hesitated, looked at me and shook her head. She went on to finish her sentence.

"Then I know I am strong," Margaret sighed.

I said nothing, anxious for her to leave. I took a paper towel from the wall dispenser and patted my face dry, intending to go into a stall, so that Margaret might get the hint that I needed privacy. But she remained standing in my way, preventing me from doing so. She began to talk again, speaking words so compelling that I had no choice other than to listen to her.

"I lost my baby, too," Margaret said. "I don't know how,

but after some time, I get stronger. I still care, but don't feel so bad anymore. After you realize, I can't do anything to change what happens, you feel better. That's life. You are right about that."

It was a pessimistic outlook, and I wasn't exactly stunned to hear this from her. Yet, Margaret had never been so personal. I knew nothing of her life. She'd seemed to be all business in class, focused on learning as much as she could, and hoping to advance in her job. But now, I saw her determination and strong personality differently. Had Margaret, who'd seemed always so much in control, capable, and ambitious, adopted this way of being in order to keep her deepest feelings of hurt at bay? Is this what I would have to do, too? Unlike Margaret, I'd always tried to clarify my feelings, and to express them. I thought I did so successfully, most of the time.

"First day back is the hardest," Margaret said.

That's what Dr. Aviva had said at my recent appointment, when I told her I'd be starting back to work this week. I knew that there would be many difficult days ahead, especially now that Ray wanted to find my first child.

"My baby girl was adopted," Margaret went on. "Too many girls in China."

"Oh, Margaret," I said, moved by her revelation, and thinking of my own adopted child. I could not tell her though. "That's awful. I'm so sorry you went through that," I said, knowing in my bones, how that had been for her.

"Long, long time ago, but thank you," she said. "American couple took her. Maybe they live in Boston," she said shrugging. "I don't know. I will never know. That's what I think."

Hearing Margaret's story did inspire a bit of fortitude. I knew what she felt. She was a kindred soul. She wanted to help. She didn't know it, but she had already helped me, making me realize that I had the opportunity to find my child, while she did not. Ray wanted to help in a search, wanted to know his child.

I saw another way she might help. Margaret knew Carlene's story from the semester before, when she'd been incorrectly placed in the same class with her, simply because the correct course had not been available at a time when Margaret could get away from her job to attend classes. *Something better than nothing*, she'd said, when I told her she belonged in a much more advanced class. Margaret had helped that day when I hadn't understood and was trying to interpret Carlene's plan to send her baby to China. It was Margaret, who had straightened me out, when I'd thought that Carlene was saying that she would be going on a family vacation, so that the child could meet her grandmother. I explained to Margaret what had just happened in the classroom that had set me off, bringing on this bout of sadness.

Margaret shook her head in recognition of the irony of this happening today, my first day back after losing the baby. No doubt she also saw the irony in Carlene getting pregnant again after making such a detailed plan for care of the child she had now, so that she and her husband could keep working without the cost of day care.

"Are you on lunch break? Could you come talk with her?"

I thought she might take Carlene for a walk, let her know about the lab report, so that I wouldn't have to be the one to interpret and discuss it with her, I explained. I didn't think I could do it, without breaking down again.

"I just can't. She wants to know what the report says, but it's too soon for me to talk about this with her. It hurts too much to think she won't want this baby, when I wanted mine so much."

"I'm on break," Margaret said. "I can go back with you, talk to her, take her out to the coffee shop, some place she can stay and not go back to class. She won't want to go back when she finds out. She will be upset, too."

Margaret had stepped up again to help, just as she had before with Carlene, and also on the day when Martin had come to pick me up, to take me to Dr. Aviva. I was especially thankful for her help that day I'd had to leave class in pain, the miscarriage taking place, and Margaret rising to the occasion, taking over, teaching the class, reviewing the medical terms with the others. If I were the office manager, I'd give her the promotion she so deserved. I felt very grateful to have her as a student and ally—a friend really. How would I have ever handled this situation today, if she hadn't appeared and offered to help. I might have lost this contract, if I hadn't gone back to class. The students might have been so worried that they'd go to HR, reporting that I'd left class and hadn't come back. They would have wanted only to know if I was all right, but HR might have felt that I'd abandoned my responsibilities.

We waited a couple of minutes before returning. Margaret, seeing that my eyeliner was smudged, offered to fix it. After she did, I tried to make myself look presentable, combing strands of my hair with Margaret's comb. I took a few deep breaths and then we went off together down the corridor, back to the classroom.

Although the students looked curious, no one asked what the matter was. Perhaps they'd figured it out, while I was gone. Carlene might have showed the lab report around and some of them might have been able to interpret it. But if they had, Carlene looked like she was still waiting for me to tell her what it meant. Maybe none of the others wanted to break the news to her.

Carlene held the white business envelope in her hand, and looking at me, raised her eyebrows slightly, a reminder that I should pick up where I'd left off with her.

Seeing her expression of expectation, Margaret spoke to Carlene in Mandarin, asking her, I hoped, if she wanted to leave to have coffee with her. Margaret pointed at the envelope and Carlene picked it up then, looking at me, as if I ought to be able to understand what Margaret had said, even though I didn't know the language. But then, I thought that she was waiting for me to confirm that she was free to go, that it was all right for her to leave with Margaret.

"Okay?" Margaret said.

I nodded.

"Thank you," I said, as the two of them headed out the door.

If I'd expected to get right into the lesson I'd prepared, it was not to be. Mei Lin began presenting yet another problem for discussion, another situation to straighten out. Hopefully this would be ordinary, and could take my mind off the pain of loss that had overtaken me just now. Because I felt emotionally spent, it was actually better to continue the sharing of news, when the students took over. Carlene's situation had been an exception. News sharing generally required less effort than if I were to introduce a new lesson.

There was always something challenging for my students in negotiating their new lives. Last week, it was a charlatan dentist, but another week, it might be a car dealer, a landlord, a school principal. In one instance a miscommunication had even led to a student's arrest. On days like this one when there was a student with an extreme situation to deal with, I generally felt that it was simply a waste of time to have carefully planned lessons.

Once all the students' questions had been answered, I fought off thoughts of Ray and his desire to search for our child. I was planning to talk him out of it during dinner. It was the reason I'd agreed to meet him after class. But now, after my talk with Margaret, I thought of how sad she was, never able to know what became of her daughter, since the adoption had happened in China. I had the opportunity now to find my daughter, with Ray's help. I just didn't know if I had the courage to accept what might result from our search. It was a real possibility that my marriage could be in jeopardy, once Martin learned that what we had, had been built on dishonesty. He'd been thinking these ten years that Danielle was the only child I'd ever parented.

I quickly distributed the books and announced the page for practicing dialogues employing the past tense, wanting to review the last lesson I'd taught before my leave. I would let the textbook lead the rest of the class. My heart wasn't in teaching today.

Twenty

Ray

I took a look at myself in the rearview mirror before getting out of the car in the Chinatown garage. I looked bedraggled, which was no surprise. After I'd left Clare, I went back to my office, and found a message from my father's doctor. He'd called to say that my father had only a couple of days left to live. His death hadn't sounded imminent, so I'd decided not to go to the hospital today, that I had my life to attend to this afternoon.

I'd never expected to hear what Clare had told me. I had, for years, believed that my unanswered letters had been a message that she no longer cared about me and had moved on, not that she'd been sent away to have a baby—our baby—how unbelievable this all was! How terrible that my letters to her were most likely destroyed by her father, so she'd had no idea of my whereabouts, and no explanation whatsoever for why I'd left without her. Somewhere out there I had a child, a teenager. I was running on empty right now. There was a burning in my chest: the questions, the confusion, too much coffee, and missing lunch—and a longing for what might have been—all of it fueling a feeling of anxiety.

I was on my way to meet Clare, walking quickly down busy sidewalks, dodging older shoppers strolling along, or stopping to inspect crates of fruit spilling out onto the sidewalk from produce stores. I skirted around clots of young men outside restaurants and small cafes, not wanting to be late. I wondered if she considered that I might not show up.

I didn't have to wait for her. She was already standing beside the archway of red and gold at Chinatown gate, where we'd agreed to meet after class. She looked worried and vulnerable, as if letting go of her long-kept secret had sucked the spirit right out of her.

"You knew I'd come, right?" I said when she looked startled

to see me.

I guess she was lost in thought, just as I'd been.

"Well, you didn't come that other time," she said. "It crossed my mind that all I've told you might have been just too much for you."

I reached for her to hug her. I couldn't help myself. She didn't resist. I wondered how she ever got through her class this afternoon.

I held on a long time, before she pulled away. I saw that she was crying and thought of the night I'd told her I was leaving for Canada, reminded that she'd cried at dinner at the restaurant, then after, pleaded for me to take her with me. And I'd promised I would, yet I'd gone on without her. I could only imagine how awful that was for her, and how much more difficult it became once she'd learned that she was pregnant.

I couldn't imagine how she'd lived with such a secret until now, not telling a soul, she said. What did it mean about her marriage, to have hidden something so big from her husband? What kind of person was he to her, that she'd be afraid to tell him, I wondered. He seemed to me like a good man. He'd been invested in Eric's case.

"Here I am, just as I said. I'm showing up," I said. "You know, I did want to wait for you that other time, but I was told it was too risky to try to cross the border with a van full of guys and just one girl."

"I suppose that would have raised questions," she agreed. "But at the time, I didn't think of that. I was thinking only about me, about what I was going through."

"We can understand things now that we didn't back then," I said.

"Do you understand?" she asked. "Seems to me, that things get more complicated as time goes on."

"I don't mean to lessen what you went through at the time, or after—not at all. It must have been very difficult," I said. "I'm sure it still is, especially now."

"I was thinking, maybe I should just go home now, Ray," Clare said. "I don't know how to make things right. I don't think I can," she said.

"You can, if we find her."

"But we might not," Clare said. "Then, where would that leave me? Can't you think of me? Of my life?"

"We'll go back to Cambridge. We don't have to eat dinner here. We'll figure things out."

"I don't know about that," she said. "I don't think we can."

We were walking toward the parking garage. As we approached, I saw Clare look around, as if she were disoriented. But she knew Chinatown, had told me she'd taught here for years, and that her students often treated her to Dim Sum and pastries from restaurants and bakeries here. But, if I were honest with myself, I felt, too, as if I were walking in some dream, or on another plane of reality. Clare's demeanor probably meant she felt the same way, suddenly not grounded, like there had been some major shift in her reality. Neither of us knew what would result from this reunion and what I now knew, but I was grateful at least, to try to set things straight with Clare, if she would let me. It seemed to be her purpose as well, in telling me. I wasn't sure though, that she'd feel she had set things right. She was still keeping her secret from Martin and the others. Setting things straight meant for me, that I would try to find our daughter. Clare thought that such a search would do just the opposite for her, causing a major disruption in her marriage and family life with Danielle.

It was rush hour, so the ride across the Charles took much longer than usual. We rode in silence. When I finally drove into Kendall Square, she said, "It's better to be back in Cambridge."

I headed to Mass. Ave. at Central Square, turning off, heading toward my apartment.

"Where are you going?" she asked. "What restaurant are you thinking of?"

"Chez Moi," I said. "I've got stuff to eat, if you're hungry," I said. "You must be."

I knew that neither of us had eaten anything for lunch, as we'd planned to picnic on the waterfront. Once we began to talk that never happened.

"No, maybe I'll just eat at home. Why don't you let me out here. It's close to the subway. I can get home on my own," Clare said.

I kept driving, and when I got to my apartment building, I

parked the car. Clare moved, as if she were going to get out.

"Please wait. Let's talk," I said.

"I have to figure this out without you," she said.

"Clare, I can't ignore what I know now. I can't push this away, as you did."

"You blame me, don't you?" she asked.

I shook my head, exasperated, not knowing how to read her.

"I'm confused. Don't you get that? This isn't just about you, you know. I actually thought you'd walk away, hearing what I had to tell you, and instead, you want to know your daughter. I thought maybe you cherished your freedom too much."

"That's true. It's not just about me. There's a girl out there somewhere, who doesn't know who her parents are."

"Maybe she doesn't want to," Clare said. "Have you considered that? Maybe her life is just fine without the two of us crashing into it, complicating things for her. She might be better off, not knowing either of us."

"Too many maybes," I said. "And I for one, won't be better off not knowing. And I doubt you will be either."

"I have others to think of. I'm not a free-wheeling jazz musician. Even though I've lost our baby, I have a home, a family—a husband and his daughter that I'm a parent to, and I don't think you're considering that."

A car pulled up beside us, seeing the lights on, and the two of us inside, the driver waited, figuring we were leaving. I waved him away.

I shut off the ignition and the lights. The interior light came on and then went off automatically. We sat there in the dark, countering each other's reasons, neither of us sure of what would come of Clare's revelation.

"You don't really think that now that you've spilled your secret to me, that you can live continuing to pretend to the others, do you? You'll still be keeping the same secret. And maybe it's worse that those closest to you don't know your lie."

"It's not a lie," she said, angrily. "It's a secret."

"A lie to protect a secret," I said. "Martin thinks that the only baby you lost is his, and that's not true. You've perpetrated a lie, don't you see? And what does that say about trust and intimacy between you?"

Clare wasn't crying anymore. She was simply trying to defend herself from the truth. She looked at me straight on, and I thought that perhaps she was realizing something important, that the truth could be dealt with, even if it was painful. She could face up to whatever might come of it.

"You don't have to justify why things happened as they did, but you can still make things right going forward," I told her.

"I don't know. I don't know if I'm strong enough," she said.

I laughed.

"Not strong enough? Wow. Think of what you've had to deal with. You don't think you're strong?"

I gestured toward the front entrance of my building. "Come, have something to eat with me. You'll feel better. Let's keep talking."

She stopped resisting then, and I wasn't sure why. I hoped I'd reached her, that I'd persuaded her to really make things right, for herself and for others.

My apartment was on the top floor and we climbed the stairs. I saw that she was lagging behind, hesitant when we reached the second floor landing.

"I rented the penthouse," I said, joking.

When we got there I unlocked the door. It was hot inside; the windows had been closed all day, so I went around opening them. As I did, Clare walked around the apartment, looking into a few rooms, seeing how I lived, I guess. On the walls there were framed photos taken at Clubs in Montreal, and some at the University in Toronto. She asked about them, and I gave her the stories to go with them. In the kitchen, she opened the fridge to see what there was to eat.

"There's always grilled cheese," she said.

"I can do better than that. In the freezer there are several slices of real pizza from a good Italian place in the North End. We can heat them up, and I've got the makings of a salad, I'm sure."

I figured we could both use a stiff drink and so I poured a couple of strong vodka cocktails. We sat drinking them in the den, waiting for the pizza to get hot. When it was, I found two glasses and opened a bottle of red wine to have with dinner—such as it was—and set everything on the table. Maybe it was the fact that Clare hadn't had lunch, so the wine went to her head, but she began to let down her defenses as we kept talking about our daughter. As if fortified by drink, she announced that she would no longer resist me. I thought she meant that she'd given up her argument against finding the girl.

She stood and walked behind me, and when I turned to point and said "on your left," thinking it was the bathroom she was after, I saw her standing in the bedroom, looking out the window at the sunset.

"Well?" she said, turning back to me. "Come see."

It was more than sunset that had lured her into the bedroom.

"Did you think we'd end up here?" she asked, tilting her head.

"Is that why you thought I asked you to come upstairs," I said. "Is it why you agreed?"

Maybe I was an ass not to realize she'd have expected I'd set this up, that I was interested in her, not our daughter—or that I wanted both, for the three of us to be together. In fact, the more she wavered about finding our daughter, the more I wanted to.

Although I hadn't planned this and I doubted she had, I wasn't averse to seeing where it might lead, allowing that that might be the best thing to do, even knowing that the ramifications of such a frolic would be complicated and even difficult. I remembered someone once saying to me, quoting someone else no doubt, *you'll never have relationships like those of your youth*. It was true that not a single lover I'd had since her, was a match for the excitement of my encounters with Clare. My affairs were pleasurable but fleeting. I wondered about a couple of my friends, who'd married high school sweethearts, whether they'd sustained that heady feeling of being in the throes of love. Were they the long-married? I thought perhaps they were.

If I felt willing but somewhat hesitant, Clare seemed sure of herself. I would let her lead And I'd follow her inclination.

I didn't light the candle although it was getting dark and

there was one on the nightstand next to the bed.

"Let's just lie here," she said.

And we did for a long time. She let her head rest on my shoulder.

"I fit right in the nook of your shoulder," she said. "I can hear your heart. So loud and beating very strong. Maybe too fast?"

I listened to her breathing, heard how after a few minutes it became regular, and then mine did, too, and we were in synch with each other.

"I'm content just like this," I said.

I did not want to take advantage. I wanted it to be her choice, if anything more than this were to happen. I thought maybe she wanted only comforting, some relief from her troubles, but I wondered what that might mean to her. I knew I felt differently with her than with Veronica, and differently too, than when we were together in our youth. For me, there was no longer that naïve hopefulness that marks young love.

It got dark as we lay there. The longer we did, my feeling grew stronger, that here was something I had been missing. There was an openness between us, and I thought she felt that, too. Lying together seemed a test of it, the waiting. She lifted her head then and turned toward me, letting me know that any confusion she might have felt before had vanished, the same as any hesitance on my part.

I touched her body as a blind man might. Fit and muscular, she was no longer the delicate girl I remembered lying with. She had a woman's body now, full and imbued with substance. We weren't fumbling teenagers in the backseat of my dad's Galaxy, Clare's arm pinched against the door handle and one of my legs off the seat, reaching down to the floor. We were experienced lovers. We were adults with accomplishments and responsibilities. I hoped she wouldn't think too much about the latter.

We had room to allow our bodies the freedom we never had as teenagers. A bed was a glorious thing. It not only gave us space to move, it held us firmly, and allowed me to offer Clare the pleasure she wanted, the comfort of this moment. I didn't fall asleep after and stayed alert. Clare seemed to be completely sober, but I was afraid that guilt would set in for her. She had enough of that. Yet, I couldn't help saying what I felt.

"You don't have to go home now," I said.

"Oh, I do actually. I definitely do. I didn't intend to take this beyond talk."

"I enjoyed it, but I wanted what you wanted. And it wasn't my intention either, bringing you here. Once I heard about our daughter, it changed everything I might have been thinking about you. If you have to go, let me take you home."

"You'd better not."

"I'll drop you around the corner from your house. We can be discreet," I said.

Clare stood before the bureau mirror, leaning into it, as if examining the circles under her eyes, a tell-tale sign that she hadn't been sleeping well. Or was she looking for evidence of the effects of this day and what more might come of it? And was she wondering, too, whether her eyes would be telling to Martin, or if she could hide this secret, too.

She fluffed her hair and asked if I had a comb. I found one and began gently combing her hair. She took me in her arms and we held each other.

"I wish you didn't have to go," I said.

I held her away from me, held her hands as I looked at her pretty face. I could still see in it, that girl I knew so long ago.

"I know you do. I know," was the last thing she said, and then we went out of the house and down the stairs to the street. She insisted on taking the subway, and I had to let her go.

Twenty-One

Martin

The call from Danielle came when I was going over Ray Newell's statement on behalf of Eric Belmonte. He'd done an excellent job of depicting his old friend as a decent human being. I left a message for him, that I'd deposed Eric's psychiatrist, but that the prosecution wanted an independent evaluation for Eric, and the judge had agreed, meaning that he was being sent to the State Hospital for observation. I let Newell know that if he'd been planning to visit him again, as he'd written in the note included with the witness statement, that he was already on his way there.

I found the message slip on my chair. That was what Dorothy did for messages she thought were important, not wanting them lost in the stacks of papers and other messages on my desk.

Call me immediately, was the message, and Dorothy had written N.B. next to the time of the call from Danielle. Now what? I looked at my watch; she'd called fifteen minutes earlier. I hoped this was nothing serious. If so, a lot might have happened in fifteen minutes.

When Danielle answered, she sounded out of breath.

"What's wrong? Are you all right? Is Clare all right?"

"No, I'm not all right. Nothing is. You'd better come home, not work late tonight."

Before I could ask, *What's going on*, she'd hung up.

I packed up a few files and left a note on Dorothy's desk to let her know I was gone for the day. For once, I was glad she was away from her desk, so I didn't have to explain what I didn't know. Ever since Clare had lost the baby, whenever calls came from home, Dorothy—or whoever else was covering the desk—would offer support, asking if everything was okay. And if I had to leave early after a call, they'd wish me *Good Luck*. I appreciated their empathy, but it seemed that these days, all anyone thought of when they saw me, was some crisis they thought I must be dealing with—except, of course, clients and witnesses, and prosecuting attorneys, who put more and more demands on my time and energy. Pleasure, or just living on an even keel for a while, seemed impossible now. I was needed at home more, and found it increasingly difficult to be there, with my work load as it was. When I was there, I wasn't there; I was buried under papers in my study.

Getting home, I walked in the door and Danielle, who'd been waiting to pounce, it seemed, demanded, "Where's Clare?" I hadn't even taken my jacket off.

"How about a *Hello*, Danielle?" I said. I explained that Clare was with her students in Chinatown. "They're having a *Welcome Back* dinner for her."

"Well, it seems she'll have some welcoming back to do herself," Danielle said.

"What's going on here, Danielle?" I asked.

She was holding a large manila envelope, and flapping it around.

"A girl came here this afternoon. She left this for Clare."

She slapped the envelope with her free hand, like it was a stranger offering unwanted attention.

"Hey, sit down, kiddo. Calm down, Danielle," I said, as gently as I could manage, putting an arm around her shoulder to lead her over to a chair.

She pulled away and went to sit on the couch. I sat opposite her in the chair, perplexed by her outburst and wondering what could be in the envelope that had set her off like this. Perhaps the girl had been rude to her. But no, that wasn't it. It had to do with what was inside the envelope.

"I opened it," she said. "Maybe you think I shouldn't have, but I did. And I'm glad I did. Because, if I hadn't, both of you would probably continue to keep this secret from me."

"What are you talking about? Calm down, will you? Tell me what's going on here," I said.

She pulled at the fringe on the pillow she was leaning on, tying it in knots. She fidgeted like that, when she was really upset, a nervous habit.

"Don't pretend to me anymore. I don't want anyone doing that to me anymore. Not my mother, not you, and not Clare. This is your secret, too, but I know now."

I reached for the envelope, mystified, as to what she could have possibly learned from what was inside.

"Give it to me. And you're right. You shouldn't open mail that belongs to other people. It's a federal offense."

"It was hand delivered anyway," she said. "So it isn't. And now you're doing the same thing I did, by opening it."

I took out of the envelope, a sheaf of legal-looking documents, and saw that they were adoption papers. The name on them—*Judy Kneeland*—meant nothing to me. I looked up at Danielle, saw that she was tapping impatiently on the wooden arm of the couch, waiting for my response. I examined the papers and saw that Clare's name was listed on the line for *Mother*. The word pulsed with questions, for me, too.

"This must be for someone else," I said. "Who is this? Who is she? This girl? What did she say about Clare?"

"Seriously? You didn't know about this? Maybe the real question is, who is Clare? I feel like I don't even know her."

I felt a tightness in my chest, and I tried to take deep breaths. They sounded like sighs. I hadn't even taken my jacket off. I did now, and I loosened my tie. I glanced again at the birth certificate, afraid of what else I might discover.

February 1969. Clare would have been seventeen then. The line for *Father* was left blank. This can't be, I thought. There must be some mix-up, some other Clare Rantel must be the mother of this girl.

Danielle persisted.

"So, tell me. Why has this been a secret you've kept from me?"

"I knew nothing about it," I said. "I don't know what else to tell you, Danielle."

I heard footsteps on the stairs.

"We'll find out what this is," I promised.

When Clare entered the apartment, the two of us were sitting in silence, still in the living room, waiting for her. Neither of us had turned on a lamp, although daylight had waned. She seemed more upbeat—perkier—than she'd been in recent days. I wondered what she'd had to drink—maybe one of those strong umbrella cocktails. Or, did her mood maybe have something to do with this Judy Kneeland? Maybe she didn't have dinner with her students at China Pearl after all.

"Is everything okay? You two are looking pretty serious. And why are you sitting here in the dark?"

She switched on the overhead light and it felt like we were in a police interrogation room.

I cringed at the brightness.

"Shut that off!" Danielle hollered at her.

Clare shut it off and put on a table lamp instead. She gave Danielle a stare that meant she thought she was out of line, and she looked to me for some correction of Danielle, though I didn't offer one.

I handed her the envelope, not letting on that Danielle and I already knew of its contents.

"Not sure what this is, but some girl Danielle's age was here this afternoon apparently, and dropped it off for you. You've met," I said.

"Oh, must be work related. Diamond Street probably."

She opened the envelope, looking, and then quickly put the papers back inside, obviously rattled. She fastened the clasp.

"Just a resume from a girl who wants to volunteer to tutor," she lied. "She'd written to me, saying she'd drop it off."

"She lies! What did I tell you?" Danielle said, turning to me. "I know what's in that envelope," she went on. "That's not true. And I talked to the girl who left it. She lied, too. She said her mother had died. But she didn't die, did she Clare? That was her adopted mother who died, wasn't it? I don't want any more secrets!" she yelled.

Danielle stormed out then, not waiting for Clare to answer, leaving me to it.

"Wait, Danielle!" she called to her. "She talked to you? I can explain everything, Danielle. Please," Clare begged.

We heard the bedroom door slam shut.

I was shocked and angry, too. If the papers were meant for some other Clare Rantel, she'd have expressed confusion, acted baffled, inspecting them.

"How can this be, Clare? Why would you ever keep something like this from me?"

Clare collapsed in the chair across from me. She looked tired and any perkiness she'd had, when returning from dinner, had dissipated.

"Did she find you—this Judy Kneeland? Is that why you called to say you wouldn't be home, that you were having dinner with your students? Is that who you were with? Was that a lie, too, or were you with someone else maybe?"

I wondered, if this girl hadn't shown up now, would Clare have ever told me about her? What kind of trouble was the girl in anyway? What did she want from Clare, showing up now, after the mother who'd adopted her had died?

"Martin, please," she said. "I'll tell you everything. I was afraid. I didn't know if she'd ever come back, especially after so long. I had no idea where she was, who'd adopted her. So, why would it matter if I kept it secret? That's what I was thinking."

"Is this why you didn't consider us having a child until this year? After ten years of marriage? I thought you wanted a child—for us—*not* to make up for one you thought was lost. How could you?"

"I did. I did want that child for us. I was afraid," she said through tears.

She said she hadn't intended to keep the child a secret from me, that at first, she was afraid that I'd think less of her, if I knew of her past, that telling me might be the end of us.

"And I was afraid, too," she said, "that you'd always be thinking of me in that situation, when I was so young and scared and sad, and that you might feel pity or sympathy for me, because of what I went through. I didn't want that. I wanted our marriage to be about us, not what had happened to me in the past."

She explained that she thought she'd tell me after Danielle had gotten used to her being around, and when Veronica had accepted the shared custody arrangement, and Danielle had adjusted to the divorce. But Danielle hadn't really ever become adjusted to being shifted back and forth between households, so finally, she said, she'd realized that if she were ever going to have a child with me, that she'd better hurry up and get pregnant.

"It took a long time for me to get to that point. I'm still not sure that Danielle ever really accepted me. And now she has real evidence to feel justified in that. I've tried with her. I've really tried. You know that, Martin."

I got up and picked the envelope up off the coffee table.

"Don't," she said.

"I trusted you. How can I now?"

I paced the floor. I couldn't sit down. Comfort was not possible right now. I thought I'd be questioning the truth of everything she told me from here on in. Next time she'd tell me she was going to have dinner with her students, I'd wonder where she really was. Now I thought, where had she been tonight?

"Were you with your students tonight? Or with this girl? Or was it someone else? You see? How can I believe anything you tell me now? Ten years we've been married, and I'm just learning you have a child! And not from you! A girl as old as Danielle! Unbelievable!"

I paused to swallow, and now I did sit down. I felt defeated, feeling as if the blood were draining out of me.

"I don't know how you could have lived with yourself, keeping such a secret from me," I said.

I opened the envelope again and looked for the father's name. Not finding it, I waved the papers around.

"Tell me," I said, "why is there no father listed on the birth certificate? Who was he? I'm sure you know. And why is his name missing from the document?"

As I said this, I had an awful thought that this child could possibly have been the result of a rape, or some abuse by a family member even, and that that might be the reason for not identifying him on the form. How cruel that would have been for her, if her family had forced her to have a child that was the result of a rape. Suddenly I remembered that having the child and giving it up would have been the only legal alternative back then. If that were not the reason, I doubted that Clare would have been so promiscuous, to have slept with so many different men that she had no idea who the father might be. What was the reason for leaving his name off the certificate of birth?

When she finally began to speak, Clare didn't answer my question about the father, but began at the beginning, finally giving me the saga of her boyfriend leaving the country before she knew she was pregnant.

"I thought I loved him then," she said. "It wasn't anything we'd planned though. It was an accident. But he was leaving the country, and at the time, I didn't know when or if I'd ever see him again."

I thought she was going to tell me that he'd died in Vietnam, as my own brother had. I softened a bit, thinking of him.

"Did he die in Vietnam?" I asked.

She was crying harder now, and hugging the throw pillow she'd reached for, on the chair beside her.

"I was sent off to the other side of the country, to a home run by nuns. My father said he'd put me out, if I didn't go. I couldn't have taken care of a child. I had no one, and no money. I was seventeen. What was I to do? I've never known what happened to her. This is the first I've heard of her."

"Danielle told me the girl said she'd met you," I said.

Clare shook her head, *No.* But hearing this she got up off the couch and picked up the envelope from the side table where I'd put it. What I'd said had prompted her to open the envelope, to look for some explanation, I guess. She found a note, neither Danielle nor I had seen. She read it aloud.

"*I didn't know how to tell you before. I had to find you. I have no one. Maybe you want me now.*"

Clare read the name on the birth certificate again.

"I did. I did meet her," she said, realizing it suddenly. "She came to see me. She said she wanted to volunteer at Diamond Street. I had no idea who she was then. She didn't let on about who she was to me. And she never showed up for the orientation. Instead, I got a letter from her, saying her mother had died."

She paused as the full realization hit her.

"Her adoptive mother died," she said.

"So, the father?"

She let out an exasperated sigh.

"Ray Newell. Ray Newell is the father," she said.

It was yet another blow. She must have stayed in touch with him. So this was the real reason why he'd come home. The old flame. Had they stayed in touch all the years we'd been married? None of this seemed possible. I'd never imagined Clare would have kept anything so important from me. Who knew what else she was hiding? This was not the Clare I thought I knew.

"Danielle needs to know this," I said.

She was looking away when she answered.

"I suppose she does," she said.

I'd been a fool to think that what we'd had was lasting. Maybe all those nights, when I was working late, she'd been with him. I'd neglected our marriage, trying to support Veronica and Danielle and Clare, pushing myself to afford it all, overextending myself at work.

I waited for more, but Clare did not elaborate. It was clear she was going to say nothing else about Newell. I looked at her, shaking my head. I could imagine what would ensue now that the girl was back.

Clare said she felt now that way one of the witnesses for the prosecution must feel, when being questioned during an interrogatory or a courtroom trial, the way Danielle said I sometimes made her feel, facing a barrage of questions from me.

I sighed long and hard. It felt like my marriage was in big trouble now. I wanted to go to Clare. She was obviously hurting, too, but I couldn't bring myself to do it.

"I don't know what I'll do now," she said. "I just don't know."

I didn't know either. It seemed as if whatever held us together was broken, or seriously frayed, and maybe couldn't' be fixed. I had no idea how we might figure this mess out. Right now I was too angry to want to.

"Danielle," I hollered, "get out here now!"

I was surprised when she came right away.

Scrunching up her forehead, she said, "What?"

She was about to get a worse bit of information. I knew how taken she'd been with her Mr. Newell, the cool sax player.

"Sit," I said. "And listen to what Clare has to tell you."

She told her then, asked her to please try to understand, that she was very young when all this had happened.

"I was only a year older than you are. Can you imagine yourself in my situation at that age?"

Danielle was speechless. I could see a row of questions in the furrows of her forehead, and in her slackened mouth, an expression of disbelief. Her mind was running with all she'd learned today. Saying nothing to Clare, except with her affect, she looked away from her and at me, and said,

"I'm calling my Mom to come pick me up."

"Fine," I said. "But do not say a word about any of this—not about the girl or about Mr. Newell—to your mother. This is not yours to reveal."

She got up to leave the room, turning back she looked at Clare and shook her head. She went into the kitchen then, and I heard her talking quietly on the phone. I trusted she would say nothing to Veronica. I hoped I was right.

Like Danielle must have realized, I knew this situation with Clare's daughter coming back would mean an outcome that would somehow involve, not just Clare, but Ray Newell, too, since he was here.

"She needs help apparently," Clare said, avoiding any further discussion of him.

"What kind of help could you give her? I mean, you don't know anything about her."

She told me I sounded "cold." There were too many questions right now, to act like any plan could be put in motion for us, or for this girl. Every possibility was potentially disruptive. If the girl really was in trouble, Clare would most likely feel that she had to bear total responsibility to help her, if Newell wanted out of the picture. And if not? If he were around—if Clare stayed in touch with him—anything might happen.

I stood up. I needed to sleep. I'd taken on yet another new

case, and I was exhausted.

"The chickens always come home to roost, don't they?" I said, as I walked out of the room.

"I'm sorry, Martin," Clare said. "It's late, I know, and this is too much to take in for one night. You must be exhausted."

She put on her coat again. I didn't know where she was going, but I let her go.

Twenty-Two

Clare

I stuffed my work tote with what I'd need for an overnight: a sleepshirt, hairbrush, toothbrush, makeup, and clean clothes. Martin hadn't asked where I was going. If he had, it wouldn't have mattered. I didn't know when I went out the door. I didn't know either, if I'd be back to stay. I didn't know if Martin would want me back, now that he'd learned who the father was, whether he or Danielle would ever understand, now that everything was out in the open.

I realized that my students at Diamond Street would be just arriving for their tutoring sessions, so I decided to go there, see if the director was in, and discuss returning to work at the Center. I'd delayed going back, not ready for such an intimate situation. The tutors had been on their own while I'd been out on leave. The place was still the tight-knit community it had been since its founding in the sixties, although the students and some of the staff had changed. I hadn't had to worry that a substitute would replace me, like at the Medical Center. At Diamond Street, one of the regular staff had taken on the responsibility of greeting the students and the tutors had been fine without me for a while. I'd trained them well.

I knew everyone would have questions, would want to express their sympathy for my loss, and I hadn't thought I was ready to accept any of it. But now, I wanted that affirmation that they cared about me, that someone did. I also needed to be occupied with work. I knew my students would not reject me, as I felt my own family maybe had. I wanted to be with people who knew me as someone they could trust, someone they counted on to help them. I wanted to be with people who saw me as reliable, and knew that I would do the right thing for them. I thought of why I'd chosen to work with these students at Diamond Street, or at the Medical Center, rather than teaching others at some prestigious college or university. I felt a bond with them, and I think they recognized that in me, even if I hid it pretty well. I knew what it was to experience great loss from a young age, as so many of them had, leaving behind their loved ones, coming to a foreign country, trying to negotiate what was to them, a strange culture.

After I'd given up my child, I was like them, needing to learn how to be among others who didn't know or understand the kind of loss I'd experienced, losing someone I knew was still out there somewhere, but someone I might never see again.

At Diamond Street, I was greeted warmly, when the staff saw me coming in the door. Amelia of the Many Stories, usually the first student to arrive each night of tutoring, was reliably already at the desk, chatting up Norman, while waiting for her tutor.

"Clare!" she called and came running to hug me.

I soaked up her appreciation, and Norman's, too.

"You back now!" Amelia announced, more a statement than a question.

It was fitting that Amelia would be the first of the students to welcome me. I'd missed her and her stories, missed them all really. Amelia's tutor arrived and we exchanged greetings and then they went off together happily, to have a lesson.

Although the director wasn't in, Norman said there was someone else I could talk to, and I thought he meant, her assistant. He pointed though to the corner of the reading room by the window, where there was a desk in a cubicle. I assumed that this was someone who'd come in off the street, inquiring about being a student or tutor in the program, that he'd told her to wait until all the tutorials were in progress and that then he would help her complete an application.

Hearing my footsteps on the wood floor, the girl turned around, and I saw that it was not someone new who'd come to ask about the program, but the same teenaged girl, who'd come to see me, supposedly wanting to volunteer. This was Judy Kneeland, who'd confessed in the note that accompanied the adoption papers she'd left with Danielle, that she'd been incognito. I'd read her confession. This was my daughter.

I caught my breath, never expecting that she'd be here. Did fate draw me to this place tonight? I had not planned to return yet, had come here for want of somewhere—anywhere—to be, after leaving Martin and Danielle. Judy had been stalking me, hoping to catch me here at work. I didn't think that I was prepared for this, and with all that had happened today—in one day—and it wasn't over yet. I couldn't escape or delay my responsibility for my child, and here, where her ruse about wanting to volunteer was believed by staff, I had to be professional; the organization expected that.

"I read your note. And I received the papers," I said. I pointed to the stairway down to my office. "Wait at the top of the stairs for me. I'll find the key."

We walked down to the basement together in silence. I unlocked the door and let her in. I hit the light switch. I reached for her to hug her but she pulled back. When she did, I got a good look at her, saw her worry, her sadness. She had just lost the only mother she'd known, and here she was with me, her true mother she didn't know.

"How did you find me?" I said, when were seated at the conference table.

I reached my arm across the table, and again she resisted me.

I'd imagined a more hospitable place for our meeting, a quiet, church-like atmosphere with soft, incandescent lighting for such a solemn reunion, and with comfortable chairs. We sat on the dreaded plastic bloody-red chairs, fluorescent lights blaring above us in a room painted like a snowstorm.

"Does anyone in your family know where you are?" I asked.

"What family?" she replied.

I took a deep breath. Was I her only family now?

"I mean your father," I said.

Just as I'd assumed, she'd come here to find me because he was out of the picture. I was perplexed. Had he been mean to her, or abused her in some other way, so that she fled after her mother's death? She'd said, too, that the couple that had adopted her hadn't adopted any other children, so she had no siblings, as far as she knew.

"They got divorced," she said. "He married someone in England, someone he'd met on business over there, my mother told me. We never heard from him after. I was little. You know he's not my real dad anyway. But I do want to know that, who he is. And I want to know you."

I saw her eyes were watering. I was her only hope right now.

Slinking down in my chair, I crumpled, thinking of what all this would mean.

"So no one knows you're here?"

"Who would there be to know? Do you think I want Child Services to know where I am?"

Yes, Child Services would want to know her whereabouts; she was just sixteen, Danielle's age. I felt the walls I'd put up trying to forget my daughter, thinking I'd never see her again, begin to crumble. This was my daughter. Not my stepdaughter, but my flesh and blood, and she was in trouble.

She seemed smart, to try to escape that fate, of being placed in a foster home. Parenting Danielle, I knew how difficult it often was for her, a teenaged girl, and I wondered how another family would approach taking on a child at her age. It was better for her to run. But what could I do for her? What did she want? Could she live with me? With Ray? Right now, I didn't even know where I was going to live. Martin had every right to divorce me, but would he? I didn't think he'd put me out of the house. I saw how much support he'd given Veronica after their divorce. I wanted to believe he'd do the same for me. And he knew all I'd put up with, parenting Danielle. We'd had no child together, so if he no longer trusted me, what reason would there be for him to have anything more to do with me, never mind to accept Judy.

There'd be time to hear Judy's story of how her mother had found out where I was, and how it happened that she let Judy know about me before she died. I looked at her. She had Ray's dark hair color, and it was fine in texture, a little bit curly most of the time probably, but frizzy in this humidity, like mine. Her brown eyes were full of my own fear and longing now. She was my girl. I'd been witness to years of milestones with my stepdaughter, yet I'd missed out on everything with Judy. It was just unbelievable that she'd finally come back to me. I'd helped so many others, not just Danielle—my students here and elsewhere. I had to help her, I knew. My daughter. My own flesh and blood. Unlike my student Margaret Kwan, who would probably never know who'd adopted her daughter in China, never know her, I had a chance to try to make up for all that time without her, a chance to be a parent now to the child I'd given birth to.

"Where are you staying?" I asked, when she told me how her mother—her *adopted mother*, she corrected herself—had left her enough money to come here to find me, once she was gone.

I was sitting at the head of the conference table, as I would have been for an advising session with a tutor or student.

"Haven House gave me a place to stay. No questions asked. It's okay. But I know I can't stay there forever. If you live there long-term, you have to have a job. That's the rule. I want to go back to school. I don't want to stay there anyway," she said.

"Oh, Judy," I said, reaching out to her.

I got up and went around the table to her, and leaned down to hug her. She let herself be taken in my arms now. How must it be, to be staying in that place? It was a shelter really. How could I let her be there, after just losing the only mother she'd ever known, while I was living just a few miles away?

Suddenly she pulled away from my hug. She looked at me straight on.

"Why didn't you want me?" she asked.

She was crying. Her question was a stab to my heart. I was unprepared for how it would feel, hearing her ask that obvious question. I'd expected it, but hadn't been able to imagine how it would feel to be asked it directly by my daughter. She had just lost the only mother she'd known, after she'd first been abandoned by me.

"I did. I did want you," I cried. "I had no choice. Everything was decided for me. My father was cruel. My mother was gone. She'd died several years before."

"What about *my* father? He didn't want me either?"

"I didn't have the chance to tell him," I said softly. I was crying now, too. "Vietnam got in the way," I said, hesitating before telling her the whole story.

"He died? Oh, no!"

"No, no. He didn't die. You're right to think he might have; many did die—58,000—young men his age mostly— were killed in that war. He didn't want to die, not for a war he didn't believe in. He was honorable, even though he didn't serve. Your father, Ray Newell, went to Canada, like many others did, to resist being drafted as a soldier. A couple of weeks later, I went for my college physical exam, and the doctor discovered I was pregnant with you."

"So you told him about me?" she asked.

She was desperate to know that someone might want her.

"That war tore families apart—like your father's," I said. "It kept your father from me, and both of us from you. I was so young, just a year older than you are now. Where was I to go alone, without anyone, without any money. How could I take care of you? My father would have put me out. He gave me an ultimatum."

"Why didn't you go to Haven House or something, like I did?"

Judy had no idea how much had changed since 1968. I looked at her and saw that. She couldn't imagine how it had been for girls back then.

"There weren't places to go then, like Haven House. Young women who weren't married would be shipped off to homes to have their babies, and then forced to give them up, without any connection to them after. An open adoption wasn't even a possibility."

I was trying not to sound defensive, but there was no way really, not to. She wanted answers. I wanted some, too, and so I asked for more about her mother.

"Do you mean that your mother never told you that you were adopted, not until she knew she was dying?"

"She had to then," she said. "She didn't want me to think that I was going to inherit what got her. It was hereditary. She knew I'd worry, she said, if I thought it was going to kill me, too."

She looked away from me, for a moment, as if trying to get the courage to finish what her mother had said.

"She wanted me to find you, because she wanted someone to take care of me. Do you know where my father is now? What happened to him? Maybe he wants me in his life, if you don't."

Hearing that dealt another blow to my heart. I wanted her to understand that I did want her now, but she couldn't hear that. Not yet. I hoped she would.

"My father would have put me out rather than allow me to raise you in the family, or to search for your father, who had to leave this country in secret," I said. "So, I was sent away by the time he wrote to me, and my father never forwarded the letters. Not being married, and having a baby, my father believed as many others did then, that I'd embarrass the family in the community. That is what he thought."

I realized as I spoke these words that, though truthful, they seemed so inadequate to explain what that year of my life had been like. But Judy was now in almost the same predicament as I would have been, had I defied my father's wishes and decided to keep the baby. Now, as a runaway from foster care, she was left to fend for herself, except she wasn't pregnant, as far as I knew.

"So, you're saying you don't want me, and my father doesn't know about me, so no one will want me?"

She put her head down on the table and covered it with her hands, as if she were giving up.

"Please, Judy. I didn't say that. I do. I do want you in my life. I have always thought about you. What I'm trying to say is that I just need to figure some things out," I said. "I want to, but I can't bring you home tonight."

Hearing me say that I wanted her in my life, she lifted her head up off the table and stared at me, as if examining my eyes and my expression, to check if I was being truthful. Then she seemed to accept what I'd said, letting out a deep breath, which I interpreted as relief.

"I know, I know, I just crashed into your life. But you have a life, and right now, I have nothing," she said.

"I'm not working right now. I just came here to check on some things," I said. "Let me give you a ride back to where you're staying for the time being. You should be safe there, right? Until I can work something out? Hopefully soon. I'll come back tomorrow morning, but try to get some sleep. You look very tired. You're sure you're okay there? They won't alert the authorities?"

"Yes, it's called a safe haven, the only place to go around here, if you aren't eighteen," she said.

Safe haven. That was the phrase used now for places like

hospitals, fire or police departments or churches, where new mothers without money or support could leave their newborn children on the doorstep, to be cared for by someone else. At least I hadn't done that. From all indications, Judy had had a good mother to care for her.

***

After I got to Boston and left Judy off at the place where she was staying, I drove directly to Ray's apartment. I hit the buzzer for him to let me in.

"Who's there?" he demanded, rather gruffly.

He sounded as if he'd been awakened.

When I said who I was, he said, "Clare?"

He buzzed me in. I'm sure he was puzzled to find that I'd returned tonight.

When I made it up the stairs he was standing, waiting for me in the open doorway. As I went in, the apartment was dark, except for a small lamp, a night light, on the kitchen counter. I had awakened him.

"What's up? What's happened?"

He rubbed his eyes. He looked like he'd been crying and not asleep.

"Are you okay?" I asked, stepping back for a moment, from my own trouble.

"I didn't think you'd be sleeping so early," I said, pretending I didn't notice that he was crying.

He walked over to turn on the floor lamp in the living room, rather than put on the kitchen overhead light. He came back and looked at me, squinting.

It was only nine-thirty, so I was sure that I hadn't awakened him.

Realizing probably, that with the light on, his tears were obvious, he said, "My dad died. The doctors thought he might have had as much as a couple of days left, when I got a call this afternoon. But after you left, another call came, that he'd passed this evening."

I didn't hand him the adoption papers right away, as I'd intended to do, but tried to respond to his grief.

"I'm sorry, Ray. So sorry you couldn't patch things up with him before he was gone."

"I tried," he said. "I came back for that, not knowing about his dementia. Otherwise, I might not have returned. And then, if I hadn't, I wouldn't have found you."

"Or our daughter," I said. "I'm glad you did come back. We have a chance now, to fix something else, because you did."

I had the envelope with the adoption papers in hand, and I gave it to him.

"Here. Look."

I pointed toward the living room.

"Can we sit in there to talk about this?" I said.

"Sure, but what is this?" he said, holding the envelope out.

He led me to the couch, and sat down next to me.

The envelope was on his lap and he looked at it, then at me, raising his eyebrows.

"Open it," I said.

He scanned the first page of the documents, shaking his head as he read.

"Where did you get this?"

"Go on," I said.

Then, he rifled through the other pages, stopping when he came to the birth certificate. He gasped.

"My name is missing."

He turned to me for an explanation.

"I was instructed by my father not to list a name, and told that if I did, it would be erased."

"How could they do that? An official document? I guess no one other than the Kneelands looked at it."

"Until now," I said.

Ray looked at me with an expression of both shock and bewilderment.

"Where did you get this? We just decided to look for her—or I did anyway—you were uncertain."

I sighed, exhausted by the amount of explaining I'd had to do tonight, and all that I still had to do.

"She found me," I said. "And she wants to find you, too. I

wanted to tell you first. She has no one else. The father is out of the picture—has been for many years."

He turned back to the sheaf of documents, shook them at me.

"Have you had this all along and didn't tell me, because you didn't think you wanted to find her? And now, that she's shown up, you have to show me?" he demanded.

"No, no. Ray, listen. She dropped them off this afternoon, gave the envelope to Danielle. I know it's strange for her to show up now, but I can explain. Her mother has died. She'd never told her she was adopted, or that she'd found out where she could find me—not until she was dying of some inherited disease and didn't want our daughter to think she would die from it as well. She has no one else."

I was crying as I told him this, and about how she felt threatened with being sent to a foster home, and the shelter where she'd been staying, and how she'd come to see me at work a while ago, pretending to be someone wanting to volunteer for my program.

"Our daughter," he said, pulling me close to him.

I didn't pull away, but I knew that what we had once could not be, nor could we take this any further between us, or continue what he might think we'd started earlier in the evening.

"I had too much to drink on an empty stomach earlier. It was a mistake to let anything happen between us tonight. You've been free to tour and move from job to job for your music. But I've put down roots here. You need to realize that."

"I understand you'd feel that way, but this is my child, too, Clare," he said. "Maybe I'm tired of roaming. I could stay put. I could be her father. I am her father, you say."

"You've had no responsibilities," I repeated.

I knew I sounded accusatory, perhaps even envious of his freedom, and that wasn't what I meant. He wasn't to blame for any of this. It was just that I had harbored this sadness alone all these years, and now I had to figure out how to share it, maybe let go of it, so there could be something else instead.

"That's not fair," he said. "I have had responsibilities—maybe not to a family. No. But I'm here. I came home to see to the care of the father who'd disowned me sixteen years ago, in spite of all the anger and sadness—it was sad, leaving back then, Clare—and then sadder still, to come home to help him, and find out his condition. And I'm pretty sure I'd have stepped up to my responsibility for our child, and for you, if you had let me know what was happening."

Now I felt like he was blaming me.

"We've already been through this thing about your letters not being forwarded. I don't want to argue," I said. "I need your help to figure this out. And I don't think I can go home now. Martin saw the papers just tonight. He never knew either, as I told you. He says our marriage was built on a lie."

He didn't want to talk about my problem, though. He was thinking, he said, about having to deal with the burial arrangements for his dad. There was no one else to take care of that.

"Where is she now?" he asked, about Judy.

"I drove her to Haven House, where she has a safe place to stay, so she wouldn't be put in a foster home. She's only sixteen, you know, so technically, she's a runaway. No father in the picture. He's remarried, living in the U.K. since she was very young. She never really knew him, so a foster home, it would be."

"Except she has us," he said.

I didn't know how he could say this so matter-of-factly, but I reminded myself that he was free and I wasn't, so that made a difference.

"You're not imagining we could be together to care for her, are you? I'm not going to give up my marriage—although I have to admit that Martin may have given me up, after hearing I'd kept all this from him."

Ray sighed and said, "I did wonder, if maybe, after earlier this evening, there might be something between us still."

"It was a mistake," I repeated. "I shouldn't have had all that I had to drink. But I sure did sober up fast when I got home and Danielle and Martin confronted me with the papers. Danielle got a look at them, even before I did, when Judy—our daughter dropped them off at the house. She'd showed them to Martin. Then I walked in. You can imagine the scene, being set upon like that. They ganged up on me. Danielle stormed out. But once I'd told Martin you were the father, he called her to come out of her room, said we had to tell her."

"He knows?" Ray said.

"He knows," I said. "And Danielle knows. She called her mother and told her to come get her, promising us she wouldn't tell her what was going on. I hope she doesn't. Telling Veronica something you're going to have to do, before Danielle does."

"Oh," he said. "What a mess!"

I was crying more now. I felt the situation was hopeless. I knew that I couldn't support this girl on my own, and even if Martin took me back, could I ask him to do that for me? For Judy?

"I'm sorry," Ray said. "Maybe I should have been the one to explain our connection to everyone. They might have been easier on you."

Martin, having met Ray when he asked for his help with his case, had told me he thought Ray was a decent guy. But learning tonight who Ray was to me, had surely altered that impression. Would he think that Ray had intended to find me once he was back to deal with his father's healthcare, assuming that he would have looked for me, even if he hadn't met Veronica and Danielle?

"I should never have kept this secret from Martin."

"I'll talk to Martin. Tomorrow. And Veronica. Listen, Clare, why couldn't we share custody, the way Veronica and Martin share responsibilities for Danielle," he said. "They shouldn't object to that. You've done so much for Danielle, it would be hypocritical, if they did, wouldn't it?"

I was stunned at this suggestion.

"It sounds like double jeopardy to me," I said.

"Think about it, Clare," Ray said. "It makes sense."

"But would Judy want that? We need to ask her what she wants, don't we?" I said.

I hadn't thought of this possibility, and the more I did, it seemed like something they all might find acceptable—even Danielle, who'd finally have the sister she'd always said she wanted.

"Maybe," I said. "Danielle would have an ally, and that would be good for her. And Judy. First though, we need to talk to Judy. Let's not get ahead of ourselves. No use in bringing that up with Martin, if it's not something she wants."

I was still debating about whether or not to accept Ray's offer to have me stay the night.

"No hanky-panky," he promised. "I'll sleep here. This couch has a fold-out bed."

I wanted to sleep this whole day off, to wake up with a clear head. But I longed for the comfort of my own bed. I didn't know though, how much rest I'd be able to get, given my worries. I wanted Martin. I wanted him to understand. Only he could bring me solace now. Tomorrow was Saturday and I was glad. He wouldn't be going to the office. There was the opportunity for a family meeting to try to work things out.

Would it calm Martin to know that Ray was willing to help with the girl, to be the father she needed now, and that I wouldn't have the entire responsibility for her care? I thought that he would be relieved to be told that Ray was only interested in helping our daughter. I was sure he'd feel sympathy for Judy, too, once he'd heard her story. After all, Danielle was the same age, and I'm sure he could imagine how awful Danielle would feel if she were the one threatened with foster care. I was counting on the fact that I'd known Martin as an empathetic man. I'd seen the work he chose for his profession, seen how much he tolerated from Veronica, and that he was a good father to Danielle.

We all had an opportunity to do something good in this situation, something I felt certain would not just help this girl, who was our daughter, but something that would help all of us.

"Clare, like you, I missed out. You did have Danielle though, and I haven't been a parent to any child. I didn't think I wanted that. I thought my career was enough, after I lost you. If I can't have you, the way I'd foolishly allowed myself to think I might, maybe we can have something else, maybe we can be parents together. I'm tired of roaming, Clare."

I did spend the night at Ray's apartment, but not sleeping much. We drank several cups of coffee, but skipped breakfast; neither of us felt like eating. I had promised Judy that I'd see her at Haven House this morning, and we'd begin to figure things out. We wanted to get on with our plans.

***

I made the decision to leave my car parked outside Ray's apartment building, feeling too shaky to drive. He was going to drop me off in Boston and then return to Cambridge to see Martin. He'd come back to meet Judy later. What would happen after that, we didn't know.

It was raining hard, and that slowed things to a crawl at the crazy Charles Street intersection; so cars were backed up across Longfellow Bridge.

"None of this seems real to me," I said, as we sat in traffic over the river.

"I'm worried, too," Ray said.

The windshield wipers squeaked as they went back and forth.

"I think they need adjusting," I said.

"I can put the radio on, if you want," he said.

"No, don't," I said, wanting to keep my mind on the seriousness of what we had to do.

I knew there were many ways Ray's conversation with Martin might go. I tried not to imagine the worst.

"It really is better that you're going alone," I said.

"I get that," he said.

"And it's better that I see Judy before you show up. To try to prepare her a bit," I said. "And don't forget. If things go well, ask Martin when he might want to meet Judy."

"If things work out," he said.

"Since he isn't working today, maybe ask him about this afternoon," I said.

"So soon?" Ray said.

"Tell him it might not happen this afternoon, though. We have to see how it goes when you meet her."

"Right. It might not happen," he said.

"Better to get it done though," I said.

"If things go well," Ray said.

He double-parked. I looked at him and sighed.

He said, "Good Luck."

"Same to you," I said.

I hadn't gone inside Haven House, when I'd dropped Judy off the night before. In daylight now, I saw the place was one of those old Boston brownstones. I headed up the granite steps and rang the doorbell. There was a sign that said, *Ring Then Enter*.

Inside there was a clump of backpacks parked in the hallway at the bottom of the staircase, as if several people were moving in or out. I asked the first person I saw if she would let Judy know that she had a visitor.

"She's expecting me," I said.

The young woman didn't ask my name, but looked me over then disappeared. I thought that maybe she was just another temporary resident, like Judy.

After waiting a few minutes I saw her—my daughter!—turn the corner onto the second floor landing and my breath caught as I watched her descend the stairs to where I was waiting for her. She looked tired, as if she hadn't slept much either. Her hair was a little damp, as if she'd just showered and towel dried it.

I went to her and put my arms around her, giving her a big hug. Her hair smelled like grapefruit.

"Good Morning," I said, trying for cheery.

"Hi. You came," she said. "I didn't know if you would."

"I said I would."

She looked directly at me, as if she were still trying to confirm my commitment.

"Have you had breakfast yet?" I asked.

"Well, we don't have kitchen privileges here. They give us a restaurant voucher for dinner. But we're on our own the rest of the day," "I usually save some food from dinner for the morning or for lunch, to try to save my money."

"I haven't had breakfast either," I said. "So let's find a diner where we can eat and talk."

I opened the umbrella I'd borrowed from Ray and held it above us, putting one arm around Judy's shoulders as we went down the front steps. It was a golf umbrella, so it was ample protection for the two of us, but a bit large for Boston's quaint brick sidewalks.

"I'm glad you have a rain slicker," I said.

"And I'm glad you have an umbrella. I forgot to pack one," Judy said.

I made note of the time on the clock tower near the corner. I didn't think Ray would be with Martin too long, and I figured it would take him at least a half hour to get over the river on a Saturday at midday. Having a little more than an hour before he returned, would give us time to eat, to hash things out, and get back to meet him at Haven House.

"There's a deli a little further down," she said. "It's not bad. I went there a couple of times."

It was windy and I struggled to keep the umbrella from going airborne.

"Have you seen much of Boston?" I asked her.

With the wind and the rain, only small talk was possible.

"Not really. I've mostly been hanging out in Cambridge," she said.

"Do you like it better?" I asked.

"It's easier there to meet people. Here people are hurrying around to get somewhere."

We reached the deli, and there was a short wait since it was Saturday morning. I grabbed a couple of menus from the hostess and gave my name for our party of two. I handed a menu to Judy.

"You should have whatever you want. It's my treat."

"Thanks," she said.

I saw her smile for the first time since I'd been with her. All along, I'd been smiling through my worry, but I knew it would take time to build trust between us. It was right for me to be meeting her alone. There was so much to know about each other, but a lot would have to wait while we figured out how to meet her basic needs. I hoped with all my heart that Martin would find it in his heart to help with Judy. As a lawyer, his advice would be so helpful, if we were to get custody of Judy, especially since paternity had to be established for Ray.

I was sure the authorities must be looking for Judy by now. If not, they would be soon. She said she'd been gone for a little over a week. I presumed that an Amber Alert would be issued nationwide, since she'd be considered a runaway.

When a booth was ready for us we sat across from each other in a corner at a window. We had a little more privacy there than if we'd been seated in the middle of all the activity. There was the aroma of good coffee and the customers were buzzing.

"This is good. We can talk," I said.

Judy looked nervous. I noticed her hair starting to frizz as it dried. She noticed mine was, too.

"You have hair like mine," she said.

I laughed.

"Kind of a curse sometimes, but you'll get used to it. I actually like mine now," I said.

Judy raised her eyebrows at that.

"I know what I want," she said.

We both ordered everything bagels with cream cheese and smoked salmon.

"With capers, please," I said.

"Me, too," Judy said.

Then we got down to talking. I told her I'd seen her father after leaving her off the night before. I gave her all the details about how he'd stayed in Canada long after he'd been able to return, and that he'd had a life there but had come home to help with his father's care.

"Is he married?" she asked. "And does he have other kids in Canada?"

I suppose she was thinking that if so, he'd be going back to them.

"No," I said. "You're his only child. And he isn't married."

Her big hazel eyes grew larger.

I told her that Ray's father had been very ill and had recently died, so she was worried he'd be going back to Canada.

"Oh, he was my grandfather," she said.

I felt stupid to think that I hadn't been more sensitive in telling her that. Of course she'd be curious about her family, thinking she might meet him.

"Well, it seems that your father wants to stay here, that he doesn't see any reason not to, especially now that he knows about you, that you're here," I said. "He has work teaching at the Conservatory. And he's been playing out. He's a sax player."

She gasped. She looked at me in disbelief and then broke into a big smile that warmed me.

"At the Conservatory?"

I shook my head.

"He's pretty good," I said. "Been making a name for himself."

She told me then that she'd been playing trumpet for several years and had been in the school band. She said that to pass the time since she'd been in Boston, she'd be going over to the Conservatory and sitting in on rehearsals sometimes. There was a sax player coaching a quartet she'd heard.

"I just take a seat in the very back of the hall, trying to be inconspicuous. Sometimes, when they aren't getting it, he picks up his horn and plays the piece for them, the way it should go. This guy is really good," she said.

"That could be him. You never know," I said.

I was relieved, thinking that her interest in music could be a real ice-breaker when she met Ray.

I told her then, what we'd talked about the night before, of the possibility perhaps of some shared custody situation, only I called it a "blended family," which sounded much more welcoming.

"We don't know how to do this. You know, I'm married, and we need to involve my husband. He's the father of the girl you met when you dropped the papers off at my house."

"Danielle," she said.

"Yes, Danielle. It's all pretty complicated to work out, but we're hopeful. Martin—my husband— is a good man. I'm hoping that he'll want you to live with us some of the time."

"And what about my father?"

"Well, he's a good man, too. And he does want you to live with him some of the time."

She looked across the table at me, and I saw a serious expression come over her face. She seemed wary. She was quiet for a minute, taking it all in.

"I never had two parents," she said. "Not that I remember anyway. I never knew my father. I don't know what it would be like to live with my father."

I didn't mention Danielle's mother, not knowing what might happen between Veronica and Ray. I thought now that it could certainly help, if something were to come of their relationship, and she had some step-parenting for Judy. Who knew though, what was going to happen with any of this?

"Martin is a lawyer," I said, "and if he thinks you can live with us—and I'm really hoping he will— he'll help getting legal custody, I'm sure. You have the papers to prove that I'm your mother. But as you know, your father's name was omitted from the record. I don't know, but Martin will probably have some ideas."

"I have a lot to think about," Judy said.

"Of course," I said.

She paused then before going on.

"But I have no one. I mean, I have you, but you don't know yet, if I can live with you."

I explained that her father was at that very moment talking with Martin, trying to explain that he knew nothing until the night before.

"Were you ashamed of me?" she said.

"No. No. That isn't it. I don't know. I don't know why I never told Martin. I should have. I was trying to forget the sadness of losing you. I thought you were lost from me forever, that I'd never know you," I said.

She scrutinized me. I wasn't smiling anymore. I felt overwhelmed by how complicated I'd made things, being so secretive.

We finished our breakfast, and it was time to head back to Haven House, to wait for Ray to return.

"I think you'll like your father when you meet him," I said.

Inside Haven House, I saw her get a glimpse of herself in the hallway mirror. She tried to tamp down her hair a bit.

"You look great," I said.

"Do you think I'm okay?" she said.

I hugged her. It felt so good to do that.

"You're more than okay. You're great," I said.

Twenty-Three

Martin

When rain pelting against the bedroom windows and the empty birdfeeder swinging back and forth against the glass woke me, I was surprised to find that I'd been sleeping at all, never mind so soundly. I'd gone to bed at midnight, but had stayed awake for what seemed like hours, attempting to understand why Clare had kept her past from me—something so important as her child—her own flesh and blood. I was worried, too, about where she was now.

She had not come home and I had no idea where she'd spent the night. Although I wanted to believe that she'd stayed with a friend or checked into a hotel, my first thought this morning was that she was with Newell. That possibility made me want to find her, bring her home. But I had no idea where he lived. Although Veronica would know his address, I didn't want to involve her, was hoping that Danielle had done as I'd asked and not spoken to her about Newell's part in this. She'd know soon enough. No need to complicate matters further, when so much was uncertain at the moment.

I went to the kitchen to make coffee. Last night's dishes were still in the sink. Pots with leftover rice, and the water from the steamed asparagus, were still on the stove. I felt powerless in the face of so many questions. All I knew was that Clare wanted to help her daughter. She said she wanted to offer her a home. How she intended to do that, she said she didn't know. Did she mean a home with me or a home with Newell?

After I'd had enough coffee, I decided to get out of the house, do a few errands. It felt like a prison where I was locked in with anxious thoughts about the end of my marriage.

But then the doorbell rang. I didn't think that Clare would ring, if she'd come back. She had the key, unless she'd forgotten to take it with her. I hoped it was Clare. There wasn't a window that gave me a view of the front steps, to see who was there.

I opened the door to find Newell standing there. He was alone. Perhaps Clare hadn't stayed with him after all. He had stepped back, away from the door. Wearing no hat and not carrying an umbrella, the rainwater dripping from the overhang of the entry roof had wet his shoulder-length hair. He was soaked, wearing only a light jacket that obviously wasn't rain gear. He must have parked down the street. I felt no sympathy for him though. Had he stepped back from the shelter of the doorway, afraid I'd hit him, when I saw him. I wanted to hit him for his dishonesty, pretending to have come home only to take care of his father's needs, while finding a way to get to Clare.

"Can we talk?" he said.

"You think that's going to change anything?" I said.

"I never knew any of this," he said.

I looked at him and shook my head.

"You expect me to believe that?"

"It's true, what I told you when we met about Eric, that my father was the reason I came home," he said.

I let him in and led him into the kitchen. It was a warm day, even though it was raining. No windows were open in the apartment. The room was beginning to smell like garbage, from the unwashed dishes with their remnants of dinner. I was exhausted, not sure that I had the energy or the desire to talk to this man who had insinuated himself into so much of my life. The anger of the night before hadn't entirely vanished, but had mostly turned to pessimism this morning.

Newell had a paper cup of coffee with him.

"I should have brought one for you, too," he said.

"I have coffee," I said, pointing to the pot on the counter, not wanting him to think I expected anything from him.

Neither one of us said anything for a minute. Was he waiting for me to speak?

"You came to talk. So, talk," I said.

"I didn't know anything. I came back to settle things for my father. Nothing else. I had no plan to work here. I figured I'd get him settled, and then go back to Canada. But it didn't work out that way."

"And is he settled?" I asked.

Newell gave a cynical little laugh.

"Sure is," he said. "He died last night."

That caught me off guard, and I softened a bit.

"I'm sorry," I said.

He shrugged.

He seemed more relieved than saddened by his father's death. I remembered some of the guys I'd counseled at the Meeting House, how they'd had to break ties with their families when they objected to the War and didn't serve. But he'd come back here after so many years, and that made me suspicious. Maybe he'd come to help his father, and maybe he'd come to find Clare. Or maybe he did really come to help his father out, and then when he had to stay, decided to look for Clare. I had no idea.

"I have other things to settle for him now, but there's this stuff about a living human being—the daughter I just found out I have—I have to take care of that first, and that's why I'm here," he said.

I shook my head, not believing him. I wanted to, but what were the chances really that he'd just serendipitously met Clare again. I knew stranger things had happened, but this seemed impossible.

"It's true. So much is unbelievable, I know, starting with coming back here after being away for so long, coming back to take care of the old man who'd written me off years ago. Do not think for one minute that I insinuated myself into your family's life to get to Clare. When I found out I'd have to stay for a while I had to find work, had to pay for some place to live. I couldn't pay rent here and for my apartment in Montreal. Not without work. And teaching is what I've always done to support my music. I had no idea that taking on your daughter as a student would lead to any of this."

I was angry at him for disrupting my life, but I considered how awful it must have been for Clare, being so young, and with him gone, being pregnant, and having no say about what she wanted to do about that.

"Well, your father and others might have thought you were a coward, going off to Canada instead of Vietnam, but you know what I think? I think it was worse for you to leave Clare like that, when she was going to have a baby. Your baby. So young. What did you think was going to happen to her? You knew her mother had died. Did you think her father would help her raise the child? How could you? It was 1968 when you left her, and didn't you know what became of an unmarried woman having a baby on her own in 1968?"

"I didn't leave her," he said. "I left this country."

He shook his head and I thought that he was realizing he'd been irresponsible, that he had a lot to answer for.

"Martin," he said, "like you, I never knew about Clare's child—our daughter. I found out yesterday. I didn't even know that she was pregnant when I left. She didn't know either."

Now, I was really shaking my head.

"But how was it that she was out of your life after you left?"

My voice cracked. He'd forgotten about her? Just like that?

"You didn't write to her?"

I thought that maybe the reason was that he didn't want anyone knowing about his whereabouts, at least not until he was safely settled in Canada, that he'd been afraid he'd be found out, sent to Vietnam.

"She couldn't tell me. She didn't know how, didn't know where I'd ended up," he said. "I was gone. And then, when I did write, she was gone, so my letters never reached her, her father sending her off like he did. He probably burned them in the fireplace."

Suddenly I felt very sad for Clare. And I wondered how it must feel for Newell, to be faced with this news, so many years later, a freewheeling musician suddenly learning he had a grown child. By now he'd have resigned himself to being childless probably. If what he'd said was true, that he hadn't known anything, hadn't come back here to find Clare, I thought that he must be as shocked as I was. I stared out the window above the sink, watched the large evergreen in the yard next door, shaking as if the wind were inside its trunk, shaking every limb.

"You are very lucky," he said. "Lucky to have what you and Clare have. Until now, I've had no one all these years I've lived in Canada. I mean, I have friends and colleagues, but you have a family. I have yet to meet Judy. Clare says she's scared and desperate, but she's been well-cared for and seems like a good kid. I need to accept my responsibility for her care."

I moved my chair and one of the legs scraped the wooden floor.

"How will it work? You tour, don't you? Different places all the time," I said.

"You make me sound like I'm part of a traveling circus. How much touring I do can change, if it has to," he said.

I knew that since he'd been back he'd put together a group that had been playing at a local club. I wondered if he'd keep teaching at the Conservatory as well. I thought he'd told me he had a temporary position there, when I interviewed him for Eric's case.

"It's been temporary," he said, "but there might be a more permanent opening for Fall."

I wondered if Veronica had arranged something, wanting him to stay around.

He got suddenly quite serious, sitting up straighter in his chair, and he looked at me dead on. Was he willing to give up his life as he'd known it, to leave Canada where he'd made his home, to threaten his career by limiting his touring, all for the sake of a daughter he'd never known he had? I didn't have to ask.

"You see," he said, "I have a chance to do something good. To be a father for my daughter. Just think about Clare, how important it is for her to be a mother to her daughter, when she needs her. Can you imagine what it must have been like for her, knowing nothing about her, missing every milestone, while caring for your daughter? And then to lose the child she thought she was going to have—your child— and so recently?"

It wasn't money that was worrying me, Clare taking on Judy, expanding our family further and adding to our financial responsibilities, if that is what Newell wanted, adding another shared custody arrangement. He was what worried me. Having him around.

"I don't want to lose Clare," I said.

"You're lucky to have each other," he said.

I surprised myself, saying it out loud. But it felt good to say it. I was glad I did, and relieved hearing that he recognized our commitment. I wanted to believe he had no intention of breaking up our marriage. Did he really want a family, without wrecking mine?

"It hasn't been easy, sharing Danielle with her mother, you know," I said.

"You and Clare have made it work though. Danielle is great," he said.

I wondered if Danielle would see Judy like a sister, almost a twin. They would have each other as allies, something that might be good for both of them.

He stood up. I did, too.

"I'm going to go meet her now. Clare was with her this morning. We'd like you to meet her," he said.

It still felt weird, his alliance with Clare. Would it continue to be so strange? I wondered. He seemed to be saying that the outcome for Judy depended upon me.

"Is that what Clare wants?" I said.

"She asked me to find out if you want to meet her this afternoon."

He extended a hand. We looked each other in the eye.

"This afternoon will be good," I said, "if that's what Clare wants."

"It is. It's what she wants," he said.

Twenty-Four

Ray

At Haven House I followed instructions on the sign, ringing the bell before opening the door.

"Are you the guy?" a young woman walking by said to me.

"I'm Ray Newell," I said, "here to meet Judy Kneeland, if that's what you mean."

I wondered just what Judy had told people about me.

Looking over the woman's shoulder before she walked away without saying another word to me, I saw Clare seated in a chair next to the staircase, raising her hand, so I'd know she was here. I went to her.

She raised her eyebrows at me. She looked anxious and I wondered how her conversation with Judy went. I touched her shoulder lightly. Seeing how worried she looked, I wanted to hug her but thought better of that. I remembered our talk the night before, when she said she had no intention of having anything more between us, than the two us being parents to Judy and friends supporting each other in that responsibility. That and Martin's questioning of my motives, meant that I would keep a respectful distance.

"Everything all right with Judy?" I said.

"Fine. What about Martin?"

"It went okay. I think we'll work things out," I said.

Clare took a very deep breath and let it out loudly.

"But what about meeting Judy?" she said. "Did he say?"

"This afternoon will be fine," I said.

"Thank God!" she said.

The woman who'd let me in was passing by again, and turned and stared at us, hearing Clare's exclamation.

Her relief must be deep, I thought.

I looked around at the place. It wasn't too bad for a halfway house or whatever it was called. Someone was tinkering with a piano in an adjacent room. It didn't sound like anyone who really knew how to play, just someone who was fooling around.

"Where is she anyway?" I said.

"She went up to get something in her room," Clare said.

A few minutes later when Judy Kneeland came down the stairs, it was like seeing Clare at sixteen again, the teenager I'd known before my life got crazy. Her features, her height, and her hair, all sent me back in time.

I looked away toward Clare, wondering if she saw herself in her daughter. She smiled forlornly.

"You look like your mother did, a couple of years before you were born," I said.

She smiled back at me, not openly. She seemed a little nervous. We were both nervous, looking each other over. I was glad we were the only people in the entry room now. Clare took over the formalities, introducing us.

"Judy," she said, "this is your father, Ray Newell. He's a musician. A saxophone player."

"Judy. Hello," I said.

It was just the right thing for Clare to have said that I was a sax player. Judy relaxed and perked up.

"I played trumpet in the school jazz band," she said.

She'd found common ground. Now I was relieved.

"But I must have lost my instrument now. I can't go back. I'm not. Ever," she said.

"We'll get you another trumpet. And you won't have to go back. Or stay here either, if we can help it."

The nervousness evident before in her smile subsided, and she grinned widely now.

"It's so good to see you smiling," Clare said.

I had made a promise that we didn't yet know how to fulfill. There was a lot to straighten out, not the least of which was that she was a runaway from a foster home. It worried me, too, that my name wasn't on the birth certificate, and I knew that dealing with that would involve complicated legal proceedings that wouldn't be resolved overnight. I hoped Martin would help with that. I knew that paternity could be determined in a lab, believed that custody for both of us should be within the realm of possibility.

In the few minutes I'd been there, the hallway had gotten busier, with a steady stream of people passing by, heading up or down the staircase, into one of the first floor rooms, or out the front door.

"Can we go somewhere quiet where we might have a bit more privacy, to get to know each other? Brunch maybe?" I said.

Clare said she wasn't very hungry, that it hadn't been long since they'd had breakfast. Judy didn't respond, but I thought she probably could be persuaded to eat something, being a teenager.

"All I had this morning was coffee," I said.

Since Clare and Judy would be going to meet with Martin, I suggested we drive back across the river to Cambridge.

"How about we find some place to eat there? I'll drop you and Clare off after," I said to Judy. "You can meet Martin then."

Judy was a fine kid, needy right now, and scared and sad, too, given the circumstances, but we all got along well.

When she'd gone upstairs at Haven House, it had been to get a photo album to show us while I ate lunch, Clare had coffee, and Judy had another breakfast. It was heartbreaking for Clare, looking through the photos, tears streaming down her cheeks. These were photos from Judy's childhood of so many milestones. Clare had missed them all. I had, too. But because I'd never known about this child of mine, I hadn't spent years thinking of what I was missing out on and wondering for her well-being, as Clare had. That loss would have been alive for her, as she watched Danielle, mothered her through her own milestones. I was sad for myself though, as much as for Clare, troubled, realizing that even if Clare had been able to let me know, I didn't think there would have been any possibility for a different outcome back then. If I'd returned to the States, I'd have been sent off to Vietnam, and Clare's father would have set in motion the same plan, sending her away and forcing her to give her child up.

Judy had had a happy, well-cared for childhood, if the photos were true to life. She smiled out at us as we turned the pages, seeing her at birthday parties, on camping trips, sailing with the family of one of her friends, playing badminton with her adoptive mother, swimming at lakes and in the ocean, performing in school plays and Christmas concerts.

After I left Clare and Judy off to talk with Martin, I went back to my apartment. I didn't want to leave them, but I had phone calls to make. I needed to find a funeral home to take care of my father's burial. There would be no calling hours or services. I was the only family he had left. He'd never had any connection to anyone in my mother's family, since she'd come east to get away from them, and they'd stayed put in the Mid-West. Like me, my father had been an only child. Once I left for Canada, I knew nothing about his life in New Hampshire after his retirement—whether he and my mother had made new friends there. It was after she died, that he decided he'd move back to Charland. But after living in New Hampshire for ten years, he'd lost touch with his Charland colleagues from Town Hall, where he'd worked for decades. Probably some of them had already passed, or moved in with their children in other places, or moved to Florida or Arizona for better winter weather.

After a few phone calls to choose the undertaker, I went to my father's apartment building in the town's senior living complex. I had no key, so I stopped first at the office to find the building manager to let me into his place. I explained that I had to look for the papers related to the cemetery plot that he and my mother had purchased long ago. I asked also about whether my father had had a car, and the manager, who also took care of parking permits for residents, said he did not. I wondered if he'd taken the train or a bus or if some ride had been arranged for him on the day he'd come into Boston for an appointment at the VA clinic and then ended up at Mass General.

The apartment held little furniture and belongings. I opened the refrigerator and it was empty. I searched through his bureau drawers. Under a neatly folded pile of *Fruit of the Loom*, I found the file folder holding the information I needed to drop off at the funeral home.

Leaving, I decided to go to the cemetery first. I found the plot. I had never been to my mother's grave, and I felt shaky and a deep sadness came over me, seeing her name on the headstone. I had missed her terribly after leaving the country and not hearing from her, although I wrote often. Learning of her death, that there was no possibility of seeing her ever again, I'd been overcome with sorrow. I was barely able to teach at the time. And then, knowing that my father had not let me know of her death, that I'd had to learn of it so long after, and from an old friend, I felt, too, anger rising in me. Somehow, I had found my way again through my music. Music saved me. What I felt now, seeing her headstone, was resentment, that he had made sure he'd have my attention in his last days, left me to deal with things after his passing, while having denied me contact with my mother. It rattled me a little, too, that my father's name had already been chiseled on the granite headstone. I thought of my dad, having my mother's dates engraved, asking the stone carver and engraver, to add his name and birth date as well, in anticipation of his own passing. I guessed it was more efficient, and maybe less costly to have done that then, only his own date of death needing to be added now.

I read my mother's name, *Flora S. Newell*, over and over. The name was foreign to me; she was Mum or simply Mother. My dad always called her "Daisy."

Twenty-Five

Danielle

Waking up at my mom's house, at first it seemed that the craziness of the night before had been a real nightmare, that it hadn't actually happened. I wished. I was glad I'd escaped being in the middle of it. Mum must have been missing me, I thought, or she thought I was missing her; she hadn't asked me a single question about why I'd come to stay with her, when it was supposed to be my weekend with my dad.

When I got out of bed, I didn't hear her moving about in the house. I'd found her note on the kitchen counter. Before leaving she'd baked cherry and chocolate chip scones and she let me know where to find them—*They're good!*—and she wrote, too, that she didn't know how long her orchestra rehearsal was going to go. I guess she really did miss me, and she thought I was here because I wanted to hang out with her.

I was glad she wasn't home because otherwise I might have slipped and told her what had gone down at my dad's house. My dad said that it wasn't my business, that it was up to Clare and Ray to tell her. It was hard though, not having anyone to talk with about what was going on. I thought it was my business as much as anyone's. My Mom was probably going to be hurt by the news that Clare and Ray had a baby, even if it was a long time ago. That was a good reason for me not to be the one to break the news to her. But I didn't know Ray's side of the story. She might not be so hurt, hearing it. It was all pretty crazy stuff.

I ate a scone, drank a glass of milk and then took a shower. I was packing up my books for studying this afternoon when the phone rang. Chris had called already and we'd arranged to meet, so I didn't think he'd be calling. I figured it was probably just a student calling for my mom, or one of her friends. It might even be Ray calling her, to set up a time to see her. I definitely didn't want to talk to him right now. I stopped what I was doing to listen to the message. It was Judy Kneeland calling for me.

I picked up the phone.

"Hi," I said. "What's up?'

"I'm at my mom's," she said.

Her mom's. That was so weird, hearing her call Clare her mom.

"Is my dad there?" I said.

"He's right here. Do you want to talk to him?" she said.

"No. No I don't," I said.

Wow. If he was there with her, and Clare, too, maybe things were getting straightened out.

"What's up?" I asked her again.

"I'm going to be staying here with my mom and your dad."

"Is my dad staying there?" I said.

"Why wouldn't he be?" she said.

"No reason. Just wondering what's up," I said.

Obviously, there'd been some major developments since I'd left.

"Do you want to hang out? This afternoon?" she said.

I didn't really want her hanging out with Chris and me. And besides we really did plan on studying for most of the afternoon. Sitting and reading in a corner carrel at the library probably wasn't her idea of hanging out anyway.

"I'm meeting a friend. To study," I said.

"Oh."

She sounded disappointed and I felt bad.

"But not for lunch," I said. "Do you want to come over just for lunch? I'm meeting him a little later. I need to leave right after lunch though, to talk to him before we go to the library."

"Sure. Lunch would be good," she said.

She laughed. She told me that she and Clare had had breakfast at a deli in Boston, and after, she said Ray had come to meet them to tell her that he was her dad— and then, she'd had a second breakfast with him and Clare at some place in Harvard Square.

"Are you even hungry?" I said.

"I could eat something," she said.

I wondered if she was so hungry because she hadn't been having enough to eat since she got to Boston.

She put her hand over the telephone receiver. I could hear her saying, *Yes. Can I get a ride?* The response was muffled and I couldn't figure out if it was my dad or Clare answering her, or what was said.

"I can get a ride with Clare," she said.

"Okay then. Come over soon, so we have time before I have to leave. You can see where I live when I'm not with my dad."

A few minutes later, the bell rang, and when I opened the door to let Judy in, I saw Clare's car pulling away from the curb.

Judy gave me a half smile, like she was nervous.

"Your mom has a really nice house," she said as she walked through the living room to the kitchen, looking around.

She nervously smoothed her hair that had frizzed from the rainy day.

"You have hair just like Clare's," I said.

"I know. I hate it. I mean, I don't hate because it's like my mom's. She actually looks fine with it. But it's just that it's a pain."

"Yours looks okay," I said.

We went into the kitchen. I had already raided the fridge and the pantry to put out sandwich stuff.

"I thought you could make your own. I don't know what you like." I pointed to what was in the white paper wrappers and got a couple of knives for mayo and mustard. "There's turkey, ham, cheese, and there's lettuce and tomatoes in the colander in the sink. And this is good bread," I said, sliding the loaf over to her. "My mom gets it some place downtown."

"Wow. This seems like normal, eating in a real kitchen and having choices," she said.

She told me about a food voucher thing she'd been given at the place called Haven House, where she'd been staying,

"This is definitely better," she said, and laughed.

"I bet," I said.

And then she started to cry and I didn't know what I should do.

"What's the matter?" I said.

Then I realized what a stupid question that was. Everything was the matter. I tried to make her feel better.

"You found Clare. She's the real mother you didn't know about," I said.

"I know. I didn't know. But I loved the mom who raised me."

"I'm sorry," I said. "You'll get used to Clare though. She's great."

I did mean that, saying Clare was great. I was sorry now that I'd screamed at her the way I had the night before, accusing her, before I hadn't even given her a chance to tell me what had happened, so I'd understand that it wasn't her fault.

Judy shrugged and turned away as if embarrassed, crying, with me there.

"I think she wants me," she said about Clare. "But still, I miss my mom."

"Of course Clare wants you. Can you imagine? You were taken away from her right when you were born? She must have been always thinking about you."

She looked at me through her tears then.

"Do you like avocados?" I said, taking one from the bowl at the other end of the counter. "I think this one is ripe."

I held it out to her and she took it from me, and squeezed it.

"It is. It's good to eat now. I love avocados," she said.

I took a napkin from the holder on the table and gave it to her, so she could wipe her eyes.

"Sorry, we're out of Kleenex," I said.

"Do you have any honey?" she said. "I like honey and mustard on my turkey sandwich."

"We always have honey here," I said.

I went into the pantry cupboard and found the bear bottle.

Judy laughed when I brought it to the table.

"My mom buys the good stuff in the summer at the Farmer's Market," I said, "but she always has the bear on the shelf, in case we run out. Ever since I was little, because I loved the bear," I said.

"Me, too, my mom always bought the honey bear," she said.

I realized that hearing her talk about her mom who'd just

died— and Clare— and calling them both her mom, that she was a little like me, having two moms.

"I have a real mom and an extra mom, just like you did," I said.

Then I worried she was going to start crying again, but she didn't. She was eating now, as if she hadn't already had two breakfasts. She was thin and I wondered if she'd lost weight, only getting one meal a day with that voucher thing, or if she was always skinny.

"When are you moving into my dad's?" I said.

"I think today," she said.

"Today?"

"My dad has to talk your mom, so she knows. Then I can. She doesn't know anything, right?"

"I didn't say anything. I told my dad and Clare I wouldn't. I didn't," I said.

"I hate staying at that Haven House place," she said.

I shook my head, agreeing it must not be ideal.

While we were eating our sandwiches, she told me that Ray's father had died.

"So, I don't get to meet my grandfather," she said.

"He died?" I said, wondering if that would mean he'd go back to Canada and Judy would go stay with him there some of the time. Clare might be sad.

"He's moving here permanently, he said," Judy told me.

She explained then, that legally she couldn't stay with him, not here or anywhere, until some court thing happened and he got custody for her, for some of the time—shared custody, like my mom and dad had for me.

"But I can still see him sometimes, legally, your dad says."

As we finished our sandwiches I told her I had to go soon to meet Chris. I invited her to come with me to the Square if she wanted to hang out there, that I was taking the bus.

"I have an extra umbrella you can use," I said.

"I've been in Harvard Square a lot lately," she said. "My mom said she would pick me up and that we could go to Haven House to maybe get my stuff, tell them I'm leaving."

Judy finished eating and then got up to call Clare, to ask her to pick her up. She turned back to me and said, "Maybe she'll give you a ride to the Square, and you won't have to take the bus."

"Probably. But I need to call my mom first. Before I leave. So, tell her to wait ten minutes before she comes to get you."

I went upstairs to my mom's study, where there was another phone. I checked the calendar above her desk, to see how long her rehearsal was supposed to go. It would be over by now, and hopefully I'd catch her in her office before she left the Conservatory.

Hearing from Judy, that Ray would be in my life in a big way, there were so many reasons now to think that it didn't matter anymore, if my mom were seeing him. I would be seeing him with Judy at my dad's house anyway. Maybe he'd come to dinner, and maybe I'd be invited to go places with Judy sometimes, when she was with him. So why shouldn't my mom keep seeing him, and why shouldn't I go back to having lessons with him? And if they got more serious about each other, he might even move in with us—or at least stay over sometimes. And that would probably mean that when he got custody, Judy would stay with us, too, which would make it not so awkward when he was here with my mom, if they got together. Chris already thought that I was lucky to have a chance to study with him. I wanted my mom to know now that I'd go back to my lessons, and I would tell Chris this afternoon, what I'd decided.

I rarely called her at work, and I hadn't at all in a very long time. Talking to her these days I felt as if some imaginary hedge had been planted, separating us, and we had to talk to each other while standing on tiptoes, looking over it.

"Mum," I said, when she said *Hello, this is Veronica Harris.* "It's just me, Mum."

"Is everything okay?" she asked.

"Everything's fine," I said.

"Good. Good," she said. "I'll be home shortly."

She seemed pleasantly surprised to hear from me, and I felt a little bad telling her I wouldn't be home when she got here.

"I'm going to the library to study," I said. "But I wanted to tell you I want to go back to my lessons."

At first, she didn't think I could possibly mean saxophone

lessons, knowing that I'd been worried about her seeing Ray.

"I hope that Morrison hasn't filled your spot since you left," she said. "He's such a great teacher and musician."

"No, Mom. Not Morrison. Not cello. I meant saxophone. I'm done with cello, I told you before," I said.

"Oh?" she said. "Well, I can look for another teacher then. I'm sure I can find someone else."

"Why would I want that? I already started with Mr. Newell, and he's a great musician. I can learn a lot from him," I said.

"Well, okay then. I'll talk to him for you," she said.

Her offer was a little less enthusiastic, and I thought that maybe she was thinking that if I went back to lessons with him, it would mean she couldn't see him anymore, if she had broken her promise and been continuing to do that, hiding it from me. Then I thought that maybe she was just looking for a reason to call him, that maybe she had kept her promise to me that she wouldn't see him anymore.

"I'll call him myself," I said. "I have his number."

"Oh," she said, sounding both surprised and disappointed.

I had actually been thinking that she was going to happy, hearing me say that I willing to take responsibility for arranging one of my activities, something she was always saying I needed to do more, rather than always relying on her.

"Well, you'll be waiting to start lessons until September then?" she said. "The Dineens will be leaving for the Cape as soon as school gets out, won't they?"

As far as she knew I was still taking the nanny job in Falmouth, going to help with the kids I babysat for during the school year in Cambridge.

"I've decided to stay here," I told her. "I've been looking for a summer job. Steph heard of a few places in the Square that were hiring. I told Molly that I'm not going to the Cape with the family. She was disappointed to have to look for another nanny, but she understood."

"She'll find someone else," Mum said. "And I'm very glad you'll be going back to lessons with Mr. Newell."

"It sounds funny, you calling him Mr. Newell, instead of

Ray," I said.

She ignored my comment and then she got kind of sad.

"I'm glad you're not leaving Cambridge for the summer, that you'll be around. I'm grateful to have any time with you now, Danielle. In another year, you'll be off to college, and I'll be alone," she said.

"Maybe I won't leave Boston for college," I said. "I don't know what I'll do. You don't know either."

"Well, I was only remembering that before, you weren't interested in schools in the Boston area. But really, Danielle, who knows where life will take you? Either for college or after. Hey, you might end up halfway around the world, like my friend Mary Sarno's daughter, teaching English in South Korea," she said.

She was running with the gloom now.

"I'm not planning to go half-way around the world, you know," I said, hoping to change her mood. "Unless it's just a vacation."

I thought now, how lucky I was to know my real mother, even when she's a pain sometimes. Like Judy, I had two mothers, but I knew from the beginning, which one gave birth to me.

I hoped that Ray would talk to her today, as Judy said he was going to do. She'd be happy again, to see him. Then I remembered what Judy had told me.

"I just found out, Mum, that Ray's father died, and thought you should know."

She was silent. I guess surprised, figuring I was telling her, so she'd be able to offer him condolences.

When she spoke again, all she said was, "Thanks for telling me."

"I have to hang up. I'm meeting a friend to study with at the library," I said.

I almost told her that *the friend* was Chris. She didn't even know that I'd been getting together with him after school some days, or that maybe he'd begin taking lessons with Ray. But then I didn't tell her, wanting to keep it from her, because I didn't know if it would last. It didn't seem real yet, and I didn't want her asking me about him all the time. I realized suddenly, that feeling this way made me believe what she'd said to me, about why she hadn't told me about Ray, why she was keeping him a secret. She'd said she felt she didn't want to jinx anything, by talking about it. I did want to tell her about Chris, but I wanted to wait, just like she had.

Twenty-Six

Ray

That afternoon I had to meet a student at the Conservatory for a lesson, and later, there was practice scheduled for a performance of my quartet. My student never showed; that happened on Saturdays sometimes, so I went to my office to wait until it was time for the rehearsal. Veronica had come by, and left a note. She was on campus for a rehearsal, too, but hers was over by now, and she was probably long gone. She was wondering if I'd want to meet her for a drink this evening. I tried calling her at home, but got no answer.

At the rehearsal, the quartet went through the play list for our next gig, and when we got it down, I packed up my stuff, and drove back to Cambridge. I didn't feel like going home to an empty house, so I headed to a café near MIT for a while, just to be among others. It was crowded, and I was lucky to get the last empty seat. I drank coffee, but not knowing anyone, I felt lonelier still.

I went out of the air-conditioned café and a blast of heat hit me. The rain had stopped but it was so humid. Slowly, I walked to the street where I'd parked.

Thinking that Veronica might be there, I drove to a pub where the two of us used to go for a drink or sometimes dinner after classes. I hoped that I wouldn't regret my decision, and I hoped she'd be there. I knew I needed to tell her what was going on before she heard it from someone else.

It wasn't easy finding parking in busy Central Square—ever—especially at this hour on a Saturday afternoon. I drove around, down Mass. Ave, taking side streets back over to Prospect and around the corner a few times, before giving up on the idea of finding a place close to *Pearl's* I turned onto a residential street, where I knew some houses had off-street parking, which might increase the likelihood of finding a space there. After a couple of times around the block, I found one not far from Mass. Ave.

I walked briskly down crowded sidewalks, weaving in and out, through clogs of Saturday shoppers and students just coming up out of the subway from Boston, or off buses. Now that the rain had stopped, everyone was out. I went into the pub, grateful to be back in air-conditioning, sitting down at an unoccupied corner table by the window.

My eyes adjusted to the darker room, and I scanned the tables around me, and then the half-moon bar, where most spots were already taken. From my seat, I had a view of the entire room, as well as the entrance. When I didn't see her, I figured that, if she had been here earlier, not seeing me, she was probably gone, thinking I'd decided not to come.

A waiter approached. "Hendricks martini with a twist?" he remembered.

"Hello. Yes, thanks," I said, and the waiter, trying to keep up with the growing crowd, breezed away, no time for ingratiating chat.

I slowly sipped my drink, while perusing my calendar of lessons and appointments for the rest of the week, trying to have something to do, while sitting here alone. Once in a while, I lifted my head and gazed nonchalantly toward the entrance to see who was coming in, or I looked out the window, scanning the sidewalk, hoping to see Veronica.

I was about to give up, when suddenly she appeared—not in the doorway, but emerging from a rear corner of the room. She'd been in the Women's maybe, and that was why I hadn't seen her at first, or someone might have been standing behind her at the bar, blocking my view.

"Ray," she called out, seeing me.

I raised my hand, stretching it high, so that she'd see I knew where the voice had come from.

She looked surprised that I'd come, but happy. She pointed to a back booth where she'd been sitting, and I picked up my drink and headed there.

"I didn't know if you got my message," she said.

"I left late," I told her. "I figured you'd already left. Tried you at home. When you weren't there, I thought I'd see if I'd find you here."

"Sit," she said.

And I obeyed. I was very glad to see her, while nervous about what I had to tell her.

She raised her eyebrows, looking at me. I raised mine, not knowing what she meant by that, wondering what her question was.

"I have to talk with you," I said.

I wanted to get it over with. I let out a deep breath.

She took a deep breath, too, and exhaled. She shook her head. I wondered what she thought I was going to say. Certainly not what I was about to reveal. Since Danielle had given up her lessons, we hadn't seen each other, except in passing— in the corridors at the Conservatory, or at nearby cafes, where students and faculty from the Conservatory went for lunch or coffee.

We were shadows of each other now, mimicking the other's body language, as if we were just getting to know each other, and we were shy. I didn't really speak until it became too uncomfortable. Then I said, "This is really something, what I have to tell you. I need you to listen. I hope you will."

She leaned on an elbow and looked at me intently. Her devilish smile appeared, an expression I'd seen only when we were going to make love. She was going to fall hard, hearing what I had to tell her. I hoped she would hear me out.

"I'm a father," I said.

"What? Can you repeat that?" she said.

She squinted, an expression that could only mean, *what kind of craziness is this?*

I took a sip of my drink, and then another. Fortification. I put the glass down.

"It's true," I said.

"Oh, don't tell me. Please. You have a family in Canada I didn't know about?" she said.

"No, no, that it isn't it. No," I said.

I moved and my jacket slid off the seat and to the floor. I reached down and picked it up.

"Don't leave," she said.

"I'm not," I said. "I never thought I'd be a father ever, never mind that I already was one."

Veronica just kept shaking her head.

"I have to begin at the beginning or else it won't make any sense," I said. "You know I left for Canada, because of Vietnam, right? Well..."

I hesitated.

"Well," I said, "Clare was my high school girlfriend."

She held her head in her hands, and looked up at the ceiling as if some angel might be there to save her from what I was telling her, throwing her head back against the booth.

"She was your high school girlfriend? " she said, still not looking at me.

It was a declaration that sounded like she was repeating something I'd said in a foreign language.

"I know, I know, I should have told you when I found out she was Danielle's stepmom," I said.

She moved on the bench and turned and looked at her raincoat hanging on the pole above the booth.

"Don't go. Please, listen. I didn't come home to find Clare. I had no idea. I wasn't planning to find her. I was going to see to my father's stuff and then go back. When his care required me to stay longer, a friend got me the Conservatory gig. I needed the money. I had a place in Canada I was paying for and an apartment here. You were the one who found me, remember? You asked me to teach Danielle. That's how I met Clare again."

"None of that explains you having a child and what Clare has to do with that," she said. "Where is this child? And how old? And, where is she—or he? And who's the mother?"

I told her the whole story then, how Clare had been pregnant and didn't know at the time I left for Canada, that her father had sent her away to have the child and give it up to another woman, and that cruelly, he had never forwarded any of the letters I'd written, so Clare didn't know how to reach me.

"I never knew about the child," I said several times, just as I had with Martin.

As I spoke, Veronica put a hand to cover her mouth, as if to prevent a scream from escaping.

When I finished, she did speak, and asked about what I had not yet told her.

"Ray," she said. "Does Clare even know what happened to her child?"

I took another sip of my drink, and Veronica lifted her wine glass to her lips.

"Well, that's just it. She's here. In town. And you can't imagine how happy Clare is to meet her. Especially now, after losing the baby she and Martin thought they were going to have," I said.

"Her. A daughter. Here? Now? Why, she must be as old as Danielle now! Did she just show up out of the blue?"

"It's sad," I said. "The circumstances. Judy—Judy, that's her name. Her adoptive mother had been ill for a long time and died. So, it's not just Clare and Martin who've been through a big loss lately."

"And you, too," Veronica said. "Danielle called and told me about your father. I'm so sorry."

I didn't want to talk about my father now. I said only, "right." Veronica got the message and dropped it.

"Well, now Judy has Clare. And Clare has her daughter back," she said.

"Judy said it was her illness—something your children could inherit, though we don't know what exactly—that's the reason her mother finally told her she was adopted. She might not have known otherwise," I said.

Veronica gasped.

"God, to be hit with that knowledge, when you'd believed something else your whole life? And at sixteen? She must be about sixteen? Right? Like Danielle?"

"Sixteen," I said. "And all that time for Clare to be wondering about her, yet Judy didn't even know she existed."

"And you didn't know about her?"

"Never. No one knew. Clare kept it secret, all those years. I've only known since she was here to tell Clare. Two days. That's all," I said.

Veronica talked then of Danielle, of Clare being a stepmom to her after losing her own daughter, and of these last weeks, when Danielle had tossed her aside. How painful it was, she said.

"How does a mother keep going after the loss of her child, thinking it's forever?" Veronica said.

I thought of my own mother, of when I'd left the country. She must have been grieving. I would like to believe that my father had given her the letters I wrote to her, but I had my doubts. And, if she hadn't read my letters, he might not have let on either, that I'd been sending those postcards I sent, intending to always keep her apprised of my whereabouts. My father would have wanted my mother to *get over it*. *Get over it*, was one of his favorite phrases, when anyone expressed sadness over a loss, disappointment, or regret. Clare seemed not to harbor any bitterness, no matter that losing Judy had happened to her when she was so young.

"Clare must be very strong," Veronica said.

I agreed.

I wasn't going to ask the big question, the one that had been on my mind for way too long.

I kept myself from saying, *should we maybe try again?* I wondered if Danielle could handle it now. I held back, afraid to wonder aloud, if getting together again would be possible, now that any involvement we might have with each other seemed to be overshadowed by new developments. Who knew what they were going to mean for Clare and me—and for Martin, too.

Veronica said that she'd made some mistakes, and she thought it had to do with the fact that I'd been the first man she'd even "cared to carry on with in a very long time."

"Well I hadn't exactly been involved in what you'd call a long-term relationship with anyone either," I said. "Short lived? Yes. Sometimes, it just took one date for me to decide not to pursue anything more."

"Well, I know about that. I skipped the online stuff. Can't imagine that, although several friends of mine have met future husbands or long-term partners that way. I always preferred to believe I'd find opportunities with people I'd have more in common with, without having to troll through what I think of as a sad yearbook of profiles on some of those dating sites," Veronica said.

"I did think things were different for me with you," I said.

"It's strange," she said, "knowing about your past."

"For me, too," I said.

I asked if that changed anything for her.

"Maybe," she said. "Danielle made the decision to go back to her lessons with you. I wonder if she's heard of this, and that's why. I suppose it means you'll be involved not just as her teacher. She's going to call you, but don't tell her I told you."

"Ah, secrets," I said. "More secrets. But she already called me this afternoon. I talked to her while I waiting around for my quartet to show. My student stood me up, so I went back to my office to wait."

She laughed.

"You know, I have nothing but admiration for Clare," she said. "Imagine—giving up her daughter, and parenting mine—seeing Danielle through all the milestones she was missing with her own daughter. So gracious," Veronica said, shaking her head as if it was unbelievable to her that anyone could be so strong, so generous.

She hesitated, as if totally feeling the sense of that realization. When she spoke again, it was to focus on Judy, as if she understood that she, too, was foremost on my mind.

"Which one of you does she look like?" she asked.

Danielle, she explained, favored Martin's family looks. She was almost a brunette.

"She has the darker, olive-toned skin—especially in summer—of the Italian side of his mother's family, and not my own pale, British and Scandinavian coloring and blond hair."

"When I first saw Judy coming down the stairs at that place she'd been staying, I was right back in high school. She looked just like Clare did at that age, I thought. But Clare thinks she looks a little like me, too, though I don't know," I said. "She has darker hair, like mine."

"She must be very good looking then," Veronica said. "You know, I'm really sorry about what happened. I should have listened to you and told Danielle. All those questions you kept asking about Clare. I didn't know what that was about, so I didn't want to tell her about us. I thought maybe what we had wasn't going to last. It was just..."

I interrupted. I reached across the table then, and put an index finger to her lips and shook my head, *No*.

She colored, and sighed, but it wasn't a sigh of defeat. It sounded like one of relief.

"How could you know why I was so interested in Clare?" I said. "It's not your fault that you mistrusted me. Of course, it was weird for me to be with you, and be asking about your daughter's stepmom—your ex-husband's wife. Really, I get that now."

"Yes, really," she said, smiling. "But," she said, "I admit, that I've been known to be inclined to jealousy, when I want to hold onto someone."

"I'm glad to hear you want that," I said. "Good. Not good that you' re inclined to be jealous, but I mean, I'm glad you want to hold onto this, whatever we might have left between us."

There. I'd said it, finally. We both had. We'd admitted what we wanted. It felt good to be honest about what I felt. It was freeing.

"What are you doing this evening?" I asked.

Veronica looked at her watch, as if suddenly reminded of a responsibility. She'd been thinking of Danielle, she said, that she ought to check in with her, see if she was planning to eat dinner at home with her.

"I'd vowed to make her a priority after what happened, and I especially wanted to keep to that pledge, since we're on speaking terms again," she said.

"Isn't she with her dad tonight?" I asked. "When she called me today, she left a message to call her at her dad's this evening."

Veronica counted back to the last weekend, when Danielle was with her, and then the days before that, realizing that I was right. It was Martin's weekend to have her with him, and she realized now that things were getting sorted out, and she'd probably be going back there.

"I got confused because she stayed with me last night. She never explained why, and I was so happy to have her choose to be with me, that I didn't even ask what was up. You're more familiar with Danielle's schedule at the moment than I am," she said.

She laughed. When I told her that Clare and I were planning on co-parenting Judy, when some legal issues were straightened out, she said that Martin and I were going to learn first-hand what it had been like for Clare as stepparent to Danielle. I let her know that for the time being, she'd be staying with Clare and Martin.

"Come on," I said, gently pulling her elbow as I stood. "Let's get out of here. Come."

I could hardly believe it. It was the miracle of living, that things could happen so suddenly to change the course of your day, your life. Too often, since coming home to deal with my father's situation, I'd thought only of the flipside of what was happening now, of how quickly things could fall apart, how loss was always waiting just around the corner.

We walked to my apartment, which wasn't far from where I'd parked my car. I decided not to move it. It might be daylight before I drove away. When I kissed Veronica as we passed the corner coffee shop, a small boy seated with a woman, who might be his mother, sat at a window table and saw us. Reflexively, he covered his mouth with one of his hands, and elbowed his mother, while pointing to us, kissing. I read his lips, "Look!" he exclaimed. And then the woman looked up from her coffee to see what it was he'd noticed. She saw us, just as we broke our embrace. She smiled out at us.

Twenty-Seven

Martin

I met Clare at the subway station in Harvard Square, after her classes at the Medical Center were finished. We were finally going to see Troy's house on Fern Hill. Remarkably, it was still for sale. Both of us had figured that we'd probably missed our chance, since we'd delayed so long, going to see it, the events of the past couple of months sidetracking our search for a new place to live. But I'd called Troy this week, since we felt that the time was right to start looking again, now that Judy would be in Clare's life.

"There must be something wrong with it," Clare said.

She'd only heard me say positive things about the house, and she was worried, I knew, that my desire to please her was fueling my enthusiasm. I knew, too, that she'd be letdown if she didn't think we should make an offer on the place.

"He must not have been showing it," I said, trying to explain why it might still be on the market.

"Since you told him you were maybe interested in it, did he think that we were a sure bet, and so he stopped bringing people in to see it?"

"He has a busy practice, you know," I said.

Clare just wasn't ready to buy into my optimism. I looked away from the wheel to see her expression. Her caution showed in the firm set of her mouth. I slowed the car a bit, though I didn't do it intentionally, and didn't even realize at first that I had.

"You'll keep an open mind, I hope. There isn't much out there—and as I said, this house was an unexpected inheritance for him. He doesn't need the money, so it doesn't matter to him, when he sells it. But at the same time, he does want to be rid of it, and he doesn't want to sell it to one of those developers. He said he wants a family to have it. There'd be room for Danielle. And Judy," I added. "They'll probably both be at college in another year, but we'd want to have a room for them to come home to—and there'd be an office for each of us.

"Judy," Clare said. "My daughter."

She was still getting used to the fact that she had come back to her by some miracle.

When we arrived at the house we saw Troy sitting, reading the newspaper in his car parked out front. There probably wasn't any furniture inside, nowhere for him to sit in the house, and he'd arrived early. We pulled up in front of his car, and I looked in the rear view mirror and saw that he was folding the newspaper and putting it down. Then, he got out of the car to greet us.

"It's good of you to meet us here in the afternoon," I said, after I'd introduced him to Clare.

"No problem. Did a little rearranging of the schedule, and I'm happy to show it to you," Troy said.

He paused and lowered his voice.

"And I'm very sorry about your loss," he said, quite seriously, and looking Clare in the eye. "Martin told me," he added.

Clare looked at me as if I'd violated her privacy, letting him know. But, when we didn't show up for a viewing the day Clare had to see Dr. Aviva, I told him she'd lost our baby, as a way of explaining why I hadn't called to cancel. I took her hand and squeezed it.

"Have you had many lookers?" I asked.

"Well, to tell you the truth, I haven't been advertising widely, just reaching out to people I know. It's a busy time for the practice. Had a few calls, but no serious interest. People not ready to take on owning. Couples as old as you even. You'd think that, getting into their mid-thirties, they might consider it. But I have feeling about you two. I'd like to see you have your own place, get out of that apartment, Martin."

I raised an eyebrow at that. He was giving us the hard sell.

"You're being very persuasive," Clare said.

"You don't have to think of it as forever. It can be a stepping stone to something even better, at a later date," Troy offered.

He was persistent. I thought he sounded more like a real estate agent than a lawyer.

"What kind of law is it, you practice?" Clare asked, picking up on that.

Troy smiled and led us inside.

"This is why I wanted you to come during the day," he said, flicking the light switch on the living room wall, so that we'd see that the electricity had been shut off. "No reason really, to be giving money to the electric company, when no one's living here."

"Well, it's still bright and sunny at this time of day in this season," Clare agreed, looking around, obviously pleased by the many, long, old-fashioned windows—floor to ceiling—in the front two rooms.

It was much brighter than our apartment, which was blocked from receiving sunlight by the houses on both sides, built on lots too close to our house. Troy seemed to be taking great pleasure in showing the architectural features that made this house what was called "Philadelphia Style." Maybe it was a technique to distract us from focusing on the kitchen and bath. Although clean and in good repair, they looked like they hadn't been updated since the nineteen-fifties.

Troy watched as I ran water in the bathroom sink, flushed the toilet, and moved on to the kitchen, opening the dishwasher—at least there was a dishwasher. I turned the crank on the windows above the sink to open them, and the room filled with the voices of young children playing outside in the yard next door.

"They're a nice family," Troy said. "Well-behaved kids. My client never complained about them being next door—and she was an older woman, in her eighties, when she passed," he said.

"I don't mind kids," Clare said. "It's nice to hear them having fun."

It was almost old-fashioned to hear kids playing in a backyard in the city. It was what I'd thought, too, about this neighborhood, the day when I'd come to see where the house was located, doing a recognizance mission. I'd been reminded of my own childhood neighborhood, after my family had moved to Providence. I had to admit that I liked the house, as well as the location, but I was trying to withhold any outward enthusiasm, at least for now, afraid to get Clare's hopes up, just in case she thought the asking price was beyond our means. I refrained for now, with Troy present, from asking what Clare thought about the house.

Then, perhaps thinking that I might not have told her about the circumstances that gave him ownership of this house, Troy began explaining that he'd never expected to be paid in kind or otherwise, that he'd represented Mrs. Crosby *pro bono*, because she'd been a close friend of his aunt, and had fallen into financial difficulty after her husband's death. "She never thought he'd be the one to go first," he said.

Suddenly I broke caution and firmly said, "I could live here. I can imagine it."

I knew that both of us would feel so much better waking up in summer, the windows open, hearing children or birds chirping, rather than rush hour traffic building on Ridge Road. Outside, I had not noticed any smell of exhaust fumes, or heard sirens or honking cars. There were trees here and all sort of plants and flowers growing.

Troy took us out the back door to the porch and pointed out the old plantings in the backyard—tea roses all along the property line, marked by a genuine New England stone wall.

"There's even a grape vine. Concord grapes, the ones with lots of flavor. Every fall. The owner told me she smuggled a cutting in from Greece, returning from a vacation there," he said.

I wondered about that. Concord grapes, from Greece? Perhaps it was the same fruit, but had a different name in Greece, or was a similar variety. Or perhaps Troy had invented the smuggling story.

I looked around, noticing hydrangea bushes budding. I recognized them by their leaves, and the very light green buds on thick stalks.

Troy suggested there was even room for a kitchen garden in front of the back porch. I agreed, and thought that a small patio under the grape arbor would be a nice place to sit and have a glass of wine on warm summer evenings, and a place to entertain friends for lunch or a barbecue.

In the car we rode in silence to Elephant Parade, which we agreed served some of the best Vietnamese cuisine in all of Cambridge.

Neither of us felt like cooking after working, and then going to see the house. Besides, being at this place gave our conversation a sense of importance. At this restaurant, I'd first promised Clare we'd find a new and better place to live than the apartment on Ridge Road, and before that we'd eaten here when she'd given me the news that she was pregnant. The restaurant had been packed that night, so it wasn't the intimate setting she'd imagined for the telling, she'd said. Tonight was a Monday night and the place was nearly deserted, so we were able to talk comfortably, not to have to try to be heard over the din of many conversations happening at once, or competing with music that came from speakers tuned to high in different places around the room. With fewer customers, tonight the volume was set much lower.

Once the waiter had brought each of us a beer, Clare said, "I'm sure the asking price must be out of our range. Too bad."

"Well, maybe not. I haven't asked yet what he wants for it. I thought we needed to talk first. We need to decide how much we want it."

"But no matter," Clare interrupted, "no matter how much we want it, we can't have it, if we can't afford it."

I took another sip of my Singha and slowly swallowed. When I spoke again, my voice was calmer.

"Listen, Clare, he doesn't really want to hold onto the house. He never expected to have it at all. You heard him. And he confided in me, when I called him, telling me he'd be willing—as the seller—to finance it. Real estate in Cambridge is picking up. He figures in ten or fifteen years, when he'd expect we could pay it off, that we'd want to sell anyway, and by then, he thinks real estate prices are going to go through the roof."

"Why?" Clare asked. "What makes this place so special?"

She had never really settled into living here. She liked it all right, but some days, she said she wished that she could live somewhere that felt more like the small town where she'd grown up. Everything here was always about being better, more successful, and there was so much wealth and privilege in Cambridge. It wasn't the real world.

"Well, for starters, look at the parks we have, for one thing, and all there is for kids—and adults. And it's only across the River from Boston. There's a certain cachet, so people want to live here," I said.

I knew that a place to live was more than that. It was about community. Having a home of your own connected you to a place. I felt that if we had a house, she'd feel like she had a home.

"There's so much competition. And ordinary people seem to disappear," she said. "Or they're pushed out, leaving a city full of people who seem sometimes just a little too special, if you ask me."

She paused, but then suddenly, as if hearing what she was saying, she began again.

"Do I sound bitter?" she asked. "Oh, my God, I'm becoming a bitter woman."

"You're not bitter. You've just had a lot happen. Think of it. And Clare, stop thinking you're not good enough to live here. That's what this sounds like. You're getting it wrong. It's a welcoming place. It's got history. You're talking about the People's Republic. Remember?"

I reached across the table and took her hand.

"We have to think positively about this," I said.

"I suppose you're right. What else do we have in terms of a nest egg? Nada," she said, giving in to a half-smile.

The loss of the baby had shaken her, and I knew she was nervous about changes coming in her life. But both things made me feel that we needed to make some definite plans for the future, to avoid the kind of bitterness that did seem to be surfacing in her, once in a while. Until Judy came along, after losing the baby she'd acted as if her goals and dreams were passing out of reach, that she was becoming, not dissatisfied with what she hadn't achieved, but adjusted to it. That bothered me; I didn't want her to be complacent. But then, Judy appeared, and I thought that maybe we could have what we wanted, only it would be different. Clare could be a parent. She could assume the role she'd relinquished so many years before.

I told Clare that Troy had agreed to have papers related to the sale ready for us, should we decide that we wanted to take the leap. We could look them over, see what, if anything, we wanted to negotiate.

"He said that he just had a feeling that the place would be perfect for us, " I said.

Getting home, we found Danielle and Judy watching a movie. I was happy Danielle had decided to return for the weekend, and Judy obviously was. They'd made a huge bowl of popcorn and we're both diving into it when we walked in. Clare sat down with them.

"What you are watching," she said.

I went into my study to check phone messages. Veronica had left one, to rsvp for the welcome dinner that Clare was planning for Judy. She added that she'd talked to Ray, and that he was planning to come as well. Clare would be pleased, having all of us together.

Twenty-Eight

Clare

By the time Friday came, there was a lot to celebrate at dinner. Not only was the family expanding to include Ray and Judy, but Martin and I had also made an offer on the house and Troy had accepted it. There was an air of general amazement, engendered by the fact that we were all sitting down together at the same table. The idea of being a stepmother or stepfather or half-sister—or ex-lover or ex-wife or husband—whatever—was disregarded in an unspoken consensus. We were simply: family. Veronica and I had never shared a meal together, even though we had, for many years, mothered the same child, and here we were now, seated across the table from one another. Danielle and Judy both seemed proud of their connection to Ray—Judy's father being a *cool* musician—and they both looked at him with the starry eyes of a fan's admiration. They were as well, obviously delighted to know that they were *sisters*—sort of—and it seemed they'd bonded immediately, as teenagers often will, in spite of any differences in upbringing.

There was champagne—lots of it—several bottles were consumed. Even Danielle and Judy were allowed to raise a glass, making them giddy. We were all rather giddy, partly from nervousness about this new family. Except Martin: he looked to me like the anointed patriarch of a new clan, pleased as punch that we were hosting the occasion. I realized now, how stressed he'd been, trying to please everyone always, and not accepting that sometimes you just can't. He was clearly relieved to have peace in his home, all the players in his little family drama, now present and seemingly happy to be with each other. He went around filling the glasses after each toast, and there were many. He stood over Veronica and Ray to fill their glasses, and I saw him notice when he did, the way Veronica looked at Ray. Ray had taken her hand and was holding it under the table, and Martin looked down and saw that, too. Seated again, he proposed a toast to "a new idea of family."

I saw that Ray continued to hold Veronica's hand during the toast and through every good wish that was voiced each time we raised the crystal flutes.

How could it be that this was an event we would not have imagined before, this kind of civility between our families? Before, it was always: Martin and Veronica and Danielle, or Martin and Clare and Danielle, or just Martin and Clare, and Veronica solo—until Ray came along, and then Judy.

Being adopted by this family was no doubt a bit overwhelming. No one mentioned that. Ray said that he thought this change had come for him when he really needed it, after the loss of his father. It was all so strange, especially that the daughter he'd never known existed, had appeared now, at this time, and at the time of my loss as well. Life certainly was full of surprises. He'd talked with me about a night in Montreal during the series of blizzards that had hit Canada hard. It was the week when someone from the hospital had called about his father naming him *next of kin*. In one of the many conversations I'd had with him since Judy surfaced, he'd told me he'd been lonely and anxious to find a place that felt like home, not knowing then, how to make that happen.

With the main course of the meal finished, I got up to clear the dishes from the table. Veronica joined me, helping to remove the serving plates, collecting the silverware. In the kitchen there was cake—almost like a wedding cake, it was so elegant.

"Martin said, when I asked a couple of times about bringing dessert, that because we had things to celebrate at dinner, that you were taking care of dessert," Veronica said.

I stood at the sink, running water over the dinner plates, and loading them into the dishwasher.

"Well, you certainly have taken care of it!" Veronica exclaimed, admiring the cake.

It was a cake of many layers. She counted aloud.

"Five layers!"

"Six actually," I corrected her. "One for each of us!"

The cake frosting was all white and made with real cream, no garish pink, yellow, red or blue flowers, but delicate white ones, and a scrolling vine design on the edges and sides. The implications of buying a cake that looked like it would be more appropriate for a wedding banquet were many, but Veronica didn't mention that.

"It's beautiful," was all she said about it.

"It's from The Cake House, in Chinatown near the Medical Center. My students buy them to celebrate the end of each semester, and I've begun buying them for special occasions; they're so delicious."

"It's a very special cake," Veronica said.

"It's a very special occasion," I said.

We stood there, looking at the cake and nodding in agreement. I handed Veronica candles, sixteen of them.

"You put them on the cake and I'll light them, as you do."

I took the box of long wooden matches from the shelf above the stove.

"I didn't realize it was her birthday?"

"It isn't, but it feels like it to me," I said.

"It's so pretty, though. I hate to pierce it with candles," Veronica said.

"It'll be fine," I assured her. "More festive."

When all the candles were lit, I lifted the plate and started to walk slowly toward the door into the dining room.

"Sixteen years of not knowing, Clare. How strong you were," Veronica said. She reached over, as if to give me a hug, something she'd never done. But I was holding the cake plate, so that was impossible. I was sure we'd find time for a hug later. I knew she appreciated that I'd been a good mom to Danielle, in spite of her sometimes histrionics.

I didn't say anything. I just shook my head, acknowledging her gesture.

"You go in first and sit down," I said to her. "And hit the light switch off, as you pass by, will you?"

Veronica complied and took her seat next to Ray. I watched, and saw him reach over and touch her knee, massaging it. She looked at him and smiled. I could see that she was happy he was beside her.

No one spoke and then Danielle started to sing *Happy Birthday* and the others joined in, as I walked through the door, carefully carrying the cake, so the candles would stay lit.

Judy laughed, amused.

I put the cake down in front of her, kissing the top of her head.

"I know this doesn't make up for all we've missed, but I'm so happy to have you with us now," I said. "We all are."

Everyone raised a glass, with a cheer of "Here, here!"

Judy turned around, standing to acknowledge me, hugging me.

"I don't want to let go," she whispered.

"Oof! The candles are dripping and melting all over that lovely frosting," Veronica interrupted.

We broke our hug then, and I took my seat between Judy and Martin, reaching out to take their hands.

***

Once everyone had gone home—including Danielle, who went back to stay with Veronica for the weekend—and after the dishes were put away, Martin sat down to read. I stayed at the sink, filling a pitcher of water for the houseplants.

At the window I pinched a dried bloom from the Phalaenopsis I'd bought in Harvard Square while doing errands on the way back from Dr. Aviva's office, the same day I'd received the news that I was pregnant. I had spotted the orchid with its tiger yellow flowers. It had been outstanding for its height and elegance in a crowd of showy begonia, lighting up the sidewalk out front of Brattle Florist. I went into the shop, paid for it, and asked the clerk to hold it for me until later in the day, when I'd return to pick it up on my way home, after the doctor visit. The plant had been vital then—buds the size of strawberries on steroids—and I'd believed it would flourish in the kitchen window. For weeks it had bloomed, but now the flowers had shriveled, and several of the deep green, long-tongued leaves, had split and dried. I carefully pulled them off, trying to preserve any growth that might burst through the tough stalk. I believed the plant was only dormant; that it would have its season again, if I cared for it well.

Since Judy had left the house with Danielle, Veronica, and Ray, the words of Kahlil Gibran were running around in my head.

One particular passage: *On Children*. I hadn't thought of Gibran in years, but now it came back to me, how diligently I'd studied those words while a college student! They'd brought some consolation after loss. *Your children are not your own. They are the sons and daughters of life's longing.* My friends and I had read *The Prophet* in the early seventies, the way we'd read and memorized prayers for Sunday Mass, first in Latin, and then in English. That was before we threw off our religion. When we did, Gibran became gospel truth.

Your children are not your own. They are the sons and daughters of life's longing. Most of my friends considered those words as justification for resisting what their parents expected of them, determined to make their way in the world on their own terms. But my interpretation was different, having by then been denied the opportunity to make what had been the biggest decision of my life, denied the choice to decide on my own terms, about the baby. I'd wished I'd been able to recite Gibran's words to my father, as my college friends would later, exerting their independence from their parents. But when I first read those words as a college student, they were heavy with a different meaning for me. I'd been struggling, so deeply affected by my loss, my life's longing, while trying to convince myself to accept that my child was not mine. I realized then, how hard I was going to have to work to discover within me, the kind of self-determination my friends seemed to have been born with and never had squelched, the way it had been for me. *Getting into trouble*—that was the way people talked then, about what had happened to me, and to other young women in the same situation. And it certainly was trouble. *Your children are not your own. They are the sons and daughters of life's longing.* I knew in my heart the truth of those lines, the folly of thinking of a flesh and blood child, as one's own, the pull in my gut remaining for my daughter *of life's longing.*

Finished watering the plants, I poured a glass of wine, and went out to the small, screened-in porch, to join Martin. This was a favorite place to think. Ours was the only house in the surrounding neighborhood with its old-fashioned porches preserved. Others in the houses all around this one had replaced theirs with decks. In the years I'd lived here with Martin, I was glad the landlord seemed to have no desire to demolish this worn refuge, to make way for the new. I wondered how some people could so easily let go of the past. I couldn't shake the strangeness of feeling that my past was alive for me now in the present moment. I asked Martin for the *Living* section of the newspaper.

"I'm still reading the Metro," he said, removing the pages I wanted and handing them to me.

I scanned the front page. I didn't really want to read. I put the paper down on the table next to the chair, and I reached over and took Martin's hand. He let the section he was reading fall to his lap. He clasped my hand tightly.

Acknowledgments

There are so many people I want to thank. First and foremost, what would I have done without the support and unwavering belief in my work from my husband, Mark Pawlak, and my son Gianni? I would like to express my gratitude to John Dufresne, Gish Jen, Caroline Leavitt, Mary E. Mitchell, Annie Pluto, and Rosie Sultan, for their willingness to read the manuscript and for offering such generous comments; your own work inspires me. Thanks to Amy Holman for guidance, encouraging me to stay with the project, even through the darkest days of the pandemic. (Also, to Christine Evans and others who joined in for the Silent Writers Room on Zoom during that time.)

I'm grateful to BFFs Joan Eisenberg and Nancy Sawyer for reading early drafts; for Karen Burke's friendship and for introducing me to Laura Huckestein, whose house above the bay in the easternmost town in the U.S. provided respite and an ideal place to work on an important edit; to Sheila Pleasants and staff of VCCA (Virginia Center for the Creative Arts), which has been crucial to this novel, from idea to completion during residencies at Mt. San Angelo and Moulin a Nef in Auvillar. I am grateful, too, for studio space at the Writers Room of Boston, my "at home residency." I have appreciated each person who listened while I read selections from the work-in-progress and especially those who offered comments: other residency fellows, Warren Wilson MFA Alumni at Conferences, and those who tuned in for several reading series Zooms or attended in-person events. Grazie to Nicola Orichuia, owner of I Am Books in Boston's North End and the Boston group of the Italian American Writers Association (especially Jenn Martelli and Julia Lisella) for providing a wonderful venue for local writers to share and market their work. Thanks to Dorothy Derifield, Sandee Storey, and David Miller at Chapter and Verse in J.P. Thank you to my School Street Sessions cohort.

Thanks to John Skoyles who reminded me at a book launch for another writer, "You were going to write a novel. What happened?"

I appreciate the many kindnesses of my dear friends Marilyn Arnold, Mike Sussman, Helena Minton, Richard Hoffman, Kathi Aguero, Dick Lourie, Abby Freedman, Renee Caso, Paul "the Man" Horan, Edward P. Jones, Dalia Ardon, Maureen Walsh, Lee Post, Tomas O'Leary, Larry Aaronson, Deb Hamilton, Nancy Donahue, Jean D'Amico, Sue Hand (R.I.P), Maureen Rogers, Tino Villanueva, Rachel Walker, Annette Rafferty, Frank Kartheiser, Kathie Roche Goggins, David Kohn, John Roemer, Kathy Sweeney Long and the women of the class of 1968, and the rest of my large Worcester tribe.

Many writers offered support in many ways, among them Pam Painter, Amy Sutherland, Kim Church, Mary Elsie Robertson, David Huddle, Steve and Ewa Yarbrough, Laurette Viteritti-Folk, Louie Cronin, Elizabeth Searle, Helen Fremont, Camille DeAngelis, Lee Prusik, Carla Panciera, Nora Paley, Jessica Keener, Jaime Zuckerman, Gert Van der Kolk, Danielle Legros Georges (R.I.P.) Henry Ferrini, Nan Cuba, Jean Flanagan, and Marc Eichen.

A special thanks to Anne Starr and Margery Gans in "our little group."

A very special thanks to Teresa Lagrange for her beautiful cover, and Allison O'Keefe for production.

Gratitude to Abbi Sauro for responsibly and generously keeping my website current, and to my stepson Andrai Pawlak Whitted for making sure I had one.

Thank you Penelope Louise Sauro for giving me hope for the future.

And....thank you, Gloria Mindock, for always being in my corner, and for publishing beautiful books; and for Bill Kelle for helping to make the Press what it is. I'm proud to be a Červená Barva Press author.

About the Author

Mary Bonina is both poet and prose writer. *My Way Home* is her debut novel. She is the author of *My Father's Eyes: A Memoir*, and three published poetry collections: *Living Proof, Clear Eye Tea*, and *Lunch in Chinatown*. Her poem "Drift", won the UrbanArts "Boston Contemporary Authors" prize, and is engraved on a granite monolith, a permanent public art installation in the City. She has been honored as a fellow and awarded several residencies at the Virginia Center for the Creative Arts, including at the VCCA retreat in Auvillar, France. Her collaborative art experiments with composers, visual artists, and sculptors, have expanded poetry's vocabulary and reach. A longtime member of the Writers Room of Boston, where she served on the Board of Directors for more than a decade, Bonina is a graduate of the M.F.A. Program for Writers at Warren Wilson College